Okay, if this is the first book of mine you're going to try, stop now. Return it. Grab another. It's okay. I'll wait.

If you're still here, please know that I haven't read *Miracle Cure* in at least twenty years. It is my second published novel, one I wrote in my early twenties when I was just a naive lad working in the travel industry and wondering if I should follow my father and brother go to (shudder) law school.

I'm hard on it, but aren't we all hard on our early stuff? Remember that essay you wrote when you were in school, the one that you got an A plus on, the one your teacher called "inspired"—and one day you're going through your drawer and you find it and you read it and your heart sinks and you say, "Man, what was I thinking?"

That's how it is with early novels sometimes. This one is a bit preachy in spots and sometimes dated (though in truth, I wish the medical stuff was more dated, but that's another matter). You might think I based part of this on a "real-life" situation. I didn't. This book predates that event. I won't say more because it could be a spoiler.

Finally, flawed and all, I love this book. There are an energy and risk-taking in *Miracle Cure* that I wonder if I still have. I'm not this guy anymore, but that's okay. None of us is stagnant with our passion and our work. That's a good thing.

Enjoy.

continued . . .

ALSO BY HARLAN COBEN

HARLAN COBEN

MIRACLE CURE

A SIGNET BOOK

SIGNET
Published by New American Library, a division of
Penguin Group (USA) Inc., 375 Hudson Street,
New York, New York 10014, USA
Penguin Group (Canada), 90 Eglinton Avenue East, Suite 700, Toronto,
Ontario M4P 2Y3, Canada (a division of Pearson Penguin Canada Inc.)
Penguin Books Ltd., 80 Strand, London WC2R 0RL, England
Penguin Ireland, 25 St. Stephen's Green, Dublin 2,
Ireland (a division of Penguin Books Ltd.)
Penguin Group (Australia), 250 Camberwell Road, Camberwell, Victoria 3124,
Australia (a division of Pearson Australia Group Pty. Ltd.)
Penguin Books India Pvt. Ltd., 11 Community Centre, Panchsheel Park,
New Delhi - 110 017, India
Penguin Group (NZ), 67 Apollo Drive, Rosedale, Auckland 0632,
New Zealand (a division of Pearson New Zealand Ltd.)
Penguin Books (South Africa) (Pty.) Ltd., 24 Sturdee Avenue,
Rosebank, Johannesburg 2196, South Africa

Penguin Books Ltd., Registered Offices:
80 Strand, London WC2R 0RL, England

Published by Signet, an imprint of New American Library, a division of Penguin
Group (USA) Inc. Previously published in an SPI Books edition. Published by
arrangement with the author.

ISBN 978-1-61793-215-1

For Corky,
the best mommy in the world

PROLOGUE

FRIDAY, AUGUST 30

DR. Bruce Grey tried not to walk too fast. He slowed his pace, fighting off the temptation to sprint across the soiled floor of Kennedy Airport's International Arrivals Building, past the customs officials, and out into the humid night air. His eyes shifted from side to side. Every few steps he would feign a soreness in his neck to give himself the opportunity to glance behind him and make sure he was not being followed.

Stop it! Bruce told himself. *Stop lurking around like a poor man's James Bond. You're shaking like a malaria patient, for chrissake. You couldn't look more conspicuous if you wore a sign.*

He strolled past the luggage carousel, nodding politely at the little old lady who had sat next to him on the flight. The old woman had not shut her mouth during the entire trip, gabbing on about her family, her love of flying, her last trip overseas. She was sweet enough, just somebody's grandmother, but Bruce still closed his eyes and pretended to be asleep in order to get a little peace and quiet. But, of course, sleep had not come to him. It would not come for some time yet.

But maybe she wasn't just some sweet, little old lady, Brucie boy. Maybe she was following you . . .

He dismissed the voice with a nervous shake of the head. This whole thing was turning his brain into sewer sludge. First, he was sure that the bearded man on the plane had been following him. Then it was the big guy with the slicked-back hair and Armani suit at the telephone booth. And don't forget the pretty blonde by the terminal exit. She had been following him too.

Now it was a little old lady.

Get a grip on yourself, Brucie. Paranoia is not what we need right now. Clear thinking, old pal—that's what we're looking for.

Bruce moved past the luggage carousel and over to the customs official.

"Passport, please."

Bruce handed the man his passport.

"No luggage, sir?"

He shook his head. "Only this carry-on."

The customs officer glanced at the passport and then at Bruce. "You look quite different from your photograph."

Bruce tried to force a tired smile to his lips but it would not hold. The humidity was almost unbearable.

His dress shirt was pasted against his skin, his tie loosened to the point of being nearly untied. Beads of perspiration dotted his forehead. "I . . . I've gone through a few changes."

"A few? You're a dark-haired man with a beard in this picture."

"I know—"

"Now you're a clean-shaven blond."

"Like I said, I went through a few changes." *Luckily, you can't tell eye color from a passport photo or you would want to know why I changed my eyes from brown to blue.*

The customs official did not appear convinced. "Were you traveling on business or pleasure?"

"Pleasure."

"You always pack this lightly?"

Bruce swallowed and managed a shrug. "I hate waiting for checked luggage."

The customs official swung his line of vision from the passport photograph to Bruce's face and then back again. "Would you open your bag, please?"

Bruce could barely keep his hands steady enough to set the combination. It took him three tries before it finally snapped open. "There you go."

The customs official's eyes narrowed into thin slits as he rummaged through the belongings. "What are these?" he asked.

Bruce closed his eyes, his breath coming in short gasps. "Some files."

"I can see that," the official replied. "What are they for?"

"I'm a doctor," Bruce explained, his voice cracking.

"I wanted to review some of my patients' charts while I was away."

"Do you always do that when you're on vacation?"

"Not always."

"What type of doctor are you?"

"An internist at Columbia Presbyterian," Bruce replied, telling a half-truth. He decided to leave out the fact that he was also an expert in public health and epidemiology.

"I see," the official replied. "I wish my doctor was that dedicated."

Again Bruce tried to smile. Again it was a failed attempt.

"And this sealed envelope?"

Bruce felt his whole body quake. "Excuse me?"

"What is in this manila envelope?"

He willed a casual look on his face. "Oh, that's just some medical information I'm sending to a colleague," he managed.

The customs official's eyes locked onto Bruce's bloodshot ones for a few long moments. "I see," he said, slowly putting the envelope back in the bag. When the customs official finished going through the rest of the carry-on, he signed Bruce's customs declaration and handed him back his passport. "Give the card to the woman on your way out."

Bruce reached for the bag. "Thank you."

"And, Doctor?"

Bruce looked up.

"You might want to visit one of your colleagues," the customs official said. "If you don't mind a layman giving medical opinions, you look awful."

"I'll do that."

Bruce lifted the bag and glanced behind him. The little old lady was still waiting for her luggage. The man with the beard and the pretty blonde were nowhere in sight. The big guy in the Armani suit was still talking on the phone.

Bruce moved away from the customs desk. His right hand gripped his bag with excessive vigor; his left hand rubbed his face. He handed the customs declaration to the woman and walked through the sliding glass doors into the waiting area. A sea of anxious faces greeted him. People stood on their toes, peering out from all points with each swish of the glass doors before lowering their heads in disappointment when an unfamiliar face approached the threshold.

Bruce moved steadily past the waiting friends and relatives, past the bored limousine drivers with name signs held up against their chests. He made his way to the Japan Airlines ticket counter on the right.

"Is there a mailbox near here?" he asked.

"To your right," the woman replied. "By the Air France desk."

"Thank you."

He walked by a garbage can and casually dropped his torn-up boarding pass into it. He had considered himself very clever to book the flight under an assumed name—very clever, that was, until he got to the airport and was informed that you could not have an international ticket issued under a different name from the one on your passport.

Whoops.

Luckily, there had been plenty of space on the flight. Even though he had to purchase another ticket for himself, reserving one under an alias had not been such a dumb idea. Before his actual departure date, no one could have found out what flight he was booked on because his name was not in the computer. Pure genius on his part.

Yessiree, Brucie. You are a regular genius.

Yeah, right. Genius. Bullshit.

He located the mail slot near the Air France desk. A few passengers spoke to the airline representative. None of them paid him the slightest attention. His eyes quickly checked the room. The old lady, the bearded man, and the pretty blonde had either left or were still going through customs. The only "spy" he could still see was the big guy in the Armani suit, who now moved hurriedly through the sliding glass doors and out of the terminal.

Bruce let loose a sigh of relief. No one was looking at him now. He turned his attention back to the mail slot. His hand reached into his bag and quickly slipped the sealed manila envelope down the chute. His insurance policy was safely on its way.

Now what?

He certainly could not go home. If anyone was searching for him, his apartment on the Upper West Side would be the first place they would look. The clinic was no good at this hour of the night, either. Someone could nab him there just as easily.

Look, I'm not very good at this. I'm just your average run-of-the-mill doctor who went to college, went to medical school, got married, had a kid, finished residency, got divorced, lost custody of the kid, and now works too hard. I'm not up to playing I Spy.

But what other choice did he have? He could go to the police, but who would believe him? He had no real evidence yet. Hell, he wasn't even sure what was going on himself. What could he tell the police?

Try this on for size, Brucie: "Help! Protect me! Two people have already been murdered and countless others may join them—including me!"

Maybe true. Maybe not. Question: what did he really know for sure? Answer: not a hell of lot. More like nothing. By going to the police, Bruce knew he would do little more than destroy the clinic and all the important work they had accomplished there. He had dedicated the last three years to that research and he was not about to give those damn bigots the weapon they needed to kill the project. No, he would have to handle it a different way.

But how?

He checked once more to make sure he was not being followed. All his enemy spies were gone now. That was good. That was a nice bit of relief. He hailed a yellow taxi and jumped into the backseat.

"Where to?"

Bruce thought for a moment, mulling over every thriller he had ever read. Where would George Smiley go, or better still, Travis McGee or Spenser? "The Plaza, please."

The taxi pulled away. Bruce watched out the back window. No cars seemed to be following as the taxi began its journey down the Van Wyck Expressway toward Manhattan. Bruce settled back, letting his head rest against the seat. He tried to breathe deeply and relax, but he still found himself trembling in fear.

Think, goddamn it. This is no time to catnap.

First, he needed a new alias. His eyes moved left and right, finally resting on the taxi driver's name on the displayed license. Benjamin Johnson. Bruce turned the name around. John Benson. That would be his name until tomorrow. John Benson. Just until tomorrow. Now, if he could just stay alive until then . . .

He dared not think that far ahead.

Everyone at the clinic thought he was still on vacation in Cancún, Mexico. No one—absolutely no one—knew the whole vacation idea was merely a diversion. Bruce had played the role of happy traveler to the utmost. He had bought beachwear, flown down to Cancún last Friday, checked into the Cancún Oasis Hotel, prepaid for the week, and told the concierge that he would be renting a boat and could not be reached. Then he shaved his beard, cut and bleached his hair, and put on blue-tinted contact lenses. Even Bruce had trouble recognizing the image in the mirror. He returned to the airport, left Mexico, checked in at his true destination under the name Rex Veneto, and began to investigate his horrible suspicions.

The truth, however, appeared to be more shocking than he had imagined.

The taxi slowed now in front of the Plaza Hotel on Fifth Avenue. The lights of Central Park twinkled from across the street and to the north. Bruce paid the driver, tipping him no more or less than the proper amount, and strolled into the lush lobby of the hotel. Despite his designer suit, he felt conspicuously sloppy. His jacket was heavily creased, his pants completely wrinkled. He looked like something left in the bottom of a laundry hamper for a week—hardly what his mother would have called presentable.

He began to walk toward the reception desk when something he barely spotted out of the corner of his eye made him stop.

It's just your imagination, Bruce. It's not the same guy. It can't be.

Bruce felt his pulse quicken. He spun around, but the big guy in the Armani suit was nowhere in sight. Had he really seen the same man? Probably not, but there was no reason to take chances. He left the hotel by the back entrance and walked toward the subway. He purchased a token, took the 1 train down to Fourteenth Street, switched to the A train to Forty-second Street, cut cross town on the 7 train, jumping off the car seconds before the doors closed at Third Avenue. He changed trains haphazardly for another half an hour, jumping on or off at the last possible second each time, before ending up on Fifty-sixth Street and Eighth Avenue. Then "John Benson" walked a few blocks and checked into the Days Inn, a hotel where Dr. Bruce Grey had never stayed.

When he got up to his room on the eleventh floor, he locked the door and slid the chain into place.

Now what?

A phone call was risky, but Bruce decided to take the chance. He would speak to Harvey for only a few moments, then hang up. He picked up the phone and dialed his partner's home phone. Harvey answered on the second ring.

"Hello?"

"Harvey, it's me."

"Bruce?" Harvey sounded surprised. "How's everything in Cancún?"

Bruce ignored the question. "I need to speak to you."

"Christ, you sound awful. What's wrong?"

Bruce closed his eyes. "Not over the phone."

"What are you talking about?" Harvey asked. "Are you still—?"

"Not over the phone," he repeated. "I'll talk to you tomorrow."

"Tomorrow? What the hell is going—?"

"Don't ask me any more questions. I'll meet you tomorrow morning at six thirty."

"Where?"

"At the clinic."

"Jesus, are you in danger? Is this about the murders?"

"I can't talk anymo—"

Click.

Bruce froze. There was a noise at his door.

"Bruce?" Harvey cried. "What is it? What's going on?"

Bruce's heart began to race. His eyes never left the door. "Tomorrow," he whispered. "I'll explain everything then."

"But—"

He gently replaced the receiver, cutting Harvey off.

I'm not up for this. Oh, please, God, let my mind be playing tricks on me. I'm not up for this. I'm really not up for any of this. . . .

There was no other sound, and for a brief moment Bruce wondered if his overactive brain cells had indeed imagined the whole thing. Maybe there had been no sound at all. And if there had been a noise, what was so strange about that? He was staying in a New York hotel, for chrissake, not a soundproof studio. Maybe it was just a maid. Maybe it was just a bellhop.

Maybe it was just a big guy with slicked-back hair and a custom-made, silk Armani suit.

Bruce crept toward the door. The right leg slid forward; then the left tagged along. He had never been much of an athlete, had never been the most coordinated guy in the world. Right now, it looked like he was doing some kind of spastic fox-trot.

Click.

His heart slammed into his throat. His legs went weak. There was no mistaking where the sound had come from this time.

His door.

He stood frozen. His breathing reverberated in his ears so damn loudly that he was sure everyone on the floor could hear it.

Click.

A short, quick click. Not a fumbling sound, but a very precise click.

Run, Bruce. Run and hide.

But where? He was in a small room on the eleventh floor of a hotel. Where the hell was he supposed to run and hide? He took another step toward the door.

I can open it quickly, scream my brains out, and run down the hall like an escaped psych patient. I could—

The knock came so suddenly that Bruce nearly screamed.

"Who is it?" he practically shouted.

"Towels," a man's voice said.

Bruce moved closer to the door. *Towels, my ass.* "Don't need any," he called out without opening the door.

Pause. "Okay. Good night, sir."

He could hear Mr. Towel's footsteps move away from his door. Bruce pressed his back against the wall and continued to make his way to the door. His whole body shook. Despite the room's powerful air-conditioning, sweat drenched his clothing and matted his hair down against his forehead.

Now what?

The peephole, Mr. James Friggin' Bond. Look through the peephole.

Bruce obeyed the voice within his head. He slowly turned and put his eye against the peephole. Nothing. Nada, as the Mexicans say. There was no one there, not a damn thing. He tried to look to his left and then his right—

And that was when the door flew open.

The chain broke as though it were a thread. The metal knob slammed against the point of Bruce's hip. Pain shot through the whole area. Instinctively he tried to cover his hip with his hand. That proved to be a mistake. From behind the door a large fist came flying toward Bruce's face. He tried to duck, but his reflexes were too slow. The knuckles landed with a horrid thud against the bridge of Bruce's nose, crushing the bones and cartilage. Blood flowed quickly from his nostrils.

Oh, Jesus, oh, sweet God . . .

Bruce stumbled back, reaching for his nose. The big guy in the Armani suit stepped into the room and closed the door. He moved with a speed and grace that defied his great bulk.

"Please—" Bruce managed before a powerful hand the size of a boxer's glove clamped over his mouth, silencing him. The hand carelessly knocked against the flattened nostrils, pushing them upward and sending hot surges of pain through his face.

The man smiled and nodded politely as if they had just been introduced at a cocktail party. Then he lifted his foot and threw a kick with expert precision. The blow shattered Bruce's kneecap. Bruce heard the sharp cracking noise as the bone below the knee snapped. His scream was muffled by the man's hand tightening against his mouth. Then the giant hand pulled back just slightly before slamming up into Bruce's jaw, fracturing another bone and cracking several teeth. Gripping the broken jaw with his fingers, the man reached into Bruce's mouth and pulled down hard. The pain was enormous, overwhelming. Bruce could feel the tendons in his mouth ripping away.

Oh, God, please . . .

The big man in the Armani suit let Bruce slide to the floor like a sack of potatoes. Bruce's head swam. He watched through a murky haze as the big man examined a bloodstain on his suit. The man seemed annoyed by the stain, upset that it would not come out at the dry cleaner. With a shake of his head, the man moved toward the window and pulled back the curtain.

"You picked a nice, high floor," he said casually. "That will make things easier."

The big man turned away from the window. He strolled back toward where Bruce lay writhing. He bent down, took a solid hold on Bruce's foot and gently lifted Bruce's shattered leg into the air. The agony was unbearable. Jolts of pain wracked his body with each slight movement of the broken limb.

Please, God, please let me pass out . . .

Suddenly Bruce realized what the man was about to do. He wanted to ask him what he wanted, wanted to offer the man everything he had, wanted to beg the man for mercy, but his damaged mouth could produce only a gurgling noise. Bruce could only look up hopelessly with pleading, terror-filled eyes. Blood streamed down his face and onto his neck and chest.

Through a cloud of pain Bruce saw the look in the man's eyes. It was not a wild-eyed, crazed look; not a hateful, bloodthirsty look; not the stare of a psychotic killer. The man was calm. Busy. A man performing a tedious task. Detached. Unemotional.

This is nothing to this guy, Bruce thought. *Another day at the office.*

The man reached into his jacket pocket and tossed a pen and a piece of paper on the floor. Then he gripped Bruce's foot, one hand on the heel, the other on the toes. Bruce bucked in uncontrollable agony. The man's muscles flexed before he finally spoke.

"I'm going to twist your foot all the way around," the big man said, "until your toes are pointed toward your back and that broken bone rips through the skin."

He paused, gave a distracted smile, and repositioned his fingers in order to get a better grip.

"I'll let go when you finish writing your suicide note, okay?"

Bruce made the note brief.

I

SATURDAY, SEPTEMBER 14

SARA Lowell glanced at her wristwatch. In twenty minutes she would make her national television debut in front of thirty million people. An hour later her future would be decided.

Twenty minutes.

She swallowed, stood slowly, and readjusted her leg brace. Her chest hitched with each breath. She had to move around, had to do something before she went nuts. The metal of the brace rubbed against her, chafing the skin. After all these years Sara still could not get used to the clumsy artificial constraint. The limp, yes. The limp had been with her for as long as she could remember. It felt almost natural to her. But the bulky brace was still something she wanted to toss in a river.

She took a deep breath, willed herself to relax, and then checked her makeup in the mirror. Her face looked somewhat pale, but that was nothing new. Like the limp, she was used to that. Her honey blond hair was swept back from her beautiful, delicate features and large doll-like green eyes. Her mouth was wide, her lips sensual and full to the point where they looked almost swollen. She took off her wire-rimmed spectacles and cleaned the lenses. One of the producers walked over to her.

"Ready, Sara?" he asked.

"Whenever you are," she said with a weak smile.

"Good. You're on with Donald in fifteen minutes."

Sara looked at her costar, Donald Parker. At sixty he was double her age and a billion times more experienced. He had been on *NewsFlash* since the early years, before the fantastic Nielsen ratings and a market share that no news show had ever seen before or since. Simply put, Donald Parker was a legend in television journalism.

What the hell do I think I'm doing? I'm not ready for something like this.

Sara nervously scanned her material for the millionth time. The words began to blur. Once again she wondered how she had gotten this far so fast. Her mind flashed through her college years, her column in the *New York Herald,* her work on cable television, her debates on public TV. With each step up the ladder, Sara had questioned her ability to climb any higher. She had been enraged by the jealous chatter of her colleagues, the cruel voices that whispered, "I wish my relatives were famous . . . Who did she sleep with? . . . It's that damn limp."

But no, the truth of the matter was much more simple: the public adored her. Even when she got rough or sarcastic with a guest, the audience could not get enough of her. True, her father was the former surgeon general and her husband was a basketball star, and maybe her childhood pain and her physical beauty had also helped her along the way. But Sara remembered what her first boss had told her:

"No one can survive in this business on looks alone. If anything they're a drawback. People will have a preconceived notion that because you're a beautiful blonde you can't be too bright. I know it's unfair, Sara, but that's the way it is. You can't just be as good as the competition—you have to be better. Otherwise they're going to label you an airhead. You'll get blown off the stage if you're not the brightest person out there."

Sara repeated the words like some battle cry, but her confidence refused to leave the trenches. Her debut tonight featured a report on the financial improprieties of Reverend Ernest Sanders, the televangelist, founder of the Holy Crusade—a big, slippery (read: slimy) fish. In fact, the Reverend Sanders had agreed to appear for a live interview after the report was aired to answer the charges—on the condition, of course, that *NewsFlash* display his 800 number on the screen. Sara had tried to make her story as evenhanded as possible. She merely stated facts, with a minimum of innuendo and conclusions. But deep inside Sara knew the truth about the Reverend Ernest Sanders. There was just no avoiding it.

The man was pure scum.

The studio bustled with activity. Technicians read me-

ters and adjusted lights. Cameramen swung their lenses
into place. The teleprompter was being tested, no more
than three words to a line so that the audience at home
would not see the anchor's eyes shifting. Directors, producers, engineers, and gofers scrambled back and forth
across a set that looked like a large family room with
no ceiling and only one wall, as though some giant had
ripped apart the outside so he could peer in. A man Sara
did not recognize rushed toward her.

"Here you go," he said. The man handed her several
sheets of paper.

"What's this?" she asked.

"Papers."

"No, I mean what are they for?"

He shrugged. "To shuffle."

"Shuffle?"

"Yeah, you know, like when you break for a commercial and the camera pulls away. You shuffle them."

"I do?"

"Makes you look important," he assured her before
rushing off.

She shook her head. Alas, so much to learn.

Without conscious thought, Sara began to sing quietly. She usually restricted her singing to the shower or
the car, preferably accompanied by a very loud radio, but
occasionally, when she was nervous, she began to sing in
public. Loudly.

When she got to the chorus of "Tattoo Vampire"
(*"Vampire photo suckin' the skin"*), her voice rose and she
started playing the air guitar. Really into it now. Getting
down.

A moment later she realized that people were staring at her.

She lowered her hands back to her sides, dropping her well-tuned air guitar into oblivion. The song faded from her lips. She smiled, shrugged. "Uh—sorry."

The crew returned to work without so much as a second glance. Air guitar gone, Sara tried to think about something both distracting and comforting.

Michael immediately came to mind. She wondered what Michael was doing right now. He was probably jogging home from basketball practice. She pictured all six feet five of him opening the door, a white towel draped around his neck, sweat bleeding through his gray practice jersey. He always wore the craziest shorts—loud orange or yellow or pink Hawaiian ones that came down to his knees, or some whacko-designed jams. Without breaking stride, he would jog past the expensive piano and into the den. He would turn on a little Bach, veer toward the kitchen, pour himself a glass of freshly squeezed orange juice, and then drink half of it in one gulp. Then he would collapse into the reclining chair and let the chamber music sweep him away.

Michael.

Another tap on her shoulder. "Telephone call." The same man who had handed her the sheets of paper handed her a portable telephone.

She took the phone. "Hello?"

"Did you start singing yet?"

She broke into a smile. It was Michael.

"Blue Oyster Cult?" he asked.

"Yeah."

"Let me guess." Michael thought a moment. " 'Don't Fear the Reaper'?"

"No, 'Tattoo Vampire.' "

"God, how awful. So what are you up to now?"

Sara closed her eyes. She could feel herself beginning to relax. "Not much. I'm just hanging around the set, waiting to go on."

"Play any air guitar?"

"Of course not," she said. "I'm a professional journalist, for God's sake."

"Uh-huh. So how nervous are you?"

"I feel pretty calm actually," she replied.

"Liar."

"All right, I'm scared out of my mind. Happy?"

"Ecstatic," he replied. "But remember one thing."

"What?"

"You're always scared before you go on the air. The more scared you are, the more you kick ass."

"You think so?"

"I know so," he said. "This poor guy will never know what hit him."

"Really?" she asked, her face beginning to beam.

"Yeah, really," he said. "Now let me ask you a quick question: do we have to go to your father's gala tonight?"

"Let me give you a quick answer: yes."

"Black tie?" Michael asked.

"Another yes."

"These big stuffy affairs can be so boring."

"Tell me about it."

He paused. "Can I at least have my way with you during the party?"

"Who knows?" Sara answered. "You may get lucky." She cradled the phone between her neck and shoulder for a moment. "Is Harvey coming to the party tonight?"

"I'm going to pick him up on my way."

"Good. I know he doesn't get along with my father—"

"You mean your father doesn't get along with him," Michael corrected.

"Whatever. Will you talk to him tonight?"

"About what?"

"Don't play games with me, Michael," she said. "I'm worried about your health."

"Listen, with Bruce's death and all the problems at the clinic, Harv has enough on his mind right now. I don't want to bother him."

"Has he spoken to you yet about Bruce's suicide?" Sara asked.

"Not a word," Michael said. "To be honest, I'm kind of worried about him. He never leaves the lab anymore. He works all day and night."

"Harvey has always been that way."

"I know, but it's different this time."

"Give him a little more time, Michael. Bruce has been dead only two weeks."

"It's more than just Bruce."

"What do you mean?"

"I don't know. Something to do with the clinic, I guess."

"Michael, please talk to him about your stomach."

"Sara . . ."

"Talk to him tonight . . . for me."

"Okay," he agreed reluctantly.

"Promise?"

"Yes, I promise. And, Sara?"

"What is it?"

"Kick some Southern-fried reverend ass."

"I love you, Michael."

"I love you too."

Sara felt a tap on her shoulder. "Ten minutes."

"I have to go," she said.

"Until tonight, then," he said. "When I have my way with a famous TV star in her childhood bedroom."

"Dream on."

A sharp pain ripped across Michael Silverman's abdomen again as he replaced the receiver. He bent over, his hand clutched under his rib cage, his face scrunched into a grimace. His stomach had been bothering him on and off for weeks now. At first he had thought it was just a flu, but now he was not so sure. The ache was becoming unbearable. Even the thought of food now made his stomach perform backflips.

Beethoven's Seventh Symphony drifted across the room like a welcome breeze. Michael closed his eyes, allowing the melody to work like a gentle masseur against his aching muscles. His teammates gave him unlimited shit about his musical taste. Reece Porter, the black power forward who cocaptained the New York Knicks with Michael, was always goofing on him.

"How can you listen to this shit, Mikey?" he would ask. "There's no beat, no rhythm."

"I realize that the musical ear of a Chopin does not

compare with that of MC Hammer," Michael would reply, "but try to be open-minded. Just listen, Reece. Let the notes flow over you."

Reece paused and listened for a moment. "I feel like I'm trapped in a dentist's office. How does this shit get you psyched for a big game? You can't dance to it or anything."

"Ah, but just listen."

"It doesn't have lyrics," Reece said.

"And your noise pollution does? You can understand the words over all that racket?"

Reece laughed. "Mikey, you're a typical whitey snob," he said.

"I prefer the term *pompous honky ass*, thank you."

Good ol' Reece. Michael held a glass of freshly squeezed orange juice, but the thought of even a sip nauseated him. Last year the knee, and now the stomach. It didn't make sense. Michael had always been the healthiest guy in the league. He had gone through his first ten NBA seasons without a scratch before tearing apart his knee a little more than a year ago. It was tough enough trying to bounce back from reconstructive knee surgery at his age . . . The last thing he needed was this mystery stomach ailment.

Putting down his glass, Michael moved across the room and made sure the VCR was set. Then he turned off the stereo and turned on the television. Sara would be making her *NewsFlash* debut in a matter of minutes. Michael fidgeted in his seat. He twisted his wedding band around and around and then rubbed his face. He tried to relax, but, like Sara, he couldn't. There was no reason

to be nervous, he reminded himself. Everything he had
said to Sara on the phone was true. She was an amazing
reporter, the best. Very sharp and quick. Well prepared
and yet spontaneous. A bit of a wise-ass sometimes. A
sense of humor when it was called for. A bulldog almost
always.

Michael had learned firsthand how tough an interviewer Sara could be. They had met six years ago when
she was assigned to interview him for the *New York Her-*
ald two days before the start of the NBA finals. She was
supposed to do a personal, non-sports-related piece on
his life off the court. Michael did not like that. He did
not want his personal life, especially his past, splashed
across the headlines. It was none of anybody's business,
Michael told Sara, resorting to more colorful terms to
get his point across and then slamming down the phone
for emphasis. But Sara Lowell was not so easily thwarted.
To be more precise, Sara Lowell did not know how to
give up. She wanted the interview. She went after it.

A jolt of pain knocked aside the memory. Michael
clenched his lower abdomen and doubled over on the
couch. He held on and waited. The pain subsided slowly.

What the hell is wrong with me?

He leaned back, glancing at the photograph of Sara
and himself on the shelf behind the TV. He stared at the
picture now, watching himself hunched over Sara with his
arms locked around her small waist. She looked so tiny,
so achingly beautiful, so goddamn fragile. He often wondered what it was that made Sara appear so innocent, so
delicate. Certainly not her figure. Despite the limp, Sara
worked out three times a week. Her body was small, taut,

athletic—*dynamite* might be a better way to describe it. Sexy as hell. Michael examined the photograph again, trying to look at his wife objectively. Some would say it was her pale porcelain complexion that accounted for her unaffected appearance, but that wasn't what it was. Her eyes, Michael thought now, those large green eyes that reflected frailty and gentleness while maintaining the ability to be cunning and probing. They were trusting eyes and eyes you could trust. A man could bathe in those eyes, disappear forever, lose his soul for all eternity.

They were also sexy as hell.

The phone interrupted his thoughts. Michael reached behind him and grabbed the receiver. "Hello?"

"Hi, Michael."

"How's it going, Harvey?"

"Not bad. Look, Michael, I don't want to keep you. I know the show is about to go on."

"We got a couple of minutes." There was a crashing sound in the background. "What's all that noise? You still at the clinic?"

"Yep," Harvey replied.

"When was the last time you got some sleep?"

"You my mother?"

"Just asking," Michael said. "I thought I was going to pick you up at your apartment."

"I didn't have a chance to get out of here," Harvey said. "I had one of the nurses rent me a tux and bring it here. It's just so busy right now. Eric and I are swamped. Without Bruce here."

Harvey stopped.

There was a moment of silence.

"I still don't get it, Harv," said Michael carefully, hoping his friend was finally ready to talk about Bruce's suicide.

"Neither do I," Harvey said flatly. Then he added, "Listen, I need to ask you something."

"Shoot."

"Is Sara going to be at the benefit tonight?"

"She'll be a little late."

"But she'll be there?"

Michael recognized the urgency in his old friend's voice. He had known Harvey almost twenty-four years, since a second-year intern named Dr. Harvey Riker took care of an eight-year-old Michael Silverman, who had been rushed to Saint Barnabas Hospital with a concussion and broken arm.

"Of course she'll be there."

"Good. I'll see you tonight, then."

Michael stared at the receiver, puzzled. "Is everything all right, Harv?"

"Fine," he mumbled.

"Then what's with the cloak-and-dagger phone call?"

"It's just . . . nothing. I'll explain later. What time you picking me up?"

"Nine fifteen. Is Eric coming?"

"No," Harvey said. "One of us has to run the store. I have to go, Michael. I'll see you at nine fifteen."

The phone clicked in Michael's ear.

DR. Harvey Riker replaced the receiver. He sighed heavily and put a hand through his long, unruly, gray-brown hair, a cross between Albert Einstein's and Art Garfunkel's. He looked every bit of his fifty years. His muscle had turned to flab from lack of exercise. His face was average to the point of tedium. Never much of a hunk to begin with, Harvey's looks had soured over the years like a two-dollar Chianti.

He opened his desk drawer, poured himself a quick shot of whiskey, and downed it in one gulp. His hands shook. He was scared.

There is only one thing to do. I have to talk to Sara. It's the only way. And after that . . .

Better not to think about it.

Harvey swiveled his chair around to look at the three photographs on his credenza. He picked up the one on the far right, the picture of Harvey standing next to his partner and friend, Bruce Grey.

Poor Bruce.

The two police detectives had listened to Harvey's suspicions politely, nodded in unison, jotted down notes. When Harvey tried to explain that Bruce Grey would never have committed suicide, they listened politely, nodded in unison, jotted down notes. When he told them Bruce had called him on the phone the same night he leaped from the eleventh-floor window at the Days Inn, they listened politely, nodded in unison, jotted down notes . . . and concluded that Dr. Bruce Grey had committed suicide.

A suicide note had been found at the scene, the detectives reminded him. A handwriting expert had confirmed that Bruce Grey had written it. This case was open and shut.

Open and shut.

The second picture frame on the credenza held a photograph of Jennifer, his former wife of twenty-six years, who had just walked out on him forever. The third photograph was that of his younger brother, Sidney, whose death from AIDS three years ago had changed Harvey's life forever. In the picture Sidney looked healthy, tan, and a touch on the chubby side. When he died two years later, his skin was pasty white where it was not covered with purple lesions, and he weighed less than eighty pounds.

Harvey shook his head. All gone.

He leaned forward and picked up the photograph of his ex-wife. He knew he had been as much to blame (more) for the failed marriage as she was. Twenty-six years. Twenty-six years of marriage, of shared and shattered dreams, rushed through his mind. For what? What had happened? When had Harvey let his personal life crumble into dust? His fingertips gently passed over her image. Could he really blame Jennifer for getting fed up with the clinic, for not wanting to sacrifice herself to a cause?

In truth, he did.

"It's not healthy, Harvey. All that time working."

"Jennifer, don't you understand what I'm trying to do here?"

"Of course I do, but it's gone beyond the point of obsession. You have to take a break."

But he couldn't. He recognized that his dedication had gone off the deep end, yet his life seemed so minor when he considered what the clinic was trying to achieve. So Jennifer left. She packed and moved to Los Angeles where she was living with her sister, Susan, Bruce Grey's ex-wife. Yes, Harvey and Bruce had been brothers-in-law as well as partners and close friends. He almost smiled, picturing the two sisters living together in California. Talk about fun conversations. He could just hear Jennifer and Susan arguing over which one had the lousier husband. Bruce would probably have gotten the nod, but now that he was dead the girls would raise him to sainthood.

The truth of the matter was that Harvey's entire world, for better or for worse, was right here. The clinic and AIDS. The Black Plague of the eighties and nineties. After watching his brother ravaged and stripped to brittle bone by AIDS, Harvey had dedicated his life to destroying the dreaded virus, to wiping it off the face of the earth. As Jennifer would tell anyone who would listen, Harvey's goal had become an all-consuming obsession, an obsession that frightened even Harvey at times. But he had come far in his quest. He and Bruce had finally seen real progress, real breakthroughs when . . .

There was a knock on his door.

Harvey swiveled his chair back around. "Come in, Eric."

Dr. Eric Blake turned the knob. "How did you know it was me?"

"You're the only one who ever knocks. Come on in. I was just talking to your old school chum."

"Michael?"

Harvey nodded. Eric Blake had become a member of Harvey and Bruce's team two years ago when they realized that two doctors could no longer carry the patient load by themselves. Eric was a nice kid, Harvey thought, though he took life way too seriously. It was okay to be serious, especially when you dealt with AIDS patients all day, but a person had to be just a little loose, just a little quirky, just a touch loony to survive the daily ordeal of death and suffering.

Eric even looked tightly wound. His most distinctive feature was his neat, scouring-pad, red hair. When you looked at him, the term *clean-cut* came to mind. Polished shoes. Good dresser. Eric's tie was always pressed and tied properly, his face freshly shaven even after forty-eight hours on call.

Harvey, on the other hand, had his tie loosened to somewhere around his knees, believed in shaving only when the growth began to itch, and would need a hand-gun to shoot his hair into place.

Eric Blake had grown up on the same block as Michael in a New Jersey suburb. When Michael first became Harvey's hospital patient, little redheaded Eric Blake visited him every day, staying as long as the hospital would allow. Back in those days Harvey was an overworked intern, but he liked to spend any free moments he could muster in the hospital with Michael. Even Jennifer, a hospital volunteer then, found herself drawn to the child. Very quickly Harvey and Jennifer formed a special rapport with this irresistible young boy caught up in a world of constant abuse.

Over the years Harvey and Jennifer watched Michael grow from childhood through adolescence and into manhood. They went to his basketball games and music recitals and award dinners, applauding his achieve-

ments like proud parents. They were there to comfort
him after his beatings, after his mother's suicide, after
his abandonment by his stepfather. Looking back on it
now, Harvey wondered if their close relationship with
Michael magnified their own major marital problem: no
children.

Maybe so. They tried, but Jennifer could never carry
to full term. Perhaps if she had, things might have been
different.

Doubtful. Very, very doubtful.

Harvey wondered if Jennifer still kept in touch with
Michael. He suspected she did.

"Did you tell Michael—" Eric started to ask.

Harvey interrupted him with a shake of his head.
"Not yet. I just wanted to make sure Sara was going to
be at the party tonight."

"Is she?"

"Yes."

"What are you going to tell her?"

Harvey shrugged. "I don't know yet."

"It doesn't make any sense. Why when we're so
close—"

"We're not that close."

"Not that close?" Eric repeated. "Harvey, look out
there. People are alive because of you."

"Because of this clinic," Harvey corrected.

"Whatever. When we let the results go public, we're
going to go down in medical history next to Jonas Salk."

"I'm more worried about the present."

"But we need the publicity so that we can raise enough
money to continue—"

"Enough," Harvey broke in, glancing at his watch. "Let's make a quick check of the charts and head over to the lounge." He smiled tiredly. "I want to watch Sara's report on Reverend Sanders."

"No friend of the cause, that one."

"No," Harvey agreed. "No friend."

Eric picked up a photograph from the credenza. "Poor Bruce."

Harvey nodded but said nothing.

"I hope his death means something," Eric said. "I hope Bruce didn't die for nothing."

Harvey moved toward the door, his head lowered. "So do I, Eric."

GEORGE Camron removed his gray, pin-striped Armani suit, carefully folded the pants at the creases, and placed it on a wooden hanger. He had been forced to burn another Armani two weeks ago, and that upset him very much. Such a waste. He would have to be more careful with his wardrobe. Bloodstained silk suits raised overhead and increased expenses.

George, a very large man, enjoyed the finer things in life. He wore only custom-made suits. He stayed in only the most luxurious hotels. He frequented only the finest gourmet restaurants. His slicked-back hair was styled (not cut, styled) by the world's most expensive hair designers (not beauticians, designers). He enjoyed manicures and pedicures.

He walked over to the hotel phone, picked up the receiver, and pressed seven.

"Room service," a voice said. "Is there something we can get you, Mr. Thompson?"

The Ritz always referred to its guests by their names when they called. The personal touch of a very fine hotel. George liked it. Thompson was, of course, his current alias. "Caviar, please. Iranian, not Russian."

"Yes, Mr. Thompson."

"And a bottle of Bollinger, 1979. Very cold."

"Yes, Mr. Thompson."

George hung up the phone and relaxed on the king-sized bed. He was a long way from his humble beginnings in Wyoming, a long way from his military days in Vietnam, a long way from Thailand, the country he now called home. A wide variety of elegant hotel rooms was George's home now. The Somerset Maugham suite at the Oriental in Bangkok. The harbor penthouse at the Peninsula in Hong Kong. The corner suite at the Crillon in Paris. The presidential suite at the Hassler in Rome.

George checked his watch, turned on the television with the remote control, and switched to Channel 2. In a few minutes *NewsFlash,* with Donald Parker and Sara Lowell, would be on. George wanted to watch that show very much.

The phone rang. George picked it up. "Hello."

"This is—"

"I know who it is," George interrupted.

"Did you get the last payment?"

"Yes."

"Good," the voice replied.

The voice sounded nervous. George was not sure he liked that. Nervous people had a tendency to make mistakes. "Is there something else I can do for you?" he inquired.

"As a matter of fact . . ."

Another job. Excellent. George had no idea who his employer was, nor did he care. He did not even know if the voice on the other end of the phone was calling the shots or merely a go-between. It did not matter. This was a job where you asked no questions. George did his work, collected his pay, and moved on. Questions were irrelevant.

"I'm listening," he said.

"The last job I gave you . . . it went smoothly? There were no problems?"

"You read the papers. What do you think?"

"Yes, well, I just wanted to make sure. You have Dr. Grey's files?"

"Right here," George said. "When do you want to arrange a pickup?"

"Soon. Have you been wearing the gloves and a mask like I told you?"

"Yes."

"And nothing else happened?"

George wondered for a moment if he should tell his employer about the package Bruce Grey had mailed at the airport. But no, it was none of George's concern. He had been hired to kill the man; make it look like a suicide; grab any files or papers he had on him; cut a page out of his passport; and leave all money, personal effects, and identification untouched. Period. Nothing about mailed packages.

Except, of course, it *was* his concern. He should never

have let Grey mail that package. It was a mistake, George was sure of it, but there had been no way to stop him. He shook his head. Maybe he should have done some more background checking before he signed on for this job. Something about it was not right.

"Nothing else," George said.

"You sure?"

George cleared his throat. Dr. Bruce Grey had made the job painfully easy. His checking into a high-rise hotel had been a blessing for George; it gave him the license to use whatever means he wished to elicit pain and solicit the suicide note. Any physical trauma inflicted on Dr. Grey would be hidden in the splattered mess on the pavement.

"I'm sure," George said. "And in the future, don't make me repeat myself. It's a waste of time."

"I'm sorry."

"You said something about another job?"

"Yes," the voice said. "I want you to eliminate another . . . person."

"I'm listening."

"Is someone else with you?"

"No."

"I hear voices."

"It's the television," George explained. "*NewsFlash* is about to go on. Sara Lowell's debut."

The voice on the phone sounded startled. "Why . . . why did you say that?"

A strange reaction, George thought. "You asked about the voices," he replied.

"Oh, right." The voice tried to steady itself, but the

strain was unmistakable. "I want you to eliminate someone else."

"When?"

"Tonight."

"This is very short notice. It will cost you."

"Don't worry about that."

"Fine," George said. "Where?"

"At Dr. John Lowell's house. He's having a large
charity formal tonight."

George almost laughed out loud. His eyes swerved
back toward the television. Dr. Lowell. Former surgeon
general. Sara Lowell's father. That explained the bizarre
reaction. He wondered if Sara would be at the party.

"The same method as the first two?" George asked.

"Yes."

George took his stiletto out of his pocket, snapped it
open, and examined the long, sleek blade. It would be
messy, no question about that. He considered his wardrobe and settled on the green Ralph Lauren polo shirt he
had picked up in Chicago. It was a little too tight around
the shoulders anyway.

2

DON'T be nervous. Don't be nervous. Don't be nervous...

"Five seconds."

The announcement tightened Sara's stomach. For a fleeting moment she almost started singing again. She forced her mouth to close, adjusted her spectacles, and waited.

I'm going to do fine. I'm going to kick some ass. I'm going to...

"Four, three, two..." The hand pointed toward the two people sitting at the desk.

"Good evening, I'm Donald Parker."

Please don't sing... "And I'm Sara Lowell. Welcome to *NewsFlash.*"

DR. John Lowell's estate in the Hamptons was enormous. The Tudor mansion sat majestically atop ten handsomely landscaped acres. There was a grass tennis court as well as indoor and outdoor swimming pools, three Jacuzzis, two hot tubs, a spacious cabana, a helicopter landing pad, and more rooms than Lowell knew what to do with. The house had been his grandfather's, a capitalist who had, according to liberal textbooks, raped and pillaged the land and its people for profits. John's father, however, chose to bypass the family business and become a surgeon. John had followed suit. He made a good living, though practicing medicine was not nearly as profitable as raping and pillaging.

In a few hours, the east wing would be packed to capacity with some of the wealthiest people in the world, all of whom had donated thousands to the Erin Lowell Cancer Center for the right to attend. John would have to smile a lot and be solicitous. He hated doing that. During his controversial tenure as surgeon general in the early eighties, John Lowell had never learned much about diplomacy or political subtlety. He crusaded zealously to crush cancer, bulldozing whatever and whomever stood in his way. He declared war on cigarette smokers, claiming in an angry remark on national television, *"Cigarettes are murder weapons, plain and simple. I feel no pity for smokers who give themselves lung cancer. They don't care if they make other people sick with secondhand smoke or even if they give their own children a deadly disease. It boggles the mind how we put up with people who are so selfish and destructive."*

The remark sent shock waves throughout the country. The tobacco industry lobbied to have John Lowell removed from office. They failed, but not from lack of trying. Battle lines had been drawn on that day, and even though John was no longer surgeon general, he continued to fight.

"Hi, Dad."

John Lowell spun toward his elder daughter, Cassandra. She was wearing a bathrobe and sandals. "Cassandra, where are you going?"

"Just taking a quick dip in the pool," she replied.

"But your sister is going to be on in a few minutes. All the houseguests are coming inside to watch."

Cassandra's eyes clouded over, but John did not appear to notice. "I'll only be a moment."

"You should come in with the rest of us and watch Sara."

Once again he failed to acknowledge the defiant glare in his daughter's eyes. "You're going to tape the show, right?" she asked.

"Right."

"So I'll be able to watch my sister over and over again. Lucky me."

"Cassandra . . ."

She ignored her father and strode away. Sara. For Cassandra's whole life her younger sister's name surrounded her like thousands of tiny birds. "Sara is sick." "We have to take Sara to the hospital." "Don't play so rough with Sara." To her father, Cassandra was never as pretty, never as kind, never as ambitious, never as smart as Sara.

Her mother had been different. Erin Lowell had loved Cassandra just as much as prettier, kinder, more ambitious, more hardworking, smarter Sara. God, how she missed her mom. It had been more than a decade now, but still the pain was fresh, constant, and occasionally all-consuming.

The heat was stifling again today and many of the guests had escaped the humidity with a dip in the pool. Most were beginning to head into the house to watch wonderful Sara's debut on *NewsFlash*. But seeing Cassandra striding toward the pool, several of the men froze.

Cassandra was tall and wild-eyed, with wavy dark hair and olive skin. She differed so from Sara that no one would ever suspect that they were sisters. To put it simply, Cassandra was hot. Burning hot. Dangerously hot. Whereas Sara's eyes could best be described as gentle ponds, Cassandra's smoldered like coals.

Cassandra arrived at the pool and kicked off her sandals. With a slight smile she slipped her robe down off her shoulders. It fell to the floor, revealing a sleek one-piece bathing suit that struggled to contain her voluptuous curves. She stepped onto the diving board, knowing that all eyes were following her, and sauntered to the front. Then, stretching her arms over her head, Cassandra dove in, the cool water tingling her skin all over. She began to swim the length of the pool, her long torso reaching forward with each stroke, her well-toned legs kicking ever so slightly. Her body sliced through the water effortlessly, leaving barely a ripple.

"It's almost eight o'clock," a voice from the house called. "*NewsFlash* is about to start."

Once again the women began to move toward the house, but the men could not free themselves so easily from Cassandra's spell. Oh, they strove to look casual, silently sucking in their paunches or putting shirts over all-too-obvious flaws. They walked by her slowly, trying desperately to sneak one last peek.

Cassandra stepped out of the pool and slowly made her way toward a chaise longue. She did not bother to dry herself. Reaching into the pocket of her robe, she withdrew a pair of sunglasses, put them on, and lay back, crossing her legs. Cassandra appeared to be resting quietly, but behind her sunglasses her eyes were very much on the move.

She spotted chubby Stephen Jenkins, the sixty-two-year-old former senator from Arkansas. Stephen—Uncle Stevie, she and Sara called him—was an old family friend. He and John Lowell had gone to Amherst together, their wives had hosted parties together, their children had gone to summer camp together. It was all very sweet and nice. And—let's be frank here—having sex with the conservative minority leader of the United States Senate had been something of a challenge for thirtysomething Cassandra. A sexual thrill, however, it was not.

"Hello, Cassandra," Jenkins called out.

"Hello, Uncle Stevie."

Cassandra had considered seducing the senator's handsome, single son as well, but Bradley was kind of a pain in the ass. And worse, he was Sara's friend. Every time they saw each other, the two of them gabbed for hours, ignoring Cassandra completely. If Sara and Bradley had been lovers, Cassandra might have considered it. But they weren't. From the day of her marriage two years ago, Sara was dedicated to Michael to the point of absolute boredom.

Cassandra poured some suntan oil into her cupped hand and began to massage it onto her legs. From across the pool Senator Jenkins watched, his eyes wide and hungry.

"Stephen?" Mrs. Jenkins called. "Bradley?"

The senator looked away regretfully. "One minute, dear."

"Hurry, everyone! Sara's on!"

The crowd moved quickly now. In a few minutes everyone was inside, watching the television. Cassandra lay back and closed her eyes. Sara was on national TV. *Who gives a rat's ass?*

SARA felt a knot form in her stomach. She knew that the Reverend Ernest Sanders was sitting in the next room, waiting to be interviewed. He was good in an interview—slick as a greased pig. If the Reverend Sanders did not like a question, he dodged it by an old, proven method: he ignored it. He could frustrate and fluster an interviewer with the best of them.

Most of Sara's report on Sanders and his Holy Crusade was taped, so she removed her glasses, took a deep breath, and willed herself to remain calm. She had gone over the report so many times that she knew every word by rote memory. She sung softly to herself and only listened to bits and pieces of the story.

Starting twelve years ago with only a few dozen members, the Reverend Ernest Sanders, former member of several white supremacy groups, built the Holy Crusade into a powerful movement encompassing thousands of mem-

bers throughout the country. Combining what Sanders calls "deep, religious values" and "traditional American rights," the Holy Crusade has been blanketed in controversy from its inception . . .

. . . the IRS has confirmed that neither the Reverend Ernest Sanders nor his wife, Dixie, has filed an income tax return in twelve years . . . Reverend Sanders has spent as much as ten thousand dollars a day on himself and several young women during "missionary" trips to Caribbean islands without a single new member of the Holy Crusade to show for it . . . millions of dollars in Holy Crusade donations are missing . . . the FBI is investigating corruption in the upper ranks of the Reverend Sanders . . .

When the taped portion of the story was finished, the camera swung to pick up the familiar and comforting face of Donald Parker. Sara stopped singing altogether.

"We have the Reverend Sanders here in our studio," Parker stated. "Reverend Sanders, good evening."

Ernest Sanders appeared on a screen, rather than in person. As on Ted Koppel's *Nightline*, guests rarely if ever sat in the same room as the interviewers. A toll-free number appeared below his image.

"Good evening, Donald." Sanders' voice was pleasant, relaxed. Sara felt the knot in her stomach tighten. The minister wore a light blue, three-piece suit, an obvious hairpiece, and a gold wedding band. No watch. No other jewelry. Nothing ostentatious. His face was gentle, trusting—the face of a dear uncle or friendly neighbor. His bright smile, one of his biggest assets, was firmly set.

"Thank you for joining us."

"Thank you, Mr. Parker."

Donald Parker asked the first question. "You saw the report, Reverend Sanders. Do you have any comments?"

Sanders' face was so damn calm that Sara wanted to scream. "I am a man of the Lord," he said in a smooth, Southern drawl. "I understand human desires."

"I'm not sure I follow you, sir."

"It's clear to me and the God-fearing people around the nation what is going on here. I do not think I need to lower myself to Miss Lowell's level by answering her charges."

"No charges were leveled, Reverend Sanders," Sara broke in, putting her wire-rimmed glasses back on her face. "Are there facts in the report you would care to dispute?"

"Do not be so sly, Miss Lowell. I know what you are really after."

"What is that, Reverend Sanders?"

He smiled. "A name for yourself. A quick reputation. What better way than to try to drag the good name of a simple preacher through the mud? A man who preaches the Bible in all its glory, who helps those less fortunate—"

"Reverend Sanders," Sara interrupted, "your personal income last year is estimated at over thirteen million dollars, yet you paid no income taxes. Can you explain this?"

The remark did not faze him. "Unless I'm mistaken, Miss Lowell, your family is not exactly economically strapped. I seem to recall that your father has a rather spacious mansion of his own. Should his finances be questioned, too?"

"My father declares his income every year," she replied. "My father can explain where every penny comes from. Can you do the same?"

"Of course," he stated emphatically. "Your lies and innuendos do not fool God's chosen people. Many have tried to distract the righteous from the path of the Lord, but the Holy Crusade will march on. The Holy Crusade will not allow Satan to succeed."

"Can you address these supposed lies?" Sara asked. "Can you be more specific?"

Sanders looked up and shook his head. "Satan uses words to twist goodness and righteousness and make it appear evil," he explained like a schoolteacher lecturing an insubordinate student, "but we will not be fooled. We live in a society today that is overrun with immorality, but we stand firm. What has happened to family values and ethics in this country, Miss Lowell? God-fearing people like my wife, Dixie, and I can't raise our children in this society anymore. Children are forced to attend public schools where God has been expelled but homosexuals are welcome. Does the Lord not tell us—"

"Excuse me, sir, but you were about to address the issues raised in our report."

"What issues? Your show does not address the real issue in America. I'm talking about Armageddon, Miss Lowell. The members of the Holy Crusade understand what is happening. They understand that we are living in an era of Sodom and Gomorrah, that heretics and infidels are attacking God. Dixie and I are doing the Lord's work, but He helps us along. He gives us signs which you choose to ignore."

"The report spoke of your financial—"

"Take what you call the AIDS virus, for example," Sanders interrupted, his voice rising to a fever pitch. "What you call the new phenomenon of AIDS is just the final chapter of Sodom and Gomorrah. God is clearly striking down the wicked, immoral homosexuals and perverts with His plague."

"Reverend Sanders—"

"Why is that so hard for you to believe?" he asked quietly, his smile brighter now, his eyes twinkling. "Most Americans believe in the Lord's work as transcribed in the Bible. Why, then, is it hard to believe He can still act in our present age? We have no trouble accepting the plagues of ancient Egypt. So why is it so hard to accept the plague of modern America? And woe to him who does not take heed. The sinners, Miss Lowell, there is no place left for them to hide. If AIDS is not a sign of what is to come, if AIDS does not make you accept the Lord as your only salvation and repent, then nothing will show you the light. You are doomed."

Sara closed her eyes and tried to keep her temper in check. She knew that she should keep to her line of questioning, that it would be a mistake to get off the subject of his financial improprieties. But her temper had other ideas.

"And what about the other victims, Reverend Sanders?" she asked, struggling to maintain an even tone.

"The other victims?"

"Yes, what about the so-called innocent victims of AIDS, the newborn babies born with the deadly disease or the people who contract the virus through blood transfusions? How do you explain the fact that AIDS is now the leading cause of death among hemophiliacs?"

Again that damn smirk of a smile. "I do not explain it, Miss Lowell. I explain nothing. The Bible does it for me. Read the Lord's words and you will see for yourself. The Bible tells us that not all living creatures in Noah's time were cruel and heartless, yet the Lord chose to save only the creatures upon Noah's ark. And in the story of Moses, why were the innocent forced to suffer through the hosts of plagues that besieged Egypt? The Bible gives us a simple answer, Miss Lowell. The Lord moves in mysterious ways. Who are we to question His ultimate plan? I know, I know, it's an old cliché, but it happens to be true. You cannot deny that the vast majority of those stricken with God's plague are abnormal people with perverse lifestyles, but yes, the innocent must on occasion pay for the sins of their brethren. That is why I ask all of you to return to God now, repent before it's too late. God will not allow a cure to be found until he rids the planet of the immoral—"

Nice move, Sara. She had played right into his hands, allowing the butthead to get on his soapbox and preach. It was time to knock him off. "Reverend Sanders, why have you not filled out an income tax form in twelve years? Why have you and your wife, Dixie, not paid a penny of income tax in all that time?"

Donald Parker sat back and watched. He did not want to interrupt. The show's director signaled for a commercial break, but Donald waved him off.

"Miss Lowell, you know the law as well as I do. This

great country of ours works to protect religious freedom, despite what some communists and atheists try to do. You may have temporarily succeeded in throwing God out of school and murdering unborn children, but the tide is changing—"

"Thank you, Reverend Sanders, but we were talking about your taxes. Please try to answer the question."

"I am answering your question, Miss Lowell. Dixie and I are law-abiding citizens. We pay our fair share of taxes."

"How much income tax did you pay last year, Reverend Sanders?"

"Churches do not have to pay taxes. It's called separation of church and state. You can read all about it in the Constitution."

Sara readjusted her spectacles. "I've read the Constitution, Reverend Sanders, but with all due respect, sir, you are not a church. You would certainly not suggest that people who work in the church should slide by without paying taxes, forcing hardworking Americans to carry the load for them, would you?"

His smile wavered, and for a brief moment there was a crack in the facade, allowing a quick peek at the cold soul beyond the smile. "Of course not," he said. "You twist everything around to suit your purposes, and the righteous know that. The righteous will not be swayed off the path of the Lord by your lies. I repeat what I have said all along. I have paid my fair share of taxes. This whole issue is nothing but a play by secularists to ruin my good name."

Donald Parker finally broke in. "Thank you, Reverend

Sanders. Well take a break and be back after this message. Don't go away."

"D R. Lowell? May I speak with you for a moment?"

John Lowell looked up, obviously annoyed. "Can't it wait until after the show, Ray?"

"There's a commercial on now," Raymond said. Dr. Raymond Markey worked for the Department of Health and Human Services in Washington. A small man, his arms and legs looked too short for his body. Thick glasses magnified his small dark eyes fivefold, making him look more like a classic movie nerd than a medical doctor. In truth, Markey rarely practiced medicine anymore. His job as assistant secretary of the department threw him more into the political realm than he cared to admit.

With a deep sigh, John Lowell stood and walked out of the room. The two headed down the hallway together. When they were alone, Lowell said, "Okay, what is it?"

Raymond Markey's giant eyes scanned the hallway like two searchlights across a prison courtyard. "He's coming to your party tonight."

Lowell's face turned red. "What? I don't want that man in my house. I thought I made that clear."

"You did."

"It's too dangerous," he whispered. "The timing of this party, everything."

"It doesn't matter," Markey said. "He'll be here. I thought you should know."

Lowell cursed silently, his hands clenching into fists. "That son of a bitch is going to destroy us all."

*   *   *

AS the party got into full swing, the group of men surrounding Cassandra fought for center stage like vain actors. But Cassandra, used to such scenes, couldn't have
cared less. She merely smiled brightly, seductively, nodding now and again but never really listening. Yes, they
were all important men. Randall Crane owned a large
chunk of several conglomerates. He had been featured
on the cover of *Fortune* magazine looking very distinguished and serious. But he was boring. They were all
deadly boring. If these men had not possessed staggering
amounts of money, nobody would even pretend to listen
to their self-indulgent horse manure.

The crowd of well-dressed patrons buzzed about
Sara's debut on *NewsFlash*. Cassandra's eyes swept over
the mansion's large ballroom, recognizing most of the
nearly three hundred guests. *Hypocrites,* she thought.
Like they really gave a flying shit about fighting cancer.
They were here to be seen, to mingle and impress. If that
meant coughing up some money for charity, well, that
was the price of admission. Being seen was the thing.

Randall Crane interrupted her thoughts. "Do you
know how I arrived here tonight, Cassandra?"

She barely glanced in his direction. "No, Randall.
Why don't you tell me?"

"By private helicopter," he said proudly. "I just
bought the bird. Seats eight. I have my own full-time
pilot, copilot, and stewardess."

"Stewardess?" Cassandra repeated. "On a helicopter?"

Randall Crane nodded. "We traveled from the roof

of my high-rise on Forty-seventh Street to here in under an hour."

"I'm very impressed, Randall."

The older man beamed. "Do you want to take a ride in it? You won't believe how fast it goes."

She had bedded Randall Crane more than three years ago, and he had lasted about as long as a fifteen-year-old boy on his first time out. The man had barely gotten his pants off.

"You should learn to slow down, Randall," she said with a wicked smile. "Speed is not always a good thing, you know."

Watching Randall's face turn red, Cassandra spotted Michael in the back corner, standing in a corner with that nothing doctor friend of his.

Michael looked so damn handsome in his tux, the only man at the party who would dare to wear a purple flowered bowtie and matching cumberbund rather than the standard black. But that was Michael. He was always a little off center. Cassandra had not seen him for nearly six months, but he still looked fantastic.

It was strange, really. Over the years Cassandra had stolen all of Sara's boyfriends, starting with her first high school beau, Eddie Myles. Cassandra had orchestrated the seduction so that Sara would be sure to walk in on them.

Which she did.

Sara's eyes widened when she saw her boyfriend's pants lowered to his ankles, Cassandra kneeling in front of him. Her face had crumbled into anguish. But Eddie was only the first. It became a game to Cassandra. A new challenge. Every time Sara risked trusting someone, her sister would pounce on him. With each seduction Sara's wounds bled anew. Insecurity began to nestle into her psyche. Sara became more self-conscious about her health problems. Her confidence withered away. Sarcasm became her defense. Cassandra watched her sister distance herself from the outside world. She dedicated herself to her studies, staying alone in her room, blasting that awful heavy metal music. Eventually, there were no boys left for Cassandra to chase away.

But Sara had been playing possum. Somehow the sly bitch had landed the best of men.

Michael, the bastard. The gorgeous, wonderful bastard.

Cassandra stepped forward. "Excuse me a moment, gentlemen."

The men parted to allow her to pass. Cassandra could not take her eyes off Michael. Six months had passed since they had last seen each other. And a lot of things might have changed in six months.

Cassandra moved toward Michael.

SITTING in the back of a studio limousine, Sara could not keep still. She tried to unwind from the excitement of the show, but the constant flow of adrenaline would not allow it. She rocked back and forth in the plush leather seat, her mind whirling with anticipation. She had moved from Blue Oyster Cult into the more contemporary sounds of Depeche Mode, but she still wasn't slowing down. Midway through "Blasphemous Rumors," the limousine driver raised the soundproof window between them.

Good.

Soon she would see Michael. Corny to say, but the best part of days like these was reliving each detail with her husband. Wincing, Sara snapped off her brace and rubbed her foot. Leg braces had improved dramatically over the years, from the days when she wore a heavy metal one that gripped like a power-vise to the modern fiberglass kind that felt more snug than compressing. Still, the brace was cumbersome and her leg throbbed painfully when she wore it a long time. She massaged her foot and lower leg with knowing hands. The blood began to circulate again.

Born two months premature, Sara had been a sickly child from the start. Infections settled into her lungs, causing pneumonia and a childhood of health complications. The difficult birth had also permanently damaged a nerve in Sara's left foot. As a child Sara had needed a brace and metal crutches to walk. Now the crutches were gone, but the brace and occasionally a cane were still in evidence.

Her youth was filled with constant hospital visits and trips to medical specialists and therapists. During endless sunny summer days Sara was forced to stay shut up in her bedroom rather than play outside with other children. Tutors visited the house or the hospital because of all the school she missed. She had few friends. Schoolmates never teased or taunted her, but they shunned the strange child and treated her like some sort of outsider. Sara was not allowed to take gym class. She had to sit on the steps during recess. Other children eyed her warily, almost frightened by the fragile, pale girl as though she represented death in a place that only understood immortality.

No matter how hard she tried not to be, Sara was always different, always coddled, always behind. She hated it. As she got older, Sara learned that the limp and brace were not as difficult to overcome as people's perceptions. Whenever she suffered a setback, teachers were quick to offer her health as an excuse.

"It's not your fault, Sara. If you were in perfect health . . ."

But Sara wanted to scream every time they said that. She did not want to hear excuses or use them to justify her shortcomings—she wanted to overcome them. Check that. She wanted to blow them away.

The chauffeur turned off the road and headed up the driveway. There were cars parked everywhere—Rolls Royces, Mercedes, stretch limos of all varieties, cars with special government license plates. Some chauffeurs stood around the driveway, smoking cigarettes and chatting with one another. Others stayed in the car and read newspapers.

When the limo reached the house, Sara snapped her brace back on, grabbed her cane, and proceeded as gracefully as she could toward the front door.

MICHAEL took another sip of Perrier. There was a steady ripping pain in his abdomen, but he did not mention it to Harvey. He had planned to say something, but Harvey was so distracted tonight that Michael decided to wait. He watched Harvey's eyes shift nervously over the guests in the large ballroom. His overall appearance, always a touch disheveled, was a complete mess.

"Are you all right, Harv?"

"Fine," he replied quickly.

"Something on your mind?"

"I . . . What time is Sara supposed to show up?"

It was the third time he had asked. "Any minute now," Michael said. "What the hell is the big deal?"

"Nothing," Harvey answered with a tight smile. "Your wife and I are having a torrid affair behind your back, that's all."

"Again? I hate it when you steal my women, Harv."

Harvey patted his paunch and tried to arrange his wild hair. "What can I say? I'm a stud."

Michael took another sip of his water. "What do you have planned for next week?" he asked.

"Next week?"

"Your birthday, Harv."

"Oh," Harvey said, "that."

"You only turn fifty once, big fella."

Harvey sloshed down the rest of his martini. "Don't remind me."

"Fifty years old," Michael said with a whistle. "Five big decades."

"Shut up, Michael."

"Half a century. The golden anniversary. Hard to believe."

"You're a pal, Mike. Thanks."

Michael grinned. "Come on, Harv. You've never looked better."

"Yeah, well, I do get tired of beating off the women with a stick." Harvey glanced over Michael's shoulder and spotted Cassandra walking toward them. "Speaking of beating them off with a stick."

"What?"

"Sister-in-law alert."

"Where?"

Cassandra tapped his shoulder. "Hello, Michael."

"Right behind you."

"Thanks." Reluctantly, Michael turned toward Cassandra. "Good evening, Cassandra."

"Long time, no see, Michael," she said, "Very long. Six months, I think."

"About that. You remember my friend Harvey Riker?"

"Ah, yes. The doctor."

Harvey stepped forward. "Nice to see you again, Cassandra."

She nodded slightly, ignoring him, her eyes never leaving Michael's face. "So how do I look this evening, Michael?"

"Nice."

"Nice?" she repeated.

Michael shrugged.

"Kind of noncommittal," Cassandra noted.

He shrugged again.

Cassandra turned her attention to Harvey for the briefest of moments. "Dr. Riker, do you agree with Michael's assessment?"

Harvey cleared his throat. "Uh, a lot of words come to mind, Cassandra. *Nice* is not one of them."

She smiled briefly, her gaze back upon Michael. "Michael, can we talk for a moment?"

"Look, Cassandra—"

"It's okay," Harvey interrupted. "I need to freshen my drink anyway."

They both watched him walk away. In front of the ballroom the band Dr. Lowell had hired finished their rendition of "Tie a Yellow Ribbon" and moved on to "Feelings." The lead singer sounded like a cat caught in a Cuisinart.

"Care to dance?" Cassandra asked.

"No, thanks."

"Why not?"

"I'm not in the mood. What did you want to talk to me about?"

"Stop being rude, Michael. I'll get to it in a minute. Pretend this is foreplay. You've heard of foreplay, haven't you?"

"I think I read something about it in *Cosmo*."

"Good. How do you like my dress?"

"Divine. What do you want?"

"Michael—"

"You're not really going to start this shit again, are you?"

"What shit?"

"You know what shit, Cassandra."

"I do?"

"I'm married to Sara, for chrissake. You remember Sara—blond, petite, gorgeous, lousy taste in music, your sister."

"So?"

Michael rolled his eyes. "So why do you keep both-ering me? Why do you always come on like some soap opera harlot?"

She looked at him. "You don't approve of me, do you, Michael?"

"It's not my place to approve or disapprove."

"So what do you think of me, then?" she asked, sip-ping her drink. "Really."

"I think you're great," he said. "You're beautiful and funny and smart, but when you act like this"—he shrugged—"you kind of make me sick."

"You're so sweet." Her hand reached out and rested on Michael's chest. Then she winked at him, leaned for-ward, and kissed his cheek.

"What was that for?" he asked.

She winked and pointed behind him. "That."

Michael turned around. From the entranceway Sara stood watching them.

A few hours ago George had successfully stolen a car and changed its license plate. He circled the area near the Lowell estate for a little while, making sure he knew ev-ery possible escape route before parking in an abandoned lot several miles away. He spread goose liver pâté on a piece of toast and poured himself a red wine. Very young. Beaujolais-Villages.

A perfect picnic.

When George had finished, he tidied the car, checked his watch, and drove back toward Dr. Lowell's mansion. He reached into the pocket of his Banana Republic khakis and took out his stiletto. He pressed the spring-release button with his thumb. The long, thin blade shot out with a sleek pop.

Very nice.

He closed the blade and put it back in his pocket. Enough games. Enough wine and song.

It was time to go to work.

3

HARVEY Riker helped himself to another martini. His third. Or was it his fourth? He was not sure. Harvey was not a heavy drinker, but lately he had found himself eyeing the bottle with new respect and desire. So much had happened the past few weeks. Why now? Why when they were on the brink of cornering and even destroying the AIDS virus did all this have to happen?

He handed the glass back to the bartender. "Another," he said simply.

The bartender hesitated but then took the glass. "Last one, okay?"

Harvey nodded. The bartender was right. Enough was enough. He spun back toward the crowd. Michael was still talking with Cassandra. Man, she was something else. Talk about sizzle. A guy could get sunburn just standing near her. Make that sunstroke.

And how old is she, Harvey? Young enough to be your daughter, I suspect.

He shrugged. No harm in fantasizing, was there?

But his mind quickly returned to the other matter. *The* matter. His bloodshot eyes scanned the room, but there was still no sign of Sara.

"Hello, Dr. Riker."

Harvey turned toward the familiar voice. "Hey, Bradley, how you feeling?"

Bradley Jenkins, the senator's son, smiled at Harvey. "Much better, thanks."

"Any problems?"

Bradley shook his head. "Right now I feel great. It's like some sort of a miracle . . . I just don't know how long it will last."

Harvey looked at the soft-spoken young man. Sara had introduced Harvey to Bradley years ago, well before Bradley had become his patient or even suspected he had AIDS. "Neither do we, Bradley," he said in a serious tone. "The important thing is to continue the treatment. Stopping in the middle can be more dangerous than the disease itself."

"I'd be crazy to stop."

"When is your next visit?"

Bradley never answered because his father stepped between them. "Not another word," Senator Jenkins hissed at Harvey. "Follow me."

Harvey did as the senator asked. He followed him down the long corridor, keeping a yard or two between them. Senator Stephen Jenkins stopped at the last door, opened it, glanced back down the corridor to make sure no one was looking, and then waved for Harvey to enter. He closed the door behind them.

They were in Dr. Lowell's library now, a huge, two-level room jammed from floor to high ceiling with thick, leather-covered books. There was a sliding ladder to facilitate getting volumes from the higher shelves and a catwalk that circled the room like a running track. Dark oak was the color of the shelves, the floor, the furniture.

Senator Jenkins began to pace. "You should know better than to speak to my son in public."

"We were just talking," Harvey said. "This is a party. People talk."

"Do you know what would happen if people found out the truth about Bradley?"

Harvey paused. "Peace in the Middle East?"

"Don't get cute with me, Riker."

"Nuclear Armageddon? The end of *Friday the Thirteenth* sequels?"

"I owe you, Dr. Riker, but don't push me."

Harvey's tone was brisk. "You don't owe me anything."

"You saved my son's life."

"We don't know that. Only time will tell for sure."

"Still," the senator said, "it is encouraging. I'm very grateful."

"I'm touched."

"I also heard about the death of your partner, Dr. Grey. My condolences."

"Care to make a public donation to his favorite charity?"

The senator chuckled without humor. "No."

"Then how about getting the Senate to vote us more funds?"

"You know I can't do that. The media and my opponents will tear me apart."

"For helping cure a deadly disease?"

"For spending the voters' hard-earned tax dollars to help a bunch of immoral, limp-wristed perverts."

"Like your son?"

The senator lowered his head. "Low blow, Riker. Very low. If it ever got out that Bradley was . . ." He stopped.

"Gay?" Harvey finished for him. "Is that the word you're looking for? Well, it won't. Not from me, at least."

"Then I'll do what I can to help the clinic—discreetly, of course." Senator Jenkins paused for a moment, thinking. "Besides," he continued, "there are other ways to raise more money without involving me."

"Like how?"

"Make your results public."

"It's still too early."

"It's never too early," Jenkins said. "You don't think there're rumors about your success in Washington? How do you think I found out about it? All you have to do is show the media some of your test cases. Show them that Krutzer kid or Paul Leander."

Harvey almost smiled. "What about Bradley? The son of a senator would certainly draw more attention than a couple of unknown gays."

"You can't use him."

"Even if it means saving more lives—or is your son the only homosexual worth saving?"

"You cannot use Bradley, Riker. That's final. Do you understand?"

"I understand, Senator. I understand that some things are more important than human lives—like reelection campaigns."

The senator stepped closer. He was a big man and he towered over the smaller doctor. "I'm getting a little tired of your moral outrage, Dr. Riker. You're out of your league here, and I've seen smaller mistakes ruin a man."

"Are you threatening me?"

"No, I'm warning you. Someone might decide to step on you if you become too bothersome."

Harvey returned the senator's glare. "You must be mistaking me for somebody who gives a shit," he replied evenly. "If my clinic goes down the tubes, a certain right-wing, narrow-minded senator from Arkansas would go with me."

Senator Jenkins shook his head. "You're so goddamn blind, Riker. You don't even understand what you're involved in here."

"So tell me."

"Your cause has more than its share of enemies," Jenkins continued. "There are plenty of people who would not mind putting an end to your research. Powerful people."

"Like you?"

Jenkins stepped back and shook his head. "I'm just trying to save my son's life," he said softly. "But there are important people who want the clinic closed . . . permanently."

"I'm aware of that. I can handle it."

Senator Stephen Jenkins walked toward the door and opened it. "No," he said, "I don't think you can."

SARA stared at Michael and Cassandra. Her hand gripped her cane to the point where her knuckles turned white. She fought off the desire to bash Cassandra with the same cane. She closed her eyes for a brief moment. Sara knew that she was playing into her sister's hands, that Cassandra was just trying to bait her. But Sara still felt a flush of anger and jealousy that colored her cheeks red.

Lord knew she should be used to Cassandra by now.

Sara cleared her throat and began to step toward them when somebody blocked her path.

"Good evening, Miss Lowell."

Sara looked up, surprised. "Good evening, Reverend Sanders."

"Please," the minister said, his famous smile spread across his face, "a moment of your time."

He escorted her toward the empty corridor and out of view.

"I didn't expect to see you here," Sara began.

And what the hell are you doing here anyway?

"The Holy Crusade is a large contributor to your father's organization," he explained. "Your father had no choice but to invite a representative from our organization. Since I've always wanted to meet the prestigious Dr. Lowell, I decided to be that representative."

"I see," Sara replied.

"Yes, Miss Lowell, despite your biased hatchet job on the Holy Crusade and what we believe as God-fearing—"

"I did not mention beliefs in my report," Sara interrupted. "I discussed finances and taxes."

Sanders smiled. "You think you are so clever, don't you, Miss Lowell? Do you really think that your petty report can hurt my ministry? You are a stupid woman. In trying to destroy me, you have done the very opposite."

Sara leaned against her cane. "I don't know what you're talking about, but if you'll excuse me . . ." She began to hobble back toward the party, but Sanders reached out and gripped her elbow firmly.

"The money has been pouring in since we went off the air, Miss Lowell. My eight hundred number is ringing like crazy. The free publicity from the show—"

"Let go of me or start singing soprano."

His grip tightened. "Your attacks on me have mobilized my supporters. The righteous see a threat, and they are rising to help—"

"Is there a problem here?"

Sanders released Sara's arm and spun quickly toward the voice. His smile was back in place. "Why, you're Michael Silverman! The basketball star! I'm a big fan of yours. Pleasure to meet you, sir."

Sara watched as Sanders stuck out his hand. Michael's eyes were burning, his temper just barely reined in. Sara moved toward Michael and caressed his shoulder. Michael's muscles were taut and knotted. He continued to ignore the reverend's outstretched hand. A few seconds later Sanders withdrew it, his smile faltering just slightly.

"Yes, well, it was nice chatting with you all," Sanders rambled, "but I really must be going back to the party now."

"Oh, must you?" Michael countered.

Sanders was sweating profusely now. "I look forward to seeing you both at the party," he said. "Good-bye, Miss Lowell."

"Good-bye, Reverend."

Sanders turned toward Michael. "Oh, by the way, Mr. Silverman, the Holy Crusade is a big supporter of Israel. I thought you should know."

Michael watched Sanders disappear down the corridor. "Permission to beat his head in."

"Permission denied . . . for now."

"You never let me have fun anymore," Michael said, beginning to relax a little.

"I'm sorry."

"And he's a big supporter of Israel. Isn't that nice, hon? I bet some of his best friends are Jewish."

Sara nodded. "He probably wants to convert."

"I'll perform the bris."

Michael hugged Sara tightly. "You all right?" he asked.

"Fine," Sara replied. She took off her glasses and wiped them with Michael's handkerchief. "So what have you been up to tonight, my valiant hero?"

Michael shrugged. "The usual—saving small children from fires, fighting crime in the streets, getting pawed by your sister."

Sara laughed. "Cassandra can be a tad aggressive."

"Just a tad—like Napoleon. You weren't upset, were you?"

"Me?" Sara asked. "Never. I did, however, feel this strong desire to bash her head in with my cane."

"That's my girl."

"You fought her off bravely, I suppose."

He put his fist to his chest. "My chastity remains intact."

"Good."

"By the way, you were great tonight."

She arched her eyebrows.

"I meant on the show, silly girl. No wonder Sanders was pissed off. You tore his ass to pieces."

"But he's probably right, Michael. All the exposé will do is galvanize his supporters and gain him a few new ones."

"In the short run maybe. But even imbeciles learn eventually."

"They're not imbeciles. A little gullible perhaps . . ."

"Whatever," he replied, taking her hand. "Ready to face your adoring public?"

"Not really."

"Good. Then follow me, my little kitten."

"Where?"

"You mentioned something earlier in the evening about my having my way with you."

"Did I? I don't remember."

"It was right after you referred to me as the Stud Machine."

"Oh," she said, moving toward the stairwell. "Now I remember."

"SENATOR Jenkins!"

Stephen Jenkins turned toward the voice. His painted, vote-getting smile, already applied to his jowly face, was holding up quite nicely. "Hello, Reverend. How wonderful to see you!"

Senator Jenkins and Reverend Sanders exchanged firm handshakes. Sanders, the senator knew, was one of the most influential men in the South. Over the course of the past decade, the religious right had been crucial in Senator Jenkins' reelection campaigns, and no one delivered their votes like the Reverend Ernest Sanders. If Sanders was on your side, he praised you as a descendant of the Prophets. If he was against you, well, Satan received kinder treatment in his sermons. Luckily for Jenkins, the reverend had backed him. Without his grassroots support, the senator might have lost in the last go-around to that upstart liberal the Democrats had pitted against him.

"Thank you, Stephen. Quite a party, isn't it?"

"Oh, yes," Jenkins replied.

Without so much as a head nod or knowing glance, the two men stepped down the long corridor, out of earshot and sight. Their smiles quickly dissolved away. Ernest Sanders leaned toward Jenkins' ear, his face tight and set. "I'm not very happy about the guest list for this party," he said.

"What do you mean?"

"What the hell is Dr. Harvey Riker doing here?"

"He's very close to John's daughter," Jenkins explained.

"This is not good, Stephen. His being here . . . it helps give him a certain legitimacy, don't you think?"

The senator nodded, though he really did not agree. He also knew his old friend John Lowell was a hell of a lot more upset at Sanders being here than Riker. John had made it very clear he did not want anyone to know of his association with the televangelist.

"A lot has been happening lately," Sanders continued. "We'd best prepare ourselves. I think we should all meet next week."

"Where?"

"At Bethesda."

The senator nodded again. "Are you in town for long, Reverend?"

"No," Sanders replied. "I'm leaving tomorrow afternoon. I only came up for the interview and . . . how should I put it?" He paused, thinking. "To keep the holy coalition together."

Jenkins felt something cold skitter down his back. "I don't understand."

Sanders looked straight at Stephen Jenkins. "Nothing to worry about, Stephen," he said. "I'll take care of everything."

S E V E R A L hours later Harvey Riker spotted Sara standing by herself near the bar. *Finally,* he thought, as something akin to relief drifted through him, *a chance to speak with her alone.* For the past fifteen minutes Harvey had watched Sara and Bradley Jenkins engage in what appeared to be a serious conversation. They were interrupted by Bradley's father, who moved between them and pulled Bradley away. No surprise there. Harvey knew that Bradley confided in Sara. Senator Jenkins probably did too.

Sara was leaning against her cane, sipping lightly at

her drink. Harvey approached her. "There you are," he began. "I've been looking for you all night. Congratulations on the show."

She kissed his cheek. "Thank you, Harvey. How are you doing?"

"Fine."

"And the clinic?"

Harvey shrugged. "Okay."

"Did Michael speak with you yet?"

"About what?"

"About his stomach."

"No," he replied. "What about it?"

Sara frowned. "I'm going to kill him."

"What's wrong with his stomach?"

"He's been having terrible stomach pain for over a week now."

Harvey nodded, finally understanding. "That explains his grimacing all night."

"I can't believe him," Sara continued. "He promised me he would speak to you."

"Don't blame him, Sara. I haven't been the most approachable company this evening. He probably thought it was a bad time."

"So what's wrong?"

"I need to talk to you about something important." Despite Harvey's earlier vow, he had gone well beyond that fourth martini. He took yet another swish, enjoying the feel of the cool liquid circling in his mouth before he swallowed. He might have been a little tipsy earlier, but his mind became sober and alert now. "It involves the clinic," he began slowly, weighing each word in his head before it passed his lips, "and I think it involves Bruce's death." He stopped.

He motioned with his hand. "Let's take a walk." They moved through the French doors and out onto the broad expanse of landscaped grounds. Many guests were outside now, the party spilling from the crowded ballroom onto the lawn and formal gardens beyond. The two strolled in silence past the pool, the cabana, the tennis courts. Sara led Harvey down toward the barn where her father kept the horses. She opened the barn door, releasing the smell of hay and animals. They entered. A horse neighed.

"This is a beautiful estate," Harvey said.

"Yes, it is."

He stroked the broad forehead of a large gray horse. "Do you do much riding?" he asked.

Sara shook her head. "Cassandra's the rider in the family. The doctors did not like the idea of me on a horse as a child, so I never got into it."

"Oh."

"So why don't you tell me what's up?"

"You're going to think I'm crazy."

"Nothing new there."

Harvey chuckled and then scanned the area to make sure that no one was around. "All right," he said slowly, "here goes. As you know, Bruce and I have been running the clinic for almost three years now, trying our best to keep all results secret and avoiding the press at all costs."

"I know," Sara replied, "but I never understood why. Clinics and doctors usually crave media attention."

"Usually, yes. And I, for one, am never against seeing

my smiling face on TV. But this is something different, Sara, something big. First, our treatment is experimental. In such cases even a rumor of success brings on expectations which probably cannot be met. Second, we are working with only forty patients, many of whom do not want their cases made public for obvious reasons. AIDS is still the evil plague in our society, one that inspires prejudice and discrimination of the highest order."

"I see."

"But a few new factors have entered the game."

"Such as?"

"Money," he stated flatly. "We're running out of it and we need more badly. Without some public pressure on the federal government to extend our grant and without some outside donations, the clinic won't survive much longer, and . . ." He stopped. "And there's something else," he said. "Something you have to swear to keep to yourself."

"Go ahead."

"Swear."

She looked at him, puzzled. "I swear."

He sighed deeply. "You've probably heard some of the rumors, Sara. No matter how hard we tried to keep things quiet, the word began to leak out. It started with the success of the drug on the isolated virus in the lab. Then we injected it in mice. Over time, the HIV was destroyed in virtually every instance. The same thing happened when we moved up to monkeys."

Sara swallowed. "What are you trying to say?"

"You can't keep something like this a secret for very long," he continued, "and frankly speaking, we felt it was time to let the facts be known—a little bit at a time, of course."

Her mouth dropped open. She had heard a vague rumor or two and dismissed them as wishful thinking. "Do you mean . . . ?"

He nodded. "We have found a cure, or at the very least a strong treatment, for the AIDS virus."

"My God."

"It doesn't work all the time yet," he continued quickly, "and it is not a wonder cure in the classic sense. It is a long, often painful regimen, but in a number of cases we have had great success."

"But why would you want to keep that secret?"

He removed a handkerchief from his pocket and dabbed the sweat from his face. Sara had never seen Harvey look so tense and strained. "A good question," he replied. "HIV, the so-called Human Immunodeficiency Virus, is a very tricky bug. It was hard to know for sure if we were truly blocking its effect or if the virus was just taking it easy on us for a little while. HIV is constantly changing, mutating, even hiding inside human cells. We didn't know about the true, long-term effects of what we were doing. Imagine, Sara, if we came out claiming to have a cure for AIDS only to find out we were wrong."

"It would be catastrophic," she agreed.

"To put it mildly. Plus we have the HHS to contend with."

"The Department of Health and Human Services? What do they have to do with this?"

"Everything. They're a giant bureaucracy and bureaucrats have a way of slowing things down to a crawl. The

Public Health Service—hell, the Food and Drug Administration, the Centers for Disease Control, the National Institutes of Health—all that is under the goddamn control of the Department of HHS."

"Bureaucrats on top of bureaucrats."

"Exactly. That's one of the reasons we kept our safe house out of the country, where no one from Health and Human Services could interfere whenever they got bored or somebody's ego was bent out of shape."

"I'm not following you."

"You know that I served as a medic in Vietnam, right?"

She nodded.

"Well, I spent a lot of time in Southeast Asia. It's a quiet society. Mysterious. No one interferes with your business. Bruce and I decided to keep all our lab tests—tissue specimens, blood samples, that kind of thing—in Bangkok, where they would be not very accessible."

"To avoid some of the bureaucracy?"

He nodded. "While their function is certainly justifiable, the FDA, for example, has a habit of testing drugs for years to make sure they're safe. You've probably read about all the experimental drugs the FDA won't allow AIDS patients to take."

She nodded. "Never made much sense to me."

"It's a complex debate, but I agree with you. If AIDS is a terminal illness, what harm can it cause a poor bastard who's already on death row to experiment? What we at the clinic hoped to do was to provide the FDA with so much evidence that any unnecessary delay would be prevented. At the same time we could test our compound without the panic and media attention that our results would cause."

Sara thought for a moment. "But couldn't you just show the government your results in secret? They'd be sure to allocate more funds once they saw some positive results."

He smiled. "You forget that the people who decide these matters are politicians. Can you picture a politician being closemouthed about something this big? No way, Sara. They would try to milk this for all the votes it could get them."

"Good point."

"And one other thing. Not all the bigwigs are in favor of our program. Your father, for one."

"My father's objections to your clinic are different," she snapped defensively. "If he knew that a cure was being found—"

"Perhaps I spoke too hastily," he interrupted. "Your father is a dedicated healer and I would never question his commitment to stop human suffering. I don't agree with his stand on AIDS, but I understand that it is a difference of opinion, not ideology. But there are others, Sara—men like that bastard Sanders and his lobotomized followers—who would do anything to stop our research."

"But I don't see what all this has to do with Bruce's death. If you were so close to reaching your goal, why did he kill himself?"

Harvey lowered his head. His bloodshot and tired eyes stared down at his shoes. "That's just the point."

"What is?"

He fiddled with the mixing straw in his glass. "Let's say I wanted to prove to you that we really have found a cure for AIDS. What could I show you to prove our claim beyond a shadow of a doubt?"

"Case studies."

He nodded. "In other words, patients who have been cured, right?"

"Right."

"Bruce, Eric and I saw it the same way. The major part of our research is our patients, Sara. Obviously, if we can present to the world patients who are fully cured—patients who are no longer HIV positive—then we have the evidence needed to support our claim."

"Understood."

"The problem is that two of our best case studies—Bill Whitherson and Scott Trian—are now dead."

"AIDS-related?" she asked.

He shook his head. "Murdered."

The word hit Sara like a sharp slap. "What?"

"They both died of multiple stab wounds within two weeks of one another."

"I didn't read anything about this."

"The murder of gays is hardly front-page stuff, Sara."

"Did you talk to the police?"

He nodded. "They thought it was an interesting coincidence but nothing more. They pointed out other similarities between the two men—both were gay, lived in Greenwich Village, had brown hair, et cetera, et cetera."

"They could be right," she said. "It could be just a coincidence."

"I know," he agreed. "I thought that too."

"But?"

"But now Bruce is dead."

"And you think his suicide is related to this?"

He paused and let out a deep breath. "I don't think Bruce committed suicide, Sara. I think he was murdered."

Sara felt her mouth go dry. "But how can that be? Wasn't a note found?"

"Yes."

"And wasn't it in Bruce's handwriting?"

"Yes."

"So how—"

"I'm not sure how it worked. It could have been a clever forgery or something—I don't know."

Sara's face twisted into a look of puzzlement. "Then you're saying that Bruce was thrown through the window?"

"I'm saying that it's worth looking into. Bruce was supposed to be in Cancún on vacation. What kind of man flies home early from a vacation to kill himself? And something else."

"Yes?"

"A few minutes before Bruce died, he called me on the phone. He sounded scared shitless. He said he needed to talk to me in private about something important. I'm sure it was about the murders. We only spoke for a minute or two before he suddenly hung up."

"Did Bruce tell you where he was?"

"No."

"Let me ask you something else," she continued, her mind racing now. "Are there other good case studies you could present besides the two murder victims?"

"Yes. At least four others. I know this whole thing sounds crazy, Sara, and yes, I know there are a million more rational solutions to all of this. There could be a psychotic gay-basher hanging around the clinic who followed Whitherson and Trian home and killed them. It could even be another patient or a staff member. But, Sara, this is so big, so important. If—and I admit it's a big if—if someone murdered them because of their affiliation to the clinic and if that someone does the same to the others, it could mean a delay in proving that the treatment works. That delay could cost thousands, maybe hundreds of thousands of lives."

"I see your point," she said, "but why are you telling me?"

Harvey smiled, though his face still looked weary. "I don't have much, Sara. I'm divorced. I have no kids. My only brother died of AIDS. My father died years ago and my mother has Alzheimer's. I work all the time, so I don't have a lot of friends." He stopped now as if trying to summon up some additional strength. "Michael has always been like a son to me. That makes you, well, the best kind of daughter-in-law. Whether you like it or not, you and Michael are my family."

"We like it," she said softly. She took hold of his hand. "Have you told anyone else about this?"

"I'm going to tell Michael, but I wanted to speak to you first. Eric, of course, knows. He's been wonderful since joining the clinic last year. I depend on him for everything."

"I'm glad he worked out so well."

"Yeah, well, Eric and I are both starting to question

our sanity over this whole murder mess. We're not sure if we're complete lunatics or just a pair of paranoid conspiracy nuts. Working on a disease like this one can make you a little batty after a while. Will you help me investigate this?"

"I'll get on it right away," she said. "I have a friend in homicide, a Detective Max Bernstein. I'll speak to him about it. But I have another suggestion."

"What?"

She hesitated. "Let me do a story on the clinic."

"Huh?"

"We'll run it live on *NewsFlash*. The positive publicity will force the government to refinance the clinic."

"I don't know, Sara," he said. "It might piss off Washington."

"So what?" she countered. "You'll have all of America on your side after this report. The politicians wouldn't dare close you down."

Harvey looked down and said nothing for a few minutes.

"Harv?"

"Can you keep our location and identity a secret?" he asked. "No names of doctors, no names of patients, nothing like that? I won't risk a patient's confidentiality."

"No problem."

He looked around, his eyes misty and afraid. "If you think it will work . . ."

"It has to," Sara urged. "Like you said before, it's time to let the world know."

Harvey nodded. "Okay, then. Do it." He shook his head, in some vain attempt to clear it. His face fought to look cheerful. "Now let's change subjects for a while. How are you doing?"

"Actually," Sara said with a hint of a smile, "I need a small favor."

"Name it."

"I need you to find me a good obstetrician."

Now it was Harvey's turn to look surprised. "Jesus, Sara, are you . . . ?"

She shrugged, trying to contain her excitement. She wanted so damn much to say yes, to see Michael's face after a positive test result came back. "Right now, I'm just late."

"Maybe this is an insensitive question, but what about your career?"

"No problem there. I can still tape the shows up until the birth and the networks love the publicity of a maternity leave. Boosts ratings through the roof."

"Can you be at Columbia Presbyterian tomorrow morning at ten?"

"Yes."

"Good. Ask for Dr. Carol Simpson. She'll know you're coming." He paused, his voice becoming serious. "I know you and Michael have been trying for a long time, Sara. Have you told him?"

She shook her head. "I'd rather wait for the results of the test. I don't want to build up his hopes if it's just another false alarm."

"Do you mind if I meet you there?"

"I'd like that."

"Great. I'll see you then."

"Harvey?"

"Yes?"

"Don't forget to talk to Michael about his stomach. He won't say anything, but it's really giving him some problems."

"I'll speak to him right away."

GEORGE sat in his car behind lush shrubbery at the foot of Dr. Lowell's driveway. He checked his gold Piaget. Getting late. The party was winding down now. Most of the guests had already left.

George had been sitting in the car for hours, watching while his intended victim drove up the driveway in a shiny limousine. The poor soul was in the large mansion now, enjoying Dom Pérignon champagne and foie gras, hobnobbing with the jet set, never knowing that in a few hours the knife in George's hand would slit open his arteries and extinguish his life forever.

He examined the stiletto blade front and back. Even in the dark, it gleamed menacingly.

A limousine drove down the driveway and past him. George looked up. He recognized the license plate immediately. The familiar adrenaline coursed through his veins.

He turned the ignition key and followed.

4

I T was a two-on-one fast break. Michael had faced hundreds of them in his career, maybe thousands. He watched as the New York Knicks' number one draft pick, a scrawny black kid from Memphis State named Jerome Holloway, dribbled toward him with lightning speed. On Jerome's left ran the Knicks' second-round pick, Mark Boone, a big white guy from Brigham Young who looked like a giant farmhand. The two kids bore down on the old veteran with determination in their eyes.

Come to Papa, Michael thought.

Michael knew better than anyone how to defend two men against one: confuse them—especially the man dribbling the ball. The key was to make the Holloway kid throw an errant pass or to stall him long enough for Michael's teammates, his reinforcements, to arrive.

Michael head-faked back and forth, alternating between blocking Holloway's trail to the basket and picking up the free man, Boone. He looked, he thought, suspiciously like a man having a fit. But that was okay—better to shake up the rookies.

Jerome Holloway headed straight toward the basket. At the last moment Michael stepped in his way. Jerome leaped, his eyes desperately seeking Boone streaking down the other side. Michael almost smiled. Once Holloway's feet had left the ground, he had committed. A mistake. A pure rookie mistake. Predictably, the kid looked panicky and began to move his arms toward his chest, preparing to throw the ball to Boone.

Like taking candy from a baby.

Michael slid between the two, readying himself to steal the pass and head back down the court for a fast break in his favor. He had done the same thing countless times before. Games had been decided by such a switch in momentum. Michael stepped forward and extended his hand into the passing lane, just as Holloway was about to release the ball.

But Holloway pulled back. The passing movement and panicked expression had been a fake. Completely out of position now, Michael watched while Holloway grinned, cupped the ball between his hand and forearm, and glided toward the cylinder. The dunk crashed through the basket with remarkable force. The backboard vibrated from the assault.

Holloway landed and turned toward Michael. The grin was still on his face.

Out of breath, Michael managed, "I know, I know. In my face, right?"

Jerome shrugged. "You said it, old dude, not me. But I do love playing against legends."

"This is just practice, kid. We're on the same team."

"Knicks to the end. By the way, nice shorts."

"You don't like them?"

"Pink and aqua flowers? Very hip."

They ran up court. Sweat soaked all ten players running through the scrimmage. Their bodies glistened in the dim light. Michael felt hot, tired, and a touch out of shape. His stomach was not helping matters much.

The upcoming season would be Michael's twelfth with the New York Knicks. He had begun, like Holloway, as a number one draft pick. Coming out of Stanford at age twenty-two, Michael had been a superstar his first year in the NBA, winning the Rookie of the Year Award and making the All-Star team. That same year the Knicks went from last place in the Eastern Conference to second place—a twenty-game swing-around. The next year Michael led them to the finals, where they lost in a seven-game showdown to the Phoenix Suns. Two years later he collected his first NBA championship ring. He had won three in his career with the Knicks, been named to the All-Star team ten times, and been the league's leader in steals and assists for eight seasons.

Not bad for an old dude.

Michael, an all-purpose shooting guard, did it all. There were many who could score like him, a few who could rebound like him, a couple who could pass like him, but next to none who could play defense like him. Add it all up and you had the kind of player every championship team needs.

"What's the matter, Michael? Feeling your age? Haul ass!"

Michael could hear himself suck in air. The voice belonged to the Knicks' new head coach, Richie Crenshaw. Richie had been a second-round pick by the Boston Celtics the same year Michael was drafted by the Knicks. There had been something of a rivalry between the two during Crenshaw's playing days, but for the most part it was an amicable rivalry. The two men always got along off the court. Now Richie Crenshaw was Michael's coach and still his good friend.

Eat shit, Richie, Michael shouted. But only to himself.

His lungs burned in his chest; his throat was dry. He was getting older, goddamn it—even though the gods of health had smiled upon Michael for his first ten-plus NBA seasons. No injuries. He had had a boating accident a few years ago, but that took place off-season, so it didn't count. Only two games missed in almost ten full seasons and those were the result of a minor groin pull. Remarkable, really. Unheard of. Then something must have really pissed off the gods. Michael had landed wrong in a game against the Washington Bullets, twisting his knee. To make matters worse, Big Burt Wesson, the Bullets' 270-pound enforcer, crashed into Michael on the play. Michael's foot remained firmly planted on the floor. His knee did not. It bent the wrong way—backward in fact. There was a snapping sound, and Michael's scream filled the stadium.

Out of basketball for more than a year.

The cast on his leg had been enormous and about as comfortable as wearing a jockstrap made of tweed. He hobbled around for months, listening to Sara tease him. "Stop imitating my limp. It's not a very nice thing to do."

"Great. I married a comedienne."

"We can be a comedy team," Sara had enthused. "The Gimpy Couple. We'll limp our way to laughter. We'll be as funny as a rubber crutch."

"Awful. Horrendous. Not even remotely funny. Stop."

"Not funny? Then we'll become a dance team. Limp to your left. Limp to your right. We can switch leg braces during a tango."

"Stop. Help. Police. Somebody shoot."

Michael and Sara had both recognized that he might not be able to come back; they were prepared for it. Michael had never been a stupid jock who thought that a basketball career would last forever. There was talk in the Republican Party about running him for Congress when he retired. But Michael was not ready to call it quits. Not yet anyway. He worked hard for a full, painful year with the therapist Harvey had found for him and rebuilt his shattered knee.

Now he was trying to get himself back into playing condition at the Knicks' preseason camp. But while the knee felt okay in its viselike brace, his stomach was slowing him down. He had promised Harvey last night that he would swing by the clinic before three o'clock for a complete checkup. With a little luck, Harv would take a few tests, see it was just some stupid bug again, give him a shot of antibiotics, and send him on his way.

Harvey. Jesus Christ, what was going on? Michael and

Sara had gotten little sleep last night. They drove home, made love again in a tangle of party clothes, then sat up and analyzed what Harvey had told them. If what Harvey said last night was true, if he had indeed found a treatment for the AIDS virus . . .

One of Michael's teammates set a pick for him. Michael used the screen and ran from the left side of the court to the right. He caught a glimpse of the wall clock and saw it was ten. Another hour, and then he would go uptown and see Harvey. At the Clinic. Capital C in his mind.

Michael was not looking forward to that visit. Immature to say but the place gave him the creeps. He was not sure if it was the magnitude of the disease or his not-so-latent homophobia, but the place intimidated him. Terrified him actually.

To be honest, Michael had never been all that comfortable with gays. Yes, he believed that homosexuals should be treated like everyone else, that their private lives were their own business, that discrimination against someone because of his sexual preference was wrong. He recognized that Sanders and his gang of mentally malnourished bigots were deranged and dangerous people. But still, Michael found himself making the occasional gay joke, referring to someone effeminate as "that big fag," keeping away from someone who was a "blatant fruit." He remembered when his teammate Tim Hiller, a good friend and apparently a ladies' man, shocked the sports world by admitting he was gay. Michael had stood beside him, supported him, defended him, but at the same time, he distanced himself from Tim. Their friendship did not crumble; Michael just let it slowly slide away. He felt bad about that.

Back on the court the ball was passed to Reece Porter, Michael's closest friend on the team and the only Knick besides Michael who was over thirty. Reece spotted Michael and tossed him the ball.

"Do it, Mikey," Reece cried.

Michael made a beautiful fake on the rookie Holloway, dribbled down the middle of the key, and laid up a soft shot. As Michael watched the ball float gently toward the basket, Jerome Holloway came flying into view. The rookie smacked the ball with his palm, sending the orange sphere off the court and into the seats. A clean block.

Again the rookie grinned.

Michael held up his hand. "Don't say it. Faced again, right?"

The cocky grin strengthened. "The word *Spalding* is imprinted on your forehead, old dude."

Michael heard the laughter. It was coming from Reece Porter. "What the hell are you laughing at?"

Reece could barely control himself. "Old dude," he managed between cackles. "You going to take that shit, Mikey?"

Michael turned back toward Holloway. "Take the ball out of bounds, hotshot, and dribble up while I cover you."

"One-on-one?" the kid asked in disbelief.

"You got it."

"I'll blow by you so fast you'll wonder if I was ever there."

Michael grinned. "Yeah, right. Come on, hotshot."

Jerome Holloway caught the ball. He took two dribbles and began to accelerate toward Michael. He was six feet past him when he realized that he no longer had the ball. "What the—?"

Holloway spun in time to see Michael making an uncontested layup. Now it was Michael's turn to smile.

Jerome Holloway laughed. "I know, I know. In my face, right?"

Reece whooped and hooted like a lottery winner. "Bet your sweet ass, brother. You've been faced something awful."

"Guess so," Holloway agreed. "You know something, Michael? You're a smart old dude. I bet I can learn a lot watching you."

Old dude. Michael sighed heavily. "Thanks, Jerome."

A whistle blew. "Take five," Coach Crenshaw shouted. "Get a quick drink and then I want everyone to take fifty foul shots."

The players jogged toward the water fountain—all save Michael. He stayed where he was, bent forward, his hands leaning on his knees. Richie Crenshaw walked over. "I've seen you look better, Michael."

Michael continued to draw in deep breaths. "Appreciate the pep talk, Coach."

"Well, it's true. You wouldn't want me to lie to you, would you?"

"Maybe a little."

"The knee giving you problems?"

Michael shook his head.

"You look like something's bothering you."

"I'm—" The next word never came out. A surge of white-hot pain pierced right through Michael's abdomen. He let loose a loud, short cry and clutched his belly below the rib cage.

"Michael!"

The shout came from Jerome Holloway. Wide-eyed with fear, the rookie sprinted back on the court. Reece Porter quickly followed.

"Mikey," Reece asked while kneeling beside him, "what is it?"

Michael did not answer. He collapsed to the floor, writhing in agony. It felt like something was raking at his insides with sharpened claws.

"Call an ambulance!" Reece shouted. "Now!"

D R. Carol Simpson escorted Sara to the waiting area in the Atchley Pavilion. Located next to Columbia Presbyterian's main building, the Atchley Pavilion housed the private offices of the medical center's many physicians. When Harvey had taken Michael and Sara on a tour of Columbia Presbyterian Medical Center last year, Sara remembered being awestruck by the size of the center, to say nothing of its reputation. There was Babies Hospital, the well-known pediatric hospital, and the Harkness Pavilion, where the private patients stayed. The Neurological Institute and the Psychiatric Institute, both housed in their own buildings, were considered the best in their field anywhere in the world, not to mention the Harkness Eye Institute, New York Orthopedic Hospital, Sloane Hospital, Squier Urological Clinic, Vanderbilt

Clinic, and the massive, newly completed Milstein Hospital Building.

And all of this medical brilliance had been jammed west of Broadway between One Hundred Sixty-fifth and One Hundred Sixty-eighth streets in Spanish Harlem.

A block or two farther west and north was student housing for Columbia College of Physicians and Surgeons, again one of the most reputable and selective medical schools in the country. But another five blocks farther north was J. Hood Wright Park, a respectable name for one of the original crack alleys, where passersby can witness or partake in drug trafficking. Its proximity to the hospital, Harvey had half joked, made it a convenient place to overdose.

One of the newest and smallest sections of the medical center, almost hidden from view, was near One Hundred Sixty-fourth Street. From the outside one would never guess that the broken-down edifice was dedicated to healing and experimental medicine. Named Sidney Pavilion after Harvey Riker's brother, this area of epidemiological study was cloaked in secrecy and security. No one could enter without the permission of Dr. Harvey Riker or Dr. Eric Blake. Staff and patients were kept to a minimum, and all had been specially selected by Riker and the late Dr. Bruce Grey personally. The medical center's board members rarely, if ever, discussed the new section in public.

Dr. Simpson showed Sara to a chair and then went to a window where she handed a test tube filled with Sara's blood to a nurse. "Take this to the lab. Have them run a beta HCG stat."

"Yes, Doctor."

"A beta HCG?" Sara asked.

"Fancy talk for a pregnancy test," Carol Simpson explained. "Doctors like to use code words no one else understands. Makes us sound more intelligent, don't you think?"

Sara liked Carol Simpson. Unlike so many others in her profession, there was nothing stuffy or intimidating about her. Her relaxed attitude put Sara at ease.

"If you say so," Sara replied.

"Well, we have to do something to justify all the years of schooling and internship and residency—besides having the M.D. license plate so we can park illegally in front of Macy's."

"You do that?"

"Only during a sale."

At least forty other patients sat biding their time in the waiting room, sneaking glances from their magazines and wishing their doctor would call their name.

"Give me a ring this afternoon," Carol said. "The results should be in by then."

"Great," Sara said.

"And try not to worry. I know you're anxious, but try not to think about it too much. Do what I do when I need to distract myself: shop till you drop."

"Well, hello there, ladies."

Sara and Carol turned and saw Harvey coming toward them. His entire person emanated exhaustion, Sara thought. His head tilted slightly to the side as though he were dozing; his back had curved into a slump.

"Hello, Harvey," Dr. Simpson said.

"Hello, Carol. How's my favorite patient doing, Doc?"

"Very nicely. We should know the test results in a few hours." Dr. Simpson turned her head toward the people in the waiting room. "Mrs. Golden?"

A massive-bellied woman looked up. "Over here."

"Come on down. You're the next contestant."

Harvey and Sara said good-bye and headed for the elevator. "You're in good hands," Harvey said. "Carol Simpson may be young, but she's already considered one of the top obstetricians in the country."

"I like her."

"Listen, Sara, about what I said last night . . ."

"Yes?"

"Well, in the light of day, my conspiracy theories always seem a little more wacko. Don't have me committed, okay?"

"Not yet anyway. Has the clinic really found a cure?"

"In some cases—maybe most cases, yes. Like I said last night, it's still in the developmental stage and it hasn't worked on everyone but—"

Harvey's beeper went off. He looked at the LCD digits coming onto the screen. "Oh shit."

"What is it?"

But he was already sprinting toward the nurses' desk and picking up the phone. "That number means it's an emergency." He dialed and the phone was picked up on the first ring. "Dr. Riker here." Pause. "What? When?" Another pause. "I'll be right there." He replaced the receiver.

"It's Michael. They just rushed him into the emergency room."

*   *   *

THE corpse was in the trunk.

George drove onward. Last night the body in the trunk had been filled with life. He had hopes, dreams, goals, desires. Like most people, he probably just wanted to be happy, to find his niche in this world. He was probably a person struggling through life, trying to do his best, grasping at the few joys life offered and trying to dodge the many hardships. Now he was dead.

Dead. Gone. Nothing.

He was no more than decaying tissue, useful only to medical students and worshipped by only the grieving family. Why, George wondered, did people care so much about the empty shell of a man, the facade? Why did they treat the worthless flesh as something invaluable? Was it man's innate inclination to see only the outward mask of the human being and not acknowledge the soul? Or was George being too harsh on his fellow man? Maybe man just needed to take hold of something tangible when he was faced with the ultimate intangible.

Heavy stuff, George. Very deep.

He chuckled and lit a cigarette.

After Dr. Lowell's gala last night, George had followed the limousine until the long, silver automobile dropped the victim off at his apartment in the city.

Perfect.

A true professional, George had already cased the building and surrounding area. He knew his victim lived in apartment 3A. He knew there was no doorman. George parked the car across the street and moved into the apartment building. Taking the stairs rather than the elevator, he stopped in front of a door with a faded 3A nailed to it. George wondered why, with all his money, his victim chose to live in this quasi-dump. He could live anywhere—Fifth Avenue, Central Park West, the San Remo Building, the Dakota, anywhere. George shrugged, dismissing the thought. It was none of his concern.

His fingers searched his pocket and removed a small tool. He jimmied the lock twice, just as he had done at the Days Inn with Dr. Bruce Grey. This time, however, he did not allow the sound of the lock being disengaged to be audible. Surprise in combat, George had learned long ago, always gave you the upper hand. Bruce Grey had been suspicious, so a simple knock on the door would not have brought him in front of the wooden portal unaware. For Bruce Grey had been prepared for an attack and was on his guard. But having the door smashed against him during a brief moment when he felt safe, when he thought the door was secure and no one was in front of it, that had been all George needed.

This victim, however, would not be suspicious. Unlike Grey, he had no idea that death had crept down his hallway. A knock was all George would need.

With the lock made useless, George put the small device back in his pocket and knocked.

A voice called out. "One moment."

George heard the victim coming to the door. He wondered whether the man was so stupid he would open the door without asking who it was. But the voice called out again.

"Who's there?"

George knew that the man was standing right behind the door now, probably leaning forward to look through the peephole. Without hesitation, George threw his full weight into the door. The wooden planks crashed against the man standing behind them, knocking him to the floor on the other side of the room.

George moved quickly. He closed the door and pounced upon his prey. His hand gripped the man's neck and he began to squeeze. There was a quick, choking noise and then silence. The man struggled, lashing out with his hands and kicking, but his blows were wild and imprecise. They did not bother George.

Maintaining his grip on the man's throat, George lowered his face to within inches of his victim's. "There is only one way I will allow you to live," George said, his voice chillingly monotonous, as though he were reading a prepared text. "And that is if you do everything I tell you. Deviate from what I say and you will die. Do you understand?"

The man's eyes bulged out from lack of oxygen and a surplus of fear. He managed a nod.

"Good. I will let you go. Call out or try to escape and you will know a pain very few have ever experienced."

He let go. The man rolled back and forth, retching uncontrollably.

George stood and watched the man's agony with something approaching boredom. "We are going down to my car now," he said, when he thought his victim could understand, "just like a couple of buddies cruising the town. Do as I say without question and you won't be hurt."

The man nodded. His immediate obedience made things so much easier. If George had been forced to kill the man here, he would have to clean up the blood, get rid of any possible clues, and worst of all, drag a body to his car without anybody seeing. Much more difficult.

They crossed the street together and George opened the trunk. "Get in."

"But—"

George grabbed the man's hand and squeezed, breaking two bones. With his free hand George covered the man's mouth and snuffed out his scream. Then George readjusted his grip on the shattered hand, squeezed a little tighter, forcing the broken bones to scrape against each other and rip at the tendons. The man's face went white.

"I told you to do what I say without question. Will you remember that now?"

The man nodded quickly and ducked into the trunk. George knew the man wanted to ask if there would be enough air once the trunk was closed, but he did not dare. He had experienced pain. Pain, George had learned, can be a greater threat than death.

George looked down the street. Three men had just circled the corner and were coming toward them. They looked pretty wasted, each walking a wobbly line that more often than not crossed the others'. George closed the trunk and drove away.

He found an abandoned road that he had used for this purpose before. He parked the car and grabbed the knife from the glove compartment. As per the instructions given to him on the phone, George slipped on surgical gloves and a mask. He felt like a doctor, preparing for a major operation.

"Scalpel," he said out loud. He laughed at his own joke.

George got out of the car and went toward the trunk. This was the part of the job George found most intriguing. He always wondered what was going through the victim's mind. A little earlier, his world had been normal, average, seemingly safe. Suddenly, he had been threatened, assaulted, and locked in a trunk. No longer did he have any say in what happened to him.

What was going through his mind?

It was a fleeting thought. In the end, George knew it didn't matter. For George only the finished job mattered.

When George opened the trunk, the man looked up at him with the eyes of a trapped animal.

"Wh-wh-what . . . ?"

George put his finger to his mask-covered lips. "Shhh."

George reached down and grabbed the man's head to hold still. Then he gripped the knife and placed it below the man's nose, the cool blade directly below the nostrils. He lowered the handle toward the mouth, almost touching the lips, and drove the blade upward. It sliced through the thin tissue, through the cartilage, and into the brain. Blood gushed freely. The body spasmed, but death was instantaneous. The man's final gaze was locked on George, his eyes wide and uncomprehending.

George tugged the knife out, and just as he had with the first two jobs, he stabbed the body two dozen times.

Wet, ripping sounds accompanied his methodical under-
taking. George's face remained calm as he drove the knife
home over and over again.

It was all very messy.

George knew that he would have to keep the body
in the trunk for the night. Then he would be able to
dump it in the appropriate area. With the others, it
had not mattered where the corpse was found, but the
voice on the phone had given specific instructions to
leave this one in the alley behind a gay bar called Black
Magic in Greenwich Village. At night, George knew,
such places were filled with all sorts of bizarre happen-
ings. They were crowded. He decided it would be safer
to dump the body in the daytime when the area was
empty.

Early the next morning George awoke refreshed from
a wonderful, dreamless sleep. He drove back into the
city and pulled up behind the Black Magic bar. A sleazy-
looking dump, he thought. It reminded him of Patpong
Street in Bangkok. Patpong, Bangkok's famed red-light
district, catered to heterosexuals, but everyone knew
about the area two blocks farther north devoted exclu-
sively to homos. And Pattaya, the popular Thai beach
resort not far from Bangkok, had a whole street jammed
with little boys who served their male customers without
question or hesitation.

Pretty sick, George thought.

He stopped the car and stepped out. He glanced
about the alley. No one. Dozens of stuffed plastic trash
bags were piled by the bar's rear entrance. Rear entrance,
George mused. How appropriate.

Taking one last look, George hefted the corpse out of the trunk, dumped it by the trash bags, climbed back in the car, and drove off. He had traveled three blocks when he glanced at his reflection in the rearview mirror.

Damn. His hair looked horrendous.

5

SARA limped along after him as Harvey sprinted toward the emergency ward. Ten yards in front of the entrance he almost slammed into Eric Blake, who was making a blind turn in the same direction.

"They paged you too?" Eric asked.

Harvey nodded. The two men barely broke stride as they crashed through the door and into the waiting area. They immediately spotted Reece Porter.

It was Harvey who reached him first. "What happened?"

"Don't know. Mikey just grabbed his stomach and collapsed. He's in there."

"Come on, Eric."

The two doctors disappeared behind a guarded door reading "No Admittance." A moment later Sara hobbled into the emergency ward.

Reece looked up, surprised to see her at the hospital already. "What are you doing here?"

She ignored the question. "Where is he? Is he all right?"

"The emergency room doctor is already with him. Harvey and Eric are in there too."

"What happened?"

"I don't know. We were scrimmaging like always, making jokes and all that stuff. We stopped for a break and a minute later . . ."

"A minute later what?"

"Mikey collapsed on the floor holding his stomach. We called an ambulance and I drove over with him. The pain seemed to let up a little on the way. When we got here, I told the nurse to page Eric and Harv."

"Is he conscious?"

"Yeah, he's awake. I bet it's just some food poisoning or something—all that Chinese food he's eating all the time. Now answer my question: what are you doing here?"

"I had a doctor's appointment next door."

"Are you okay?"

His voice rang with the warmth of genuine concern. In the background Sara could hear children whisper, "Look, Mom, that's Reece Porter!" Reece's six-eight frame was about average for the NBA, but it was semi-freak anywhere else. His height always drew fascinated glances.

"I'm fine," Sara said, hugging him tightly. "Reece, thanks for going with him."

Reece shrugged. "He's my friend," he said simply.

"And don't worry too much about Mikey. The man is blessed. Remember how scared we were the last time we met in a hospital? All that blood and everything?"

Sara did. Every year when basketball season ended, she and Michael joined Reece and his Eurasian wife, Kureen, for a get-away-from-it-all vacation. Five years ago, when Michael and Sara were first getting serious, the four decided to charter a small cruise boat out of Florida and explore the Keys and the Bahamas. The past basketball season had been a particularly long one, ending when the Knicks bested the Seattle Supersonics in a grueling, bruising seven-game showdown. All four of them had been anxious to escape the world, the fans, and the press.

On the third day of the voyage Michael and Reece had gotten up early, hired a kid with a speedboat, and gone waterskiing. The kid had gotten drunk and crashed the boat into a rock formation while Michael was on the water skis. He had been rushed to a local Bahamian hospital, bleeding heavily, and spent the next three weeks in bed.

"I remember," Sara said softly.

"But Mikey is—as one of the rookies would say—a tough old dude. He'll be okay."

Sara tried to take solace in Reece's words, but something kept jabbing at the back of her mind, telling her that he was not going to be okay, that nothing was ever going to be okay again.

"WHAT'S going on?" Harvey asked.

The young resident whose name tag read "John Richardson" looked up and spoke with quick precision. "We're not sure yet. He's suffering severe abdominal pain. Physical examination is remarkable for the liver being palpable four centimeters below the right costal margin. It's extremely tender."

"Hurts like hell is more like it," Michael managed from his prone position on the table.

"Vital signs?"

"All stable."

Harvey moved toward the bed. "Looking good, champ."

"Feel like shit, Coach."

"I was only kidding. You look like shit too."

Michael managed a chuckle. "I got the varsity in here now. How's it going, Eric?"

"Fine. Should I page Dr. Sagarel, Harv?"

Harvey nodded.

"See you in a bit, Mike," Eric said.

"I'll wait here for you." Michael turned his attention back to Harvey. "Who is Dr. Sagarel?"

"A gastroenterologist."

"Of course. I should have known."

"Jesus, Michael, look at your shorts. They're horrendous—even by your standards."

"I ask for a doctor. I get a fashion critic."

Harvey probed the liver area. "Does that hurt?"

"Like a son of a bitch."

Harvey straightened his back and turned toward the resident. "Have you done the blood work yet?"

"Yes."

"Get him an abdominal flat plate done stat."

"I'll also need to get a better history," Richardson said. "It could be something he consumed—"

"Can't be. He's had this pain for weeks. And his skin is jaundiced."

Eric came back into the room. "Dr. Sagarel will be here in about a half hour."

"Michael," Harvey asked, "have you noticed anything unusual in your urine lately?"

"A Datson hatchback came out the other day."

"Hilarious. Now answer my question."

Harvey saw the fear gather around Michael's eyes. "I don't know. The color's been darker maybe."

The doctors exchanged knowing glances.

"What?" Michael asked. "What have I got?"

"I don't know yet. Eric, make sure they do a hep screen on the blood. Also EBV and CMV titers. Then bring him down for an abdominal ultrasound."

"One step ahead of you."

"Now in English?" Michael asked.

"All the signs point to hepatitis," Harvey explained. "Eric and Dr. Richardson are going to take you downstairs for X-rays now. I'll see you in a little while."

D R. Raymond Markey, Assistant Secretary for Health of the Department of Health and Human Services, stared out the window at the lush green compound in Bethesda, Maryland. To him, the National Institutes of Health resembled a cross between a European spa and a military base. From his corner office the wilderness seemed to stretch for miles. But Markey knew better. He knew, for instance, that his big boss, the President of the United States, was about ten miles away, beginning his weekly brunch meeting with the Vice President. The two men met most Mondays for a light brunch and a heavy discussion. Raymond had attended a few of those brunches. He did not particularly care for the conversation or the food.

He sighed deeply, took off his glasses, and rubbed his eyes. He was excruciatingly nearsighted. When he viewed the sprawling landscape without his glasses, the world turned into a large abstract painting. The bright colors bled into one another and seemed to move in a kaleidoscope pattern.

He put his glasses back on, turned away from the calming view, and glanced at the two reports on his desk. The first was marked "Confidential!" and there were numerous seal protectors on the envelope so that Markey could be sure that no one had opened it before him. The envelope was also specially treated so that its contents could not be read by holding it up to a light. Any tampering left permanent scars. It was a lot of security, but sometimes every bit of it was needed.

The second envelope read "Sidney Pavilion, Columbia Presbyterian Medical Center, New York." The security surrounding this file, while significant, was somewhat more limited.

Assistant Secretary for Health of the Department of Health and Human Services—a long and rather unimpressive title, Raymond Markey thought. But he knew better. His office was in charge of the U.S. Public Health Service, controlling such agencies as the Food and Drug

Administration, the Centers for Disease Control, and the National Institutes of Health—hardly an unimportant or ceremonial post.

Markey reached for his letter opener and slit the confidential envelope. He then laid the reports side by side. The regular report had been filled out by Dr. Harvey Riker and for the first time Dr. Bruce Grey's signature had been omitted. Too bad. As for the confidential report . . . well, safer not to think about the source. Repeating the name of the author out loud could prove hazardous to one's health. Even fatal.

Markey skimmed the files for obvious discrepancies. One jumped out at him immediately.

The number of patients.

According to Riker's report, they had been treating forty-one patients, two of whom had been murdered in recent weeks. Riker's write-up was factual, not drawing any conclusions, but he did mention the strange coincidence that two patients had died of multiple stab wounds within a couple of weeks of each other. Markey also noticed that Riker never referred to Grey's death as a suicide but as a "shock" and "death that made no sense."

Curious description, Markey mused.

He examined the reports again. The report stamped "Confidential" stated unequivocally that there had originally been forty-two patients, not forty-one. *Why the discrepancy?* Markey wondered. Raymond doubted very much it was a mistake. No one made mistakes in these situations. There was a reason for the discrepancy. All he had to do was figure out what.

Markey thumbed back to the beginning of the confidential report. He was sure that Harvey Riker was behind the discrepancy. He knew Riker well and did not trust him. Many years earlier, when Raymond Markey had been chief of staff at St. Barnabas Hospital in New Jersey, he had first encountered a brash young intern named Harvey Riker. Even back then Riker hated rules and regulations. And now that those rules and regulations came from the government, Markey knew Riker was even more apt to bend them. The man had tremendous talent but very little discipline. He needed to be watched. Closely.

Ah, here it was. On page two.

Page two of the confidential report listed all the staff members and patients at the Sidney Pavilion. Markey sifted through Riker's report until he found the patient list. He counted them. Yes, forty-two in the confidential report. Forty-one in the doctor's report. Which name was missing from Dr. Riker's file?

It did not take long to find. The name might as well have been underlined.

His hand shaking, Raymond picked up the phone behind his desk. The office phone was probably bugged, but he carefully screened his private line on a daily basis. *Can't be too careful.* He dialed. The receiver on the other end was picked up after three rings.

"Yes?"

"I have the confidential report. It arrived this morning."

"And?"

Markey swallowed. "I haven't had a chance to go

through it completely yet, but I think we better move fast. They're getting close."

"Then we might have to send someone to Bangkok. When can I get a copy?"

"I'll mail it out today."

"Good."

"There's something else."

"Yes."

"Dr. Riker is secretly working on an important patient," Markey said. "He left the name out of his report."

"Who is it?"

"Bradley Jenkins. The senator's—"

"I know who he is." There was a brief silence. "That explains a lot of things, Raymond."

"I know," Markey said.

"Get me that report right away."

"I'll send it out immediately. It'll be on your desk tomorrow morning."

"Thank you, Raymond. Good-bye."

"Good-bye, Reverend Sanders."

STILL leaning heavily on her cane, Sara hobbled toward Michael's room. So much was going on, so much happening at one time. Michael's illness, the possibility of being pregnant, and this weird mystery surrounding Harvey's clinic. Two patients murdered. Coincidence? Maybe, but Sara did not think so. She made a mental note to call Max Bernstein when the opportunity arose. He might know something.

She turned the corner and pushed open the door to

Michael's room. Her foot felt stiff today, more like an attached club than flesh and bones. Michael looked up from the bed. His face brightened when he saw her. She moved over to the bed and kissed him lightly.

"Feeling better?" she asked.

"Much," he replied.

"You scared me half to death, you know. I called my father. He should be here soon."

"Sara," he said, "what were you doing at the hospital today?"

She hesitated. "I didn't want to say anything to you until I was sure."

Michael sat up, his voice unsettled. "Sure about what? Are you okay?"

She nodded. His concerned, tender gaze plucked at her heart. "You know about my time of the month?"

"I guess so," he replied. "It was pretty well covered in seventh grade health class."

She chuckled but the anxiety still would not leave Michael's face. "Well, mine is six weeks late."

His eyes widened. "You're pregnant?"

"I don't know yet. The test results should be back in a few hours."

"Jesus, Sara, why didn't you tell me?"

She sat next to him on the bed and took his hand in hers. "I didn't want to get either of our hopes up if it was just another false alarm. I hate to see the disappointment in your face . . ." She turned away, but Michael gently tilted her face back toward him.

"Sara, I love you. Not being able to have kids is not going to change that."

She nestled her face into his chest. "Mean it?"

He chuckled. "Yeah, mean it."

"You got a lemon when you married me."

"Yeah, but a pretty foxy lemon. Great in the sack too."

"Fresh. You're supposed to be sick."

"I can still have a lewd thought now and again. Doctor said it's good for me."

"Funny, I didn't hear him say that."

"What did you hear him say?"

"Something about the fact that your skin was jaundiced and you may have hepatitis."

"Well, is it true? Does my skin look jaundiced?"

She examined him. "You look like a Ticonderoga pencil."

"Thanks."

"But a cute pencil."

There was a sharp knock on the door and then Sara's father peeked his head through the opening. "Am I interrupting something?"

"Come in," Michael called out. "I could use all the doctors I can get ahold of."

John Lowell entered the room. He was of average height and extraordinarily good-looking. His neatly parted, full head of gray hair was the very definition of *distinguished*. His face boasted cheeks that dimpled when he smiled and a cleft chin, but one's gaze was immediately drawn to his eyes—eyes as bright green as Sara's. He crossed the room, kissed Sara, and shook Michael's hand. "I think I'm a little out of my field of expertise here. Who examined you?"

"Harvey and Eric—you remember my friend Eric Blake?"

"Of course. I hear he is working with Dr. Riker at . . . at the clinic."

John Lowell's face shadowed at the mention of the clinic. Sara and Michael both noticed it. Michael decided to let it slide; Sara did not.

"Yes, he is," Sara said. "The clinic is making marvelous progress."

"Good," her father said, his tone clearly ending any discussion of the clinic. "Now, then, Michael, what seems to be the problem with you?"

"They're running some test, but they think it's hepatitis."

"What specialist is Harvey recommending?"

"Dr. Sagarel."

John nodded his approval. "Good man. Listen to what Sagarel says, Michael, not those two epidemiologist friends of yours."

Sara said, "You know Harvey Riker is an exceptional physician, one of the top men in his field."

"I'm sure that is so—"

"And the clinic is on the threshold of a major breakthrough in the war against AIDS."

"I'm happy to hear that," John replied without enthusiasm. "The sooner, the better. We need those funds elsewhere."

"How can you say that?"

"Let's not start this again, okay?" he said. "It is a simple question of economics."

"Economics?" Sara repeated. "Economics is more important than saving lives?"

"Please do not use that preachy, simplistic argument on me," her father replied evenly. "I've used it too often myself in front of Senate subcommittees to fall for it now. The truth of the matter is that only X amount of dollars goes into health care and medical research. X amount. Period. Some goes to the Heart Association, some to my own Cancer Center, and then there is muscular dystrophy, rheumatoid arthritis, senior citizens, whatever. We all compete for funds. Now AIDS comes along and gets an astronomical—not to mention disproportional—slice of that pie."

"You make it sound like some sort of contest," Sara said. "Doesn't compassion—"

"This is the real world," her father interrupted. "In the real world you have to deal with economic realities. Fact is, every dollar spent on AIDS is taken away from those other organizations."

"Wrong," a voice pronounced. John Lowell turned. Harvey Riker stood in the doorway. "Donations toward AIDS research are often raised separately," Harvey continued.

"Some, perhaps," Lowell replied, "but Liz Taylor and her friends can just as easily hold garage sales for the Heart Association or the Cancer Center. And let me ask you, Dr. Riker, who is the major contributor to your clinic here at the hospital?"

Harvey paused. "The federal government and the hospital board."

"And where would that money go if not to your clinic? Toward the cure of cancer or arthritis or heart disease, that's where. Many people will die of AIDS this year, but how many thousands more will die from either cancer or heart disease? Innocent victims who do not indulge in self-destructive and immoral activities—"

"Listen to yourself," Harvey interrupted. "You sound like Reverend Sanders."

Lowell stepped toward Harvey, his eyes blazing. "I don't know Sanders personally, but don't you ever compare me to that money-hungry pig, do you understand? And stop playing the naive academic. You know that there have to be priorities in medical research—to deny that is to deny reality. Some illnesses have to take precedence over others."

"And you don't think AIDS should be a priority case?"

"The disease is almost one hundred percent preventable, Dr. Riker. Can you say the same about cancer? About heart disease? About arthritis? That's why I voted against funding your clinic at the board meeting. Innocent people—people who weren't screwing strange men behind sleazy bars or jamming needles filled with poison into their veins—are killed in horrifying ways. People who weren't engaging in sexual acts that boggle the mind—you're not stupid, Dr. Riker. You know that the gay community ignored all the warning signs. Epstein-Barr ran rampant through them, but they ignored it. Cytomegalovirus and a host of other viruses infected a frighteningly high percentage of the gay community, but they chose to maintain their wanton lifestyles."

"So promiscuity should be punished with death?" Harvey shot back. "Is that what you're saying? Then a lot of heterosexuals better beware too."

"I'm saying simply this: they were warned. Anyone who spoke out against their wild sexual behavior—anyone who tried to tell them to slow down—was labeled a bigot and homophobic. With viral infections plaguing the entire gay community for years, what did they expect to happen?"

"That's ridiculous."

"Is it? Weren't these men responsible for their narcissistic and dangerous activities? Weren't they in some way asking for this?"

"Dad!"

Harvey's voice was cool. "They never asked to die, Dr. Lowell. Try as you might, you cannot get rid of this disease by denying its existence. We're not talking about something that affects animals or strange creatures or some sort of subhumans. Thousands of living, breathing human beings are dying horrible deaths from AIDS."

"I know that," Lowell said, "and Lord knows, I hope those boys are cured. But the money being spent on AIDS is outrageous when self-control will stop its spread."

Harvey shook his head. "You're just plain wrong, Dr. Lowell—even economically speaking. Do you know how much AIDS is ultimately going to cost us if we don't find a cure for it? Do you have any notion of the enormous expense in treating AIDS patients? Every social and medical program will be drained. Whole cities will go bankrupt from the medical bills."

"The patients should foot the bill themselves," Lowell replied. "There are other priorities, other ways the board could have spent that money." His voice began to crack and Sara knew what was coming next. She closed her eyes and waited. "I watched cancer kill my wife," he continued. "I watched it eat away at my Erin until . . ." He stopped then, his head lowered, his face anguished.

"And your commitment is admirable," Harvey replied. "I, however, never got the chance to see my brother die. Sidney suffered alone while lesions and infections engulfed and destroyed his body. He was shunned, made an outcast by his own family—including me. Most of these young men—boys in their twenties and thirties, for chrissake—die the death of a leper. If this disease had hit any other segment of the population, the government would have reacted quickly and with lots of money. But everyone thought it was merely a 'fag' disease, and who cares about a bunch of fags anyway?"

"They should have shown some self-control."

Harvey shook his head. "You can't play God, Dr. Lowell. While part of me agrees with your harsh statements on cigarette smoking, I have to ask you, sir, where do you draw the line? Should thin people get priority over obese? Should people who ignore their doctor's warning about high cholesterol be told that they 'asked for' their heart attack? Where do you draw the line, Dr. Lowell? And who gets to play God?"

John Lowell opened his mouth to continue the argument, then closed it. His face was etched in exhaustion. "The sad fact is that resources are limited. That means that tough choices have to be made."

"And who is going to make those choices, Dr. Lowell?"

John waved his hand as though dismissing the question. His voice took on a nervous, shaky edge. "Enough of this now," he said. "I want to hear about Michael's condition."

POLICE Lieutenant Max "Twitch" Bernstein hated New York in the summer. Too damn hot for a human to be in the city this time of the year. Not that Max knew anything else. He had been born and raised in Manhattan, went to college at New York University in Manhattan, lived with Lenny in Manhattan, worked as a cop in Manhattan. Homicide. Business was always good when you worked homicides in a place like Manhattan, but in the summer the whackos really came out of the woodwork.

Max parked his unmarked Chevy Caprice squad car (unmarked, his ass—like a criminal wouldn't know it was a cop's car at a glance) and moved toward the police barriers. He did not look like a homicide detective. He was too young, his hair too long and curly, his mustache too bushy, his nose and face just a little too long and thin. Actually, he looked more like he should be delivering pizzas than chasing killers.

He walked to the side of the building with a sign above the door that read "Black Magic Bar and Grill." Max had visited the Black Magic in more liberated, fun-loving days when it was called the Butt Seriously. More than once, actually. Always in disguise. Used an alias too.

He flashed his badge at a couple of uniforms and proceeded down the alleyway. Sergeant Willie Monticelli greeted him.

"How's it going, Twitch?" Willie asked.

Bernstein did not care much for his nickname. First of all he did not have a twitch. Yes, he fidgeted a lot, gestured wildly, bit his fingernails past the cuticles, played with anything he could get his hands on, blinked too much, never sat or stood still. Sure, everybody was always asking him when he had quit chain-smoking.

But there was definitely no twitch.

"Better before I got this call," he replied. "Looks like you put on a little weight, Willie."

Monticelli patted his stomach. "Nice to meet someone who's not all caught up in the diet craze, huh?"

"Great." Bernstein took out his pencil, put it in his mouth, and chewed. It already looked like a much-used dog toy. "What's the story here?"

"A garbageman found him half an hour ago. Wanna take a look?"

Already feeling his stomach churn, Max nodded and bit down harder on the pencil. He hated this part. "Have to. It's why I'm paid the big bucks."

"Yeah, I can tell by your fancy set of wheels."

Willie walked over to the still form sprawled in the garbage. He pulled the sheet back. Max swallowed away his nausea. Then he bent down and examined the mess that was once a living man.

"Jesus."

"Looks like the Gay Slasher is back," Willie said. "Same M.O. as the other two."

"With one noticeable difference," Max said almost under his breath. "And don't call him that, Willie. The press will dive all over it."

"They're gonna dive anyway."

"They ignored the first two victims," Max noted.

"They won't ignore this one."

"What makes you say that?"

"Do you know who this is?"

Bernstein looked down at the disfigured face and then up at Willie. "His mother wouldn't recognize him."

"You're not going to like it."

"I never do."

"According to his wallet, his name is Bradley Jenkins. I checked him out. His father is—"

"A U.S. Senator, I know." Max closed his eyes and turned away. He stroked his mustache.

"Right. Bradley lives on Twelfth Street. His father and mother have a house in the Hamptons. Weird, huh? Senator from Arkansas who vacations on Long Island?"

"Senator Jenkins has been living in the Northeast since he began going to school here as a boy," Max explained. "I doubt the guy has spent five straight days in Arkansas, except during election campaigns."

"How do you know so much about it?"

Max's hand ran through his thick, dark curly hair several times. "First of all, he's the Senate minority leader. Second, I read a newspaper now and again."

"And third?"

"Bradley is a good friend of Sara Lowell's. I met him once."

"Oh," Willie said. "That's too bad. Think Sara will handle the story? It'd be nice to have a member of the press on our side for this one."

"I doubt it."

"Yeah, she won't waste her time with us anymore. She's big-time now. You see her on TV last night?"

Max nodded, pacing rapidly back and forth but traveling no more than five feet in any direction. "You got today's *Herald* in your car?"

"Sure. Why?"

"Get it. I want to show you something."

Willie fetched the paper and handed it to Bernstein. Bernstein grabbed it and thumbed through the pages quickly, ripping several as he went along.

"Whoa, Twitch, slow down a minute."

"It's right here . . ."

"What's right here?" Willie asked.

Bernstein continued to riffle through the paper, the pencil still in his mouth. "Did you read the society pages today?"

"Shit, no, I don't read that crap. But I did check out the box scores."

"That should be a big help," Max said. He turned a few more pages, his right foot tapping the pavement impatiently. "Bingo," he said at last. "Take a look at this."

Willie looked over Max's shoulder. A page of photographs showed the well-dressed people who had attended Dr. John Lowell's charity ball the previous evening. Max pointed to the picture in the upper right-hand corner. "There."

"Shit on a stick," Willie whispered.

The caption read: *The luminous Sara Lowell enjoys the festivities after her triumphant* NewsFlash *debut with (right) her handsome hubby and Knicks superstar, Michael Silverman, and (left) Senator Stephen Jenkins' dashing son, Bradley.*

"It's him," Willie exclaimed, pointing to the photograph. "It's Bradley Jenkins."

"Correct."

"Not much resemblance now. Maybe a little around the ears."

"Very funny."

"God, I hate these big cases," Willie said. "Mayor'll be calling all the time. Everybody wanting answers."

"We might as well get started, then. I want you to check the neighborhood. See if anybody saw anything."

"Sure thing. Someone must have heard something— screams or a struggle or something."

Bernstein shook his head. "I don't think the murder took place here."

"What do you mean?"

"Take a look at the corpse," he continued. "Bradley Jenkins has been dead since last night, right?"

"Looks like it."

"But at night this alley is packed with patrons of the Black Magic."

"Patrons. Is that what they call them now?"

Bernstein greeted the remark with a hint of a smile. *Oh, Willie, if you only knew* . . . "Someone would have seen the murder if it happened back here last night. And there's blood only on the body—none in the area. If he had been stabbed a zillion times back here, the alley would have been sprayed with blood. No, I think Jenkins was killed somewhere else and his body was dumped here. That's where the M.O. is different. The body was moved this time."

Willie followed his young lieutenant's pacing, his head

shifting back and forth as if he were watching a tennis match. "Makes no sense, Twitch. There's a lot of places less risky to get rid of a body. Why here?"

"Don't know."

"You want me to find out if Bradley was gay?"

Max felt a powerful headache coming on and began to massage his temples with his fingertips. The son of a prominent, conservative senator found with multiple knife wounds behind a gay bar—Tylenol wouldn't put a dent in this one. "No need," Bernstein said. "I'll get the personal info from Sara."

"Send my condolences."

"Will do. I want the lab over every inch of this alley and I want this neighborhood canvassed. Ask if they saw anything out of the ordinary last night or this morning."

"Gotcha. Oh, one more thing."

"What?"

"Good luck with the press, those bastards. Next thing you know we'll have every loony tune in the area confessing or copycatting the son of a bitch."

Max nodded and clenched his teeth. The pencil in his mouth snapped into two jagged pieces, nearly cutting his gums.

It was going to be a bad week.

6

"HOW are you feeling?" Sara asked Michael for the twentieth time.

"Fine," he replied. "Ask again and I'm going to scream."

"I'm just concerned."

"Then do something constructive," Michael said.

"Like?"

"Like lock the door and get naked."

"I stepped into that one, didn't I?"

Michael nodded.

A woman's voice from behind them said, "Hello, Sara."

They both looked toward the entranceway where Dr. Carol Simpson now stood. Chopin's Concerto in D minor played from the small CD player beside Michael's bed. Reece, of all people, had fetched it from the Knicks' locker room at Madison Square Garden and brought it to the hospital, claiming, "This shit makes me sick, but it might be just what ol' Mikey needs."

"Michael," Sara said, "this is Dr. Simpson, the obstetrician I was telling you about."

"Nice to meet you, Michael," Carol Simpson said.

"Nice meeting you."

"I heard you'd been rushed in," she continued. "How are you feeling?"

"Better, thanks," he said.

"Good," she replied. "Since I knew you were both here, I thought I'd stop by personally to deliver the news."

Michael sat up. His lips felt dry. He tried to wet them with his tongue, but there was no moisture there either. "News?" he asked.

"Yes. I have the results of Sara's test."

"And?" Sara prompted.

Carol Simpson stuck out her hand. "Congratulations. You're pregnant."

Sara's hands fluttered toward her mouth. "You're sure?"

"Positive. About two months, I'd say."

Sara turned toward Michael. "Did you hear that, hon?"

Michael nodded, not yet able to speak. "Forgive me, Doctor," he managed. "It's just . . ."

"No need to apologize. It's nice to see."

Sara wrapped her arms around him and pulled him close, smothering him against her chest.

"Well," Dr. Simpson said, "I have to be going back.

Sara, I want you to stop by and see me tomorrow morning, okay?"

"Okay."

Michael pulled away. "Thanks, Doc."

"Take care of yourself, Michael. Congratulations again."

She left them alone.

Michael smiled. "Do I have to start calling you Mommy soon?"

She nodded. "And I get to call you Dad."

"Even in bed?"

"No. There I can still call you by your name."

"Hung Stallion?"

"Dream on."

"God, I can't believe it. We're going to be parents, Sara. You, me, and baby makes three."

They kissed.

"I love you, Michael."

"I love you too," he said, rubbing her still-firm stomach. "Both of you."

As they kissed again, the phone rang. Michael reluctantly reached over, picked up the receiver, and said hello. After a brief pause he handed it to Sara.

"It's for you," he said.

"Who is it?"

He shrugged. "Don't know."

Sara put the phone to her ear. A nasal, female voice said, "Please hold while I connect you."

There was one ring before the phone was picked up.

"Sara?"

"Max?"

"Jeez, you weren't easy to find. Took me over an hour to track you down. How've you been?"

"Never better."

"Glad to hear it."

She could almost see him chewing on his nails as he spoke. "This isn't a social call, is it, Max?"

"No, it's not."

"So what's up?"

Max Bernstein let go a long breath. "Bradley Jenkins was murdered. I need to talk to you right away."

THEY met half an hour later in a quiet corner in the hospital cafeteria. After a quick greeting Max said, "Everything we say here is confidential and off the record, okay?"

"Okay."

"Let me ask you something right off the top."

"Go ahead," Sara said.

"Was Bradley Jenkins gay?"

"Yes."

Max had expected that answer. He nodded, his curly dark hair swaying with the movement. He put a fresh pencil into his mouth and began to chew. Then he crossed his right leg over his left, ran his hand through his curls, put his feet back on the floor, and then crossed his left leg over his right.

Bernstein was thirty-two years old, but he looked a good five years younger. Sara knew the police department—for that matter the world at large—considered Twitch Bernstein a bit of an enigma. Despite being homicide's number one lieutenant, he had no love of danger. He hated carrying a gun and had never used one in the line of duty. He was barely adequate with his fists, did not consider himself particularly brave, and tried to avoid violence whenever possible.

What he did like, however, was solving puzzles—the bigger, the better. And he was good at it. Damn good. No one knew for sure just how he did it, but Bernstein had the rare ability to plod and putter and shift and un-nerve and fidget his way to the answer.

"My turn to ask a question," Sara said. "What happened to Bradley and why did you want to know if he was gay?"

"That's two questions."

"Max . . ."

"Just trying to keep things light," Bernstein said. "We found his body this morning behind a gay bar in the Village."

"Jesus."

"The autopsy is not in yet, but we're sure he died from multiple stab wounds. We think . . . Sara, are you all right?"

Sara's eyes were wide, her face shockingly pale. "Have there been other murders?" she uttered.

"What makes you say that?"

"Don't play with me, Max."

"We may have a serial killer on our hands," he said. "I wasn't involved in the investigation of the first two cases, but two other men were killed in the same grisly way. We suspect that the same person committed all three murders."

"And why did you ask if Bradley was gay?"

"Because the other two victims were. The killer may be targeting the gay community. Now it's my turn. How did you know that there were other victims?"

"I assume you've met Dr. Harvey Riker," she began.

"Sure."

"You know that he is operating an AIDS clinic in here?" He shrugged. "So?"

"The first two victims—what were their names?"

"Bill Whitherson and Scott Trian."

"Right. They were part of a select group of AIDS patients who were being treated in this clinic. It should be in your files."

Bernstein's leg began to shake. "To be honest I haven't had a chance to go through them thoroughly yet. I just got the case an hour ago."

"Anyway, Harvey told me about it last night. That's how I knew."

"An obvious question—was Bradley being treated here too?"

Sara lifted the coffee cup to her lips and took a sip. "I don't know," she said. "You'll have to ask Harvey."

"What do you mean, you don't know?"

"Just what I said."

"Did Bradley have AIDS?"

"It can't leave this room," Sara said.

"It won't."

"The answer is yes."

"Was he being treated for it?"

"Yes, but I don't know where. It was a big secret, and I didn't want him to tell me."

"Why not?" he asked.

"You know who his father is, of course."

"Of course."

"The senator beat the crap out of Bradley when he found out that I knew about his AIDS. Bradley's father was terrified that the truth would be exposed."

"Because it would ruin him."

"Exactly. So we tried not to talk about it."

"I see." Max stopped, looked up toward the ceiling, scratched his neck where it met the top of his chest. "Wouldn't Dr. Riker have said something to you if he was treating Bradley?"

"No way. The clinic is cloaked in secrecy. I do not know the names of any patients being treated at the clinic."

"Interesting." Max looked away for a moment, his hand moving up now to rub his face. "So why did Dr. Riker speak to you about the two murders last night?"

She hesitated. "I think you better ask Harvey that."

"Sara, you're not going to pull that 'can't reveal my source' crap on me, are you?"

"I'm afraid I'll have to for right now. But speak to Harvey. He can enlighten you better than I can anyway."

Max shrugged. "Okay. Let's find him."

AFTER passing two security checkpoints, Max and Sara found Harvey in his office in the Sidney Pavilion. He looked up from his paper-cluttered desk, his eyes red and weary.

"What's up?" he asked.

"Harvey, you remember Lieutenant Bernstein."

"Of course. Hello, Lieutenant."

"How's it going. Doc?"

"Fine, thanks," Harvey replied. "Sara, I just finished talking to Michael. As we suspected, the abdominal ultrasound showed swelling in Michael's liver."

"What does that mean?" Sara asked.

"It could mean a dozen things, but Dr. Sagarel, Eric, and I still agree that it is probably hepatitis. We should have the results of the blood test in another day or two. Chances are he'll need a couple of weeks here and at least a month of bed rest."

"And basketball?"

"Not this season, Sara. There's an outside chance he'll be able to play in the play-offs."

"He knows?"

"I told him. His reaction was a little strange."

"Meaning?"

"It didn't really bother him all that much. He told me the good news about your pregnancy. Hell, it was all he'd talk about."

"Pregnancy?" Max interrupted. "You didn't tell me."

"Hardly seemed the time."

"Congratulations," Max said.

"Thank you. Harvey, Lieutenant Bernstein needs to talk to you."

Harvey stood and moved in front of his desk. "Is this about what we discussed last night?"

"Might be," Max interjected, trying to sound professional but coming across like a bad actor in an old private-eye movie. He had never been good at the tough-guy bit. "Is Bradley Jenkins a patient of yours?"

Harvey's face twisted into a look of confusion and annoyance. "What the hell does that have to do with anything?"

Bernstein cleared his throat. "Mind answering the question?"

"As a matter of fact, I do." His line of vision swung over to Sara. "What's going on here?"

Sara looked over to Max, who nodded for her to go ahead. "Bradley Jenkins was found murdered this morning," she said.

"What?"

"Multiple stab wounds," Bernstein said. "We suspect that his death is related to the murders of two patients at your clinic, a Bill Whitherson and a Scott Trian."

"Jesus Christ."

"Now would you mind answering my question? Was Bradley Jenkins a patient at the clinic?"

Harvey moved tentatively back toward his chair like a man who had taken too many blows. He sat down and lowered his head into his hands. "Sara," he asked after a few moments had passed, "can he be trusted?"

"Yes."

His eyes tried to lock onto Bernstein's, but the lieutenant's were busy dancing about the small office. "Swear you won't let the media get it."

"Swear."

"Yes, Bradley Jenkins was a patient of mine—a very confidential patient."

"How long had Bradley been receiving treatment here?"

"Not long. Four months maybe."

"And the other two—Whitherson and Trian?"

"They were both here from almost the beginning."

"How long ago was that?"

"More than two years."

Max nodded. He finally took out his pad and used the pencil to write on it. "Now, why don't you tell me about last night's conversation with Miss Lowell?"

Harvey looked over to Sara.

"You can trust him," she said.

Hesitantly, Harvey began by telling Max his suspicions that the murders were related to the clinic. Then he explained that they were close, painfully close, to finding a treatment for AIDS. Max nodded vigorously, jotting pages of notes and listening without comment.

When Harvey stopped speaking, Bernstein said, "You said 'we' might have found a cure. Who is 'we'?"

"Mostly myself and my late partner, Dr. Bruce Grey— and a new member of the team, Dr. Eric Blake."

"Blake's a friend of Michael's, isn't he?"

"Yes," Sara replied.

Max's eyes narrowed in thought. The pencil found its way back into his mouth. "Dr. Bruce Grey . . . isn't he the guy who swan-dived through a hotel window a couple of weeks back?"

Harvey glanced toward Sara and then nodded.

"Interesting," Max said again. "So what do you make of his suicide, Dr. Riker?"

"I'm not sure I make anything out of it," Harvey replied. "Bruce committed suicide, I guess. That's what the police insist anyway. The rest of what I told Sara must have been some wild fabrications my overtired mind and overactive imagination invented. It's crazy."

Max moved toward the chair in front of the desk and sat down. "I enjoy crazy."

CASSANDRA tiptoed down the staircase. She was still a bit hungover from last night's festivities, but her headache was not nearly as bad as usual. She tried to put the pieces of the previous evening back together. She recalled some heavy-duty conversation with Michael. She vaguely remembered screwing Senator Jenkins in the cabana. She had some recollection of drinking too much.

But the part she remembered with startling clarity came toward the end of the party. Cassandra had made her way to the bar for one last shot before she called it a night. While waiting for the bartender to fill her glass, she started a conversation with a man who also seemed a bit inebriated. She knew who the man was, had met him a few times, but she had never paid him much (or any) attention. But no one else was around, and Cassandra was feeling particularly charitable.

When the guests began to leave more than an hour later, Cassandra realized that she was still talking with the same man. Talking. Not flirting, not hitting on, not being hit upon, not fucking. Just talking. And shit, she had to be seriously intoxicated. Under normal, more sober circumstances she would not waste a good spit on this guy.

But the man had been a perfect gentleman. He listened to *her*, to what she had to say. Oh, she had seen men feign interest in order to get in her pants, but somehow she knew that this guy was actually interested in what she had to say.

Strange.

Even stranger, when she finally asked him if he wanted to go upstairs with her, he answered, "Not tonight."

"Why not?" she asked.

The man shook his head and smiled. "Didn't I see this once on the *Twilight Zone*? The homely man and the gorgeous woman switch places? I can't believe I'm saying this, but here goes—I don't want to be just another notch on your belt."

"Excuse me?"

"I know, I know. I don't believe it either. Look, Cassandra, I'd give my right arm to spend an evening with you."

"So?"

He shrugged, holding up his hands helplessly. "If I go upstairs with you now, that'll be it. But if I refuse, you might be intrigued. You might want to pursue it— though I can't help thinking that once you're sober you'll think this whole conversation was a nightmare."

She smiled. "You're giving away your strategy, Harvey."

"Yeah, well, I never was very good at this stuff and I'm a bit out of practice—like twenty-six years out of practice. Do yourself a favor, Cassandra. Stay away from me. I'm trouble."

"Now you really have me intrigued," she said.

"Nothing to be intrigued about," Harvey continued. "I'm just a workaholic who spends every waking and sleeping moment in a hospital in Spanish Harlem. I have no time for a social life. It was a fun evening, a wonderful distraction, but it's time I returned to Planet Earth."

"I wish you'd reconsider," she said.

Harvey pounded the side of his head like he was trying to clear it. "I'm dreaming, aren't I?" he asked. "This whole conversation is a dream."

"Maybe. I guess we'll find out tomorrow."

Now it was tomorrow, and for some strange reason, Cassandra wanted to see Harvey Riker again. One problem—she had spent most of the morning trying to figure out what she should do next and had come up with nothing. Should she wait until Harvey called? Suppose he didn't? And talk about being out of practice—it had been years since Cassandra questioned or cared if a man called her or not.

Then a solution had presented itself when her father came home.

"Where were you?" she had asked him.

"At Columbia Presbyterian," John Lowell replied, distracted. "Michael was rushed there."

"Is he all right?"

"I think so. His friends are taking care of him."

"Harvey Riker?"

Her father nodded. "They think he has hepatitis."

"I think I'll go visit him."

"Whatever. When are you going to go?"

"In ten minutes," she said.

"Good. I have a meeting in a little while, and I don't want anyone around when my appointment gets here. Understood?"

But that had been more than an hour ago, which

was why she was tiptoeing. Her father's private meetings were just that—private. Bathed in secrecy. He would be furious if he found out she was still home. She crept down the hallway toward the garage. As she passed her father's study, she heard his voice come through the thick oak. He sounded very angry.

"Goddamn it, you shouldn't be here," her father shouted.

"Relax," another voice said, a voice Cassandra could not quite place. "You said no one was home."

"Doesn't matter. I don't want you in my house."

"Stop worrying so much. There's work to be done."

Who the hell . . . ? Cassandra carefully moved away from the door, her mind racing. The voice was so familiar. She had heard it before, she was sure of it. But where? And who did it belong to?

She was at a traffic light about a mile away when the answer came to her.

7

"WHAT I found in Dr. Grey's note," handwriting analyst Robert Swinster began, "is pretty rare."

Lieutenant Max Bernstein nodded. "I know. It might just explain everything."

"Like what?"

"Later," Max said. "I have a million things to do."

"I can take a hint. I'm as good as gone."

Max shook Swinster's hand and patted his back. "Thanks again, Bob. I really appreciate it."

"No problem, Twitch. I'm glad I could help."

Robert Swinster walked away from Bernstein's desk as Sara hobbled toward it.

"Hi, Max."

He smiled at her. "Glad you could get here so fast. Have a seat."

Sara examined the man and his desk. All the usual

signs were there—his red eyes, the ragged edges of his fingernails, the thought lines in his forehead, the fingers twiddling with the pencil, the paper clips he had snapped in half lying all over the desk, the hand constantly rubbing his unshaven face.

For two days Max and his men had investigated the sensational murder of young Bradley Jenkins by the now-infamous Gay Slasher. A distraught Senator Jenkins had gone into hiding and would make no comments to the press about the rumors swirling around his son's death. His Senate spokesman continuously spewed a standard line— the murder was clearly a ploy by certain subversive groups to destroy the senator's reputation and personal life.

Max had interviewed Senator Jenkins yesterday, after his son's funeral. Bernstein had seen during his years in homicide what a tragedy like this could do to even the strongest of men, but he was still taken aback by the senator's appearance. His skin was ashen, his eyes wide and uncomprehending, his shoulders slumped, his whole demeanor defeated. The senator had answered Max's questions in a flat, distant voice, but it seemed that the man knew very little that would help find the killer.

"Who was that?" Sara asked.

"Robert Swinster," Max replied, "a handwriting analyst. He was rechecking Bruce Grey's note."

"Did he find anything?"

The phone on the desk buzzed. Max put up a finger to signal for her to wait and picked up the receiver.

"Yes?"

"*Daily News* on line five again. ABC-TV on line eight."

"I'm not talking to the press right now," he snapped. He slammed the receiver back into the cradle. "Damn reporters," he muttered. "Enough to drive a man crazy."

"Temper, temper."

"Everyone keeps screaming how we're not doing our job. How the hell are we supposed to get anything done with the press breathing down our necks all the time? Bunch of vultures—present company excluded, of course. You know something? I think the media hopes the psycho will strike again, the sick bastards."

"Comes with the territory," Sara replied.

"I know," Max said, "but the pressure on this one is unbelievable. At the press conference the other day I felt like fresh meat in front of starving Dobermans. And that's not the half of it. The mayor's demanding answers in that holier-than-thou way of his. Every gay activist is coming out of the woodwork accusing the fascist police department of discriminating against homosexuals. I've had a dozen phony confessions today alone. Everyone suddenly wants to be the Gay Slasher." He took a deep breath. "Ah, screw it. So how's Michael?"

"Feeling better. His teammates are visiting him now."

"Good. I needed to talk this over with you right away."

"Bouncing time, eh?"

Max nodded and smiled wearily. Several years ago Sara had been instrumental in helping Max find a cop killer who had randomly gunned down four of Max's fellow officers in one week. Max had learned from that experience that he liked bouncing ideas off an intelligent listener, and Sara was about as sharp a listener as there was.

Very often they said some crazy things to each other, came up with some crazy hypotheses, even called each other crazy, but eventually the irrational statements began to mesh with the more rational facts, often forming solid solutions.

"Is this case harder for you than most?" she asked.

"Meaning?"

"You know what I mean."

He smiled nervously, checking to make sure that no one was within earshot. "It'd make an interesting news angle, huh? The fag detective in charge of finding the Gay Slasher?"

She said nothing.

"Sara, you're still the only one who knows—aside from Lenny and my mother." He swallowed, his Adam's apple visibly sliding up and down. "I wish I could say something, but do you know what would happen to me if the force found out?"

"I can imagine."

"I'd lose everything. I'd be lucky if they let me work as a meter maid."

"You don't have to explain yourself to me, Max."

He nodded, his eyes lowered to the floor. "By the way, Lenny says hello."

"How is he?"

He shrugged. "He's a nag, but I love him."

"As long as you're happy."

"You sound like my mother. Can we get back to the case now?"

"Okay," Sara said, "what have you got so far?"

"Not much. We got a wino who saw Bradley's body

being dumped behind the Black Magic early in the a.m. We also located the car the killer was driving at the time. That's about it."

"Go on."

"It seems the wino, a Mr. Louis Bluwell, was sleeping off a couple of bottles of gin under some garbage bags when he heard the car and saw a man he described as 'a big monster' get out of the car and dump the body amongst the garbage bags. Mr. Bluwell said the car was a beat-up green Chevy. We found a car matching that description abandoned on Riverside Drive around One Hundred Forty-fifth Street. There was a fair amount— make that gallons—of the victim's blood splashed all over the floor of the trunk. The car had been stolen the previous evening."

"Did the lab find anything else in the car?"

"One set of fingerprints—the victim's. A few hairs— all belonging to the victim."

"Figures," Sara said. "Anything else?"

"According to Mr. Bluwell, the man in the car was big—a mountain-sized guy with dark hair. No noticeable features."

"So what do you make of it?"

Bernstein leaned back, placing his hands together, the fingertips of his index fingers resting against his nose. He put his feet on his desk. "I find it all interesting," he remarked.

"How so?" Sara asked.

"It just doesn't make sense."

"What doesn't?"

"Okay, help me here, Sara. What do we know so far?

First, all three victims were homosexuals. Second, all three victims were being treated at the same AIDS clinic. Third, all three died of stab wounds within the past three weeks."

"So?"

"So take a look at the cases one by one for a second." Max sat up quickly, opened up his pocket pad, and read. "Victim one: Mr. Scott Trian. Trian had been found tied spread-eagle to his bed in apartment 8G at 27 Christopher Street. The corpse was found with twenty-seven stab wounds. The murderer sliced off Trian's left ear, both thumbs, and left nipple—while he was still alive, we think. He also castrated Trian."

"Unbelievable," Sara whispered.

Max nodded. "Even more unbelievable is that we've managed to keep the mutilation and torture away from the media."

"Won't last," Sara added. "Someone will open his mouth."

"True enough, but until then I can use it to cut through all these phony confessors. When pressed for details about the killings, none of the confessing Gay Slashers knew about the mutilation or torture. They only knew what they had read in the papers. But we're getting off the subject. Let's move on to the second victim."

"Okay."

Bernstein wet his index finger and turned a few pages. "Victim number two: Mr. William Whitherson. Mr. Whitherson's boyfriend, a Stuart Lebrinski, stepped out of their co-op on the Upper West Side to pick up some groceries. When he came back an hour later, Whitherson was dead. Twenty-three stab wounds. There was no mutilation or signs of torture."

"There was no time," Sara said. "The boyfriend was only gone an hour."

"Could be," Max allowed. "But now things get really interesting. Victim number three: Mr. Bradley Jenkins." Pages were once again turned before Max continued. "A limousine driver dropped Bradley off in front of his apartment building after the charity ball at your father's estate. One neighbor thought he saw Jenkins leave the building a few minutes later with another man the neighbor described as 'very big.'"

"Probably the same guy the wino saw."

"Makes sense," Max agreed. "Anyway, the next thing we know Jenkins winds up dead behind the Black Magic Bar and Grill. Several patrons of the bar recognized Bradley from his photograph, but all swear that he had not been seen that entire evening."

"So? He was at my father's party until late."

"One other thing—the lock on Bradley's apartment door was jimmied."

"The big guy probably broke in," Sara said. "I don't see what part of it doesn't make sense."

Max put down his notebook. "Put the whole thing together, Sara. First, Bradley Jenkins comes home from the party. Then some big guy jimmies the lock and breaks in. Fine, okay so far. You with me?"

"Go on."

"Now, from the looks of Jenkins' apartment, the struggle—if there was one—was painfully short. Then Bradley and the killer leave the apartment and drive off

together. Based on the tremendous amount of blood in
the trunk, we can speculate that Bradley was murdered
while lying in the trunk of the car. No mutilation, but
like the other two, approximately two dozen stab wounds
cover his face, chest, and groin. The killer keeps the body
in the trunk overnight, wakes up the next morning, and
dumps his body behind a gay bar."

"Maybe Bradley knew the guy," Sara said. "Hold on.
Skip that. If they knew each other, there would have
been no need for the jimmied lock."

Max managed a grin. "And I was all ready to jump on
you for being wrong."

"Sorry to spoil it for you."

"Never mind. But you're ignoring the more important question."

"Which is?"

"Why did the killer take Bradley out of the apartment
in the first place? Think about it. Trian and Whitherson
were both murdered in their apartments, right? The killer
got them alone, did his thing, and left the mess. But not
with Bradley. He went to the trouble of taking him out
of the apartment. That meant the killer had to go to the
trouble of stealing a car, one. Two, he had to risk being
seen leaving the apartment as well as risk being seen getting rid of the body behind the Black Magic. Why? Why
not just kill him like the others and get it over with? And
why dump the body behind a gay bar?"

Sara thought for a moment. "I see what you mean.
Look, Max, I know the heat is coming down on you,
but I can't hold back much longer. I won't say anything
about the mutilation of Trian, but I have to let the public

know about the connection of the three victims to the AIDS clinic."

"Sara . . ."

"Someone is going to dig it up soon anyway, and now Bradley's father can't be hurt any more than he already is." She gripped her cane. "More important, Harvey has decided to go public with the clinic's success. He needs to raise funds. There'll be an hour story on the success of his AIDS treatment on *NewsFlash*."

Max whistled. "Talk about a major scoop," he said. "Could be Pulitzer here, Sara. I'd hate to see you miss that."

"Not fair, Max."

"I know. My bias against the press flaring up again. Sorry."

"Forget it." She watched him start to gnaw on his finger—not the nail, the finger. "Max, don't you think the connection to the clinic is important?"

"Crucial," he answered, removing his finger from his mouth and rubbing his face with the same hand. "My people are checking out everyone involved with the place."

"That's the crux of the whole thing, isn't it?" she asked. "I mean, everyone assumes that a psychopath is targeting gays, but he could really be after AIDS patients or, more specifically, patients at Harvey's clinic."

"Could be."

"What about Harvey's fear that someone is trying to sabotage the clinic?"

Bernstein stood up and began pacing in a small, tight circle. "A possibility but a long shot. According to Harvey, nobody outside the clinic—not the FDA, you, or anybody else—knew how close they were to finding a cure. Sure, there were rumors, but people don't usually try to sabotage a rumor."

"I'm not sure I agree with you there," Sara said. "We've both seen plenty of people act on a lot less than unsubstantiated rumors before."

"Granted, but look at it this way—if someone wanted to destroy Harvey and Bruce's work, why go to the trouble of murdering all these people in such a grisly fashion? Why not just burn down the clinic? Or why not just kill . . . ?" His voice trailed away.

"Just kill?"

Max swallowed. "I was about to say, 'Why not just kill the doctors?'"

There was a long silence. "Max, what did the handwriting analyst say?"

"Bruce Grey wrote the note. No chance of it being a forgery."

"Does that mean he definitely committed suicide?"

Bernstein paused, his hand still nervously massaging his chin. "Not necessarily," he began. "Because of the note in Grey's handwriting, the suicide was barely questioned. It was an open-and-shut case."

"And now?"

"There's so many holes, Sara. I checked out Grey's history. He seemed happy enough, normal enough, no signs of depression or mental illness."

"But if Bruce wrote the note—"

"Ah, but *how* did he write the note?"

"I don't understand."

"As you know, I took the liberty of having the hand-writing analyst check the note again. But this time I had him look for other details."

"Such as?"

"For one thing, Swinster noted that the handwriting was unusually shaky. Words and letters ran into one an-other. It was definitely written by Grey—the shape and design of the letters tell you that—but it was not his nor-mal handwriting. He was in a rush or under duress or something like that."

"Isn't that normal in the case of a suicide?"

"Not really. Usually, the handwriting is slow and even and fairly normal. Grey always wrote very neatly—even when he scribbled down a prescription. The suicide note was uncharacteristically sloppy. It could have been—I said *could* have been—coerced."

Sara sat forward with her eyes opened wide. Her words came fast. "Then what you're saying is that maybe Bruce was forced to write it," she nearly shouted. "Maybe somebody put a gun to his head and made him do it."

"Calm down, Sara. We don't know anything of the sort yet."

"And if that's the case, Harvey could be in real dan-ger."

Bernstein shook his head. "Don't start building this into something it's not. There are a million better expla-nations for all of this. It could be something as simple as Bruce Grey being so cold his hand shook when he wrote the note. Or it could be that he was nervous at the thought of running headfirst through a window."

"You don't buy any of that."

Max pocketed his keys. "But it sounded good."

"Where are you going?"

"To the Days Inn. I want to check out Grey's room."

"HEY, hey, Mikey, boy! How you feeling?"

Michael looked up and smiled. Reece and Jerome piled into the room with a half dozen other Knicks. "You guys are a bunch of the ugliest candy stripers I've ever seen."

"But look what we brought you," Jerome said, holding up a brown paper bag.

"What is it?" Michael asked.

"Hospital food sucks, right?" Jerome continued.

"Bet your ass," Michael replied. "Two days of it and I'm already going crazy."

"And," Reece added, "everyone knows how you Jews love food from the Orient."

"You mean—"

"Yup," Reece interrupted, "takeout from Hunan Empire."

"I think I love you guys."

"Don't get mushy on us, old dude."

"I'll try not to break down."

"So how you feeling, Mikey?"

"Okay."

"When you coming back?"

"Probably not till next season."

"Shit."

"Yeah, tell me about it. But, guys, guess what."

There was a pause. "Reece already told us the good

news," Jerome said with a wide smile. "You're going to be a papa. Congratulations, man."

They shook hands. "Thanks."

The other players gathered around him to offer their congratulations.

"Hey, old dude, how you gonna teach me anything from a hospital bed?" Jerome asked.

"Watch old game films," Reece suggested. "See how Mikey played when he was in his prime."

"They had movie cameras back then?" Jerome joked.

Reece laughed.

"What the hell are you laughing at?" Michael asked him. "You're only a year younger than me."

"I know. That's why I want you back with the team. I don't want to be the new 'old dude.'"

"Swell. How's practice going anyway?"

"We miss you, Mikey," Reece said.

"Nice to hear."

"Yeah," Jerome added, "I miss blocking your shot and putting it in your face."

"Just hand over the food, Jerome, before my doctor sees it."

"Too late."

The tall bodies of the New York Knicks turned toward the door. Harvey stood leaning against the frame of the doorway.

"Hey, Harv," Reece said.

"How's it going, Reece?"

"Not bad."

"Would you and your cohorts mind if I have a few minutes alone with Michael?"

"Of course not."

"Good," Harvey replied. "In the meantime I'll have one of the nurses bring you hoodlums over to the pediatric wing. There's a few kids in there you fellas might be able to cheer up."

"Be our pleasure," Reece said. "Come on, guys. Let's go."

Michael's teammates bade him good-bye and left. Then Harvey closed the door and moved into the room.

"So what's up?" Michael asked.

"We just got back results of the blood tests," Harvey began. "You were HBV positive."

"Meaning?"

"You have hepatitis."

"Isn't that what you were expecting?"

"Yes and no."

"Explain, *por favor.*"

"Frankly speaking, it's all a little strange."

"What do you mean?"

Harvey crossed the room. "You have hepatitis B rather than hepatitis A."

"Is that bad?"

"Ninety percent of all hep B patients recover fully within three to four months. With a little luck and some good training, you could even be back in shape for the end of the season and the play-offs."

"Great."

"But we'd like to take a few more tests, Michael," Harvey said, "including a T cell study and an HIV test."

Michael sat up, his eyes finding Harvey's and locking onto them. "An HIV test? Isn't that—"

"Yes," Harvey interrupted, "it's a test which is supposed to indicate if you are carrying the AIDS virus."

"Why would I need one of those?"

"It's merely a precaution," Harvey continued. "We're sure you don't have AIDS or anything of the sort. You're not homosexual and you're not an intravenous drug user, which means your chances of having it are next to nil."

"So?"

"So Eric and I discussed it. We also consulted Dr. Sagarel, the gastroenterologist. The thing is no one really understands how you contracted hep B."

"Some bad seafood maybe?"

"You're thinking of hepatitis A," Harvey continued. "Hepatitis B is transmitted through blood transfusions, saliva, semen, stuff like that. Now, I know you're going to want to slap me for asking, but I have to do it anyway. It's important that you tell the truth."

"Shoot."

"I know you love Sara, but have you had any extramarital affairs? Any at all. An indiscretion during a Knicks road trip, anything?"

"No," Michael answered. "Never."

Harvey nodded. "Normally, we wouldn't think of going through with an HIV test, but when Eric reviewed your records, he came up with the fact that you had a blood transfusion after your boating accident in the Bahamas."

"But that was years ago."

"I know. If it were more recent, I wouldn't worry about it as much. Nowadays we have the technology to screen blood donations so that the chances of a patient's receiving HIV-contaminated blood are very remote. Back then the test didn't exist."

"So you're saying—"

"I'm not saying anything. Look, Michael, Eric and I have HIV-on-the-brain with the clinic and all. You don't have AIDS. I'm nearly positive of it. Under normal circumstances I would have just gone ahead and done the HIV test without telling you."

"So why didn't you? You didn't give me details about the other tests."

"Because the law requires that you sign a form, that's all."

"And Dr. Sagarel agrees with you and Eric about this?"

Harvey's face seemed to cloud over in hurt for a brief moment. "Yes, Michael. He agreed."

"Harv," Michael began, "I don't mean to question your judgment—"

Harvey waved his hand. "Don't worry about it, Michael. It was the right question to ask."

"So now what?"

"I'd like to draw some blood, if it's okay."

Michael shrugged, his eyes still scared. Then he nodded. "You guys are the doctors."

"Good," Harvey said. "Give me your arm."

"Pick a vein, any vein at all."

Harvey did so, inserting the needle into the protruding blue line. "Believe me, Michael, this is merely a formality."

"I hope you're right."

He finished taking the blood and withdrew the needle. "I am," he said. He walked over to the door, opened it, and stepped into the hallway. "Janice?"

As per Harvey's instruction, Janice Matley, his most loyal and trustworthy nurse, was waiting by the door. Harvey had brought Janice over from the clinic because he did not trust anyone with this task. "Yes, Doctor?"

He handed her the blood sample. "Give this to Eric or Winston only. Nobody else. If neither one of them is there, just wait."

She nodded and left. Harvey stepped back into Michael's room.

"When will you know the results?" Michael asked.

"In a week," Harvey answered. "Now stop worrying like an old lady. There's no reason to think you have anything other than hepatitis."

MR. Philip Adams, assistant manager of the Days Inn, unlocked the door. "Here it is," he said. "Room 1118."

"Damn," Lieutenant Bernstein said.

"Something wrong?"

Max took his finger out of his mouth. "Hangnail. It's driving me nuts."

Philip Adams watched with something near horror while the police lieutenant used his teeth to rid himself of the annoying problem. "Will there be anything else?"

"Has anybody stayed here since the suicide?"

"Actually, business has been a little slow right now, so we've kept it vacant."

"Has the room been cleaned since the incident?"

"Oh, sure."

"Can you find me the maid who cleaned it?"

"She's off today."

"When will she be in?"

"Tomorrow morning."

"I'd like her to call me when she gets in."

"Of course, Lieutenant, but why are you investigating this now? The suicide was more than two weeks ago."

"Just trying to tie up a few loose ends," Bernstein explained. "Can you also find me the receptionist who was on duty the night of the suicide?"

"Hector checked Dr. Grey in," Adams said. "The police spoke to him already."

"When does Hector come in?"

"He's here now."

"Then please send him up."

"No problem."

"Has any work been done on the room since the incident?"

Adams coughed into his fist. "We replaced the broken window he jumped through, of course."

"Nothing else?"

The assistant manager thought a moment. "No, I don't think so."

"Okay, thanks."

"Here's the key, Lieutenant."

"I'll return it to you on my way out."

"Thank you."

Left alone, Bernstein paced the room in a circular pattern, hoping to get a feel for the surroundings. Then he closed his eyes and tried to step into the good doctor's shoes. He tried to picture Dr. Bruce Grey checking into

this hotel, taking the elevator up to the eleventh floor, unlocking the door, moving into this room. Max imagined
Grey trying to force open the window and finding that
it was nailed shut. So what did Grey do next? He must
have decided to take a running start and leap through
the glass. Max pictured him backing up, sprinting forward, hurling his body against the glass, shattering it into
small shards, slicing himself in the process. Not exactly a
neat suicide. Very messy, in fact. And painful—jumping
through glass could not have been a lot of laughs.

Something's wrong here, Twitch.

He nodded to himself. Why here? Why a leap? Why
jump through glass? It did not add up. The man was
on the verge of a major medical breakthrough. He had
been divorced for seven years already, had a kid he didn't
see enough, loved to read, loved to work, was more or
less a homebody. According to Harvey Riker and several of Bruce's friends, Grey rarely traveled and had only
been out of the country three times—his recent trip to
Cancún, Mexico (taking a vacation before suicide?), and
twice to Bangkok a few years back, where the clinic kept
all confidential blood and lab samples and test results.
Max had learned that Harvey and Bruce were paranoid
about leaks, sabotage, government interference, that
kind of thing—hence the decision to have a safe house
way out in Bangkok. Might have seemed like unsubstantiated paranoia at the time but now . . .

Bernstein stopped in mid-thought when he saw it.

His gaze fastened on the left side of the wall by the
door, his eyes widening. He slowly crossed the room and
examined the chain lock, which hung from the wall and

door in two separate pieces. The steel chain was snapped in two. Max was bending forward to get a closer look when a knock on the door made him jump.

"Who is it?" he asked.

"Hector Rodriguez," a voice with a Hispanic accent called out. "Mr. Adams told me you wanted to see me."

Bernstein opened the door. "Come in."

The slight, dark-skinned man moved into the room. He wore a hotel uniform and a goatee that looked like it had been penciled onto his face. "Mr. Adams said you have some questions about the suicide?"

"Hector, did anyone notice this before?"

Hector squinted at the chain lock. "I don't think so. No one's used this room since the suicide."

"Are broken chain locks a common occurrence in this place?"

"No, sir, they're not. I'll have it replaced right away."

Bernstein wondered if the lock had been broken when Grey first came into the room. Somehow he doubted it. "Do you remember Dr. Grey checking in?"

"A little," Hector replied. "I mean, he jumped out the window a few minutes after he checked in. He couldn't have been in the room for more than five minutes."

"What do you remember about him?"

"He had very blond hair—"

"I don't mean looks-wise. I mean, how did he act? How was he behaving?"

"Behaving?"

"Yes. Did he seem depressed, for example?"

"No, not depressed. I'd say nervous was more like it. He was sweating like a pig."

"I see . . ." Bernstein's hands flew forward. "Hold it a second. Did you just say Dr. Grey had blond hair?"

"Very blond."

Max's eyes squinted in bafflement. He opened his file and looked at a recent photograph of Bruce Grey. The man in the photograph had black hair. "Is this the man who checked in that night?"

Hector stared at the picture for a good ten seconds. "I can't say for sure. He looked much different. He didn't have a beard, and like I said before, his hair was blond."

Bernstein opened the file. He had tried to avoid the police photos because he was not fond of looking at splattered remains, but now he knew that he would have to look. He thumbed through the papers until he arrived at the first glossy photograph. There was not enough face left to tell if there had ever been a beard, but even through the thick patches of blood, Max could see that the dead man definitely had blond hair. Like Hector said, very blond.

Max closed both the file and his eyes. Why the sudden appearance change? A new hairdo and quick shave for a leap through a window seemed a tad bizarre, to say the least.

"Tell me what Dr. Grey said to you when he checked in."

Hector looked up, trying to remember. "Nothing special. He just said he wanted a room. I asked, 'How many nights, sir?' and he said, 'One.'"

"That's it?"

"I said, 'Will that be cash or charge?' and he said, 'Cash.' Then I gave him the key and he took off."

"Nothing else?"

"Nothing."

"You're sure."

He thought a moment. "That was it."

"He didn't have any special requests for his room?"

"No."

"He didn't ask for the room to be on a certain floor?"

Hector shook his head. "I don't even think he looked at the number on the key until he stepped into the elevator."

Cold fear slid down Bernstein's chest. His finger went back into his mouth, but there was nothing left to chew except skin. This whole thing was getting messy and complicated, too messy and too complicated. Bruce Grey had not asked for a special room. He had not asked for a room with a view or a room near an elevator or one of those new no-smoking rooms. He had not asked for a room with a king-sized bed or a queen-sized bed or two separate beds. And most of all Bruce Grey had not asked for a room on a high floor. For all he knew, he could have gotten a room on the ground level.

"Is there anything else, Lieutenant?"

"No, that's it for now."

Hector Rodriguez turned to leave and then stopped. "I saw your name in the *Herald*, Lieutenant. I hope you catch that whacko before he slices off somebody else's nuts."

Max's head shot up. "What did you say?"

"Cutting off a man's balls. Pure loco, huh, Lieutenant?"

"Where did you hear that?"

"The evening edition. Front cover. What kind of a man does something like that? City's full of sickos."

Once again, Max rubbed his face and eyes with his right hand. The press. The mayor. The gay activists.

Help.

8

THE ringing of the telephone jerked George out of his sleep. He awoke, as he always did, quickly, alert. He picked up the receiver before the second ring.

"Hello."

"Did you read this morning's paper?"

George sat up and checked his watch. The voice on the other end sounded different this time—still agitated and strained, but now there was something else. More fear. Maybe even anger. "No," George replied. "Should I have?"

"According to the *Herald,* the Gay Slasher tortured and castrated Scott Trian before killing him."

"You sound upset."

"They were supposed to die quickly, damn it! I never said anything about torture or mutilation."

"If you're unhappy with my work—"

"Unhappy? You're a lunatic. I thought I was dealing with a professional, but you're a goddamn psychopath."

"I was following your orders," George said. "The mutilation just speeds up the end result. It makes sense financially."

There was stunned silence on the other end.

George continued. "I assume you also read that everything went smoothly with Jenkins' murder. I dumped the body just where you wanted it."

"Did . . . did you disfigure him?"

"He died from the first stab wound. The same with Whitherson."

"You're sure?"

"Don't make me repeat myself."

"Then just promise me you won't hurt any of the others."

George almost smiled. "I am merely the executioner, the one who pulls the switch or drops the gas pellet. But you . . . you are the judge and jury. You are the one who ordered their deaths."

"No," the voice said slowly, "I am not."

Again there was silence. Then the voice said, "Promise me, George. Promise me that no others will be needlessly tortured."

George paused. "Okay. But I assure you it was for the best."

There was a long release of breath and then the voice said, "The situation is different now. You'll have to be more careful. The police are going to start watching."

"Watching what?" George asked. "The police force

can't guard every faggot in Manhattan . . . unless there's something else."

"Something else? I don't understand."

"I think you do," George said. "Listen, I don't care who you are. I don't care why you want these people killed. It's not my concern. But I need to know what the police are thinking. I need to know what the real connection is between the victims so that I can prepare properly. Otherwise, mistakes can be made."

Silence.

"Can I assume," George continued, "that these men have more in common than being gay?"

"They're all patients at an AIDS clinic," the voice said.

"So that explains why you told me to wear the mask and gloves."

"Yes."

"And Dr. Grey worked at this clinic?"

"Yes."

"So let me get this straight: Trian, Whitherson, and Jenkins were all AIDS patients at a clinic operated by Bruce Grey?"

"Yes."

"And the police know this?"

"They know most of it. The rest they'll figure out."

"So they may look into Grey's suicide again."

"They might."

George thought for a moment. "I have an idea, but it'll cost you."

"I'm listening."

"I'll kill a couple of random faggots—"

"No!"

"Hear me out. I kill a couple of faggots who don't have AIDS or aren't being treated at this clinic. It'll throw the cops off the track. Make it look even more like the work of a psychotic gay hater."

"No!"

"Then I'll change the way I kill the next few. I'll make it look like an accident or, better yet, a suicide. If these guys have AIDS and are on death row anyway, a suicide might not be looked into too closely."

"The police will be looking for something like that. You'll never get away with it."

"Worth a try."

"No. I want you to use the same methods unless I say otherwise."

George shrugged. "Your money."

"And remember—the only people who are to be put to death are the ones I say."

"Not put to death," George said.

"Excuse me?"

"They're not being 'put to death,'" George continued. "They're being murdered."

" DO you eat here every day?" Sara asked.

"No," Eric Blake replied. They both slid their trays along the hospital cafeteria girders. The room was packed with doctors, nurses, lab technicians—everyone dressed in white coats or blue hospital scrubs with the words "Property of Columbia Presbyterian Medical

Center—Removal from Premises Prohibited" emblazoned across the chest. Everyone looked exhausted, the
men unshaven, the women baggy-eyed. Working forty-
hour shifts can do that to a person.

Sara looked down at the hospital pizza and frowned.
"Eric?"

"Yes?"

"Is mozzarella cheese supposed to be green?"

"It's one of the better items on the menu."

"I think I'll pass."

"I can order in Chinese, if you'd like."

She shook her head. "Michael would kill me. He
hasn't eaten Chinese in two days and he's already suffering withdrawal pains."

"He always did love Chinese food."

They found a table toward the back where the room
was relatively quiet.

"How's Michael feeling?" Eric asked. "I haven't had a
chance to check in on him today."

"About the same," Sara replied. "He's taking a nap
right now. I don't know, Eric . . . he just doesn't look
right to me."

"He'll be fine." Eric carefully opened his container of
milk. While everyone around them drank directly from
the carton, Eric poured the milk into a glass and then
lifted it to his lips. "It's kind of spooky seeing Michael
here, though. Like a bad déjà vu."

"What do you mean?"

"It reminds me of when we were kids," he said. "Of
when Michael's stepfather beat him."

Sara winced. "He doesn't talk about it much."

"I know. I don't blame him. It was a bad time, Sara, best forgotten."

She nodded slowly, picturing Michael as a helpless child in a hospital bed. A flush of anguish and anger rose in her. Her mind traveled back five years to the first time she had learned about Michael's past, a few hours before she met him for the first time.

"I want you to interview Michael Silverman," Larry Simmons, *managing editor of the* New York Herald, *told her.*

"The basketball player?" she asked.

"Yup."

"Why? Basketball is hardly my area of expertise."

"I don't want a story about basketball. I want a story about Michael Silverman, the man. Look, the NBA finals are on now and everyone is applauding Silverman's skill on the court. But where did he come from? What made this Jewish kid from New Jersey become such a fantastic athlete?"

"Hasn't this story been done before?"

"Others have tried. Others have even dug up some of Silverman's tragic past."

"Tragic past?"

"It's all in the file. But I don't want you to look at it right away. I want you to start by going directly to Silverman."

"So why hasn't the story been done before?"

"Because Silverman won't talk to the press about his personal life. Ask him about a jump shot or a quick move to the basket and he'll be as poetic as Proust. But ask him about his precollege years and forget it."

"So what do you want me to do?"

"Get him to talk. Find out what he's all about. Be honest and open with him. If that doesn't work, be sneaky."

She laughed. "And if all else fails, I'll hit him over the head with my cane."

"Now you're talking."

A half hour later she called Michael's apartment in the city.

"Mr. Silverman?"

"Yes."

"My name is Sara Lowell. I'm a reporter for the New York Herald."

"Oh yes," Michael said, "I've read some of your work, Miss Lowell. I liked the exposé you did on the housing commissioner last month. Powerful stuff."

"Thank you."

"Now, what can I do for you?"

Sara was somewhat taken aback. She had been prepared for an ogre, a man more than a little wary and suspicious of the press. But this man was very polite. Gracious even. "I'd like very much to do an interview with you at your convenience."

"I see. Have you become a sportswriter, Miss Lowell?"

"Not really."

"Then what sort of story do you plan on doing?"

"Oh, I don't know. Just a general piece on Michael Silverman off the court. Your interests, your hobbies. Let the fans get to know you a little better."

"Sounds like pretty dull stuff."

"I don't think so," Sara said. "From what I hear, you're a fairly interesting person."

"So," Michael continued, "all you want to do is a light piece on how I like to go to the theater, collect rabbits, garden in my underwear, stuff like that?"

"Sort of."

"I assume, Miss Lowell, that you already know that I do not grant interviews on my personal life."

"I've heard something to that effect, yes."

"And you won't ask any personal questions? Nothing about my love life or my childhood?"

"You can always say, 'No comment.'"

Michael chuckled. "You forget, Miss Lowell, I read your column. You don't do fluff. You probe and penetrate and usually go for the kill."

"Mr. Silverman, this article is nothing like—"

"Explain something to me," he interrupted. "Why can't you reporters understand that my personal life is none of anyone's business? Why can't you just report what happens on the basketball court and leave me alone?"

"The public wants to know more."

"Frankly speaking, I don't really give a shit what the public wants. How come I never see a reporter's life story smeared across the headlines? How come I never see a story on how you lost your virginity, Miss Lowell, or about that wild college weekend where you had too much to drink?"

"No one wants to read about me, Mr. Silverman."

"Bullshit. No one wants to read about me either unless I'm scoring baskets."

"Not true."

"Listen, I'm not in the mood to be this week's tabloid story, okay? Just leave me alone. And why do you have to play all the devious head games with me? Why couldn't

you have been honest enough to admit what you were really after?"

She hesitated before answering. *"Because you would have probably hung up on me."*

"Very prophetic of you. Good-bye, Miss Lowell."

She heard him slam down the receiver. *"Eat shit, Mr. Silverman."* So much for his being a nice, easygoing fellow. She stood and headed for the door.

"Where you going?" Larry Simmons called to her.

"To Silverman's apartment."

"He agreed to the interview?"

"No. He hung up on me."

"So?"

"So sneaky didn't work. Maybe bouncing my cane off his skull will prove more persuasive."

"Before you go," Larry said, *"I think you should read his file after all."* He handed her a manila envelope.

The file was short but potent. One page to be exact. Sara skimmed the sheet. *"I don't believe this,"* she muttered.

"I thought you might find it intriguing."

She read out loud. *"Born Beth Israel Hospital, Newark, New Jersey. His father, Samuel Silverman, died in a car crash when he was five. Mother, Estelle Silverman, remarried a year later to a Martin Johnson. Between the ages of six and nine Michael had eight overnight hospital stays. His injuries were rumored to have been the result of physical abuse at the hands of his stepfather and included several broken bones and three concussions. When Michael was ten, his mother committed suicide by shooting herself in the forehead. Michael found her body. He has no brothers, no sisters. Stepfather abandoned him after the suicide. Only living relative* was paternal grandmother, Sadie Silverman, who raised Michael until her death when he turned nineteen.'" She looked up. "Jesus, Larry, you want me to go after this guy?"

"None of it has really been printed before because the details are too sketchy. Keep reading."

Her eyes found the spot where she had stopped reading. "'Michael got full scholarship to Stanford for basketball as well as piano.'" She paused. "The guy's a pianist?"

Larry nodded. "That part is fairly well-known."

"'Academic All-American at Stanford four years in a row . . . reputation of being a bit of a ladies' man—'"

"That's the understatement of the millennium," Larry interjected. "The man changes women like some men change socks." He smiled. "Hope you don't get sucked in."

"Changes women like socks? Very tempting but doesn't sound like my type."

"No one is your type," Larry replied.

"What's that supposed to mean?"

"It means," he said, "that you never date."

"I've got too much work to do."

"Excuses."

"And no one interests me right now, okay."

"Listen, Sara, I'm sixty-seven years old, have seven grandchildren, and have been happily married for forty-four years."

"So?"

"So you're going to have to find someone else. I'm taken."

She smiled. "Damn. You found me out."

"And don't be so quick to judge Silverman," he added. "Look at his past. Would you want to get close to too many people if you had his childhood?"

She put the file on her desk. "This story is beginning to sound like a piece of cheap sensationalism," Sara said.

He shrugged. "Depends on how you handle it. Fact is, Michael Silverman is a sports idol. We Jews love him because so few of us can play sports. I mean, the last time there was a Jewish athlete this famous . . . Well, you'd have to go back to Sandy Koufax."

"What's your point, Larry?"

"It's a great human interest story. A man who overcame incredible adversity to become one of the world's top basketball players. And he'd be a perfect role model for abused kids."

"Suppose he doesn't want to be a role model."

"Tough. He's news, Sara, big news. So the story is a bit sensational—so what? You're a reporter and this is a damn good story."

"All right, all right. I get the picture. I'm on my way over there now."

"Sara?"

She looked up, startled. "I'm sorry, Eric."

"Don't apologize. I know you've got a lot on your mind right now, but remember this—all Michael's problems are in the past. You two are going to have a baby together, and Michael has never been happier in his life."

Sara tried to smile, but it never reached more than the corners of her mouth. She sensed that Michael's past woes were not finished with him yet, that they were still potent enough to reach into the present and hurt him . . .

"Mind if I join you two?"

"Hello, Max," Sara said. "Max, you know Eric Blake, don't you?"

"I believe we've met," Bernstein said. "How are you, Doctor?"

"Very well, thank you," Eric replied as the beeper on his belt went off. "If you two will excuse me, I have to go."

"Emergency?" Max asked.

"No. Just time for rounds."

Max scratched his face hard, like he had fleas. "Can I ask you a quick question before you go?"

Eric stopped. "Of course."

"When was the last time you saw Dr. Grey alive?"

Eric thought a moment. "The day he left for Cancún."

"Did he look the same to you?"

"The same? I don't understand."

"I mean, was his hair still dark and did he still have a beard?"

"Yes," Eric said without hesitation. "Why do you ask?"

"No reason. Thanks, Eric."

"Anytime, Lieutenant. I'll see you later, Sara."

"Bye, Eric."

Eric Blake neatly piled the garbage on his tray before leaving. When he brought his tray to the window, he was the only one who took the time to sort his silverware.

Sara turned to Max. "I called you three times today."

"Sorry. It's been a busy day."

"Are you getting much flak about the castration story in the news?"

Max's whole body seemed to shrug. "Nothing I can't handle with a grenade launcher and tear gas."

"I can imagine. Okay, so what have you learned?"

He leaned forward, his right elbow on the table, his

left arm thrown behind the back of the chair. "First of all, Bruce Grey had blond hair and no beard when he allegedly jumped out the window. He also was wearing cosmetic contact lenses to change the color of his eyes. I checked with several of his friends, even the limousine driver who dropped him off at the airport. Bruce definitely had dark hair and the beard when he left New York."

Sara nodded. "As you would say, 'Interesting.'"

"To say the least. But there's more." He quickly told her about the rest of his conversation with Hector Rodriquez at the Days Inn. Sara sat stunned, quietly listening.

"Then Grey didn't commit suicide," she said when Max finished.

"He was murdered, Sara. I'm sure of it."

"And someone wanted to make it look like a suicide," she said.

"Seems so," Max replied.

"Hmmm. Bruce's murder has to be connected to the stabbings, agreed?"

"Agreed."

"So why did the killer want to make Bruce's death look like a suicide while doing nothing to hide the fact that the other three were murdered?"

"I don't know," Max said. He stood up, circled the table for no apparent reason, and sat back down.

"Max."

"What?"

"You're playing with your hair again."

Bernstein looked up at his right hand. Strands of hair were wrapped around his middle finger as though it were a curler. He untangled his finger and put his hands on the table. "Saves on a perm," he explained with a smile.

"So what else did you learn?"

He leaned forward. "This morning I went through the personal possessions found in Grey's hotel room. Everything was there—wallet, ID, cash, credit cards, briefcase, change of clothes—even passport."

"So?"

"There was no stamp for Mexico on the passport."

"No mystery there. You don't need to use your passport to go into Mexico. Just proof of citizenship."

"Then why did he bring it with him?"

She shrugged. "What else did you find in the passport?"

"It's what I didn't find," he said. "You know those pages where the customs officials stamp the country you're visiting?"

"Yes."

"One of those pages had been neatly clipped out of Grey's passport. You would never notice unless you looked at it closely."

Sara looked up at the ceiling. "So the killer doesn't want anyone to see what was on that page. Maybe Bruce never went to Mexico. Maybe he went someplace else and the killer doesn't want us to know where."

"My thinking exactly. So I called the Oasis Hotel down in Cancún."

"Did he check in?"

"Yes."

She waited for him to continue but he just sat there, smiling. "Max, stop playing games with me. What happened?"

"I called your old contact at customs and immigration."

"Don Scharf?"

"Right. I know I should have asked you first, but time was of the essence. Anyway, he remembered me from that case we did a few years back where that rapist fled to Puerto Rico."

"What did you find out?"

"Well, it took a while but we finally traced down where Bruce went."

"And?"

"And Bruce did go down to Cancún first. But he flew out of Mexico the very next day."

"So where did he go?"

Max smiled. "Bangkok."

"THERE'S no question about it, Eric," Winston O'Connor, chief lab technician at the Sidney Pavilion, said with his Alabama twang. O'Connor had been working for the clinic since its inception and, in fact, had not lived in the South since entering Columbia University eighteen years ago. Still, the years had not subdued Winston's deep Southern accent. "Take another look at the Western blot. The band pattern is unmistakable."

Eric swallowed and reached out his hand. The wall clock, one of those noisy kinds that schools used, read five ten a.m. When was the last time he had left the clinic? Eric did a little quick math. Forty hours ago. He needed sleep something terrible, but all of a sudden he felt wide-awake.

He glanced down at the photograph and remained silent for a moment. Eric knew what the readings meant, but he kept staring at them anyway, as though he could make the bands on the photograph slide lower or higher by just concentrating on them. "Let me take a look at the ELISA test."

Winston sighed. "We've already looked at it twice."

"I want to look at it again. You sure you used the right sample?"

Winston looked at him strangely. "Are you kidding?"

"I want to make sure."

"You were standing here when I did it," Winston said. "I don't make mistakes on these kinds of things. Neither do you."

Eric lowered his head. "I know. I'm sorry."

Winston crossed the room and opened a door that looked like it belonged on a refrigerator. His hand reached in and extracted a plate. "Here. And here's the digital readout of the optical density."

"Get me the T cell study too."

"Again?"

Eric nodded.

"Here," Winston said a moment later. "What the hell you looking for, Eric?"

Eric did not respond. He examined all the tests and studies at least a dozen more times. Somewhere in the background he could hear Winston sigh and curse under his breath every time Eric asked to look at the same thing again.

"For crying out loud," Winston half snapped, "how many times are you going to view this stuff? There's no mistake here. Shoot, we've never made a mistake on this test—ever."

"It can't be," Eric muttered. "It just can't be."

"We've had hundreds of positive HIV tests come through here," Winston continued. "Why all the double-checking on this one? I've run the ELISA and the Western on this guy twice now. There's no question about the results."

Eric moved to a chair as though stunned by a blow to the head. He slowly picked up the phone and dialed.

"Who you calling?" Winston asked.

His voice came from far away. "Harvey."

"I'll put this stuff away, then."

"No," Eric said. "Harvey will want to look at it too."

"But both of us have already—"

"He won't believe us," Eric said. "He'll have to see this one for himself."

9

HARVEY buttoned his shirt and smiled toward the rumpled bed. If Jennifer could see him now . . .

"I still can't believe you're here," he said.

Cassandra leaned back on the bed and stretched. A thin, white sheet was all that covered her body. "Why not? This is Day Number Four already, Harv."

"Happy?"

"Blissful," she replied. And it was true. From their first kiss she had felt intoxicated. It was strange, but even now she could feel her heart swell in her chest just thinking about him.

"No complaints?" he asked.

"Just one," she said. "I don't care much for your hours."

"I warned you."

"Yeah, but two hours a night?"

"Sorry."

"Not your fault, I guess," she said. "Anyway, it makes me appreciate my nine to seven at the agency more."

Harvey searched the clothes-cluttered floor, found a pair of pants crumpled in a corner, and put them on. "When are you making your presentation to the airline?"

"This afternoon. Northeastern Air. I have a meeting with their handsome marketing director. Jealous?"

"Should I be?"

She looked at him. "No."

"Good," Harvey said with a goofy grin. "Because I really like you."

She laughed. "God, you're corny."

He shrugged. "Just out of practice," he said. "So what ad slogan did you come up with?"

She thought a moment. "Fly the friendly skies of Northeastern?"

"It's been used."

"How about 'We're Northeastern Airlines, doing what we do best'?"

"Sorry."

"'I'm Candy, fly me'?"

"Might work if you show some cleavage."

"No problem," Cassandra said. "I majored in cleavage in college."

"I bet." He found a red tie crumpled into his loafer. "I probably won't be back here until the day after tomorrow."

"I have to go home anyway. I'm running out of clothes."

"And leave my palatial penthouse?"

Cassandra glanced around Harvey's sloppy, one-bedroom dump on One Hundred Fifty-eighth Street. She looked at him skeptically.

"Okay," he admitted, "Versailles it's not."

"A human dwelling it's not."

"Granted, it might need a little work."

"It might need a bulldozer."

"You are spoiled rotten."

Cassandra smiled. "Bet your ass." She sat up and put the pillow behind her head. "Harv, is it true? Do you really have a cure for AIDS?"

"Not a cure exactly," he said, tying his tie and then loosening it. "More like a treatment."

"I had a good friend die of AIDS," she said slowly. "He was my ad partner at Dunbar Strauss. God, he was so creative, so alive. I remember visiting him at the hospital until he was in so much pain he wouldn't let anyone see him."

Harvey nodded. "It's an ugly disease, Cassandra."

"How does your treatment work?"

He stopped. "You really want to know?"

"Yes."

Harvey sat on the edge of the bed and held her hands. "AIDS," he began, "or Acquired Immuno-Deficiency Syndrome, does not, in and of itself, kill people. You see, the AIDS virus, known as HIV, attacks the immune system. It causes the immune system to break down to the point where the patient is readily susceptible to illness and infection. Eventually these illnesses or infections become fatal. With me so far?"

"I think so," she said. "You're saying that the AIDS virus tears down the wall that protects you from disease."

"Exactly. How the HIV destroys the immune system is a bit complicated, so I'll try to be as nontechnical as possible."

"I'm listening."

"Okay. The HIV attaches itself to what are called T cells. It then crawls inside the cells and destroys them. Still with me?"

Cassandra nodded.

"The part of the cell where the HIV first attaches itself is called the T receptor. In other words, the HIV searches around and is attracted to T receptors. Then it latches onto the receptors and moves in for the kill."

"Got it," Cassandra said.

"What we do at the clinic is inject our patients with a powerful, addictive drug we've created called SR1— S and R stand for Sidney Riker, my brother. The negative side effects with SR1 are many and unfortunately the patient needs to take larger and larger doses over a long period of time."

"What does SR1 do?" she asked.

Harvey squeezed her hand. "Again, it's complicated, so let me try to cut through all the medical jargon. In the human body SR1 greatly resembles T receptors, so the AIDS virus is drawn to the phony T receptors."

"So," Cassandra said, "the HIV attaches itself to the SR1 T receptors rather than the real T receptors."

"Something like that, yes. It's almost like SR1 is wearing a mask and disguising itself as a T receptor. The HIV is drawn to it, latches itself onto it—"

"And then the SR1 kills the HIV."

Harvey shook his head. "I wish. One day it might happen that fast, but we're still years away from anything like that."

"So what happens?"

"Well, after the HIV latches itself onto the SR1's T receptors, they struggle. It's almost like a tug-of-war inside the immune system. At first, the HIV is really pissed off by all this. The SR1 is actually activating the virus, stirring it up. We give additional and escalating dosages of SR1 until the drug begins to wear down the virus. For a while the effects of AIDS are put into a holding pattern. Eventually, after a long, hard struggle, the HIV dies."

"SR1 wins the tug-of-war."

He nodded. "We believe so, yes. Several long-term patients have actually changed from HIV positive to HIV negative."

"Amazing."

"The problems are obvious. Aside from the dangers and addictive factors in SR1, we can save only the immune system. If a person is in the latter stages of AIDS—if a patient is already seriously ill with some AIDS-induced infection—our cure will do little if any good. SR1 can stop only HIV. It doesn't cure Kaposi's sarcoma, for example, or any of the other diseases AIDS may eventually give you. As a result, we have to catch the virus early, before infections and disease settle in. And of course, more research is needed. We've only scratched the surface."

Cassandra said, "You're sure to get the funds you need once Sara does her report."

"I hope so."

"What do you mean, hope so? Once everyone sees the evidence they'll support the clinic—even my father."

Harvey slipped on his shoes and stood. "That'll be the day."

"You'll see. He'll back you."

"Maybe," Harvey said, more to keep the peace than anything else. "But he's not the one I'm afraid of."

"Then who?"

"Dangerous whackos who are making a name for themselves off the deaths of young people. People like that Reverend Sanders—"

"You think he's out to sabotage the clinic?"

"It wouldn't surprise me."

Cassandra rolled over, exposing the long smooth curve of her hip. "He was in my father's study the other day."

Harvey spun back toward Cassandra. "Reverend Sanders?"

"Yup."

"But your father told me he didn't know Sanders personally."

"I heard him in my father's study the morning after the party. They were arguing."

"Arguing about what?"

"I'm not sure."

"Cassandra, it's important."

She tried to collect her thoughts. "I remember my father telling Sanders that he should never come to the house."

"What did Sanders say?"

"He just told my dad to relax. I remember that Sand-

ers sounded so cool. His tone was such a contrast to my
father's angry one. Then Sanders said something like
'There's still work to be done.'"

Harvey's body went rigid. "Jesus."

"That's all I heard. I left after that."

"Are you sure—"

The phone rang. For a moment neither of them
moved, their eyes locked onto each other's. Then Harvey
lowered his gaze and moved toward the phone.

"Hello."

Eric's voice came in a rush. "Get down to the lab,
Harv. Hurry."

"What's the matter?"

"It's Michael, Harvey. Oh God, it's Michael."

MICHAEL pressed the button and held it down.
Slowly and with a whir, the bed began to move, curling
his frame into a sitting position. He coughed twice into
his fist and then smiled at Sara.

"Go ahead," she said. "Take a sip."

Michael brought the plastic cup to his lips and drank.

"How's the orange juice?" Sara asked.

"Tastes like paint thinner," he replied. "What time is it?"

"Seven a.m. Did you sleep well?"

"Not really," he said. "I don't like sleeping in separate
beds."

"Neither do I," Sara said, "but my bed is only a yard
away."

"Makes it worse. Sort of like being able to see the
Holy Grail and not grasp it."

"How poetic."

"To put it somewhat less poetically, I want your bod."

"And I yours," Sara said. "Every time you stand up I see your cute little ass hanging out the back of your hospital gown. It drives me crazy."

"I know. I'm such a tease." He pushed the orange juice away and glanced up. "So tell me, how's the story on Harv's clinic going?"

"We start shooting the interviews later today. It'll be hectic as all hell, so I may not be able to stop in as much."

"Good. I'll be able to get a little peace and quiet."

"Not so fast, handsome. I'll still be able to come by around lunch and dinner. And I'll still be sleeping in that bed come this evening."

He grabbed her and they kissed. "Can't get rid of you, huh?"

"Never."

They kissed again.

Behind them, the door opened. Sara turned and watched Harvey and Eric enter. Their grim expressions seemed to magnify into looks of tremendous pain when they saw Michael and Sara embracing. Sara took a second look at their faces, at the way they held their heads, at the way their hands stayed still in their pockets. And she knew. She knew without question or hesitation. It was over. Everything was over. She held Michael closely, feeling his muscles stiffen. She wanted very much to scream.

Harvey stepped forward and closed the door. "We need to talk."

10

JENNIFER Riker lifted her face toward the sun, enjoying the feel of the warm rays against her skin. She passed a store window, stopped, took two steps backward, and examined her reflection. The late forties, she thought, had not been particularly easy on her looks. Her petite figure was beginning to spread a little. The small lines around her eyes were deepening into full-fledged (no sense denying it) wrinkles. Her neck was starting to crease. She looked again and wondered for the millionth time if she had done the right thing, if she had not, as so many had warned her, jumped out of the frying pan and into the fire.

She thought about it a moment before acknowledging that, in truth, there had been no choice. To stay with Harvey would have meant to wither away in a world of watching too many soap operas and feeling utterly worthless. To remain married would have meant playing the dutiful wife to a man who had dedicated his life to a cause and assumed those around him had chosen to do the same. Just looking at Harvey on those rare nights when he'd come home from the clinic, exhaustion blanketing his face and posture, made Jennifer feel inadequate and selfish. She had to get out.

And so she left. She made her escape before the weight of her depression had a chance to squash her spirit completely. She moved to Los Angeles, where she now lived (quite happily, thank you) with her sister, Susan, and her young nephew, Tommy. During her twenty-six years of marriage to Harvey, Jennifer had rarely ventured off the East Coast, never visiting California, not even going as far west as Chicago. She and Harvey had been snobbish Northeasterners, believing that the only cultural life of the country bloomed within the boundaries of the original thirteen colonies.

But Los Angeles had its advantages over New York, albeit they were mostly the obvious. The warmer climate, for one; the warmer attitude, for another. Jennifer enjoyed the laid-back California lifestyle—especially after the pressure of the last few years. And living with Susan had ended up being fun, almost like reliving her childhood in certain respects. Jennifer and Susan had always been close, confiding in each other even as small children. As they grew older, both sisters decided that they would always live near each other. Jennifer, older than Susan by two years, had gotten married first, to a doctor named Harvey Riker. Almost in a rush not to be left behind, Susan married another doctor, Bruce Grey, a year and a half later. Harvey and Bruce quickly became friends and even medical partners while Jennifer and Susan continued to grow closer and closer. Everything was moving along perfectly until one minor problem began to snag up the works.

Bruce and Susan started drifting apart.

After a few futile attempts to save a dying marriage, Susan left Bruce, moving to Los Angeles and taking their seven-year-old son, Tommy, with her. Jennifer and Harvey had been horrified when they heard. They started to feel isolated and afraid, and for the first time, Harvey and Jennifer began to question their own happiness and examine their own relationship. From then on, it had been only a question of time.

Jennifer closed her eyes and sighed. She took out a key, opened the door, and stepped inside the apartment. Almost immediately the phone rang.

"Hello?"

"Is this Mrs. Susan Grey?"

"She's not here at the moment. May I ask who's calling?"

"Is this Mrs. Jennifer Riker?"

"Yes, it is."

"Good morning, Mrs. Riker. This is Terence Lebrock."

"Oh, you're the executor of Bruce's will."

"That's correct. I just wanted to let you know that I sent a post office box key via overnight mail yesterday. You should be receiving it today."

"A post office box key? I'm not sure I understand."

"Dr. Grey kept a post office box in the main branch of the Los Angeles post office. I think it would be best if somebody clears out that box right away. There might be important papers in there."

Jennifer thought for a moment. Odd that Bruce had a post office box in Los Angeles. Of course it could be the same one he had used during his two-year stint in the research department at UCLA, but why would he have saved it? She shrugged. It was probably another example of Bruce's compulsive personality.

"Don't worry, Mr. Lebrock. I'll clear it out today."

THE silence was staggering. It filled the room, expanding, growing larger and larger until Sara was sure the walls around them were about to give way. First, there had been denial. How could it be? Michael had never experimented with homosexuality. He had never been an intravenous drug abuser. He was not a hemophiliac who needed constant blood transfusions. He had slept with no one but Sara for six years. Any way you looked at it, Michael should have been a very healthy thirty-two-year-old man.

Except he was not healthy. He was lying in a hospital bed with hepatitis B and a positive reading on an HIV test. His T cell count was dangerously low and the most obvious conclusion the doctors could draw was that Michael had received contaminated blood in the Bahamas after his boating accident.

He had AIDS.

She looked at him now. His handsome face showed no emotion, so strange for a man as filled with passion as Michael, a man who rarely hid thoughts and feelings be-

hind a blank expression. She thought about the first time
she had seen that face, the first time she had ever spoken
to him in person.

*The door swung open and Beethoven's Sonata No. 32 in
C minor escaped from the room and moved outside. "Yes?"
Michael said. He was surprisingly handsome, tall, of course,
with broad shoulders. There was a towel draped around his
neck, a glass of what looked like orange juice in his hand.
Perspiration matted the ends of his hair together. He wiped
his brow with the corner of the towel.*

*Sara nervously gripped her cane. She was about to stick
out her right hand for him to shake, but she suddenly realized that her palm was slick. Her honey blond hair was tied
back away from her face, accentuating her already prominent cheekbones.*

"Good afternoon. My name is Sara Lowell."

He looked at her, startled. "You're Sara Lowell?"

"You sound surprised."

"I am," he said. "You're not what I pictured."

"What did you picture?"

*He shrugged. "Something a little gruffer-looking, I
guess."*

"Gruffer-looking?"

*"Yeah. Dark, curly hair. Cigarette dangling from lip
with an ash about to fall off. Manual typewriter. Black
sweater. A little on the meaty side."*

"Sorry if I disappointed you."

*"Hardly," he said. "What are you doing here, Miss
Lowell?"*

"Sara."

"Sara."

She sneezed.

"God bless you," he said.

"Thank you."

"Have a cold?"

She nodded.

"So what can I do for you, Sara?"

"Well," she began, "I'd like to come in and ask you a few questions."

"Hmmm. This whole scenario seems a tad familiar to me. Do you have a sense of déjà vu too, Sara, or is it just me?"

"Depends."

"On?"

"On if you slam the door in my face like you slammed the phone in my ear."

He smiled. "Touché."

"Can I come in?"

"First, let me ask you a question," he said. He feigned taking a pencil out of his pocket and writing in a small notebook. "Why the cane?"

"Excuse me?"

"You heard me," he continued in his serious, reporter-like voice. "You're using a cane and you have a brace on your leg. What happened to you?"

"Playing role reversal, Mr. Silverman?"

"Michael. Just answer the question, please."

"I was born prematurely, with permanent nerve damage in my foot."

"Was it bad when you were young?"

Her voice was soft. "Not good."

She lifted her head and saw the gentle, almost soothing

expression on his face. He'd have made a great interviewer,
she thought, except there was an undeniable tension between
them, a tension that was not altogether unpleasant.

"You say you were born premature," he continued. "Were
there other complications?"

"Not so fast," she replied. "My turn. When did you start
playing basketball?"

"I don't know. When I was six or seven, I guess."

"Were you one of those kids who played all the time, who
lived on the playground?"

"It was the best place to be," he replied.

"What do you mean?"

Michael did not answer. "What were your other compli-
cations, Sara?"

"Lung infections," she said quickly. "So when did you
start playing the piano?"

"When I was eight."

"Your parents hired a music teacher?"

A humorless smile came to his lips. "No."

"Then who—"

"I think you'd better leave," he said.

"Let's change the subject."

"No."

"But I was just going to ask—"

"I know what you were going to ask," Michael inter-
rupted. "How hard is this for you to understand? I don't
want my personal life splashed all over the papers. Period."

"I just wanted to know the name of your piano teacher,"
she said. "I thought you would want to give your teacher
credit."

"Bullshit, Sara. 'Let's change the subject' is just another

way of saying you want to try to attack from another angle. You figure if you keep probing, eventually you'll get what you want—no matter what the cost."

"And what are the costs, Michael? Your story could give hope to thousands of children who are being abused—"

"Jesus, how low will you stoop to get this story?"

"Don't flatter yourself," she replied. "I want every story I'm assigned."

"Have you no ethics?"

Sara's fists clenched. "Spare me the morality play. We reporters are great as long as we're telling the world what a wonderful guy you are. We're your best pals when we pat you on the back and help you get more endorsement money. But oh, if we dare to criticize, if we dare to dig deeper—"

"My personal life is none of anyone's goddamn business."

"Afraid I'll shatter your precious image? Afraid I'll make you look like something other than Superman?"

She could see him wrestling with his temper. "Good-bye, Sara," he said with too much control. "I really didn't want to do this."

"Go ahead. Slam the door in my face. I'll be back."

"No," he said, "you won't."

"We'll see."

And then he closed the door in her face just as Sara let loose with another sneeze. Her breathing was shallow from the effects of her cold. Sara wheezed, each drawn breath a painful struggle. She turned away from the door and huffed off.

"The man is a major-league pain in the ass."

Back home, she began to reread his file. As the words passed in front of her, her anger softened and then evapo-

rated. Could she really blame him for being so defensive? His childhood read like something out of Oliver Twist. *She sat back, laced her fingers behind her head, and sneezed again. Her breathing was still labored, even worse than before. She had tried to dismiss it, but the truth was becoming more and more apparent. With something near terror, Sara knew what she had to do. She reached for the phone and called her father.*

The next morning the doctors confirmed Sara's diagnosis.

"Pneumonia," John told his daughter in her hospital bed. There were tears in his eyes. "Third time for you in the last two years, Sara."

"I know," she said.

"You have to slow down a little."

Sara glanced up at her father but said nothing.

"Are you feeling okay?" he asked.

"Fine," she replied. "How long will I have to be here this time?"

"The doctors don't know, honey. I can stay with you for a while, if you'd like."

She nodded. "I'd like that very much."

John Lowell left his daughter's bedside at nine p.m. Sara did not want him to go. Irrational as it might seem, she hated being alone at night in the hospital. Despite all the time she had spent in hospitals, Sara was still scared to close her eyes, afraid that someone or something might sneak up on her. She felt like some movie character left alone to survive a night in a haunted house. It was the hospital sounds that made her shudder, the sounds that reverberated louder in the blackness and stillness of the night: footsteps echoing much too loudly against the tile floors; the constant beeping, gurgling, and sucking noises of life-saving machines; the random moan of pain; the scream of terror; the squeak of wheels; crying.

Feeling lonely, Sara strapped on her Walkman and began to sing a little ditty by the Police. When her voice grew too loud ("Don't stand so . . . Don't stand so . . . Don't stand so close to me!"), *the nurse came in, gave her a scolding glare, and told her to quiet down.*

"Sorry."

She took off the headset and flicked on the television. She was immediately greeted by a sportscaster's voice. "Great move by Michael Silverman. What a game he's having, Tom."

"Sure is, Brent. Twenty-two points, ten rebounds, nine assists. He's playing like a man possessed."

"And Seattle calls time out. The score in this fourth game of the NBA Championship Series—New York 87, the Sonics 85. We'll be back at Madison Square Garden in New York City in just a moment."

Though not much of a sports fan, Sara watched the remainder of the game. The Knicks won by five points, tying up the NBA finals at two games apiece. The series would now move to Seattle for the next two games and then back to New York if a seventh and final game was needed. She continued to watch as the inane sportscasters spewed out as many clichés as they could come up with while reviewing the game highlights. After that there were interviews with numerous players and coaches, which lasted for another hour or so.

"Looking for me?"

Sara turned quickly toward the door. "Who—?"

Michael stepped forward from the shadows. His hair was still wet from his postgame shower. "Miss Nancy Levin," he said simply.

"What?"

"You asked about my piano teacher. Miss Nancy Levin. She was the music teacher at Burnet Hill Elementary School."

Sara swallowed, not sure what to say. "It's past visiting hours."

"I know," he said. "I promised the security guard two tickets to a game if he looked the other way. One of the advantages of fame. Mind if I take a seat?"

Sara tried to speak but had to settle for a shake of the head.

"Thanks," he said. "I called your office this morning and your editor told me you had pneumonia. He said you get it pretty frequently."

She shrugged.

"So I thought I'd pay you a visit. I hope I'm not keeping you awake."

"Not at all," she replied, finding her voice at last, "but shouldn't you be celebrating with your teammates?"

"We don't celebrate until we win four games. We've only won two so far."

"Didn't the reporters want to interview you after the game?"

He nodded, smiling. "But as you well know, I don't really like interviews."

"Not even postgame victory ones?"

"Actually, I like those."

"So?"

"So I wanted to come here and see you, okay?"

She turned away from his steady gaze, summoning some inner strength before turning back to face him. "How much does this championship series mean to you, Michael?"

"Do you always ask so many questions?"

"Occupational hazard."

"Well, how can I put it? It means everything to me. I can't tell you how many times I've dreamed about hitting the winning shot in the NBA finals. Since I was a little kid, winning the NBA finals has been my dream. Does that answer your question?"

"Yes."

"So how are you feeling?"

"Fine," she said.

"Tired?"

"No."

"Want to talk?" he asked.

She nodded.

"Under one condition," he said. "It's all off the record. We're just chatting now. None of this can be used in a story. I want your word."

"You have it."

He stood and paced. "What do you know about me?"

"The file is on the night table," she said. "Read it."

He lifted the folder and opened it. Sara watched his eyes grow large and pained as they moved across the page.

"Is it true?" she asked him.

"Yes."

"All of it?"

"Yes."

And so they talked for the next hour until the nurse, a

large black woman who was no basketball fan, found Michael in Sara's room, reprimanded him for being there after visiting hours, and threw him out.

The Knicks and the Sonics split the next two games, putting both teams at three wins apiece and setting up Game Seven at Madison Square Garden in New York. Game Seven—mystical words for sports fans. Twenty-four teams playing eighty-two regular season games each and four rounds of play-offs had come down to one final game to decide the championship.

Sara watched the game from her hospital room. She found herself cheering for the Knicks fiercely, for Michael most especially. With three seconds left and the Knicks down 102–101, the ball was passed to Michael. Sara felt her heart leap into her throat as Michael drove the lane and lofted a hook shot high over the outstretched hand of Seattle's seven-foot center. The buzzer sounded. The ball bounced on the rim twice, hit the backboard, and then dropped in for two points. The game was over.

New York Knicks 103, Seattle Supersonics 102.

New York City went crazy. Michael's teammates, led by Reece Porter, mobbed Michael. Madison Square Garden rocked in a frenzied celebration. Sara heard herself crying out with joy, her hands pounding the bed in excitement.

He had done it. Michael had done it.

"Yahoo!" she shouted.

The same nurse peeked her head through the doorway. "Miss Lowell . . ."

"Sorry."

She watched the locker room scene, the champagne being poured on everyone's head, the rare joy of winning the NBA championship. The Knick players and coaches were hooting and shouting and hugging one another in one of adult life's few moments of uninhibited, unashamed happiness. Sara tried to find Michael in the rejoicing horde, but there was too much confusion. Several Knicks were interviewed by the sportscasters, all singing Michael's praises, but the game's superstar was nowhere to be found. Some time later Sara heard footsteps approach her room.

"Hi," Michael said.

"What are you doing here?"

Sara's voice was angry. A hurt look crossed Michael's face.

"What are you doing here?" she repeated, her tone no softer. "You're supposed to be celebrating the greatest moment of your life, right? So what the hell are you doing here?"

Tears glistened in the corners of his eyes. "I don't know," he said.

"What do you want from me? You said everything was true in that file, so I know you have a hundred bimbos to choose from—"

"Sara . . ."

"So what do you want from me?"

He lowered his head. "Why are you so angry?" he asked, his tone almost childlike.

She stopped. Her reaction had surprised her. Why was she yelling at him like this? Why did she feel so strange whenever she was with him—a soaring and yet queasy feeling? Why was she acting so angry when, truth be known, she was so happy he was here? "I'm just confused, Michael. I don't understand what's going on."

He moved closer. "Neither do I, Sara."

"Why did you come here tonight, Michael? Why aren't you celebrating with your teammates?"

"I don't know," he replied. "I ... I just wanted to be with you, that's all."

And now he had AIDS.

AIDS. The word floated about the room like a poisonous vapor. Sara felt the tears come to her eyes, and once again, she began to cry.

"It's okay," Michael whispered to her. "Everything is going to be okay."

He had not cried a single tear since Harvey and Eric had told them the news two hours ago, and somehow his lack of response was the most terrifying thing. His body had shook, but his eyes stared off, lost, confused, thoughtful. *What are you thinking?* Sara wondered. *What are you feeling right now and why won't you share it with me?*

Harvey and Eric had not yet left the room. Eric sat by the window, staring out over the impatient traffic on One Hundred Sixty-eighth Street. Harvey paced.

"I want the truth," Michael said now, his hand tightening against Sara's. "Can you cure this or not?"

Harvey stopped and turned toward Michael. His gaze met Eric's for a split second before resting on Michael's face. "We want to give it a try. We believe it's very possible."

"Then let's do it."

Harvey nodded. "I'll have you transferred to the clinic today."

"Today?" Sara said. "Can't it wait—"

"No," Harvey replied. "It can't wait. The earlier we start treatment, the better. I want to warn you both now that this treatment is not pretty. You will be hooked on SR1 and the side effects will be painful and unpleasant. For a while you will be a junkie, Michael. You will feel as though you need the fix or you'll die. And you'll be right."

The room slid gently back into silence.

"You two better go now," Michael said. "You must have a thousand things to do."

Harvey signaled to Eric and they both moved toward the exit. As Harvey opened the door, he turned back toward Michael. "Think about what I said earlier, okay? You can do a lot of good."

Michael nodded. The moment they left, Sara threw her arms around Michael again, but he stiffened, his body cold and hard . . . like a corpse.

"Michael?"

"I'm sorry," he said. His eyes shifted around the room, moving quickly from item to item as though looking for an easy exit. Sara rested her head against Michael's chest, and they stayed that way in silence for a very long time. The only sound Sara could hear was Michael's steady breathing, her head rising and falling with his chest.

Finally, Michael spoke. "You should go, Sara," he said. "You have your story to do."

"I'm not going anywhere."

"You have to," Michael said. "The story is too important."

"I'll get Donald Parker to do it."

He shook his head. "You should do it."

"To hell with the story, Michael. I want to stay with you."

Michael did not say anything for another ten minutes. He just remained silent, his lips curling around his teeth. "Sara, I'm not sure I want you to go through this."

"You don't have any choice," she replied. "And don't you dare play the brave martyr with me, Michael. You're not going to die. You're not going to leave me and the baby here alone without you."

He smiled sadly and patted her stomach. "We have Junior here to think of."

"That's right."

"Sara?"

"Yes?"

"I've been thinking about this for the past few hours," he said. "And I want to go public with this."

"What?"

"What they said makes sense—"

"They should have never said anything," Sara said. "This is no time for you to be making decisions, Michael. You're vulnerable right now."

He smiled again, sweetly, sadly. "What's the point of delaying the inevitable, Sara? You know we have no choice."

Fear wrapped around her neck like a cold scarf. "Please, Michael, think this through more. Don't just throw away . . ."

"Throw away what?" he asked. "It's over, Sara. There's nothing to throw away. I never let you do the story on the physical abuse I suffered as a child, and that was a selfish thing to do."

"Michael . . ."

"No, let me finish. It's really strange, Sara. When Harvey told me the results of the test, my thoughts became frighteningly clear. I've been thinking this whole thing through. Harvey and Eric didn't say too much, but I know where they stand. They want me to go public with this."

"Give it a little time," Sara said. "You just heard. There's a lot of things to consider here. Think for a second about the discrimination. People will hate you for it. The NBA will probably say you're too much of a health threat to ever step on the court again, even if the virus goes into remission."

"So what? Look, I'm not a brave man. Maybe you were right all those years ago. Maybe the story of my childhood would have helped people understand child abuse, but—I don't know—I just couldn't live through it again. I didn't have the strength."

"It's okay," she said. "It's not your fault."

"But, Sara, this is too big, too important. I can't just sit back again. I think Harvey knows that. He sees what his cure can do for people and so he puts everything else on hold. You heard what he said. The publicity from my case could have the biggest effect on the AIDS epidemic since Rock Hudson died. I can't just walk away from that."

She just held him, her eyes squeezed shut.

"So I want this story done, Sara. And I want you to arrange a press conference for me for tomorrow."

"If that's what you really want," she said slowly, "then we'll do it. But let's not talk about it right now, Michael. Right now, I just want you to hold me."

*   *   *

JENNIFER Riker pushed open the glass door leading
to Los Angeles' main post office. The air-conditioning
pounced upon her. Poor Bruce, she thought. He had
been a wonderful person in so many ways. A lousy husband, yes, but some men are just not built for marriage.
Why had he done it? What could have been so horrible
that Bruce had chosen to end his own life?

The tragedy had been hard on them all, especially
young Tommy. Not surprisingly, Bruce's son had blamed
his mother for his father's suicide.

"You killed him!" Tommy had yelled at Susan. "It's
your fault Dad died!"

And though Susan tried to argue with him, something
inside her leveled the same accusation; something could
not help but wonder what part she had played in Bruce's
demise. Jennifer watched the guilt etch lines onto her
sister's lovely face. Susan could not sleep at night. She
barely ate. The situation reached the point where Jennifer began to raise the possibility of seeking professional
counseling to help them deal with their grief.

But in the end Susan decided against it. She thought
that what she and Tommy really needed was to get away
from the world for a while and see if time and solitude
could help them regain their ties and come to grips with
Bruce's death. They had left two days ago for a quiet
retreat outside of Sacramento where there were no tele-
phones and no outside distractions.

Jennifer walked up to the information counter. "Could
you please tell me where box 1738 is?"

"Around the corner and to the left."

"Thank you."

A few minutes later Jennifer located the correct number, inserted the key, and opened the box. It was filled to capacity with junk mail and soot. She waved away the particles of dust and began to transfer the mail from the box into her tote bag. Ed McMahon's picture was on one envelope, telling Bruce that he might have already won $100,000. Alas, the postmark showed that the letter was mailed last year. Too bad. Bruce might have been rich and never knew it.

There were also several envelopes that looked like bank statements, postmarked seven years ago, and even a couple of medical periodicals, also from seven years ago. Nothing very interesting. Nothing very current, for that matter.

Her fingers continued to sift through the box's contents until they stopped suddenly at a large manila envelope. Jennifer paused when she spotted the familiar handwriting across the front. She tried to recall whose penmanship it was, but for a brief moment the name eluded her. She closed her eyes, picturing the neatly formed letters in her head and trying to remember where she had seen them before. The answer came to her. Of course. It was Bruce's handwriting. The careful shaping of the letters was unmistakable.

Jennifer turned the envelope around and tried to read the postmark. When she was finally able to see the date clearly, her legs nearly gave way. August 30th of this year. She tried to swallow but her mouth felt too dry. August 30th. Bruce had died on August 30th. He must have mailed this letter a few hours before his death. And even stranger, he had addressed the package to himself.

Why had Bruce mailed himself a package right before he committed suicide?

Jennifer quickly dropped the package into the tote bag as though she were afraid to hold it any longer. Then she finished unloading the post office box and headed toward the exit.

She'd open the package later.

I I

HARVEY felt the onset of another in what had become a series of powerful headaches. It was sometime around two a.m., and the hallways of Sidney Pavilion were silent, sleeping, recuperating. Harvey moved slowly down a darkened, empty corridor with dim fluorescent lights that buzzed like distant chain saws. He opened the doors, each one sounding off its own unique creak, and looked in on his sleeping patients. He checked their IVs, their charts, their medications.

He walked into the last room on the floor, Kiel Davis and Ricky Martino's room. Both men were sleeping soundly. The forty or so clinic patients were broken down into two groups: inpatients who stayed in Sidney Pavilion and outpatients who came in on an almost daily basis for treatment. Usually, the members of these two groups rotated every three or four weeks so that no more than twenty-five patients were ever in the clinic on any given night. Right now there were almost thirty patients sleeping over. Most had private rooms, but because of limited space, a few had been doubled up.

The overnight schedule rarely worked exactly as planned because each patient had different needs. Take Davis and Martino, for example. Kiel Davis, a homosexual from Indiana who had relocated to New York ten years ago, had spent almost two-thirds of the last eighteen months in the clinic, while over the same period of time, Martino, an intravenous drug user from the Bronx, had slept over less than six months total.

Harvey scanned their charts, listening to the gentle, deep breathing of their slumber. He closed the door behind him, headed toward the staircase, and jogged up one flight of stairs to the third floor—his way of getting exercise. He heard himself wheezing from the effort.

Out of shape, he thought. *I should stop using the elevator altogether and always take the stairs.*

But Harvey knew that the hitching in his chest was due to something beyond poor physical conditioning. The muscles in his forehead seemed to swell now, bunching up against the sensitive nerve endings. A fluttery sensation flitted across his stomach.

He was scared.

Harvey stopped in front of the door that led to room 317, the only room on the floor that held a patient. He pushed open the door and leaned his head through the frame. The patient was at long last asleep, which had been no easy task in this case. Drugs had been necessary. Strong ones. Harvey had finally convinced Michael to take a couple of potent sleeping pills. They worked. Actually, they were potent enough to work on a charging rhino.

Long shadows came in through the windows and reached across the room like giant fingers readying to close. Sara sat in a wooden chair at the side of Michael's bed, her hand clutching his. Even in the poor lighting Harvey could see anguish tightening the skin around Sara's cheekbones. Her lips quivered as though from cold; her eyes were moist. She had not yet acknowledged his presence, though she surely must have heard him open the door. Instead, Sara continued to look down at her sleeping husband. Harvey wondered if she was lost in her own thoughts or if she had simply chosen to ignore him.

Probably a little of both.

He looked again at the figure hunched over the bed. They were confident, at least, that Sara's HIV test would come back negative. She had already taken the test less than a month ago as part of her research for a story on AIDS testing at the *New York Herald* and it had been negative. While the virus was known to remain dormant for many years, it was still encouraging news for Michael and Sara and the unborn infant.

Harvey turned away from the pitiful sight and let the door close. He knew Sara was going through hell right now, worse even than Michael. Standing aside and watching helplessly while a loved one suffered was often more difficult than the simpler task of suffering through the physical trauma. Harvey wished he could help. He wished that he could take Michael's place, that it was he rather than Michael who had to bear this great burden. But of course that was impossible.

Cruel as it seemed, Michael and Sara would have to go through this ordeal alone. Crueler still, Harvey knew, was that he saw the possible benefits he could gain from Michael's situation. When Harvey considered the positive implications for AIDS patients generally and the clinic specifically—the hope, the finances, the publicity—he could not help but hope Michael would go public with his illness. Awful as it might seem, he realized that Michael's diagnosis could in the long run save thousands of lives. Michael could do for AIDS what no one since Rock Hudson or Ryan White had done—bring it home to the public, make it real, change the perspective of thousands, perhaps millions of people.

And that was why Sara was angry with him. Harvey had really not said very much, but his feelings on the matter were clear. Michael had been handed a responsibility that was bigger than all of them. A rare opportunity to do good had been thrust upon him. He could not just toss it away. And Sara saw that. In her heart she knew what would have to be. But right now Sara's mind was too clouded by her pain for her to see what was so clear. That was certainly understandable. Right now the rest of the world did not matter to her. Only Michael mattered. Protecting him.

So steam would eventually have to be blown off. The hurt would have to run its course before they could all look at things rationally, calmly. But not tonight. Tonight they needed to be left alone to ponder their fate. Saving lives could wait for another sunrise.

Harvey moved down the hallway in the direction of the clinic's laboratory. The night was absolutely still now. Harvey could hear only two noises: the heels of his shoes clacking against the cool tile and—

—and the rustling noise coming from behind the lab door.

He froze. Winston and Eric had sealed all experiments and locked the lab door three hours ago. No one else had a key. And no one was supposed to be in there.

Don't panic. Maybe one of them came back to do a little extra work. It wouldn't be the first time.

That was certainly true. Harvey slid closer to the door. The door's window had a shade pulled over it so he could not peer in. Instead, he pressed his ear against the pane. It felt cold to the touch. He listened. Nothing. The lab was quiet. He closed his eyes, straining to hear.

The rustling sound started up again.

Okay, no problem. It's just Winston or Eric. I'll just turn the knob, open the door and . . .

His head hurt like a bastard now; the pounding in his forehead was almost audible. Harvey reached for the knob, grasped it, and turned. The door was locked. An icy coldness glided through him. His hand flew away from the door. The lab door was never locked when someone was inside. Never. He tried to peer into the room through the tiny crack where the shade did not cover when he realized something that twisted his stomach. He looked down by the floor to confirm his fears.

No lights.

There were no streams of light coming through the

shade opening or from under the door. The lights in the lab were off.

What kind of scientist works in the dark?

Seeing-eye scientists? Scientists with infrared glasses?

Sweat popped onto his forehead.

It still might be nothing. It still might be . . .

Might be what?

He had no answer to stave off his mounting panic. Acting without conscious thought, Harvey's hand reached into his pocket for the key to the lab. He took it out and moved it toward the lock. From behind the door, Harvey heard a file drawer slam shut. He swallowed in a deep breath, slid the key into the hole, and flung open the door.

The room was dark, the dim hall lights providing only a modicum of illumination. Harvey thought he saw a movement in the corner of his eye. He spun toward it, but there was nothing. Could have been just his imagination. His hand reached out blindly, finding the light switch and flicking it up. The lights came on, the sudden brightness startling him.

At first he saw nothing unusual. The lab was neat, tidy. No loose papers were visible. The microscopes were covered with plastic. The test tubes sealed. Only one thing looked different and that one thing made Harvey's eyes widen. Suddenly Harvey forgot about things like caution and wariness. Gone were the worries that a dangerous prowler might still be in the lab, hiding, preparing to pounce. He stepped forward, concerned solely for the welfare of what lay beyond the jimmied lock on the other side of the room.

That was a mistake.

Without warning, something heavy slammed against the base of Harvey's neck. His body pitched forward. Sharp slivers of pain and numbness erupted throughout his skull. Harvey grasped his head between both hands as he folded at the waist and fell to the floor. His eyes closed.

JENNIFER had a light dinner by herself, caught the latest Woody Allen movie at the CinePlex, one of those movie theaters that seemed to have more screens than clients, and arrived back at the house a little past midnight. She tossed the little airline bag filled with the contents from Bruce's post office box onto the couch and collapsed beside it. For a few moments she did nothing other than stare at the Sabena World Airways logo on the flight bag. Her mind traveled back ten years—ten years since she and Harvey had flown on Sabena to Brussels to begin a European odyssey through Belgium, France, and Holland. First-class. Champagne and caviar on board. What a magnificent trip. Alas, it had been the last vacation she had convinced Harvey to take. He, in truth, had not enjoyed himself. Relaxing, sightseeing, eating gourmet, being pampered in fine hotels—that was just not for him.

The stupid fool.

All right, so she was bitter. She had a right to be. She had loved Harvey. Still did. But the man did not know how to live. Oh sure, he could be funny and seemingly carefree and he was a far cry from some sort of bookworm, but he was obsessed with his work. With saving the world. Yes, she had married a dreamer and that had

been great while they were courting. It had been romantic, even Gothic. But it had worn on her after a while. His
selflessness began to eat away at her lust for life, leaving
her with little more than self-pity.

The stupid fool.

Bruce Grey had been dedicated too, but the man understood that there were limits. He was not nearly as naive and foolhardy as Harvey. Bruce saw reality. He knew
that the two of them could not stop the mass suffering,
only alleviate it a little. That was all a person could be
expected to do. For Bruce, that had been enough. But
not for Harvey—

Jennifer sat up suddenly. The manila envelope. The
one Bruce had addressed to himself the day he died. She
had not yet opened it. She slid over toward the Sabena
flight bag, grabbed it, and rummaged through the horde
of envelopes. It did not take her long to locate the packet
in question. It was the thickest and heaviest by far. She
extracted it from the bag and laid it on her lap. Bruce's
name and address were clearly written in his own handwriting. So strange.

She walked over to the desk, took hold of the letter
opener, and sliced open the envelope. Numerous papers,
tubular containers, and what looked like files streamed
out like candy from a broken piñata.

With a sigh, Jennifer began to read them.

"OWWW."

"Harvey?"

"My head," Harvey groaned.

"Harvey, can you hear me?" Sara asked.

Harvey's eyes opened slightly. The lights seemed particularly bright, pricking his eyes. He closed them, shaded them with his hand, and tried again.

"Harvey?"

"Yeah, Sara, I can hear you. Where am I?"

"You're still at the clinic."

"How long have I been out?"

"I found you half an hour ago," Sara replied.

His vision focused in on two faces. One beautiful, the other thin with a mustache and long nose. "Lieutenant Bernstein?"

Max nodded. "Sara called me. Are you all right?"

"Yeah, fine."

"Can you tell me what happened?"

Harvey tried to clear his head. "In the lab," he began slowly. "Someone was in the lab."

Sara said, "I caught a glimpse of someone running down the hall, but I couldn't see the face."

"Whoever it was," Harvey managed, "hit me over the head."

"Why don't we start at the beginning, okay?" Bernstein suggested, taking out his pad and pencil. "Tell us what happened."

Slowly, Harvey told them what had occurred from the moment he heard the noise in the lab until he was knocked unconscious. When he finished, Lieutenant Bernstein stopped pacing and asked, "So what was he after? What was so precious that you forgot a prowler was in the room?"

"My private files."

"Your what?"

"My private files. I keep them locked in there."

"You don't keep them in your office?"

"No. The lock and security around the lab is supposed to be much tighter than in my office. And the information I keep in those private files is usually derived from lab results. We all keep our private files in the lab."

Bernstein stared at his pad intensely. "You keep saying 'private' files. What do you mean by that?"

"They contain personal information—professional secrets, if you will."

"What kind of secrets?"

"Different things. Results from experiments, stuff like that."

"What kind of experiments?"

Harvey lay back down. "Personal ones," he replied. "You see, it pays to work closely with partners and to share all your findings, no question about it, but sometimes you need to work in private—alone and without any outside interference and suggestions. It's often the best way to make headway—the one man working in solitude kind of thing. We understood and respected each other's private work."

"Who is 'we'?"

"Bruce, Eric, and myself."

Bernstein nodded, circling to the other side of the bed and then back again. "Did Bruce Grey have private files?"

"Of course."

"Have you gone through them since his death?"

"Yes."

"Was there anything surprising in them?"

Harvey hesitated. "Not really."

"What do you mean, not really?"

"I mean there were no major breakthroughs or anything like that. Bruce wasn't very big on independent research . . ." He paused. "It might be nothing."

Bernstein leaned over the bed. "Go on."

"Well, several of his important files were missing."

"What sort of files?"

"Patient files. Trian and Whitherson's, to name two."

"How about Bradley Jenkins'?"

"That one is still there."

Max stood back up, walked to the door, fiddled with the knob. "I'd like you to give me a complete list of the missing files, and I also want to go through Grey's entire file cabinet as soon as possible."

Harvey nodded. "I suspected as much. But do me a favor, Lieutenant. Don't let anyone else go through them. The information in those files is confidential and must remain so."

"I don't understand something," Sara interjected. "Why would routine patient files be locked up with the private files?"

"There is no such thing as routine patient files in here," Harvey explained. "Everything in here is confidential. We use codes here, never names, so that no one—lab technicians, nurses, orderlies—knows a patient's name. We often keep patients secluded from one another. Except for roommates, patients never see or get to know one another."

"Did Whitherson, Trian, or Jenkins know each other?" Bernstein asked.

"No."

"What happens when visitors come by?" Sara asked. "Won't they see the other patients on the floor?"

Harvey shook his head. "This whole place is compartmentalized. First floor is offices and visiting rooms—we wheel the patients into private rooms so that the visitors never enter the actual patients' ward, which is on the second floor."

"Sounds like prison visiting hours," Max added.

"The situation is similar," Harvey agreed. "The key thing to remember is that visitors never go into a patient's room."

Bernstein scratched his smooth right cheek hard, like a dog with a tic near his ear. "Okay, so let me get this straight. The first floor has offices and visiting rooms. The second floor is the patients' ward. The third floor has the lab."

Harvey shot a quick glance toward Sara. "And highly confidential patients are also kept on the third floor," he said. "We normally keep no more than one or two patients up here."

"Was Bradley Jenkins one such patient?"

"Yes."

"Interesting." Max put his pencil into his mouth and looked up at the ceiling. "So the prowler may have been trying to find out names of patients or the prognosis of a patient."

Harvey sat up. "Could have been," he said, swinging his feet onto the floor.

"Where are you going?"

"I have to check my files."

"Wait a second," Max said, snapping his fingers. "Was there any patient recently admitted? Was there anybody whose identity you wanted to keep confidential?"

Harvey stopped.

"You can tell him," Sara said.

"Tell me what?"

It was Sara who responded. "Michael was admitted today. He has AIDS."

NOT too far from where Sara, Max, and Harvey were talking, Janice Matley, the Sidney Pavilion's most trusted nurse, knew something was wrong the moment she opened the door. She sensed it. There was something about the stillness of the bed, the way the sheet was twisted around the body, the way the head lolled limply off the pillow. Janice felt a creeping dread in the pit of her stomach.

She knew.

Janice Matley was a heavyset black woman in her mid-fifties. She had been a nurse for the better part of thirty years and had worked for Dr. Riker and Dr. Grey for the past decade. She had been crushed when Dr. Grey committed suicide, absolutely devastated. Such a lovely man, poor thing. And a great doctor. He and Dr. Riker had been perfect partners, complementing each other like no other two men could. Dr. Grey was the heart, the team player, the one with the good bedside manner, the one who felt for every patient. Dr. Riker was the brains, the leader, the drive, the one who would do what had to be done and blind himself to the personal price.

And Dr. Eric Blake? Janice was not sure where she would place him. He was a bit of a paradox, that one. He too was dedicated, spending all his time in the clinic like Dr. Riker, but somehow he seemed distant, aloof. Oh, he cared about his patients immensely and Janice knew that Dr. Blake would follow Dr. Riker to the ends of the earth and back, but he still seemed so . . . unfeeling. Maybe that wasn't fair. Just because she could not warm up to him did not mean he was not a nice man. He was a fine person, a fine doctor, and smart as they come. His patients and colleagues respected him greatly. He just wasn't . . . warm, that's all.

Janice stepped toward the patient with the blank facial expression of an experienced nurse. Inside, she could feel something tremble. She reached the bed and flicked on the reading lamp. Her knees went wobbly. The patient's eyes, glassy and uncomprehending, looked straight through her. His lips were parted and frozen. His arms felt almost brittle, like the branches on an old tree that would break rather than bend.

Janice ran for the door.

MAX stared at Sara. "Michael has AIDS?"

She nodded.

He collapsed into a chair. "I don't know what to say, Sara."

"He'll be fine," Sara said firmly.

He nodded, unsure what to say next. "Who knows about Michael's condition?"

"Aside from us," Harvey replied, "just Eric and maybe one of the hospital nurses."

"Maybe?"

"There is a good chance that the nurse might recognize his face."

"Who's the nurse?"

"Her name is Janice Matley."

"You trust her?"

"Completely."

He shook his head. "I don't care how much security you have around here. There is no way you're going to be able to keep this a secret."

"We know that," Sara said. "Michael has scheduled a press conference for tomorrow evening. It'll be covered live on *NewsFlash*."

Bernstein's eyes squinted into small slits. "Are you trying to tell me that Michael is going to tell the world he has AIDS?"

Sara nodded.

"And then you're going to do the report on SR1?"

"Not me," Sara corrected. "I'm too close to this now. Donald Parker is going to do it."

"And what exactly is Parker going to cover?" Max asked. "The AIDS cure? The Gay Slasher connection? Senator Jenkins' kid being treated at the clinic?"

"All of it," Sara replied.

Max took the pencil out of his mouth and let go a whistle. "That's going to be one hell of a story. The whole country is already talking about the Gay Slasher story. Wait till John Q. Public finds out that the murders are connected to a clinic that's found a cure for AIDS. And then add the fact that Michael Silverman has AIDS and is being treated at the same clinic." Bernstein shook his head again. "It's going to be unbelievable."

No one said anything for a moment.

"Okay," Max said, "switch gears with me a second, Doc. You said the lab door was locked when you tried the knob, right?"

"Right."

"Who has a key besides you?"

"Eric and Winston O'Connor, the chief lab technician."

"Does this O'Connor know about Michael?"

"No," Harvey replied, "Winston doesn't know the names of any of the patients in here. Like I said before, the test results are coded. The people in the lab never see the names, only numbers. In other words Winston O'Connor sees the test results, but he is 'blind' as to whom it involves. We even change their code numbers weekly so that they cannot be traced down."

"You're a cautious man, Dr. Riker."

"Almost paranoid, right?"

Bernstein was about to answer when they heard a shout. Janice Matley stuck her head through the doorway.

"Dr. Riker, come quick!" Janice shouted, though she knew it was much too late.

"What is it?"

"Code blue! A patient's arrested!"

12

JENNIFER Riker scanned the contents in the packet. Little of it made sense. First, there were the files.

Being a doctor's wife, Jennifer had seen plenty of patient files before but these were considerably more vague than most. Specifics were not jotted down—more like Bruce's overall opinions and thoughts on the patient. A journal almost. She read the neatly typed name on the label of the first file: Trian, Scott. She jumped back to the beginning of the file and saw a whole slew of numbers:

1/9	897a83
1/16	084c33
1/23	995d42
1/30	774c09
2/06	786m60

They continued in a similar pattern for two full pages. Jennifer went to the kitchen and grabbed a calendar. She guessed that 1/9 must stand for January 9, 1/16 for January 16, and so on. She checked the calendar. January 9 was a Monday, as was every other day that followed. For some reason Bruce had jotted down a five-digit number with a letter between the third and fourth numeral on every Monday.

Why?

She shrugged and continued to read. Very little of it made sense to her—a lot of medical jargon—but early on she read something that she understood all too clearly:

HIV positive. T cell count very low. Signs of Kaposi's sarcoma.

The word wasn't there, but Jennifer knew what Bruce was trying to say: AIDS. In fact she could not find the term anywhere in any of the reports, as though the very acronym should be avoided, whispered, never written in anything but easy-to-erase pencil.

AIDS.

She continued to read. A few pages later another paragraph gave her reason to pause. Bruce's handwriting was bright now, soaring, reflecting the mood he had obviously felt at this moment. She had seen what the job of medical research could do to a man, the highs and the lows, how every setback brought on depression and every breakthrough a major high. Emotions swayed on a daily, sometimes hourly, basis.

Good news. Trian appears to be getting better. His progress is remarkably similar to the animal tests which proved so successful. It is hard not to get your hopes up when you chart it. The SR1 has taken its toll on him, but for the first time he appears genuinely healthy. Is it simply remission or something much more?

And ten months later:

We are finally ready. Harvey and I will know tomorrow. I can't believe it. Both of us are so anxious that we keep snapping at one another and anyone who happens to be around us. Poor Eric. Harvey almost bit his head off for nothing. He felt bad about it afterwards, like Harv always does when he loses his temper. Then he tried to make it up to him by repeatedly complimenting Eric on his work.

I can't blame Harvey for being a little edgy. This is it. This is what we've been waiting for.

What was Bruce talking about? What were they waiting for? Jennifer noted the date. Nine months ago. So much had happened to her in the last nine months— leaving Harvey, moving to California—but when Jennifer read what happened the next day, she realized how insignificant the changes in her life had been. Bruce's words put her own private world back in perspective, and for the first time in many months she felt the hollow pang of inadequacy ripple anew from the distant recesses of her mind.

"My God," she uttered out loud. "It can't be."

She swallowed and reread the page, sure that she had misunderstood the words:

I am not ashamed to say that tears keep running down my face as I write this. Powerful emotions keep crashing over me. It's more than I can take. It's more than I ever expected to hear. But I'm getting ahead of myself, so let me go back a moment. I'll try to be as precise as possible for the sake of posterity.

Harvey and I wanted to see the Trian results for ourselves. After all, this is hardly the kind of thing you wait for the lab boys to send you a report on. So we walked toward the lab with the controlled rush of school children heading for recess under a teacher's watchful eye. Winston seemed surprised to see us. He asked what we were doing in the lab. I told him we wanted the results for 443t90. Why the rush? Winston asked. Harvey became a little impatient, which was certainly understandable under the circumstances, and told him to hand over the file. Winston did.

We were too nervous to open it in the lab so we did our "trying not to run" bit back down to my office. Janice stopped us on the way to ask a question, but we just blew right by her. She looked at us like we had lost our minds. We hustled into my office and closed the door. Harvey handed me the file. I can't look, he said.

I opened it. Trian was HIV negative. His T cell count was almost normal. My heart leapt into my throat while Harvey stood without moving. I think he was in shock. We called in Eric and told him the news. He and I began to shout and jump around like Super Bowl champs, but not Harv. He just stood to the side and looked off at nothing. What's the matter? I asked him. We've done it.

Harv shook his head. Not so fast, he said. We have a lot still to be done.

But look at the results, I insisted. He's HIV negative.

Harvey: Yes, but for how long? It's encouraging but what do we know for sure? We have to test him again.

Me: But this is just what we need to get the place going again. We needed this boost, this kick in the ass. The PHS will give us more money now. Our grant will have to be extended.

Harvey: Timing is everything.

Me: What does that mean?

Harvey: It means that we have to keep this quiet. Can you imagine the uproar if such news got out? The press, the scrutiny? We'll lose our anonymity.

Eric said nothing.

Harvey: No, my friends, for right now, we should tell no one. We will reveal little bits—enough to maintain interest and finances—but not enough for anyone to know for sure. In the meantime let's make sure everything is well documented. Send the sample to Bangkok on Friday.

Jennifer could not believe what she was reading. HIV negative? They had turned someone who had been HIV positive back into HIV negative. The disclosure hit her like a heavyweight.

They've cured AIDS.

That was probably optimistic thinking, but the evidence was right in front of her. They had done it. Somehow they had found a cure for the AIDS virus. And Harvey had never mentioned it to her.

It was all so unbelievable. The startling revelation wearied her. She put the file down and closed her eyes. She wanted just to rest them for a few minutes before continuing to read, but exhaustion got the better of her. She slid into the cusp between consciousness and slumber and her head tilted back. One question kept gnawing at the base of her brain as she glided down into a deep, sound sleep: Why had Bruce committed suicide right after mailing out this packet?

RALPH Edmund, the county coroner, rolled the stretcher past Max. Ralph looked like a coroner—to be more precise, a mortician. Sallow skin, tall, thin body, thin black hair, long fingers. On the other hand he never dressed like a mortician. He wore loud colors, polyester prints, and ostentatious gold jewelry. He also did not act like a mortician. Ralph was emotional, loud, uncouth as all hell. Even better, he had the charming habit of chewing tobacco and spitting the black-yellow juice wherever and whenever he saw fit.

"I want the autopsy done right away," Max whispered to the coroner.

"Is that why you called me down here personally?" Ralph asked.

Max nodded. "Check everything."

"Okay," Ralph replied, a thick ball of tobacco bulging in his cheek. "I'll get to it later this afternoon."

"Now. Right now. And get all the blood samples you can out of him. I want you to run a full battery of tests on him."

"Like what?"

"We'll go over it later."

"Hey, Twitch, why you whispering? He's not going to wake up. Ha!"

"Hilarious. Just find out what killed him." Max turned and moved toward Harvey. The doctor looked pale and exhausted. "Where's Martino's roommate?"

"Kiel Davis? I had him moved to another room. He's being sedated."

"I want to speak with him."

"Later," Harvey replied. He shook his head. "My God, I can't believe this."

"What's to believe?" Max asked, flipping through his

notepad. "There was no visible trauma, no blood, no stab or gunshot wounds, no signs of a struggle. The victim was a patient at an AIDS clinic, so we can assume he was in poor health. All signs point to death by natural causes, right?"

Harvey did not reply right away. "Ricky Martino was no angel," he said at last. "He was an intravenous drug abuser. He used to push drugs at a local high school."

"Irrelevant. How sick was he?"

"Actually," Harvey replied, "Martino was cured."

"He didn't have AIDS?"

"Not anymore. His last test showed he was HIV negative. He was still undergoing more treatment, of course, but he was on his way to a full recovery."

"Interesting," Max said.

"To be frank," Harvey continued, "I wasn't crazy about treating Martino."

"Why not?"

"Because he was a lousy candidate. For one thing, he was a heroin addict."

"Then why did you?" Sara asked. "With so many good candidates willing to give anything a try, why would you choose Martino?"

"Because we wanted a cross section of patients—not just gay men. So Bruce brought Martino in. Bruce liked Martino. He believed in him."

"And you didn't?" Sara continued.

Harvey shrugged. "Intravenous drug abusers, by and large, are a rather sordid group. I confess I'm no big fan of treating IVDAs—not for any moral reason but simply because they are unreliable data. Addicts cannot be trusted. On top of that, most of them are already un-healthy from a lifetime of abusing their bodies, which makes their chances of fighting the disease that much slimmer."

"Then what do you think killed him, Doctor?" Max asked.

"I don't know." He paused to gather his thoughts. "I just don't understand it. I was in this room less than an hour ago."

"Before you got hit on the head?"

"Right before."

"And Martino appeared fine?"

"He was breathing, if that's what you mean. Look, Martino was not the healthiest man alive, but he had nothing that would have led to an acute death like this. And with the prowler in here tonight and all . . . it just seems like a hell of a coincidence."

Max folded his arms across his chest, his face twisted in heavy thought. "If Martino was murdered, it puts this whole thing in a new light."

"What do you mean?" Harvey asked.

"New M.O., for one," he answered.

"No stabbing," Sara agreed.

"But what about Bruce?" Harvey said. "He wasn't stabbed either."

Bernstein nodded slowly and began to pace. "Let's slow down a minute. Five people are dead, four patients, one doctor. Three—Trian, Whitherson, and Jenkins—were stabbed to death under similar, though not identi-cal, circumstances."

"We know all this," Harvey said impatiently.

"Just bear with me, okay? What do the three patients have in common?"

"They were gay," Sara began, "and they were all being treated at the same AIDS clinic."

"Now add Martino to the list, assuming he too was murdered."

"Then we can rule out a gay basher," Harvey noted. "Martino was heterosexual." His beeper went off. "Damn, I have to go."

"I'll need to speak to you later," Max said. "I also want to see your files on the murder victims."

Harvey nodded and left. Bernstein stopped pacing and looked toward Sara gently. "You must be exhausted. Why don't you get some sleep?"

"I feel fine."

"Sara . . ."

"Don't start this shit with me, Max. Crying and moping around is not going to help. I need something to distract me."

Max nodded, understanding. "Okay, where were we?"

"Riccardo Martino."

"Right. Add him into the equation and what makes them all similar?"

"Two things," Sara answered. "AIDS and the clinic. Like Harvey said, we can eliminate the gay connection since Martino was heterosexual."

"Okay, now let's move on to Dr. Bruce Grey. Add him to Whitherson, Trian, Jenkins, and Martino. Now what is the common denominator?"

"Only one thing," Sara answered. "The clinic. Someone is targeting people associated with the Sidney Pavilion."

Max did not respond right away. He just looked off, his head slowly shaking, his teeth locating another corner of fingernail on which he could gnaw. "We're missing something here," he said finally, "something big."

"Like?"

"Hell if I know."

"Do you think someone is trying to sabotage the clinic?"

"Could be."

She glanced at the clock above the door. "I have to get back to Michael now. He'll be waking up in a little while."

"I'm going to check through Dr. Riker's patient files."

"Okay. I'll see you later."

"Sara? One other thing?"

"Yes?"

"I'm saying this as a friend, not a police officer."

"Go ahead."

"You're blocking on Michael. It's going to hit you soon."

She moved to the door. "I know, Max. Thanks."

HE could hear the running water.

"No, no, please . . ."

"Shut up, you whining punk."

Seven-year-old Michael looked up, his eyes tainted with fear. His stepfather was leaning over the tub. His blue work shirt, the name Marty sewed on the breast pocket in red script, was unbuttoned, revealing a ripped white T-shirt underneath. Marty's face contorted into a look of pure, dumb anger and hate. His breath reeked of liquor and tobacco.

"Get over here, Michael!"

"Please . . ."

"If I have to chase you, boy . . ." He never finished the sentence, allowing Michael's imagination to do it instead.

Michael tried to run, but his feet felt glued to the floor. He could not move. Marty reached his hand out and took Michael by the hair. He tugged him forward and then down, forcing Michael's head under the water.

"You gonna mess around in my room again?" Marty shouted.

Michael could not answer. He could not breathe. He flailed his head back and forth, searching for air. But there was none. Water went down his throat and he began to choke.

Marty's grip tightened. His hand held firm. "I didn't hear you, boy. You gonna mess around in my room again?"

Pressure built up in Michael's head. His lungs felt like they were about to burst. He could hear the water splash around him . . .

Michael shot up out of bed. Sweat coated his skin.

Just a dream.

He looked around, almost expecting to see Marty's face in the corner of the darkened room. But his stepfather was not there. Michael was alone in the clinic. The AIDS clinic. He had AIDS. From the hallway he could hear water running. Someone washing up. Someone cleaning out something. No reason to be scared.

He swung his legs out of the bed and stood. His body still trembled from the power of the dream, but at least he didn't feel any of the SR1 side effects yet. He wrapped his arms around his chest and moved toward the window. He looked out. Not much of a view. Just a dirty alley. Garbage strewn everywhere. Two homeless men playing cards. Overturned tin cans. Cats chewing on a chicken bone. The only thing that hinted at the sanitary conditions within the building was a startlingly clean white truck with the inscription "Recovery Corporation of America—Medical Waste Disposal" painted across its side. Michael continued to stare.

Random thoughts and emotions ricocheted through his mind. They moved so quickly that he could not make complete sense of them, like trying to read a license plate as a car speeds by you. He tried to slow them down, but it was impossible. He caught just glimpses. In the end, one word became clear, blocking out all others:

Sara.

Funny, but Michael was not afraid of dying. Leaving Sara frightened him more. Alone. With the baby. The future meant something to him now. He had a stake in it, responsibilities. He wanted to stay with Sara, with the baby. So why did this happen now? Why show him what could be only to take it away?

Enough self-pity, Michael. You're making me sick.

He thought about the press conference he would have to give tonight on *NewsFlash* and wondered what he was going to say. He could just imagine the questions the reporters were going to hurl at him gleefully:

"Have you always been gay? . . ." "Did your wife know? . . ." "How about your teammates? . . ." "How many boyfriends have you had? . . ."

And oh God, Sara, what am I doing to you? he asked himself. *All I ever wanted to do was protect you. Now I'm throwing you in the middle of this. I wish I didn't have to. I wish I could just ignore it, blind myself from the truth. But I can't. Why should you have to suffer anymore? Part of me wants to push you away, to shield you from going through this whole AIDS shit with me.*

But Michael knew he could never. Sara would never allow it. And he knew that if the roles had been reversed, there would be no way Sara could have persuaded him to let her go. None. She would want to be there, and selfish as it might be, he wanted her there. He knew he would never make it without her.

He just wished he wasn't so goddamn scared.

"Michael?"

He turned. Sara stood in the doorway. She was so beautiful, so goddamn achingly beautiful . . . He felt tears come to his eyes, but he forced them back down again. "I love you," he said.

She limped to the window and hugged him tightly.

He closed his eyes and held on. "We're going to beat this thing, aren't we?"

She pulled back and looked up at him. A smile flirted with her lips. "We're going to whip its ass," she said staunchly.

She embraced him again, trying so very hard to believe her own words.

THAT morning Lieutenant Bernstein found Dr. Harvey Riker in the lab, checking through his private files.

"Anything missing?" the lieutenant asked.

Harvey shook his head. "But someone went through them. A couple of them are out of order."

"Michael's?"

"Yes. Have you heard from the coroner yet?"

Bernstein nodded. The fingers of his right hand busily twisted a paper clip into shapes it was never intended to achieve. "There were traces of cyanide. Someone injected it into his right arm."

"So it was murder."

"Looks like."

Harvey let go a long breath. "Did you speak with Kiel Davis yet?"

"Yes. He saw nothing. He heard nothing. He knows nothing."

As Harvey was about to respond, Winston O'Connor stepped through the doorway. "Good morning, Harvey."

"Hi, Winston. Win, I want you to meet Lieutenant Bernstein."

Winston O'Connor stuck out his hand. "Pleasure, sir. Ain't you kinda young to be a lieutenant?"

Bernstein ignored the common question and busied himself studying the man. Fortyish, thick Southern accent, blond-turning-to-gray hair, average height, open smile. "You're the chief lab technician?"

"That's right," Winston twanged. "What brings you all around these parts, Lieutenant?"

"Someone broke into this lab last night," Bernstein said, purposely not saying anything about Martino yet.

"You're kidding! A break-in here? What did they take?"

"Nothing," Max replied. "Dr. Riker walked in on them."

"You all right, Harv?"

"Fine."

"Where were you last night at around three in the morning?" Max asked.

Winston's face registered surprise. "Am I a suspect?"

"No one is a suspect. I'm just trying to figure out what happened."

"I was home all night."

"You live alone?"

"Yes."

"Can anyone vouch for your whereabouts?"

"Why the hell would I need anyone to vouch for me?"

"Please just answer the question."

"No. I don't make a point of having witnesses watch me when I'm in my own home."

"What time did you leave here last night?"

"Around midnight."

"Were you the last one to leave the lab?"

"No," Winston said, his voice an octave higher. "Eric Blake was still here."

"Alone?"

"Yes. I just locked up some of the experiments, same as I do every night, and left him in here." Winston glared at the police detective, but Bernstein diverted his gaze, never allowing the man to look him in the eye. "Can I go down the hall now to get a cup of coffee, Lieutenant, or do you need my mama's maiden name first?"

"Go."

Winston spun and left.

"Kind of touchy," Bernstein remarked.

"But a good man," Harvey added, "hard worker."

"How long have you known him?"

"Fifteen years."

"How long has he lived in New York?"

"I don't know. Almost twenty years."

Max stroked his chin. "Interesting."

"What?"

"Nothing. I have a few more questions for you, if you don't mind."

"Ask away."

Bernstein's pacing commenced. He never looked in Harvey's direction as he spoke. "How many confidential patients do you treat?"

"They are all confidential, Lieutenant."

"Okay, but how many are 'very' confidential, kept away from the rest of the patients behind that door down the hall with no window on it?"

"Right now, just Michael. I came up with the idea of the secluded room when we first started treating Bradley Jenkins."

"How did you meet Jenkins?"

Harvey went back to sorting his files. "Through his father."

"And how did you meet his father?"

"He came to see me one day. Said he wanted to know more about what we were doing. I was wary, of course. Senator Stephen Jenkins is hardly one who normally sides with our cause. After a while he said he had heard rumors that we could cure AIDS. I denied it, telling him our success had been minuscule at best. But he was adamant. That's when he told me about his son."

"He admitted to you that Bradley had AIDS?"

"Yes. He was desperate, Lieutenant. He may be a bit of a fanatic, but his boy was sick and dying. He promised me he'd help the clinic discreetly if I took Bradley in."

"So you did."

He nodded and then realized that the lieutenant was not facing him. "I didn't really believe he'd help. I was more hoping he wouldn't hurt."

"Jenkins took a hell of a risk trusting you."

"What choice did he have? He wanted to save his son's life. We worked out extra security measures like we used with Michael—hidden entrances from the basement and all that."

"Besides yourself, who knows the names of the patients in here?"

"That's the weird part. Practically nobody. Bruce knew. Eric knows many of the names, not all. And . . ." He stopped.

"Who else?" Max asked again.

"Dr. Raymond Markey."

"Who's he?"

"An Assistant Secretary of Health and Human Services. We report to him directly."

"Do you trust him?"

"Not much. He's always been more of a politician than a doctor."

"But he knew Bradley Jenkins was in here?"

"No. We hid it from him."

"How did you manage that?"

"I lied."

"How?"

Harvey shrugged. "I just left Bradley's name off the patient list I sent Markey."

"And this Markey guy never questioned it?"

"No."

"Does he know you've found a cure?"

"Yes and no. We tell him just enough so he can't pull back the money."

"And he just accepts your word?"

Harvey half chuckled. "Hardly. We always back up our claims with irrefutable evidence. A good researcher always guards against a charge of tampering with results. Just the accusation of falsifying data could bring down an entire clinic like ours. That's why I set up a system where at least two doctors work on each case—always at separate times. It prevents any hint of wrongdoing."

"I'm not sure I follow."

"Take the blood work."

"The blood work?"

"The taking and handling of blood. If I did the original examination on a patient, Bruce or Eric would do the testing during the latter stages of the treatment and vice versa. Let me give you an example. I diagnosed Teddy Krutzer as having the AIDS virus three years ago. As a result, Bruce was the one who handled the blood work when we tested to see if Krutzer had actually become HIV negative. Another example. Scott Trian, the first murder victim, was first diagnosed with AIDS by Bruce Grey four years ago so—"

"So you or Eric ran the blood test to see if he had been cured or not."

"Exactly. This way, we are able to head off anyone who might want to slow us down by throwing out false accusations of tampering."

Max shook his head. "This case just keeps getting weirder and weirder."

"Not so weird," Harvey said.

"Oh?"

"I think it's pretty simple."

"Then why don't you let me in on it?"

Harvey stopped playing with the files and looked up. "Someone is trying to destroy this clinic. Someone has found out what we have discovered here and wants to prevent us from showing the world. It's what I've suspected all along. It's why I set up all these internal safeguards."

"But—"

"Look, Lieutenant, it's like I told Sara in the beginning. If I wanted to prove to you that I could cure AIDS, what would be the most convincing thing I could show you? Cured patients, right? Eliminate the cured patients and all I have is charts and graphs and tests and files that don't add up to a thing. I'd have to start all over again. A vaccine could be delayed years."

"Makes sense, I guess," Bernstein said without breaking stride. "But let me ask you this. How many good test cases are still alive?"

"Three."

"Three cured patients left," Max repeated. "Well, then, all three need protection. They should be moved to a safe house where no one will know where they are."

"I agree," Harvey said.

"Then I have a suggestion for you, Doctor, that you might not like. I want to put them in a *real* safe house."

"I don't understand."

"If this conspiracy is as big as you suspect, then anyone could be involved in this plot. They've already gone to extreme lengths and they probably won't stop now. I think it safest if no one, not even you, knows where they are. The less everyone knows, the less that can slip out. Or be forced out."

"Do you really think—"

"Five men have been murdered already," Bernstein interrupted.

"But these patients have to be watched by a qualified doctor."

"I have a doctor who has made a living keeping his mouth shut. You tell him what to do and he'll do it. If you need to see them yourself, I'll take you to the safe house. Blindfolded."

Harvey nodded. "Okay, sounds reasonable. But I want your word that the patients won't be touched without specific permission. If your doctor were to give them the wrong medication or take unnecessary tests—"

"He won't—you have my word. I'd also like to go through the medical records of the four victims."

"Of course, Lieutenant, but let me ask you something."

"Go ahead."

"If this conspiracy is so powerful, how do I know you're not a part of it?"

Bernstein stopped pacing, looked up, and twirled his hair around his middle finger. "Interesting question," he replied. And then he walked out the door.

JENNIFER Riker woke up on the couch. The contents of the packet were scattered around her. *I'll look through it later,* she thought. She showered, dressed, and poured herself a bowl of Triple Bran, the latest in a series of fad cereals that were supposed to cure everything from cancer to lockjaw. It tasted like tree bark. Her sister, Susan, bought all those crazy health foods, coming home from the supermarket exclaiming, "I just bought (fill in the blank), and my friend (fill in the blank) swears that this will make you feel one hundred percent more (fill in the blank)."

She sighed, carried the bowl back into the den, and sat on the couch. She glanced at the file she had read yesterday. Unbelievable. Harvey and Bruce had done it. Cured AIDS. Turned an HIV positive into an HIV negative. Historic.

Jennifer picked up Scott Trian's file and fingered through the pages until she arrived at the spot where she had left off. She scanned down the page. There. The spot where Trian became HIV negative. She read on. Trian's condition progressed nicely now, though not without some setbacks. Bruce noted:

> There are times when Scott is made so weak from the injections of SR1 that I fear for him. Harvey and I talked about it last night. We both agree that we have to do something to lessen the side effects.

Still, the alternative—death from AIDS—is far worse than what we are seeing in Trian.

The file held no more surprising revelations, just a few scattered notes about Trian's reaction to SR1. Bruce's last note read:

DNA? A vs. B

What did that mean? She shrugged, put down the file, and picked up another. Whitherson, William. His file was very much like Trian's. Whitherson had also been transformed to HIV negative, but he had other problems:

Bill's family is so damn unsupportive. His father won't speak to him, and his mother feels trapped between her husband and her son, afraid to talk to Bill because her husband would see it as some sort of betrayal. Horses' asses, both of them. The funny thing is Bill still loves them like mad. He calls them all the time. I hear him pleading over the phone in a hushed, defeated voice. "But don't you understand? I'm dying." Still nothing.

And the same last note:

DNA? A vs. B.

She read about Krutzer, Theodore, next. His pattern was very similar to the others' with only a few noticeable differences:

Unlike Whitherson's family, Teddy's seems positively unbelievable. His father and mother have not only accepted their son's homosexuality, they seem to encourage it. His father invites Teddy's boyfriend to the house on weekends. They go fishing together.

And then further:

Another cured patient. It's too good to be true. Krutzer's illness had never been acute, nothing worse than a bout with hepatitis and a few skin rashes. And now he's cured. Harvey made a suggestion today which I think is valid. The conversation between Harvey, Eric, and me went something like this.

Harvey: You do all the testing on Krutzer, Bruce. Don't let anyone else but yourself touch this case. You do the tests in the lab yourself.

Eric: Why?

Harvey: Independent research. If different people handle different cases, then one man cannot be accused of tampering with the results. I suggest you try to bring in Markey on this one.

Me: Okay, I'll give him a call. I doubt he'll be interested.

Harvey: At least we can say we offered him the opportunity.

Eric: I'm not sure why we have to do this. We don't have time to play lab technicians.

Harvey: It's too important, Eric. We can't let there be any holes in our research for our enemies to exploit.

The rest of the files read similarly, each with its own unique twists and turns. Nothing odd about that. What was odd, however, was that they all ended with the same strange note:

DNA? A vs. B.

Jennifer was about to reach for the last file when she remembered the small tubular containers. She glanced at them, stacked on the edge of the couch. Each one had a patient's name taped to the outside. She pried open the one that read "Trian, Scott." Inside were two small test tubes labeled A and B.

What the . . . ?

She pulled the small test tubes—more like vials really—out of the snug holders. Blood. They were blood samples. She examined the other containers. All were the same. A patient's name taped to the outside, two test tubes labeled A and B both filled with blood on the inside.

What for?

Then she noticed the small white envelope.

It had fallen under the couch and only a corner of it was visible. Jennifer reached down and picked up the

envelope. Plain white. No return address, no mark-
ings. The kind of envelope you'd buy at a five-and-ten.
Bruce had written "Susan" across the front in his familiar scrawl. Jennifer turned the envelope over. When she
read what Bruce had written across the back seal, she
felt her stomach drop into her feet. In small, plain block
letters, it said:

TO BE OPENED UPON MY DEATH

"NEED some help?"

Max Bernstein looked up at Sara. "Yeah, come on in.
Where's Michael?"

"Being treated," Sara replied. "Are those the patient
files?"

Max nodded, a fresh pencil in his mouth. "This sucker
just gets weirder and weirder."

Sara sat down, unsnapped her brace and rubbed her
leg. "I'm listening."

"Okay," Max began. "Here are the medical files for all
the victims. Let's start with Trian. He was one of the first
patients, admitted almost three years ago. Whitherson
came in about the same time. Same with Martino, the
intravenous drug abuser."

"And Bradley?"

"That's just it. Bradley is the oddball out. He was in
here less than a year. He was in the middle of treatment.
He was doing well, but he had not yet turned HIV negative. It doesn't fit. Did Harvey fill you in on our talk?"

"Yes."

"Did he tell you about his theory about someone trying to destroy the clinic?"

Sara nodded. "It made sense to Michael and me."

"Made sense to me too, but there are so many holes. Take Bradley Jenkins, for example. Let's assume that these conspiracy guys are out to get rid of the cured AIDS patients—the proof, to use Harvey's word. Then why kill Bradley Jenkins? He was a new patient at the clinic. And why move his body behind a gay bar? And another thing. If you're out to do serious damage to a place and you don't care about killing a few people in the process, why pussyfoot around? Why not go all out? Why not burn down the Pavilion? Why not just kill Harvey and Eric and destroy their records?"

"I see your point."

"I don't know, Sara. Something just doesn't fit. Why did the killer make the murders so obvious?"

"He's a psycho."

"A psycho who has penetrated the inner sanctum of this hospital? I don't think so."

"Maybe he wanted to distract everyone by making them think he was just targeting the gay community," Sara said.

"How so?"

"His first two victims were blatant homosexuals killed in a gruesome manner," Sara explained. "The press was bound to pick it up. The killer knew that. He also knew that the world would immediately assume the murders were the work of a psychotic homophobe. No one looked deeper than that pat explanation at first. The world searched for the Gay Slasher, a man who murders homosexuals randomly, not a calculating killer intent on exterminating patients at a confidential clinic."

"But the press didn't go after the story that much until . . ."

"Until they killed the son of a famous senator," Sara finished. "Which explains why he killed Bradley. It attracted media attention. Everyone finally focused in on the Gay Slasher."

Max scratched his face, thinking. "I see what you're saying, but it still doesn't jibe. Why did the killer move Bradley's body behind the gay bar?"

"So the world would know he was gay," Sara tried. "The killer wanted everyone to think he was the Gay Slasher, a man who terrorized the gay community. Trian and Whitherson were known homosexuals. Bradley's sexual preference, on the other hand, was a well-kept secret. What better way to reveal the truth than to dump Bradley's body behind a gay bar in the Village?"

"Okay," he said, "that's theory one. I'm not sure I buy it, but let's move on."

"I don't completely buy it either," Sara said, "but let me throw something else out at you. Could the killer just have been after Bradley?"

"What do you mean?"

"I mean, could the killer have murdered Trian and Whitherson to make it look like a serial killer when the real target was Bradley all along? Could someone have been out to destroy Senator Jenkins by—"

"Forget it. I thought about that already. It makes no sense. Why kill Ricky Martino after the fact? Why break into the lab? And what about the clinic connection? Are you just going to write that off as a coincidence? And what about Grey's supposed suicide—"

"Enough already," she interrupted. "I get the point. Forget I mentioned it."

"Sorry." He stacked the files and pushed them away. "Nervous about tonight's press conference?"

"Terrified. But I'm a lot more afraid of this disease."

Max nodded. "Michael's strong, Sara. Harvey will cure him."

HARVEY Riker picked up his private line. "Hello?"

"Hello, handsome," Cassandra said. "I'd like to rip your clothes off."

"I'm sorry. You must have the wrong number."

"All the better," she replied.

"How did your meeting go with Northeastern Air?"

"It's not over yet. How's your day been?"

He considered telling Cassandra about Michael's condition but quickly dismissed the thought. It was not his place to say anything. "Not good. We lost a patient last night. Murdered, we think."

"Another one?"

"Yes."

Cassandra hesitated. "Do you really think that Reverend Sanders is connected to this?"

"I wouldn't put it past him."

"And my father?"

Harvey weighed his words carefully. "It seems strange to me that the same day your father denied knowing

Sanders personally, you hear them arguing in his study. Why did he lie to us? What was he trying to hide?"

Harvey's intercom buzzed before she could answer. "Hold on a second, Cassandra." He pressed the intercom button. "Hello?"

"Dr. Riker?"

"Yes," Harvey replied.

"There's a call for you on line seven."

"I'm in the middle of something here. Is it important?"

There was a small pause. "It's Dr. Raymond Markey."

Harvey felt afraid. The Assistant Secretary of Health and Human Services never called unless it was bad news. "Hold on a second." He pressed a button. "I'll call you back, Cassandra." He pushed another button. "Dr. Markey?"

"Hello, Dr. Riker. How are you this morning?"

"Not very well."

"Oh?"

"Another one of our patients died last night. He may have been murdered."

"Murdered?" Markey repeated. "My God, Riker, how many does that make?"

Harvey caught himself just before saying the number four. "Uh, three."

"What was the latest victim's name?"

"Martino."

"Martino, Martino . . . ah, here it is. Riccardo Martino? Intravenous drug abuser?"

"That's him."

"So let's see. The other two were Trian and Whitherson. Both gay. Multiple stab wounds. The same with Martino?"

"No."

"Then what killed him?"

"An injection of cyanide."

"My God, how awful. Terrible thing."

"Yes, it is. I'm really beginning to worry about the safety of my other patients."

"Yes, well, I wouldn't worry about that too much. I'm sure this is all nothing more than a terrible coincidence."

A terrible coincidence? "With all due respect, sir, three patients all from the same clinic have been killed."

"Yes, but you're forgetting one important factor: Bradley Jenkins, the senator's son, was also found stabbed to death. According to the police, he was murdered by the same man who killed Trian and Whitherson—this so-called Gay Slasher. And Jenkins was not a patient at the clinic. I have your patient list right in front of me and his name is not on it."

Harvey froze, trapped. For some reason he was sure that Raymond Markey was smiling on the other end of the phone. "Well, yes, but—"

"So there is nothing to worry about. Now, if Jenkins had been a patient at the clinic, well, then we'd have quite a problem on our hands. Your reports would be inaccurate. And if that were the case, then everything in the reports could be questioned. We'd have to assume other discrepancies exist. All your studies would have to be reexamined and all your findings would be considered tainted. You could lose your grant."

Harvey felt something in his gut tighten. The show tonight. The report on the clinic, on the murders . . .

. . . on Bradley Jenkins.

Lieutenant Bernstein's voice came back to him.

"What exactly is Parker going to cover?" Max had asked Sara. *"The AIDS cure? The Gay Slasher connection? Senator Jenkins' kid being treated at the clinic?"*

And Sara's answer. *"All of it."*

Raymond Markey did not speak for a few moments, allowing his words to float about, settle, and then burrow into the surroundings.

The son of a bitch already knows about Jenkins, Harvey thought. *But how? And why didn't I think of this before? What the hell is going on here?*

At last Raymond Markey broke the silence. "But of course," he said, "we both know that Bradley Jenkins was not a patient at the clinic, so you have nothing to worry about. The deaths are nothing but an awful coincidence. Good-bye, Dr. Riker."

RAYMOND Markey put down the phone. In front of his desk Reverend Sanders sat smiling. Such an eerie smile, Raymond thought. So genuinely jolly, friendly, gentle. Not sinister at all. What a mask it was. Incredible really—as incredible as the man himself. Markey knew Sanders' history. Poor boy from the South. Father was a farmer who ran moonshine across state lines. Mother was a drunk. Sanders had conned, clawed, and blackmailed his way out of poverty, stampeding over anything that got in his way. He was shrewd. He knew how to manipulate people and consolidate a power base. His influence had started with the poor and uneducated and now stretched into some of Washington's most powerful circles.

Including mine, Markey thought.

"Done," Markey said, standing. He adjusted his red tie in the reflection of a picture frame. Raymond Markey always wore red ties. They had become something of a trademark over the years. Red ties and thick glasses.

"Good," Sanders said. "Has your source come up with anything new?"

"Nothing. Just what we already know. A camera crew has been hanging out at the clinic, but everything is being kept hush-hush."

The reverend shook his head seriously. "Not a good sign. They might go public with Michael Silverman's illness."

"You don't think my call will stop them?" Markey asked.

Sanders thought a moment. "I don't think Riker would dare publicize Jenkins' connection to the murders," he said. "But if they've decided to go public with Michael Silverman, I don't see how your conversation with Riker is going to dissuade them."

"Maybe we should forget this whole thing," Raymond said tentatively. "It may have gone too far already."

Sanders looked at him with burning eyes. "Are you trying to back out, Raymond?"

"No, it's just—"

"Do I have to remind you why you agreed to help me in my holy mission? You were the one who never trusted Riker, disliked him personally and professionally. And I have that videotape right—"

"No!" Markey shouted. He closed his eyes for a brief moment, his breathing shallow. His voice grew calmer.

"I'm still behind you one hundred percent, but you have to admit the conspiracy is cracking."

Sanders' smile returned. "*Conspiracy* is such an ugly word," he said. "I see it as more of a holy mission. The Lord is behind us in our crusade to do His work."

Straight from his TV show, Markey thought in disgust. Sanders' "holy mission" was to tell the world that Armageddon was upon them. And what better proof of the oncoming apocalypse than the AIDS epidemic.

After all, Reverend Sanders would shout into the microphone, *AIDS is the modern equivalent of the plagues of Egypt. It strikes down the immoral without mercy. Yes, my friends, God is preparing for the final battle. For Armageddon. God has sent down a clear sign that we cannot ignore. God has sent down this incurable plague to rid the planet of the perverted, hedonistic scum. And soon the final battle between good and evil will be upon us, amen, praise the Lord. Who will be ready? Who will bask in the light of God, and who will join the AIDS carriers in the fires of hell? We must arm ourselves for this battle, my friends, and we need your help to do it. Now is the time for those with untainted souls to give and give generously.*

Then Sanders would show a few slides of how God's plague could ravage and pillage a human body into scraps of useless tissue and marrow. His mesmerized, horrified followers would stare at the screen in terror while the contribution baskets were passed among them. From the pulpit Sanders would watch the baskets fill and then overflow with green.

Ah, but if AIDS were somehow cured, if the Lord's plague were somehow lifted . . . well, that could throw a real socket wrench into Reverend Sanders' interpretation of the Gospel.

Strange thing was, Raymond was convinced that Sanders really believed most of it. Oh, he knew how to fake a miracle and he sure liked siphoning off a lot of money, but he honestly felt that he was doing God's work here. When Sanders compared AIDS with biblical plagues, he saw a direct correlation. Why, he once asked Raymond, was it so hard to believe that God could function in the twentieth century just as well as he had in biblical times? Did people think God had lost his power over the centuries?

"The point remains," Markey said. "We're losing the base of our support."

"You're wrong, Raymond. They are still with us."

"How can you say that? Senator Jenkins—"

"Stephen is grieving right now," Sanders interrupted. "It must have been a terrible blow to find his son was an immoral pervert. He will rejoin us when he comes to his senses."

Raymond looked at him incredulously. "You can't be serious. You know what he did. He sold us out."

"Yes, I know. And I don't like it. But he is still a powerful senator and we need him. I want you to call him, Raymond. Tell him I expect to see him at our next meeting."

"And when is that going to be?"

Ernest Sanders shrugged. "Depends," he said. "If Michael Silverman goes public with his illness, then I want you to call an emergency meeting right away. All of us."

"All of us? But Silverman is John Lowell's son-in-law."

Sanders chuckled lightly. "Don't worry about Dr. Lowell. I'll take care of him." He stood, put on his coat, and walked to the door. "After all," he reminded Markey, "John Lowell is one of us."

HARVEY stormed into Michael's room, his eyes wide with panic. "Sara, thank God I found you."

She was sitting on the side of Michael's bed. Sara and Michael had been going over his press statement. They had decided to make it as brief as possible. "What's the matter?" she asked.

"Where is Donald Parker?" Harvey asked.

"He should be here in a few moments. What's going on?"

Harvey's words rushed out. "You have to speak with him. He can't mention Bradley Jenkins' connection to the clinic."

"Why not?"

"Because it could jeopardize everything." Harvey quickly recounted his conversation with Assistant Secretary Markey, his sentences stumbling against one another. "If Markey finds out I left Bradley's name off the progress reports, I could lose the clinic. All our findings would be labeled invalid."

"Could they do that?" Michael asked.

"Markey will certainly give it his best shot. He's itching for an excuse to reallocate our funds. This would be just what he needs. We can't let him find out Bradley was treated here."

Sara nodded. "I'll speak to Donald as soon as he gets here."

CASSANDRA woke up in a familiar state of disorientation and pain. The disorientation came from not knowing where she was, the pain from a massive hangover. The disorientation usually lasted only a few moments, just until her mind could scrape together enough outside stimuli to reconstruct the previous evening. The pain customarily clung to her a little longer.

"Harvey?" she called out.

No answer.

She groaned. She clasped her head between both hands, but the internal jackhammer continued to rip through her temples. By exerting herself, she was able to pry open both eyelids. She squinted in the harsh light, though the shades were pulled and all the lights were out. In fact, the room was fairly dark.

She groaned again.

It was a hotel room, not Harvey's apartment. A fancy hotel room. A travel brochure would call it "lush" and "well-appointed." In the distance a car honked its horn, but to Cassandra it might as well have been a blown amplifier from a rock concert taking place somewhere in her cerebrum.

"Shhh," she said out loud.

Her hands held her head in place, waiting until time glued her skull back together. She tried to remember what had happened. The meeting with Northeastern

Air. Had they gotten the account? Not yet. Northeastern's marketing director, a runaway egomaniac, had held
off making a decision. Then they had gone drinking at
the . . . at the Plaza—that was where she was. What had
they talked about? She couldn't remember. The marketing director, while good-looking, was obnoxious, over-
bearing, and conceited. A big-time phony. When he
opened his mouth, shit came out. She tried to recall what
he had said, but the only thing she could remember him
saying was "me, I, me, I, me, I."

Then what?

Pretty simple. The marketing director had taken her
upstairs, fucked her, and left. It started coming back to
her now. The sex was bad. He was a "poser," someone
more interested in his appearance than in what he was
doing, the kind of guy who would rather look in a mirror
than at his partner. Might as well have been making love
to himself.

Cassandra sat up and glanced about the room. Yep,
he was gone, thank God. He had left a note on the night
table. She reached for it and read:

Congratulations. You got the account.

He had not signed the note, just left his business card.
Christ.

She swung her legs off the bed and managed to stand.
The room was like so many others she had been in—
spacious, beautiful, immaculate, expensive furnishings,
clean sheets, thick towels. Only the best for Cassandra

Lowell. Never a sleazy motel. If you wanted to fuck Cassandra Lowell, you had to surround her with beautiful things. You had to take her to a classy place. She was, after all, no cheap whore.

She was a classy whore.

She headed toward the bathroom. Standing outside the shower, she turned on the hot water and waited till the water steamed before stepping under the spray. She stood there for a very long time, letting the near-scorching water pound down on her. She lathered her body and rinsed off repeatedly. Forty-five minutes later, she dried herself off. Then she sat on the king-sized bed, cried for a brief moment, got dressed, and went home.

When she arrived at the Lowell mansion a few hours later, she poured a bowl of cereal and sat down at the kitchen table.

"Good morning, honey," John Lowell said.

Cassandra looked up. Her father was wearing a charcoal turtleneck, his hair neatly groomed, his cheeks flushed. Her father was still a good-looking man, she thought, but he had not had a serious relationship with a woman since her mother's death almost ten years ago. A shame and yet Cassandra wondered how she would feel if another woman were to light up her father's eyes the way her mother had.

Spiteful, probably. That would be typical of her.

"Good morning," she replied.

"Have you heard from Sara?"

"No. Should I have?"

Her father shrugged. "I called the hospital. They told me Michael checked out this morning. I called their house, but all I got was the answering machine."

"Did you try Dr. Riker?" she asked.

Dr. Lowell nodded. "He hasn't returned my call. I don't think he will."

"Why not?"

"Let's just say that Harvey Riker and I are not exactly buddies."

Cassandra lowered her eyes. She felt something peculiar, something, she guessed, akin to shame.

"Still," Dr. Lowell continued, "it's quite strange."

"What is?"

"Michael has hepatitis B, which means he'll have to be hospitalized for at least three weeks. Why would he check out?"

"Maybe they moved him to another hospital."

"Maybe," Dr. Lowell said doubtfully.

Cassandra remembered how quickly Harvey had hustled out of the apartment after Eric's call yesterday morning. She had not picked up much of the conversation, but Harvey's tone had been grave, nervous. She had also heard him mention Michael's name before hanging up and rushing out the door without so much as a good-bye.

Is something seriously wrong with Michael?

"I have to go," her father said. "If your sister calls, tell her she can reach me on the car phone." He kissed Cassandra on the cheek and walked toward the door. He had not asked where she had been the past five nights or with whom. When it came to sexual matters, her father liked to pretend nothing was amiss—easier on the ol' morals than the truth.

Cassandra thought about Harvey. She wondered why she had ended up in bed with that Neanderthal marketing director (what the hell was his name?) when things had been going so well . . .

. . . *too well?* . . .

. . . with Harvey.

Well, c'est la vie. It could be that she and Harvey were never meant to last. Or it could be that she had too much to drink. Or it could be . . .

. . . *or it could be that you're a worthless whore, Cassandra.*

She closed her eyes. When she heard her father drive away, Cassandra stood and crept down the corridor toward his study. It was time to put last night behind her. There were other matters, more important matters, to consider.

She knew that what she was about to do was wrong. She knew that her father's study was off-limits, that she had no right to pry into his private affairs. But Harvey's words—and maybe the need to make up for last night—propelled her forward: *"It seems strange to me that the same day your father denied knowing Sanders personally, you hear them arguing in his study. Why did he lie to us? What was he trying to hide?"*

Indeed, she thought. *What was—or is—he trying to hide?* Could he really be connected with Reverend Sanders? Could her father really have something to do with the trouble at the clinic?

She reached the door to his study, turned the knob,

and entered. Her father's office was her favorite room in the house. So spacious, with a high ceiling, dark oak everywhere, thousands of books—like Henry Higgins' study in *My Fair Lady.* She crept behind the large antique desk and pulled the side drawer. It would not open. She tried it again. Locked. She sat back in the plush leather swivel chair. Now, where did he hide that damn key? Her hand felt around the underside of the middle drawer. A few moments later she felt something cool, metallic.

Bingo.

Her fingers closed around the small key and ripped away the tape. She unlocked the desk and began to rifle through its contents. In the bottom right-hand drawer, she found his file of personal letters. She skimmed through them until she found one that piqued her interest. It was from Dr. Leonard Bronkowitz, the chief trustee at Columbia Presbyterian Hospital:

Dear John,

I know this is going to upset you immensely, but the board has decided to go ahead with Sidney Pavilion. Despite your rather persuasive arguments, a slim majority of the board members seems to feel that AIDS is an illness which has been ignored for far too long. While many members agreed with your point that the pendulum has swung too far in the other direction now that the world has recognized the severity of the illness, the board also believes that Dr. Riker and Dr. Grey could make some serious headway into developing a vaccine for the virus. Aside from the benefits for mankind, such a vaccine could bring the hospital additional prestige and, in turn, finances.

I realize that this will hinder your own programs at the Cancer Center, but I hope you will support us in this new and exciting endeavor.

Sincerely,
Leonard Bronkowitz, M.D.

And there was a letter from Washington dealing with the same subject:

Dear Dr. Lowell,

The medical disbursements for this fiscal year have been allocated and I regret to say that there will be no funds for the new wing at the Cancer Center. We realize and respect the importance of your work, but the fact remains that New York City and, more specifically, Columbia Presbyterian Medical Center have already received more than a lion's share of funds, most of which have gone to the center's new AIDS clinic, operated by Dr. Harvey Riker and Dr. Bruce Grey.

Personally, I believe your work is crucial and am disappointed in this decision, but since you are a former surgeon general, I am sure you can appreciate how these things sometimes work. The AIDS virus seems to me to be the public's "Disease of the Week" or "Flavor of the Month." It's the new "in" cause for everyone to rally around. I am confident that the public's interest will wane and tire soon and then they will have the ability to view this disease more rationally.

Take heart and know that there are others who feel as we do. I would be honored if during your next visit to Washington you would call me so that we can discuss the world of medicine. I very much value your opinion on a broad range of subjects.

Yours,
Raymond Markey, M.D.
Assistant Secretary of Health and Human Services

Cassandra felt ill. There was really nothing shocking in the letters. She knew her father had been against the clinic from its inception, that he had complained bitterly about the "waste" of funds. What she had not known was the direct effect the Sidney Pavilion had had on his own cancer research. It was an either/or situation—either the AIDS clinic or the new wing at the Cancer Center. Cassandra knew how much the Center meant to her father, but how far would he go to get funding? Surely, he would never . . .

The sound of a car pulling up the driveway made her jump. A loud diesel engine. Her father's Mercedes. He was back already.

Shit! I thought he was going to be out all day!

Cassandra put the two letters back into the folder, put the folder back into the bottom drawer, and closed the drawer. In the background she heard the purr of the electric garage door opener.

What did I do with that damn key?

Her eyes scanned the desktop for the key. Nothing. She looked on the floor. Still nothing. The Mercedes was pulling into the six-car garage now. She had to get out of the office before he saw her. Damn it, where was that key? When she saw it a second later in the desk's keyhole, she wanted to slap herself for not looking there earlier. She wrenched it out as she heard her father turn off the engine and slam the car door shut.

She ripped a piece of Scotch tape out of the dispenser on the desk and taped the key back under the middle drawer. She moved quickly now, getting up from behind the desk, slipping quickly to the door, opening it, turning right, and heading down the hall.

If she had turned left instead, she would have seen her father standing at the end of the hallway, watching her with a stunned look on his face.

DONALD Parker stood with a stiff back, perfect posture, and a dark blue suit at the end of the hall. Forty years in the news business had taken him across all seven continents. Parker had covered the inauguration of every president from Harry Truman to George Bush. He had witnessed the first moon launch, the Tet Offensive, the Beijing massacre, the opening of the Berlin Wall, Operation Desert Storm. He had interviewed Gandhi, Malcolm X, Pol Pot, Khomeini, Amin, Gorbachev, Hussein. There was little he had not accomplished.

As Sara limped toward him, Donald Parker caught her eye and smiled gently. His eyes were bright blue, piercing and probing. The eyes of the perfect interviewer. "Hello, Sara."

"Hello, Donald. Did you get my notes?"

He nodded. "This is quite a story, Sara. The story of the year maybe. Why are you giving it up?"

"I'm too close to it," she said.

"Personal involvement?"

She nodded.

"Does this have something to do with the statement your husband is making before the show?"

"I'd rather not say just yet."

"Fair enough," he said. "Any new developments?"

"Another patient, a Riccardo Martino, was murdered last night on the hospital grounds."

"What?"

"I have all the details here."

He took the piece of paper and read it. "Good work, Sara."

"There's one other thing."

"Oh?"

"You can't mention Senator Jenkins' son on the air."

"I don't understand."

She explained. He listened intently, nodding. "Okay," he said when she finished, "I'll leave that part out."

"Thanks, Donald. I really appreciate it."

"And let me get something else straight. This Dr. Riker does not want to be on television?"

"Right. Dr. Riker wants to keep his anonymity. His assistant, Dr. Eric Blake, will handle the interviews."

"Okay, then, I better get this thing wrapped up. Thanks for laying all the groundwork, Sara. You've left me with the easy parts."

"No problem," she said, walking away. "And thanks for understanding about Bradley Jenkins."

Donald Parker watched her hobble away, leaning heavily on her cane. Sara was a mesmerizing girl, an awesome beauty masking an awesome intellect. She was good at her job and Donald found his respect for her growing every day.

Unfortunately, he knew, her respect for him was about to be tested. After tonight's show she would be more than disappointed with him. She would be furious. But Donald Parker had been in this business a long time, and he had developed a certain code of ethics over the years. He did not believe in ignoring important aspects of a story for the convenience of others—no matter what the possible consequences.

And he was not going to leave Bradley Jenkins out of his report.

13

CASSANDRA was about to say something she would later regret.

She had come to Harvey's office to tell him about the letters she found in her father's drawer. Instead, unplanned words poured out of her mouth.

"I have something to tell you," Cassandra began.

"Oh?"

She kept her head low, her eyes afraid to meet his. "I spent last night with another man."

A brief flash of grief rushed through him, widening his eyes. "The, uh, marketing director?"

She nodded.

"I see," Harvey said, his face calm now, showing nothing. He circled back to his desk, sat down, and began to jot notes in a file.

"Is that all you're going to say?" she asked.

"What do you want me to say?"

"It doesn't bother you?"

"Do you want it to bother me?"

"Stop answering my questions with a question."

"I don't know what you want from me, Cassandra. You come in here and tell me you slept with another man. How do you want me to react?"

"I don't know."

"Why did you tell me?"

"What do you mean, why?"

"I would never have found out," he said. "Why did you say anything?"

She opened her mouth, stopped, began to shrug, stopped, then said in a hesitant voice, "I wanted to be up-front with you."

"Fine. You were up-front. Now, if you'll excuse me, I have a lot of work to do."

"Wait a second—"

"I'm sorry, Cassandra. I really am. I thought we were happy together. I thought—I don't know—I thought we had something special."

"We do."

"Then we have different ideas about special. I can't afford to get my heart squashed again. It hurts too much. It affects my concentration, my work—"

"It won't happen again. I swear. I never meant to hurt—"

"It doesn't matter. I should have never let it come this far anyway. It was a mistake from the beginning. I was a goddamn fool to think you could ever . . ." He shook his head. "Good-bye, Cassandra." He lowered his eyes and began writing.

"Harv?"

He did not look up. His voice was more firm now. "Good-bye, Cassandra."

She felt something odd, something hard and painful, form inside her own chest. She wanted to say something more, but his cold expression stopped her.

She turned and left.

"MICHAEL'S giving a press conference in five minutes."

Reece Porter stopped lacing his high-top Nikes and looked up at his coach. "What are you talking about?"

Coach Richie Crenshaw crossed the locker room, stepping over strewn sneakers, jockstraps, and long legs. The Knicks were in Seattle's Kingdome, preparing to play a preseason scrimmage against the Supersonics. "Just what I said. Michael is making a statement at the start of *NewsFlash*."

"What kind of statement?" Reece asked.

"Hell if I know."

Jerome Holloway exchanged a confused glance with Reece. "And it's being covered on national television?"

"That's right," Coach Crenshaw replied.

"I don't get it," Reece said. "What the hell could Mikey have to say that a primetime news show would want to cover live?"

"Something about his hepatitis, I guess."

Reece shook his head. "SportsChannel or ESPN might be interested in covering something like that but not CBS."

"Besides," Jerome added, "the press already knows about his hepatitis."

Coach Crenshaw shrugged. "Beats the hell out of me. Turn on the TV, Jerome, and we'll find out."

The rookie walked over to the set and flicked the switch. Michael's teammates and coaches stopped what they were doing and turned their attention to the screen. Most of their faces displayed a sense of relaxed curiosity. But not Reece's. Something didn't make sense to him. An athlete, no matter how popular, does not make a live statement on a news show unless it is big news. Really big news. Something that transcended sports.

As Reece Porter watched Michael and Sara walk toward the podium, an awful feeling of dread flooded his chest.

GEORGE was in the middle of doing his third set of one hundred push-ups, his muscles bunching and swelling with each repetition, when he heard the advertising teaser:

"Stay tuned for a very special episode of *NewsFlash*. What's the connection between a surprise statement from basketball great Michael Silverman, the Gay Slasher, and the story of the year about the AIDS epidemic? Watch *NewsFlash* and see. Next on CBS."

George froze. Michael Silverman, husband of Sara Lowell, son-in-law of John Lowell. Silverman had been at the charity ball on the night that George killed Bradley Jenkins. Now he was going to make a surprise statement on live television.

George wanted to hear what he had to say. He wanted to hear very much.

Of course, an announcement by someone like Michael Silverman was hardly reason for concern, but what else had the TV blurb said? Something about a connection to the Gay Slasher. Well, that should be interesting. And then there was the last thing that voice on the TV had said—the story of the year on the AIDS epidemic. George shook his head. It was too much of a coincidence. Michael Silverman, the Gay Slasher, the AIDS epidemic.

Someone had tied a few loose ends together.

The real question for George concerned Michael Silverman's announcement. The police already knew about the connection between the murder victims and the AIDS clinic, so it had only been a matter of time before it leaked to the press. But what did it have to do with Sara Lowell's husband? Was Michael Silverman connected with the murders? And if so, how?

Careful, George. Your job is to eliminate them, not figure out why.

True, but a man had to watch his back. George was being forced to take greater risks than normal. The Gay Slasher had become high-profile stuff. Now that the scrutiny was intensifying, logic dictated that he should learn more about the "why" of these killings in order to protect himself.

Damn it, why hadn't he checked this whole thing out beforehand?

Sloppy work, George. Very unprofessional.

George sprang up off the floor as the commercial ended. He sat on the edge of the large bed and watched as Michael and Sara walked toward the podium. Sara Lowell was very beautiful. Incredible looking. Turning his gaze to Michael, George felt a sharp pang of envy.

That lucky son of a bitch slept with Sara Lowell every night.

George shook his head. Sometimes life was just not fair.

" I'M home," Max Bernstein called out.

"I'm in the bedroom," Lenny replied. "Did you pick up some milk?"

"Yep. And a six-pack of Diet Coke."

Lenny walked into the den and kissed Max lightly on the lips. "Tired?"

"Exhausted. How about you?"

Lenny nodded, taking the bundle from Max's arm. "I spent seven hours in court for a case that was never called."

"What happened?"

"My client didn't show."

"Skipped his bail?"

"Seems so."

Bernstein shrugged. "We cops catch them. You lawyers let them go."

"Yeah, but without us you'd be out of a job. By the way, I ordered a pizza. I figured you wouldn't want to go out."

"You figured right."

Lenny carried the bag to the kitchen. "Are you going to be working this weekend?"

"Huh?"

"Stop biting your nails for two seconds and listen. Are you going to be working this weekend?"

"Probably, why?"

"It's my weekend with Melissa."

Melissa was Lenny's twelve-year-old daughter. "I'll try to be around."

"I'd appreciate it. Oh, I rented that movie you wanted to see."

Max picked up the phone and dialed. "Can't watch it tonight. *NewsFlash* is on in a few minutes."

"I almost forgot." Lenny came out of the kitchen. "Max?"

"What?"

"Get your fingers out of your mouth before I shove them down your throat."

"Sorry."

"And who are you calling?"

"My apartment."

"Such a waste."

"Lenny, don't start."

"Why have you kept that empty apartment for six years? All you have in there is a telephone and an answering machine."

"You know why."

"Oh, that's right. You're afraid someone is going to find out you live with—gasp-oh-gasp!—a man. That you're an honest-to-God screaming faggot."

"Lenny . . ."

"So you keep your swinging bachelor pad on Eighty-seventh Street for show—no, because you're paranoid. Wouldn't it be cheaper just to tell everyone that we're two single, homo studs who happen to live together? Something like in *Three Men and a Baby*."

"What are you babbling about?"

"*Three Men and a Baby*. You remember the movie. Tom Selleck, Ted Danson, and Steve Guttenberg were all single and sharing an apartment and nobody worried about their sexual preferences. And what about Oscar and Felix on *The Odd Couple*? Murray the cop never thought they were getting it on."

No messages on the machine. Max hung up the phone. "You're a nag."

"And trim your mustache already. You look like Gene Shalit."

"Nag, nag. Did you feed Simon yet?"

"A few minutes ago. He ate eight goldfish the other day and he's downing another half dozen now. Want to watch?"

"I think I'll pass."

Lenny shrugged. "He's your snake."

Max had bought Simon, a harmless garden snake, on a whim two years ago. He thought it would be kind of cool to own a pet snake. Max, however, had overlooked one small problem—he was scared to death of snakes. He loved Simon, liked to watch him slide about his cage and slither up to the screen on the top. But he was afraid to touch him—or go near him, for that matter. And worse, the only thing Simon ate were live goldfish, which he caught in his laser-quick mouth and swallowed whole. You could actually see the outline of the struggling fish as it slid down Simon's thin body.

Gross.

Luckily, Lenny had taken a liking to Simon—a rather sick liking, as a matter of fact. Lenny enjoyed inviting friends over to watch the feeding; they bet on which fish would be the last one eaten.

Very gross.

The doorbell rang. Lenny opened the door, paid the delivery boy, and brought the pizza into the den. Max watched him, remembering how his life had changed when he first saw Lenny's gentle eyes seven years ago: 1984, a year of transition. The nights of anonymous sex, orgies in SoHo, leather bars, and Caligula-like bathhouses were beginning to melt away under the blistering heat of the AIDS epidemic. Though he had lived in constant fear of being found out, Max had participated in it all. How many lovers had he had? He had lost count. How many friends had he lost to the AIDS virus? On that number too he had lost count. So many taken away, and now the dead were little more than a blurry blend of faces, vivacious young men whose lives had been suddenly, painfully, snuffed out. They were gone now and too often forgotten.

Why, Max wondered, *did we all gorge ourselves on nameless, faceless sex? Was it merely for the physical thrill or was there something more? Were we trying to rebel? Or were we just releasing the pent-up anxieties of living too repressed for years in a straight society? What were we looking for in that mass of flesh? Or more important, what were we running away from?*

Over the past seven years Bernstein had had more than twenty AIDS tests performed on himself—all under assumed names and all negative. A stroke of luck and yet sometimes he felt guilty for not having contracted the virus, like an Auschwitz survivor wondering why he was still alive.

Lenny, on the other hand, had come from a conservative family. He married his high school sweetheart at the age of nineteen and they had a daughter a year later. He tried to suppress and deny his true sexual orientation, and for a while it worked. But by the fourth year of their marriage, he and his wife, Emily, knew that the heterosexual facade had finally cracked and broken away. The truth was revealed to their families, and Emily and Lenny parted as friends.

Max turned on the television. The two sat quietly on the couch, watching the television and holding hands.

Lenny leaned his head on Max's shoulder. "I'm the best thing that ever happened to you, you know."

"Yeah, I guess you are."

A few minutes later they watched Michael and Sara walk toward the podium.

"DAD?" Cassandra called.

John Lowell did not respond. He continued to stare down at the old photograph.

"What are you looking at?" she asked softly.

He sighed deeply and placed the photograph down gently as though it were delicate porcelain. "Nothing," he replied.

Cassandra crossed the room. As she suspected, her father had been staring at a picture of her mother. Tears flooded her eyes. "I miss her too," she said.

"She loved you very much, Cassandra. She wanted you to be happy."

Cassandra nodded, reaching out her hand and touching the image of her mother. "Sara just called."

"Where has she been?"

"She wouldn't say. She said we'd find out on *NewsFlash*."

"On *NewsFlash*? What does that mean?"

"I don't know."

John reached out, and for the first time in many years father and daughter embraced. Cassandra snuggled closer, feeling the wool sweater brush up against her. For a moment she forgot about the letters she had found in his desk. She forgot about Reverend Sanders' voice in her father's study, and she even forgot her own crazy suspicions. He was her father. She felt so right in his arms, like a small child again, so safe and warm and content and yet . . .

"You're my whole world," he whispered. "You and Sara."

They clung to each other with an odd sort of need. The need was surprisingly strong, like a ravenous hunger that grew as you ate. Neither spoke, but they both knew that they were thinking the same thing. They could not say how they knew each other's thoughts, nor could they explain the awful feeling of doom that permeated the room. This should have been a happy, tender moment, but something was lurking around the corner, something that wanted to rip and shred and destroy.

Cassandra broke away and they looked at each other uncomfortably, as though they shared an embarrassing secret. "The show's coming on."

"Right," he said.

They left the room then, no longer holding hands or even touching. Still, the warmth of his embrace stayed with Cassandra like a shawl wrapped around her shoulders. She watched her father turn on the television and felt a wave of love overwhelm her. He was such a gentle man, she told herself, a man who had dedicated his entire life to healing others. He would never hurt anyone. Never. She was sure of it. Positive. Her suspicions were nonsense. After all, a couple of letters and a meeting with Reverend Sanders hardly meant he was guilty of some sort of wrongdoing. As a matter of fact it meant nothing at all. She was glad that she had not told Harvey about the letters, that she had not betrayed her own father's trust.

Cassandra sat back now, relieved, confident, and trying like hell to ignore the irritating voice of doubt that still echoed in her head.

FLASHBULBS worked like a strobe light, giving the illusion that Sara and Michael were moving in slow motion. They reached the podium together. Michael stepped forward while Sara stood behind him and to the side. Michael's head was lowered, his eyes closed. A few moments later he lifted his head high and faced the crowded room of reporters.

Sara watched him. He looked handsome in his gray

suit with a solid blue tie, but the clothes were just not him. There were no wild splashes of color, no yellow and green paisley, no purple floral pattern, no funky polka dots—so drab and . . . and lifeless for him. His face, somber, ashen, tired, matched the look.

He took a piece of paper out of his shirt pocket. His fingers unfolded it and his palm smoothed it out against the podium. He glanced down at the statement, but he did not read the words. His hand pushed the paper to the side and slowly his face tilted upward. Then he just stood there for a few moments and said nothing.

Through the glare of flashbulbs, Sara could sense the unease in the audience. Murmurs began to stir and strengthen through the press corps. She moved closer to Michael, took his hand in hers and squeezed. The coldness of his hand startled her. Then he did something very strange. He turned toward her and smiled—not a fake or tired smile, but a genuine, beautiful Michael smile. It comforted her and frightened her at the same time. The smile slipped away from his lips slowly as he turned back to the microphone.

"Yesterday," Michael began, "I learned that I have contracted the AIDS virus."

Immediate silence. The murmurs ceased as though they had been on a tape recorder that had been switched off.

"I am entering a private clinic which you will hear more about during this program. That's all I have to say. Thank you."

He stepped back, smiled anew at Sara, and took her hand. "Let's get out of here."

The press attacked with both barrels. "How long have you been gay, Michael?"

"Sara, how long have you known your husband was homosexual?"

"Is the marriage a farce?"

"Have you had sex with any of your teammates?"

With each question, Michael involuntarily winced. Finally, he stepped back toward the podium to set the record straight. When he reached the microphone and the room fell silent, Michael turned away without saying a word. He bent down and kissed Sara's cheek.

"Like I said before, let's get out of here."

HARVEY watched the report alone.

Being alone was fine with him. That was how it should be. Cassandra had been a mistake from the start. Talk about your basic self-delusion—he must have been taking major mind-expanding drugs to think someone like her could be interested in someone like him. Besides, he had the clinic. He could not afford distractions that would hinder his concentration and affect his work negatively.

He shook his head. Enough of this. There were much more important things to worry about than his creature comforts. Harvey pushed Cassandra clear out of his mind and focused on the *NewsFlash* report.

Donald Parker was doing an excellent job, presenting the facts without too much innuendo. To help the clinic keep its anonymity, the report did not give the name or address of the Pavilion. Thank God for that. Harvey could just imagine the riots if the clinic's name and address were used in the report. Talk about bedlam.

Better still, only Eric's name was used in the report. The name of the "chief researcher" was left out. Perfect. Couldn't be better. Parker had even given an 800 telephone number and an address for those who wanted to make donations to the clinic and suggested writing or telegramming Congress to approve additional grants for the "unnamed" AIDS clinic.

Donald Parker's blue eyes swerved forward, making contact with millions of viewers. Harvey could see why Parker was considered the best in the business. His intensity made you forget that you were watching television. He became a houseguest, just a member of the family seated in the den instead of a studio.

"Even more glaring," Donald Parker's deep voice continued, "is the clinic's connection with the so-called Gay Slasher who has been terrorizing New York City's gay community for the past two months. In reality, the Gay Slasher might better be called the AIDS Slasher. Here's our report."

His voice was now on tape. "Young men found stabbed and mutilated—they had everything to live for." Several snapshots of bloodied sheets draped over bodies, an arm or leg jutting into view, flashed across the screen. "The world at large believed that a psychopath was hunting down members of the gay community. But new evidence has come to light which blows that theory right out of the water and draws a more devastating conclusion."

A proper pause. "The so-called Gay Slasher is murdering AIDS sufferers. In fact, the murder victims all had one thing in common—they were patients at the clinic we have been discussing tonight."

After another proper pause, Parker continued. "The first victim was Scott Trian." A smiling photograph of Trian came on. "Trian, a twenty-nine-year-old stockbroker, was murdered in his apartment in the most grisly fashion imaginable. He was tortured and mutilated with a knife before he finally bled to death."

Bill Whitherson's image replaced Trian's. "William Whitherson, a vice president at First City Bank, was the Gay Slasher's next prey. Over twenty stab wounds were scattered across Mr. Whitherson's face, neck, chest and groin. He was found in his apartment by his roommate, Stuart Lebrinski, who had left the victim only an hour before. The blood was still flowing from Mr. Whitherson's wounds when Mr. Lebrinski came back from the supermarket." The picture of Bill Whitherson faded away . . .

. . . and a photograph of Bradley Jenkins appeared in its place.

Harvey felt his heart constrict in his chest. "Oh God, no. Don't . . ."

"The murder of Bradley Jenkins, son of Senator Stephen Jenkins and a secret patient at the AIDS clinic, put the Gay Slasher on the map. Bradley was found behind a gay bar in Greenwich Village—"

Harvey no longer heard his words. "No," he whispered in horror. "Do you know what you've just done?"

REVEREND Ernest Sanders watched the report. It was bad, very bad, but Sanders did not get angry. Anger was a wasted emotion, one that clouded the mind, shoved away rational thought. What he needed to do was think clearly.

Dixie was upstairs in the bedroom, passed out on the bed from too much wine. Again. Third straight night. But he loved her. She was an extraordinarily beautiful woman—even his enemies confessed to that—a far cry from the Tammy Faye stereotype of an evangelist's wife. She meant the world to him and so he lavished her with expensive gifts and the best of everything. Still, she despised him. He could see it in the way she looked at him every time he came through the door. His son, Ernie Junior, had grown into a handsome young man who worked in the ministry. He had learned the Gospel well, was a passionate speaker, made a whole heap of money, and hated his father too. The repulsion in his son's face, Sanders thought, would make a blind man blush.

Luckily, Dixie, Ernie, and the two girls, Sissy and Mary Ann, all loved his money. Money was power, no question about it. Sanders remembered how his father used to recite the Golden Rule—he who has the gold makes the rules. And Sanders had the gold. The power. The control.

And he had his job. His ministry. Funny how you are what people perceive. Some considered him a savior, a prophet, a man of God. Others considered him an extremist, a cheap con man, a bigoted hypocrite.

What was the truth? Well, he had never had a vision from God like he said on his show. Jesus had never visited him in his bedroom at night. He had never heard a mysterious voice or seen a real miracle. But so what? People wanted to believe. People needed something, and he gave it to them. *We need food, we need air, we need recreation and entertainment, and we also need to believe in something.* The leftist liberals believed in their gods— secularism, academia, the media. Didn't old-fashioned Americans have the same right? They needed a strong leader, someone they could follow without question or doubt. Politicians used deception and slick packaging to create an image a person could trust. What was so wrong with a preacher doing the same?

To the critics who accused him of taking advantage of his followers, Ernest Sanders scoffed. Just take a look at his parishioners one Sunday morning, the exhilarated, rapt expression on their faces. How could you put a price tag on something like that? Take a look at how their eyes glowed as he spoke to them, their attention and trust never wavering. Yes, take a good look at these hardwork- ing Americans who asked for no more than a few min- utes of religious rapture, who wanted to believe there was something more than the boring grind they went through every day, who wanted to rely on the faith of God rather than just people.

Ernest Sanders gave them all that and more. And yes, he made a lot of money from it. Why shouldn't he? He made the world a better place and brought joy to thou- sands, maybe millions, of people. Maybe God hadn't shown him a burning bush or given him the power to walk on water. But He had given him the power to move people with his words and perhaps that was, after all, the way God intended it to be. No flashy miracles in this technological, bureaucratic era—just the simple power to communicate His message.

Perhaps, Sanders thought, he was engaged in a holy battle and God had chosen him to lead the side of the righteous, to rally His troops, to lead them into the Promised Land . . .

. . . and to rid the world of the godless scum, to fight the evildoers who would try to stop him. Even to the death.

The *NewsFlash* credits rolled by. With a sigh, Sanders reached for the phone and dialed Raymond Markey's home.

"Hello?"

"Were you watching?" Reverend Sanders asked.

"Yes."

"Very distressing," Sanders continued. "There is going to be a tremendous outcry."

"But Riker played into our hands when they mentioned Bradley Jenkins," Markey said. "Now we have proof that his reports were falsified. His findings can be labeled invalid."

"Maybe," Sanders allowed, "but don't count on it. We can use it, but it might not be enough. We might have to consider other plans."

Markey cleared his throat. "If you think it's necessary."

"It is. Now that Riker has brought Silverman into this, I don't see how we have any choice. I'll contact Silverman's stepfather."

"What do you want me to do?"

"Get on a plane to New York. I want you to confront Harvey Riker man-to-man."

"Fine." Markey paused. "There's one other thing."

"Yes?"

"The Gay Slasher killings—it's all very strange."

"I know what you mean."

Markey paused again before asking, "Who do you think is behind it?"

Ernest Sanders weighed his words carefully. "To be honest, Ray," he said at last, "I really don't know."

14

EARLY the next morning, Sara hobbled down the corridor and pushed open the door to Donald Parker's office without knocking.

"You bastard."

Donald looked up from his desk. If he had been surprised by her outburst, his face did not show it. "I've been expecting you."

"You lied to me."

"Sara—"

"You said you would leave Bradley Jenkins out of your report."

"Sara, I'm sorry but I just couldn't do it."

"Why not?"

"Because I'm a reporter," Parker said. "I was assigned to cover the story, the full story—"

"Spare me the speech."

"Hold on a minute, Sara. You were biased on this one. Your judgment was clouded."

"What are you talking about?"

Parker adjusted his tie. "It's simple. You don't leave out a vital aspect of a story to protect a friend."

"But I explained—"

"You explained what? That your friend, this Harvey Riker, lied to government officials? That he falsified reports?"

"He didn't falsify anything. He allowed Bradley Jenkins the right to confidentiality."

"Oh, come, Sara, you didn't really expect me to give up the Gay Slasher story, did you? If I left Jenkins out of the report, what was the connection between the Gay Slasher's victims? The whole idea was that they all came from Riker's clinic. I couldn't just skip over Bradley Jenkins, now, could I?"

Sara leaned against her cane. "You don't realize the consequences."

"Worrying about the consequences is not our job. You know that. We report the news and let the pieces fall where they may. We cannot choose to suppress important facts in order to achieve our personal goals. Reverse our roles for a minute. If you were doing a story and I came to you and asked you to leave out a vital part of the story in order to protect a friend of mine—a friend who tampered with government documents—would you?"

"I didn't ask you to protect a friend. I asked you to protect the clinic. Don't you see? Your report could close them down."

He shook his head. "No way. After the show last

night, the public would never allow it. The researchers at the clinic are overnight heroes. All of America is talking about them."

"You still should have told me."

"Maybe I should have," he allowed, "but I didn't think there was time." He crossed the room and stood in front of her. "I'm sorry about your husband. He must be a very brave man to go public with something like this."

She nodded and turned to go. "Thank you, Donald," she said curtly. "I apologize for barging in."

D R. Harvey Riker tried to read the report at his desk, but it was pointless. After watching the *NewsFlash* report last night, sleep had kept a safe distance away from him. Now that the evening had given way to sunrise, his mind still churned with the same questions and doubts. Had he made a grave mistake in allowing the report to be aired? It had seemed like the perfect idea, the perfect way to keep the clinic going strong, but he had forgotten to add in the Bradley Jenkins factor, a factor that could very well destroy the clinic.

What was going to happen now?

The intercom on his desk buzzed.

"Yes?"

"Dr. Raymond Markey is here to see you."

Harvey felt something twist in his abdomen. "He's here? In the clinic?"

"Yes, Doctor."

Oh God, oh God . . . "Show him in."

Harvey sat back and began to gulp down large quantities of air. He waited, staring at the second hand of the clock above his door. It moved like it was being weighed down—no sweep, just a grudging crawl.

Markey already knew. The son of a bitch knew about Jenkins before the show. But how?

"Dr. Riker?"

Harvey put on a smile that was way too broad. "Dr. Markey, come in. What brings you here?"

"You don't know?"

Harvey continued to smile, unfazed. "Should I?"

"We need to talk."

Harvey was a touch confused by Markey's tone. He had expected the man to be cool, calm, sure; instead, there was an undeniable strain in his voice. The Assistant Secretary of Health and Human Services was dressed in a blue pin-striped suit, black shoes that desperately needed a shine, and a solid red tie.

"Have a seat."

"Thank you." Markey fell heavily into the chair as though overcome by exhaustion.

"Some coffee?"

"No." He leaned back and crossed his legs. "Dr. Riker, let me get to the point. I saw the television report on your clinic last night. I found it very informative . . . and disturbing."

"Disturbing?" Harvey repeated with the same stupid smile glued to his face. He wondered how much longer he would get away with the dumb act. Not very, he surmised.

"I reread your findings and confidential reports last night," Markey continued. "While they are not exactly contradictory to what the show said, they were, shall we say, vague."

"It was not intentional," Harvey tried, his brain scanning fiercely for escape avenues. "You see, Dr. Markey, I did not want to make any wild claims before I had full documentation to back them up."

"But the show said—"

"Exactly. The show said—I didn't. You know how the press operates. They exaggerate everything out of all proportion."

"Then the TV coverage was not your idea?"

"Absolutely not. The media came to me. They told me they heard about the clinic through a leak." An idea finally broke into view. Harvey seized it. "They implied, Dr. Markey, that the leak came from Washington. Your offices, in fact."

That's it, Harv, lie like a cheap toupee. Put him on the defensive.

Markey tilted his head toward the ceiling, considering Harvey's accusation. Then he said, "Maybe the leak came from Michael Silverman or Sara Lowell? I understand that they are both good friends of yours."

Harvey shook his head. "They knew nothing about the clinic until the day before yesterday when we diagnosed Michael as being HIV positive. That reporter from *NewsFlash*—Donald Parker—knew about it over a week ago—"

Markey looked at him doubtfully. He leaned forward, "Forget that matter for a moment," he said. "I think it's time we stopped dancing around and got to the heart of the matter."

You're mixing your metaphors, Harvey wanted to scream. Panic and desperation coursed through him like tiny shards of glass.

"You lied to us, Dr. Riker. Your reports were falsified."

"Falsified?"

"You know what I'm talking about. You experimented on Bradley Jenkins. There was no mention of him in any of your reports."

Harvey cleared his throat. "A patient has a right to confidentiality, Doctor."

"Not in this case, he doesn't. There were no studies on him, no lab test results, nothing."

"But—"

"You haven't changed, Riker. You still don't understand that there are rules that must be followed."

"I know all about rules."

"No, I don't think you do. You've always been the same, always looking for the easy way."

"Not the easy way," Harvey corrected, fighting to hold back his growing fear and rage. "I look for the way with the least amount of bureaucratic bullshit to wade through. I look for the way that will save the most lives quickest." He stopped, not wanting to continue but knowing he was powerless to stop. "You'd understand that if you were more of a doctor than a pencil pusher."

Markey's eyes widened behind his thick spectacles. His whole face became two angry eyes. "Who do you think you're talking to?"

"Dr. Markey, if you'd just listen—"

"Do you understand the seriousness of your actions?" Markey interrupted. "You could have your grant revoked. The clinic could be shut down and all your findings labeled invalid."

Harvey stared at him, frozen, afraid for a moment to speak or even move. Finally, his lips parted. "Senator Jenkins forced me to keep Bradley's name out of the reports," Harvey said, grasping at anything to stay afloat. "If you try to close us down, there will be a scandal like you've never seen before."

"The senator's good name has already been dragged through the mud," Markey replied. "A little more isn't going to hurt."

"So what are you saying?"

"Simply this. I have a proposal for you."

Harvey looked at him, confused. "Proposal?"

"What I am about to offer you is not negotiable. You either take it or we close the clinic. It's your choice."

"I'm listening."

"You have falsified reports, which we both know is a very serious issue. All your findings are tainted. We could disregard them all together . . . or we could allow you to build upon them."

"I don't understand."

"Michael Silverman is your most recently admitted patient. Correct?"

"So?"

"Not much work has been done on him yet?"

"Very little. He's been on SR1 for less than twenty-four hours."

"Good. We are going to watch his progress. I am bringing in my own men to monitor everything that happens with Silverman. They will chart every detail of his treatment. When and if he becomes HIV negative, we'll be able to reexamine your other findings and begin testing—"

"It could take years!"

"You should have thought of that before you tampered with NIH reports," Markey snapped.

Oh God, oh God, what do I do now? I'm trapped . . .

"I didn't tamper with evidence," Harvey half shouted. "I tampered with a goddamn patient list—that's all. One goddamn name."

"The point remains. If you could falsify reports on one thing, you could do it for others."

"But we've already cured six patients."

"Only three of whom are still alive. And how do we know that your findings on them are not distorted?"

"Test them, for chrissake!" Harvey shouted. "I'm not going to let you get away with this. I'll do whatever it takes—"

"Simmer down."

"I'll go to the press."

Harvey was sure he saw fear in the man's face, but Markey just smiled at him. "An unwise move, Dr. Riker. First off, I'll immediately cut off your grant. Then I'll reveal to the world that you falsified reports, that you would not allow us access to your patients, that you have never cured anybody, and anything else I can make up. Our PR men will make you look like some charlatan selling snake oil. You won't be able to get a job cleaning bedpans by the time they're finished with you."

Harvey's mind battled back his mounting panic. "The facts will prove you're lying," he said.

"Eventually, perhaps—if you haven't falsified them. But by the time they do, I'll already have stalled you into the next century."

Harvey stared at him in horror. He knew Markey was semi-bluffing, that he did not want to be forced into a confrontation, but what he was saying was also true. He could destroy everything. Even if Harvey cleared his name and proved that Markey was lying, it would take months. Years maybe. And in the meantime the money would stop. A cure would be delayed indefinitely.

Raymond Markey stood and moved toward the door. "My people will be here tomorrow afternoon. Please inform your staff."

MICHAEL came to consciousness slowly. He heard the TV. A man talking. Sounded like the news. His eyes blinked open.

"Good morning, handsome," Sara said.

He felt groggy. His vision was blurred. He rolled over and kissed Sara, who was lying next to him. There was a book in her hand.

"Good morning, Nurse. You better get out of here before my wife gets here."

"Funny."

"What time is it?"

"Almost noon. How do you feel?"

He tried to sit up. "Like a small animal died in my stomach."

"Yuck. Guess what I have here."

"What?"

She held the book closer to his face. Michael squinted and read the title out loud. " *1,000 Names for Your Baby?* I already thought of a name."

"Oh?"

"Moahmar."

"And if it's a girl?"

"That is for a girl. So what's happening?"

"Let's see. What do you remember last?"

He thought. "Eric taking my blood, the little vampire."

"Well, nothing much has happened since then."

Their conversation was interrupted by the television.

"CNN Headline News. Today's major story surrounds the still-unnamed AIDS clinic that is treating basketball star Michael Silverman. Thousands of gay activists marched upon Washington today, demanding that the FDA approve nationwide testing of the little-known drug called SR1. Donations to the financially troubled institution have been pouring in from all over since the *NewsFlash* story aired last evening. According to reports, the anonymous AIDS clinic has made amazing strides in its fight to cure the AIDS virus with injections of a new drug called SR1. With us now is Dr. Eli Samuels from the Mallacy AIDS Center in San Francisco."

The doctor appeared on the screen, his left hand holding an earplug in place. On the bottom of the screen the words "San Francisco, California" appeared in white.

"Dr. Samuels, what is the reaction of the medical community to last night's *NewsFlash* story?"

"Cautiously intrigued," the doctor replied.

"Could you elaborate for us?"

"Certainly. While the press may want to have a field day by celebrating the discovery of this supposed cure, the medical community has to question the authenticity of the report. This unnamed clinic has released no results yet, no firm findings, has not written a paper for *The New England Journal of Medicine* or a similar periodical. It's all highly unusual."

"Are you suggesting fraud?"

"I'm not suggesting anything, but I do believe that the media and the medical community would be acting irresponsibly if we accepted these claims as fact without further evidence."

"Thank you, Doctor."

The anchorman spun his chair in order to face forward. "In a related story, New York Knicks basketball superstar Michael Silverman shocked the sports world last night with his announcement that he had contracted the AIDS virus. According to clinic doctors and last night's report on *NewsFlash,* Michael Silverman contracted the virus during a blood transfusion in the Bahamas several years ago after a serious boating accident. There are those, however, who doubt the story and believe that the clinic is trying to cover up Mr. Silverman's true sexual orientation."

Another face came on the screen. Michael's body stiffened.

"It can't be," he uttered.

"Michael, what is it? What's the matter?"

Michael continued to stare at the image on the screen. The face had changed very little in the past twenty years. A little gray around the temples. A little more sag on the jawline and neck. The overall appearance, however, was radically different. A tailored sports coat. Nice tie. Nice, neat haircut. Just your typical, friendly Joe.

The anchorman continued. "With us now from Lincoln, Nebraska, is Mr. Martin Johnson, the stepfather who raised Michael Silverman. Mr. Johnson, thank you for joining us."

"My pleasure, Chuck."

"Mr. Johnson, what do you think about the reports that your stepson contracted AIDS through a blood transfusion?"

Martin Johnson shrugged. "Might be. I would never want to speak ill of the boy, but . . ."

"But?"

"Well, it seems to me that there is a far greater likelihood that he got it from one of his boyfriends."

The anchorman was nearly salivating. "Then Mr. Silverman is gay?"

"Well, I wouldn't want to say that. I'd say he's more like one of those bisexuals. He's had plenty of sex with both men and women. Started at a young age. But he prefers men, I'm almost sure."

Michael flew up from the bed. "Turn it off!"

Sara grabbed the remote control and snapped the OFF button. The picture turned into a bright dot before fading away. "You okay?"

He nodded. "Lying son of a bitch. I haven't seen him since I was ten years old."

Sara flicked the switch on Michael's portable tape deck. Bach gently blew into the room, but it did little to assuage him. "It's strange," she said. "Why do you think he'd lie like that?"

"Because he's a psychopath, that's why."

Sara shook her head. "There has to be more to it."

"What do you mean?"

"I'm not sure exactly. I just have a feeling he wasn't acting on his own."

"Could be," Michael said. "So what do we do now?"

"We'll have to work some damage control, come up with a counteroffensive, prove the slimeball was lying."

"No matter what we do," Michael said, "some people are going to believe him."

"Yes, some people are going to believe him."

Michael shook his head. "After all these years, after all this time, seeing his face again . . ."

O N the other side of the country Jennifer Riker began to shake. She could not believe what she was seeing on the television screen. Like something out of a cheap horror movie, Marty Johnson had risen again. She had hoped to shut away the memory of his evil smirk forever, but now it was back, dragging painful images that would not go away into plain sight—the bruises on little Michael's body, the black eyes, the concussions, the hospital stays, the absolute terror on the boy's face.

The sick bastard was back.

Jennifer let her anger fester, mount, become obsessive. She concentrated on it, encouraged it, and hoped that it would block out the more painful fact.

Michael had AIDS.

She shook her head. That poor kid. How many times had she said that about Michael? Thousands. Despite being born with looks, intelligence, and enough talent for ten people, bad luck had still tagged along after Michael like a faithful dog.

Jennifer glanced down at the coffee table. For the millionth time she read the name Susan on the envelope and wondered what to do. Last night she had considered trying to reach Susan but had decided it was foolish. Bruce was dead. Whatever he had written in the note would not change that fact. What was the rush? When Susan came back the note would still be here.

But now Jennifer was not so sure about her decision. Something bothersome gnawed at the back of her brain. Bruce's suicide, the mysterious package mailed to an unused California post office box, the murders, the SR1 cure, the cryptic writing on the envelope:

TO BE OPENED UPON MY DEATH

And now Michael.

Her sadness at all this bad news had now transformed itself into something more, something deeper. Though she could not say specifically why, she felt frightened. No, more than that. Petrified. She chastised herself for being paranoid, for seeing conspiracy in everything. But she could not shake the feeling. Something was very wrong here, and it had something to do with Bruce's medical files and that note to Susan.

Jennifer sat back, her head reeling in a rising spiral of uncertainty.

*   *   *

HARVEY picked up his private line. "Hello?"

"Please forgive me, you great big hunk. I want to be your love slave."

He closed his eyes and rubbed them. "Cassandra, this really isn't the time."

Nervous pause. "I'm . . . I'm sorry. I'll call back later."

"Please don't."

"I said I'm sorry. I can't take back—"

"It's not that," he interrupted. "I just don't have the time to get involved with someone right now."

"I blew it, huh?"

"No. It should have never happened in the first place."

"But it felt so right. You said so yourself."

"Cassandra . . ."

"I was scared, Harv. And when I'm scared, I get stupid. I do dumb things. I . . . I have a tendency to destroy whatever I care about before it dies on me, you know?"

"I understand," he said. He stopped, took a deep breath, and then continued. "Why don't we just take it slow, okay? Go one step at a time."

"You mean it?"

He half smiled. "Yeah."

"Why the change of heart?"

"I remembered something Sara once said about you."

"My sister?"

"She said you had a heart as big as all outdoors—despite what you think of yourself."

Pause. "Sara said that?" she asked incredulously. "About me?"

"Yes. I think she wishes you two were closer."

"I think I'm falling in love with you, Harvey."

He let a small chuckle pass his lips. "Like we just agreed, let's take it slow."

"I'd like that."

"Good-bye, Cassandra."

"Good-bye, Harvey."

GEORGE picked up the telephone. "Good afternoon," he said.

"Good afternoon."

"I've been waiting for your call," George said.

"I know. I'm sorry."

"And I've been waiting for the rest of the money you owe me."

Pause. "I know that, George. I'll have it for you soon. I promise."

"Plus ten grand."

"For what?"

"Late fee. An extra ten grand a week."

His employer let loose a long sigh. "Okay. An extra ten thousand dollars."

"Fine, then," George said. "Do you have another job for me?"

"Yes. But this one is going to be very different and more than a little tricky."

"Go on."

"Did you see *NewsFlash* last night by any chance?" the voice asked.

"Of course."

"Then you'll appreciate how difficult this job is going to be."

"That's my problem," George said. "You just worry about paying me."

"Understood."

"When do you want the job done?" George asked.

"Tonight."

"That doesn't give me much time."

"This situation has changed now," his employer said. "It has to be tonight."

"Okay, but it'll cost you."

"I'll pay it. I swear."

George sighed. "So who is tonight's lucky faggot?"

From the other end of the phone, George heard a throat being cleared.

"Michael Silverman."

15

DR. John Lowell looked across his desk at the plump man. He tried to mask the naked hatred on his face, but he knew that it was pointless. Reverend Sanders could see his expression of loathing; it did not seem to bother him.

"Thank you for seeing me," Sanders began. "I appreciate you finding the time in your busy schedule."

"We only have an hour," Lowell replied impatiently. "What do you want?"

Sanders stood and strolled about the spacious study. "This is really a beautiful room, John," he began, his smile locked on autopilot. "Every time I'm in here, I feel so . . . so at home. It's a wonderful study."

"Never mind that. My daughter will be home in a little while."

"So?"

"I don't want her to see you."

Sanders reached out and picked up the picture frame on John's desk. "You have such lovely daughters, John. Gentle, beautiful Sara and the, uh, sex"—he stopped and looked up—"the, uh, sculpted Cassandra. You are a very fortunate man. You see, John, family is what it is all about. Our country was built on the principle of family values. Now that foundation is beginning to crack and crumble. It is our task, dear John, to repair the cracks and make the foundation as strong as ever."

"What do you want?"

"It's very simple. I want you to continue to help me in our crusade. I want you to stand up and do what is right."

"Will you please stop with the mumbo jumbo and get to the point?"

Sanders' voice remained unruffled, placid. "Tell me, John, why did you refuse to come to last night's emergency meeting?"

"Are you out of your mind?"

"No, John, I don't think so."

"You don't want this disease cured, do you?"

Sanders gave an amused smile. "Tell me, John, would you have wanted to cure the plagues of Egypt? Would you have tried to help Job, even though God did not want you to? Would you have told Abraham that God did not really want him to sacrifice Isaac?"

"What the hell are you—"

"Would you try to stop God's work, John? Would you try to join Lucifer in obstructing the Lord's plans?"

"Get the hell off your high horse—"

"We know that AIDS can be transmitted through bodily fluids," Sanders interrupted, "yet if you dare suggest mandatory testing of your doctor or your dentist, the liberals go crazy. They scream about constitutional rights. Well, John, what about our constitutional rights? What about our rights to remain healthy? They don't care about us. Why should we care about them?"

John Lowell just stared for a moment. "You and Markey said they weren't making any progress."

"Yes, I know. It was a surprise to us as well, John. Dr. Riker's reports never showed any hints of what we all heard on your daughter's television show last night. We were as shocked as you were."

John rubbed his forehead. Sanders' calm voice was beginning to unnerve him. "I would have never gone along with . . ."

"With what, John?"

"You know what."

Again, Sanders smiled. "The fact remains, however, that we still have a job to complete. Now it will be tougher than ever. We need your help, John."

"You're insane. My son-in-law is being treated in that clinic, for God's sake."

Sanders nodded his head solemnly, his expression suddenly grave. "I'm so sorry for you and your daughter. What an awful way to find out the truth about Michael's, uh"— again the dramatic pause—"his sexual preference."

John struggled to keep his temper under wraps. "You saw the report. Michael got the virus from a blood transfusion."

The smile came back. "Perhaps you are right, John,

but it seems awfully suspicious to me. A blood transfusion in the Bahamas? You will have to admit it's rather hard to swallow—especially in light of the statements made by Michael's very own father."

"Stepfather," John corrected. "An ignorant son of a bitch who Michael hasn't seen since his childhood."

"Is that so? How interesting. I wonder why he would lie, then."

John said nothing for a moment, and then his eyes narrowed into thin slits. "You," he whispered.

"Excuse me?"

"You put him up to it, didn't you? You paid Johnson off to say that garbage."

"Me? Why would I do such a thing?"

"To distract the media. To cast a shadow over the clinic's positive press."

"Now, hold on a minute, John. It is not very nice to hurl unsubstantiated accusations around like that."

"Get the hell out of my house."

"But there is so much more to discuss, John . . ."

"Get out."

". . . like your continued participation in our struggle."

He stood. "Jesus, you are insane. This has gone too far. It has to be stopped now before anyone else gets hurt."

"Regrettably, John, I fear it will continue." He reached into his pocket and pulled out a cassette tape. "This might help to steer you back on the road of the righteous."

The color drained from Lowell's face, turning his

ruddy complexion into something near chalk. He sat back down. "What's . . . ?"

"On the tape? A good question, John. You remember our first meeting in Raymond's office? The one where you said you would do *anything* to destroy Riker and Grey's clinic so that the Cancer Center could get the finances for its new wing? Do you remember that meeting?"

"You son of a bitch."

The smile grew broader, happier. Power always had that effect on him. "I wonder what gentle, beautiful Sara would think of her sweet little ol' daddy after hearing this tape? Or the press?"

"You'd be taking yourself down too."

"No, I don't think so, John. You see, this tape is edited. Only your voice is on it."

"I'd reveal everything."

"But you'd have no proof, John. And let's face facts. Your accusations would only strengthen my hand with the religious right. They would see me as a leader who is willing to do more than just talk. You, on the other hand, would be ruined—along with the Cancer Center."

John opened his mouth but ended up saying nothing.

"Yes, John, the Lord doth move in mysterious ways. Ah, but do not be upset with me. You are doing what is right. You are going to help destroy something that is evil, and in turn, you are going to benefit cancer research. You are truly helping mankind."

"Get out."

"I have a plan that I am sure you will find satisfactory— one that will help us all, including your son-in-law. You can find out all about it at our next meeting. Raymond will call you. In the meantime I would advise you to keep all of this to yourself. Loose lips sink ships, you know."

He winked, flashed one last smile, and then headed for the door. "After all, John, you are one of us."

After he was gone, Lowell just sat there alone in his study. He stared unseeing at a bookshelf, weighing his options. After five minutes had passed, he stood and went out of the room, closing the door to his study behind him.

After the door closed, the door to a closet swung open. Cassandra pushed away her father's Burberry coat and stepped out. She was still shuddering.

LIEUTENANT Max Bernstein headed down the Sidney Pavilion's third-floor hallway. He was about to enter the laboratory when he heard Dr. Eric Blake's voice coming from just inside the door:

"Maybe what Markey is suggesting isn't so terrible," Eric said.

There was a small pause. Then Harvey replied, "Don't you see what he is trying to do?"

"Of course I do, but maybe we can twist it into our favor."

"How?"

"If he keeps his word," Eric continued, "the government will have to finance the clinic for a few more years yet—until Michael's prognosis is determined anyway—plus we have the new donations coming in on the toll-free line. That may give us the time to perfect SR1—"

"And delay its implementation by two or three years,"

Harvey interrupted. "Markey is trying to make us start all over again."

"Well, it could have been worse. He could have closed us down all together."

Max waited to hear Harvey's response, but when none was forthcoming, he stepped into view. "Good morning, Doctors."

They were both standing over a microscope. Their heads swiveled toward the doorway at the sound of Max's voice. "Good morning, Lieutenant."

Max's eyes moved about the room. "Where's your lab chief this morning?"

"Winston O'Connor? He's taken a few days off."

Max nodded vigorously, his fingers twirling a pencil as though it were a baton. He began to circle the lab, picking up and putting down items at random. "You two look lousy," he said.

"Been a bad day," Harvey replied.

"How so?"

"I received a visit from Ray Markey this morning."

"The guy from Washington?"

"That's right."

"What did he have to say?"

Harvey recounted his conversation with Dr. Raymond Markey. Max nodded, continuously moving about the lab, his eyes never swerving in the general direction of the speaker. To those who did not know him, he appeared not to be paying attention.

He did, however, stop and examine Eric Blake as though seeing him for the first time. Nice shoes, expensive suit, monogrammed dress shirt, power tie, matching suspenders. Looked a little stiff. Acted more than a little stiff. Actually, Eric looked more like a Wall Street wheeler-dealer than an altruistic doctor.

When Harvey finished, Max picked up a test tube, examined it, and said, "Interesting."

Eric snatched the tube from the lieutenant's hand. "Do you mind?" he asked irritably. "These are important experiments."

"Sorry." Max paced off in another direction. Judging by the few sentences Max had overheard in the hallway, Eric Blake did not see Dr. Markey's visit as reason to panic. In fact, he did not seem concerned at all. Again, interesting.

You're missing something here, Max. Something big. Think, damn it.

But nothing came to him, just a steady, annoying nudge in his brain.

"So let me get this straight," he said. "Markey wants to turn Michael into a guinea pig to see if SR1 works?"

"Something like that, yes."

Once again Max nodded. "Then we can't hide Michael with the other patients. But then again, there's no reason to hide him anyway, is there?"

Eric stepped forward. "Hide him? What are you talking about?"

"It's okay, Eric," Harvey replied. "The lieutenant and I have talked it over already. We've decided to place the cured patients in a police safe house to protect them from this Gay Slasher."

"Where?"

Max smiled. "It's a secret—hence the words *safe house*."

"From us?"

"Yes."

"But I don't see why," Eric continued. "Can't we just improve security and leave them in here?"

"We could," Harvey said, "but we both felt this was the better solution. It would be much too disruptive to have a ton of policemen all over the place and try to operate a first-class medical facility. And another thing. Martino was killed in this very building while I was still here. It would be impossible to guarantee their safety."

"What about their medical treatment?" Eric asked.

"The lieutenant has assured me that he has a qualified man who will follow our very specific instructions. Right, Lieutenant?"

"Correct. We won't touch them without your go-ahead."

"And for right now I have informed the lieutenant that the patients are not to be touched or handled in any manner."

Eric said nothing.

Max cleared his throat. "Now that we have that settled, how many cured patients are still alive?"

"Three," Harvey answered. "And to answer your other question, no, there would be no reason to hide Michael from the killer since he is not a cured patient. I might suggest, however, a few extra men at the entrances."

"Okay," Max agreed. "Where are the three patients?"

"They're all here."

"Good. Did you have a chance to go through Dr. Grey's private files yet?"

Harvey nodded slowly.

"Do you have a list of Dr. Grey's missing files?"

"Here." Harvey handed Max a piece of paper and stepped back. Max glanced over the list of names. He shook his head, took the pencil out of his mouth, and scratched a line across three names:

> Krutzer, Theodore
> Leander, Paul
> ~~Martino, Riccardo~~
> Singer, Arnold
> ~~Trian, Scott~~
> ~~Whitherson, William~~

"Let me guess," Max said wearily. "The three surviving HIV negative patients are Krutzer, Leander, and Singer."

Harvey nodded.

Max pocketed the list and headed for the door. "Then let's start preparing them for the move to the safe house."

"Fine. Eric, I'll see you later."

"Okay."

After the two men left the room, Eric Blake walked toward his private file cabinet. He bent down, unlocked the bottom drawer, and reached way into the back. His fingers deftly lifted away loose papers, digging down to the bottom where they hit warm glass.

Eric quickly made sure that no one was looking before he pulled out a test tube filled with blood.

*   *   *

POLICE Sergeant Willie Monticelli was three years away from his pension. He was a twenty-seven-year veteran of the force, having worked homicide for more than a decade. Sounded like glamorous work to many but usually the job was about as exciting as watching paint dry. It consisted of running down useless leads, interviewing hostile people who knew nothing, writing up painstaking progress reports that were never read, and worst of all, surveillance.

Right now Willie Monticelli was on his second day of surveillance. The first day had produced the usual—nothing. Zippo. Subject X had not done one thing that could be labeled even slightly suspicious. Day 2, however, was another matter.

On Day 2, Subject X had flown to Washington, D.C.

Earlier in the morning Willie had followed Subject X to La Guardia Airport, where he purchased a ticket for American Airlines flight 105 to Washington. Willie did likewise. When Subject X landed at Dulles International Airport, he rented a car from Hertz. Willie did likewise. Now they were both driving down Rockville Pike. Destination—still unknown. Willie was not worried about losing the gray Chevy Camaro in front of him. He was the best tail man in the business. Willie could stick to a guy's tail like sweaty thighs to a car seat.

He shook his head. Twitch Bernstein had done it again. The kid was stranger than a duck on bad acid, no question about it, but Willie reviewed his nearly three decades on the force and could think of no better man to lead a homicide investigation. The kid was more than just smart; hell, there were a lot of smart guys in homicide. No, Willie thought, it was Twitch's very weirdness that raised him above the others. Twisted and warped realities were no problem for Bernstein. The kid understood the loony mind.

Subject X's car turned, stopped in front of a guard's post, and then continued forward. Willie stopped his car and looked at the sign.

NATIONAL INSTITUTES OF HEALTH

*   *   *

SARA undressed quickly, sat on the cold examining table and waited. She passed the time by reading Dr. Carol Simpson's medical diplomas twice and counting the tiles on the floor. Ninety-four in all.

Carol Simpson arrived with an apologetic smile. "Sorry," she said. "It's been a busy week."

"I understand."

"How are you feeling?"

"Okay."

Carol took in a deep breath, held it, and then let it go. "Look, Sara, there are two things I can do. I can dance around awkwardly and pretend I live in a vacuum and never heard about Michael's condition or I can just come out and say I'm sorry. If there is anything I can do . . ."

"Just one thing," Sara said. "Help me make Michael the father of a healthy baby."

"I'll do my best, but I have to be honest with you. This is not going to be an easy pregnancy. Normally, I would tell you to avoid stress, but I realize that would be impossible in your case. I can only urge you to minimize it as much as possible. Try to keep up with your regular routine."

"I'll be going back to work on the show tomorrow," Sara said. "Now that the treatment is getting more intense, I won't be staying overnight at the hospital anymore."

"Good."

"Dr. Simpson?"

"Carol."

"Carol, what are the chances that I'll carry to full term?"

Again, the doctor inhaled deeply, kept the air in her lungs and her puffed cheeks, and then released it slowly. "I don't know," she said at last. "The next month or two will be critical. If we can get past that, it should get easier. Now, why don't you lie back and relax?"

EXHAUSTION emanated from every fiber of Harvey's being.

He wished he could find a way to unwind, to forget this place for just a few minutes, to rejuice his flagging battery. But there was no escape, and in truth, it was because he accepted none. The clinic was just too important to diddle in the mundane or trivial.

He opened the door to his office. The room was dark. No lights on. No windows to offer illumination. He flicked the switch.

"Close the door," a husky voice commanded.

Harvey's stomach dropped to his knees as he stared at
Cassandra. She was standing in front of his desk wearing
a short white robe whose brightness contrasted beauti-
fully with the dark Mediterranean tone of her upper
thigh. Her long, black hair was slightly mussed, with a
couple of tight curls reaching down and covering one
eye. She smiled a wild, seductive, tantalizing smile that
he could feel in his toes.

"I said, close the door."

Swallowing, Harvey obeyed.

She loosened the robe and let it open slightly, hinting
at the delights that lay beneath.

Harvey swallowed again.

The robe slid off her shoulders and onto the floor.
Underneath, she wore only a black garter belt and lace
brassiere.

"I've been waiting for you," she purred.

With her torrid gaze never leaving his, Cassandra sat
on his desk and slowly lowered herself into a prone position. She rolled back, stretching her hands above her
head and arching her back. Then she turned her body to
the side, her head leaning against her hand.

She renewed her smile.

Harvey's eyes crawled over every inch of her, over every luscious curve. Her body was utterly fantastic. Mile-
long legs to a flat stomach, hourglass hips and waist, and
then her bountiful, round breasts and smooth shoulders.
Incredible. She was almost impossibly voluptuous.

He felt the familiar, unsettling stir building up inside
of him. He tried to swallow yet again, but his mouth had
gone completely dry.

"I thought we agreed to take this slow," he managed.

She laughed, threw her head back, and beckoned him forward with both a look and a demanding finger. "The slower, the better."

MAX drove the rented station wagon across the George Washington Bridge and into New Jersey. In the backseat Theodore Krutzer, Paul Leander, and Arnold Singer sat quietly. They looked, Max thought, amazingly healthy and calm. All three men had been diagnosed with the AIDS virus two years ago, but Max would never have guessed it. He kept turning around and snatching glances at them. Their good health and spirits, in shocking contrast to the many friends and lovers Max had seen ravaged by the virus, were a fresh and constant reminder to him of the importance of solving this case.

As they reached New Jersey, Max's beeper went off. He pulled into a Gulf station on Route 4 and parked next to a pay phone. "I have to make a call," he said to the three men in the backseat. He got out of the car and dialed the precinct. "Max Bernstein," he said.

"Yeah, Lieutenant, we have a call from Sergeant Monticelli. I'll connect you."

There was a clicking noise. "Twitch?"

"Yeah, Willie, it's me. Where are you?"

"Bethesda, Maryland," he said. "Guess what Southern-fried lab technician is visiting the National Institutes of Health."

Max felt a strange fluttering in the pit of his stomach. "Winston O'Connor."

"Bingo. So I checked his file real good. About his childhood in Alabama and all that crap. Everything is in order. No holes at all. Nothing suspicious. Absolutely clean. Perfect."

"Too perfect?"

"Yup. The guy's gotta be a plant."

Max nodded to no one in particular. "Thanks, Willie. Come on home. No reason to follow him anymore."

"Will do, Twitch."

When Max reached the safe house, he took Dr. Zry, his best (and quietest) medical man, aside. "I have some very specific instructions for you."

"Like?" Dr. Zry prompted.

"I want you to take some blood samples from the three patients," Max said.

"But I thought the guys at the clinic said not to touch—"

"I know what they said," Max interrupted. "That's why I want it to remain our little secret."

GEORGE entered the clinic's basement at five o'clock in the afternoon. Despite the cops crawling all over the obvious entrances, George had had no problem getting into the building through a tunnel entrance in the basement. Getting out the same way would be no problem either. He had spent most of the day studying a blueprint of the building and had come up with a plan he was sure would not fail.

Michael Silverman was in a private room on the third floor, no more than ten yards from the stairwell and the elevator. George was not yet sure which he was going to use to make his escape, but he was leaning toward the elevator. No other patients were housed on the third floor, and after eight p.m., the floor should be abandoned unless someone was still in the lab down the other end of the hallway.

Time to recheck the plan.

He took the blueprint out of his pocket and quietly unfolded it. His finger traced along the paper until it arrived at the third floor. He squinted. Michael's room was over here, the lab was way down there, two empty rooms right there, the storage closet on the right, medical supplies locked over on the left. That was it. Nothing had been overlooked. He would just have to watch the nurse, wait until she left Michael's room.

George refolded the blueprint and jammed it into his front pants pocket. He wondered if Michael Silverman was another faggot or if he had really gotten the disease from a blood transfusion. Probably another fruitcake. His marriage to Sara Lowell was for show.

He settled back against the brick wall and waited.

16

GEORGE checked his watch.

Seven forty-five p.m.

He was already on the third floor and ready to move. Just a few more minutes to go.

From his spot inside the lab doorway George watched Sara Lowell and Reece Porter leave Michael's room. Perfect. Right on time. Ten minutes earlier Dr. Harvey Riker had made his exit. Now Michael Silverman was alone in his room, probably asleep.

George listened closely, but he heard no voices. Sara and Reece were waiting for the elevator in perfect silence. Nothing to be said, he guessed.

Well, they'll have plenty to talk about tomorrow.

The familiar adrenaline rush was beginning to build inside of him, but George remained cool. No reason to rush. Rushing led to mistakes.

He knew he would have to wait a few more minutes until the nurse came by to check on Silverman. When she left his room, George would be able to waltz down the hallway and spend a little quality time with Michael. And what do you know? Lookie here. George would not have to be patient much longer.

The nurse was at Michael's door already.

NO more than two minutes after Reece and Sara had left, Janice Matley entered Michael's room. Her ears were greeted by a mixture of the soothing strings of Mozart coming from the tape deck and the gentle sounds of slumber coming from Michael.

Out like a light, the nurse said to herself. Sleeping like a baby, the poor thing. Not enough he had to have this awful virus—he had to go through it while the whole world tried to watch. Damn shame, that was what it was. Nice young fella like that.

Damn shame.

She checked his chart. According to the file, Dr. Riker had given Michael an injection of SR1 less than an hour ago. That would mean he would not have to be wakened for another four hours. Good. Lord knew the boy could use some rest. She looked at her watch. Ten minutes to eight. She would go downstairs until one a.m. Then she'd come back for his shot.

She pulled down the shade on his door window and left the room. She was just about to head down the stairs when something made her stop short. She could not say exactly what it was. There had been no sound, no voices, no rustling noises in the lab. There was only the steady hum of the fluorescent overhead lights. Damn lights made the most annoying noise. *They can put men on the moon,* she thought, *but they can't make a long lightbulb that doesn't sound like an angry bee.*

Her eyes passed over the empty corridor, but nothing appeared out of place. She shook her head in a vague attempt to clear it. What on God's green earth was bothering her? Nothing. Nothing at all. Everything was peaceful and quiet. Or maybe it was the very quiet that needled her. Maybe it was the sense of pure desolation that gave her reason to pause. And yet, when something was so quiet, so damn still, it was almost like someone was making it like that, like someone was standing so still that the whole room does the same.

Janice decided not to use the stairs just yet. Instead, she walked toward the lab at the other end of the hallway.

THIS was something George had not planned.

Shit! What the hell was the dumb bitch doing?

Relax, George. What harm can she do?

She can see me. Hell, she definitely will see me.

Then you'll have to take care of that problem, won't you?

Damn. He hated deviations from his plans, and the fat nurse was a big goddamn deviation.

Okay, calm down. There's no need to panic.

But she's coming this way!

He could clearly hear the nurse walking toward him. She stepped hesitantly but with authority. He wondered how his employer would react to the death of the old nurse. Not too happily, George imagined. Very pissed off, in fact. But George could not worry about that now. He had far bigger worries. He had to get to Michael Silverman before the damn doctor returned.

He pressed his back against the nook in the lab doorway and waited. From the sound of her footsteps, the old lady could not have been more than ten steps away. He reached into his pocket and slid out his stiletto. She was only a yard away now.

His muscles tensed in preparation.

TWO floors below Sara hobbled next to Reece Porter. "Reece?"

"Yes."

"How did he look to you?"

Reece Porter shrugged. Immediately after hearing Michael's statement, Reece had left the Knicks' locker room, taken a taxi to the Seattle airport, waited eight hours for the next available plane to New York, flown across the entire country, spent the day trying to find out where Michael was, located Sara at Dr. Simpson's office, and then obtained permission from Harvey to visit Michael.

A damn long twenty-four hours.

"Mikey looked okay," he said at last. "Just tired mostly."

"From the SR1, I think," Sara added. "I'm glad you came, Reece. It means a lot to him."

Reece shrugged. "So how are you feeling?"

"I'm fine."

"Uh-huh. Sure you are."

"What do you mean by that?"

"Your walk, for one thing. It looks like somebody did a deep freeze on your leg."

It was true. Her leg had been cramping up all day, the soreness clenching down on the very bone with sharp teeth. Every step was a new adventure in pain. "I'll be all right. It's just a little stiff."

"Then wait here," Reece said. "I'll get the car."

"I can walk."

He shook his head. "I swear, Sara, you can be as big a pain in the butt as Mikey. Just wait here and stop being so goddamn stubborn. Sit over there."

With a weak smile she did as he asked.

"I parked in the visitors' lot on One Hundred Sixty-seventh Street," Reece continued, heading for the exit. "Give me ten minutes."

"I'll be here."

She glanced about her surroundings. There were two armed security guards at the door plus two plainclothes policemen in cars outside the clinic's door. Her leg throbbed as though her heart had dropped down into the area above her ankle. She would soak it when she got home. Yes, she would take a long, hot bath, find a good book, smother herself with blankets and pillows and . . .

And what?

Lie there and worry, she guessed. When she had first been told about Michael's condition, the news did not really reach her. It was as though her mind had built a barrier—more like a sieve actually—which only let in the facts but kept out the emotions and ramifications. Unfortunately, the holes in the sieve were beginning to widen. They were opening up enough to allow reality to seep into her conscious thoughts.

Sara had done a few stories on the AIDS epidemic. She had seen what it could do to a person, how the virus could eat you alive from the inside. Her mind began to swirl with the devastating images, and like the horror AIDS inflicted, the images lunged at her in no particular order.

Wasted bodies now little more than a defenseless battle zone for disease: Kaposi's sarcoma; pneumocystis carinii; lymphoblastic lymphoma; fierce fevers over 105 degrees; respiratory infections; whole body systems collapsing; mental deterioration; delirium to the point of babbling like an Alzheimer's patient; every breath an intolerable struggle; lungs filling with fluid until a tube was shoved through the rib cage in order to drain them; getting weaker before your eyes, so weak that even eating becomes impossible; in and out of comas; a handsome young face changing overnight into a haggard skull-mask; healthy physiques disintegrating into little more than brittle bones with skin hanging off; painful and unsightly purple lesions everywhere; sores inside the mouth so thick that swallowing produces only choking sounds; no control over bowel movements; constant, inescapable agony; eyes that can actually see Death standing around the corner, waiting patiently to step forward and claim its conquest . . .

And the fear of the disease, the confusion, the discrimination. Even now, 25 percent of the American people were so ignorant about AIDS that they actually believed it could be transmitted from just donating blood.

No, there was nothing pretty about AIDS, nothing

romantic, nothing Gothic, nothing cinematic. There was just pain, horror, and death. With AIDS, your body and mind fought a constant battle against agonizing illness after agonizing illness. You suffered through one devastating bout after another, no time to recover, like a weakened club fighter who is forced to go yet another round with the champ. But against AIDS there was no chance for the one-punch comeback.

Eventually, you lost.

She replayed what Harvey had told Michael and her no more than an hour ago about his visit from Raymond Markey. And yet, when she considered the cruel severity of the AIDS virus, her mind could not comprehend his words. Could someone really be trying to prevent a cure? Could someone really be trying to turn back the clock, delaying a cure for tens or even hundreds of thousands of fellow human beings? The weight of the cruelty boggled the mind.

Could someone be so desperate to keep the AIDS virus alive that they would murder? It made no sense. And all of this just made her want to talk to Michael more, want to, at the very least, look in on him one more time before heading home.

"Hi, Sara."

She looked up. Eric was standing in front of her. Despite the fact that he had been working for fifty of the last sixty hours, he looked fresh and neat. He smiled at her warmly. "Are you okay?"

She nodded.

"On your way home?" Eric asked.

"Yes. I'm just waiting for Reece."

"I'm on my way out too. I haven't slept in . . . I can't even remember the last time I slept. I just have to run up to the lab and slide this under the door first."

"Is it anything important?"

"Not really. It's just a memo for Winston O'Connor. Harvey wants us all to meet tomorrow morning."

"I, uh, I can bring it up for you."

Eric looked at her, puzzled. "But I thought you just said you were on your way out."

"I am. I mean, I will be." She pushed down hard against the top of her cane in order to stand. "It's just . . ."

"Just what?"

She half shrugged. "I want to see Michael again."

"He's probably sleeping, Sara."

"I know. I don't want to wake him. I just . . . I don't know. I just want to peek my head in and make sure everything is okay."

Eric smiled tightly. "I understand—really I do—but I don't think—"

"Please," she said. "It's important to me."

Eric hesitated. Then: "Okay, here's the memo. If he's still awake, say good night for me too."

"I will. Thanks, Eric." She took the paper from his hand, kissed his cheek, and pushed the call button. A few moments later she was ascending in the elevator toward the third floor.

JANICE Matley saw George's sneakers first.

The toes were jutting out from the doorway of the

lab. They were black sneakers, or at least the toe part was black. With the kids and their crazy sneakers nowadays, who knew what color the rest of the sneaker was? Her grandson had a pair of Nike Air Jordans that had more colors than a rainbow.

She swallowed. "Who's there?" she called out.

Her voice, she was surprised to hear, sounded steady, confident.

"I said, who's there?"

She saw the foot slide forward. The sneaker was completely black after all. Reeboks, as a matter of fact. A man, a big man, followed the sneakers. He was dressed entirely in black. Black sneakers, black socks, black sweater, black pants. His shirtsleeves were pushed up, revealing powerful forearms the size of Popeye's. He stepped out from inside the doorway and smiled at her. The smile was wide, bright, but mostly . . . unfeeling. It touched no other part of his face. When she looked up into his dark, bleak eyes, a cold chill rippled in her belly

And once again, she knew.

"Hi," he said. "Nice night."

Janice never had a chance to react. With one hand George palmed the back of her head and yanked it forward. With the other, he flicked the switch on the side of the stiletto, releasing the eight-inch blade. The point of the thin knife penetrated the hollow of Janice's throat and sliced through her windpipe. Thick streams of warm blood spurted onto George's face as the stiletto exited out the back of her neck, inches below the spot where his hand gripped her skull.

Janice's gaze locked onto his. She could see her own

horror-stricken face reflected in the cold blankness of the murderer's eyes. His grip on her head tightened. She gargled on her blood for a moment before her eyes rolled into her head. The last sounds she heard were the buzzing of the lights and the inhuman choking noises still forcing their way past her own lips.

George watched the corpse slide to the ground, the stiletto still implanted through the neck. He calmly took out his handkerchief and wiped the blood off his face. Messy. Too messy for a pro like himself. There was blood splattered everywhere, but he had no time to clean it up now. He would have to move fast.

With a weary sigh, George dragged the body into a supply closet. Once inside, he tugged hard at the blade in order to release it from the throat area. Grudgingly, the corpse surrendered the weapon with a sucking pop. George closed the blade, pocketed it, and headed down the hall toward Michael's room.

When he reached the door, George tried to peek into the room through the shade over the door window, but it was pulled closed. Slowly, George turned the knob and pushed open the door. Like Janice Matley before him, George heard Michael's deep breathing and the violins from the cassette deck. George debated his next step and then made a decision. He would turn on the lights. He wanted to see what he was doing. Heck, the old nurse was certainly not going to mind and the rest of the floor was abandoned. A little illumination might help him along his way. Besides, what was the risk? If Silverman woke up—very unlikely anyway—George would be all over him before his first flinch.

George's fingers found the switch and flicked it up. The light was bright, startling, but Michael did not stir. His chest continued to rise and fall at the same steady, undisturbed pace. Nothing surprising in that. But now, as George stepped toward Michael's bed, something surprising did indeed happen.

George heard the elevator door opening.

DURING the elevator ride Sara had concentrated very hard on something completely inane: which would she do first, slide the memo under the lab door or look in on Michael? As the elevator doors opened, she decided to slide the memo under the lab door first. She knew that if she looked in on Michael first and then went to the lab, she would crave a second peek on her way back.

Her leg ached like a bastard as she stepped out of the elevator. She checked her watch. Reece would be another five minutes at least. Good. She was really happy he had visited today. She could tell that Michael was thrilled too. Reece meant a lot to him. They shared a special bond, one that only teammates—

Sara froze. Her eyes widened.

Oh my God . . .

She stared down the hall in the direction of the laboratory. The walls looked like some kid had fingerpainted them with red paint. Only the texture was too thin for paint, too dark for ketchup, too syrupy for anything but blood.

Maybe somebody dropped a blood sample on their way to the lab?

Then how do you explain the tiny fact that the blood was splashed all over the place?

Maybe whoever it was tripped and the blood sample went flying all over the place and . . .

And nobody cleaned it up? Good try, Sara.

Her heart pounded in her chest as another thought pushed its way through the confusion and into the front of the brain: *Michael.*

She spun back toward the door to Michael's room and hobbled forward. Her knees buckled in fear when she saw the door shade was illuminated.

Why is Michael's light on? Why the hell . . .

For a brief second the light created a silhouette against the window shade. The brief image was as clear to her as those presidential cutouts kids did in school during President's Week.

It had been the silhouette of a man.

Her leg felt anchored to the ground, but she dragged it along like an inanimate object. When she reached the door, she grabbed the knob and pushed without hesitation. She limped in, her eyes searching.

No one.

Her mind began to whirl aimlessly. There was no one in the room except, of course, for Michael. He lay sleeping. Or was he? Yes, his eyes were closed, but there was something very strange, something so obvious and yet so subtly horrifying that she felt her chest tighten. She could not breathe. If Michael was just sleeping, then how come his face was upside down? How come his head was lolling at a strange angle. And most important, how come he was lying half off the bed?

From behind her came a voice. "Good night, Sara."

She turned, but Sara never got a chance to see the man's face.

17

"DAD?"

Dr. John Lowell turned toward his older daughter.

"Yes, Cassandra?"

She licked her lips nervously. "Where are you going?"

"On a business trip. I'll be home tonight."

"Where?"

He put down his briefcase. "Why are you so interested?"

"Just tell me where."

"Washington."

Cassandra closed her eyes. "You're going to meet with them again, aren't you?"

"Meet with whom again?" he asked, his voice a mixture of annoyance and fear. "What are you talking about?"

"With Reverend Sanders, for one."

Silence. Then: "I don't know what you're talking about."

"You know exactly what I'm talking about," she replied. "I was here when you met with him three days ago. I was hiding in your closet."

His eyes widened. "You what?"

She moved closer to him. "It has to stop. You have to tell the truth before there's more bloodshed."

"Cassandra, you don't know what—"

She stepped in front of him. "Don't let him blackmail you any longer."

His face grew tight. "Stay out of this. I know what I'm doing."

"How much more blood are you going to spill? How many people have to die before you put a stop to this?"

"Get out of my way. You are talking nonsense."

"Dad . . ."

"Move!" He pushed her harder than he had intended. She fell to the floor.

"Cassandra!" He sprinted toward her. "Honey, I'm so sorry," he began. "I didn't mean to hurt—"

She sat up, her eyes burning. "Get away from me."

He backed away, his face twisted into a look of longing and anguish. "I have to go now, honey. Please trust me. I know what I'm doing. When I come home tonight we'll talk about it, okay? Just trust me. I love you."

He turned and hurried out the door. Cassandra stood. She was still unsure about what she should do. This was, after all, her father—not some evil monster. Maybe there was a reasonable explanation. She should give him the benefit of the doubt.

What doubt, Cassandra? What are you so afraid of?

Nothing. She would wait until tonight. She would listen to what he had to say first before jumping to any conclusions . . .

No.

She grabbed her purse and headed out the door. It was time to tell someone before it was too late. But not Harvey. He would never be able to look at it objectively.

It was time to tell Sara.

S O hot . . .

Michael tried to stir himself to consciousness. It was no easy task. His eyes felt stapled shut. His mind spun in figure eights. Something was wrapped tightly around his mouth, making it hard for him to breathe.

He heard boisterous sounds all about him. Very noisy. Cars. Horns honking. People shouting out like hot dog vendors at a baseball game. Loud rock music. Laughter. General chatter. He tried to concentrate on the sounds, tried to sift out some meaning in them, but he found it difficult. Some people were speaking English, no question about it, but others were talking in a foreign tongue that Michael's cloudy mind could not place. It sounded Chinese or something like that—only more lyrical, more pleasant to the ear.

What the hell is going on?

He wondered if he was perhaps dreaming, if he was not still asleep. But how often did he dream of sounds with no vision? No, he was awake. His eyes were closed. He was lying on a hard wood floor, his right ear numb from leaning against it. His whole body felt sore, as though he had been lying on this floor for a week, which, he surmised, was entirely possible.

He tried to sit up, but he fell back down upon the ground twice. His hands, he realized, were handcuffed together behind his back, pinning back his shoulder blades painfully.

After another failed attempt Michael managed to work himself into a sitting position. In the background he could hear someone shouting with a heavy accent, "Supergirl! Supergirl! Come meet Supergirl! Time of your life!" With a struggle Michael's eyes fluttered and then opened. It took him another minute or two to focus and take in his surroundings. Small room. Barren. Dirty. The walls were covered with chipped paint. A lightbulb dangled from exposed wires on the ceiling. There was a fold-out chair and ratty mattress that made the room smell of mildew, sweat, and urine. There were also bloodstains on it. Michael's right ankle was shackled to a pipe running through the room. His mouth had been taped shut with what tasted like masking tape. His eyes continued to scan the room until they stopped at something on the ceiling.

What the . . . ?

He looked again. Jammed in a hole by the door were sticks of what looked like dynamite. Michael swallowed.

Where the fuck am I?

He tried to reconstruct his last conscious hours. He had been at the clinic. Harvey had given him an injection of SR1. Reece and Sara had visited him. He recalled dozing a bit while they were still in the room and finally falling asleep. And then . . . nothing.

The heat in the room was well past tropical, the air thick and still. His body was coated with sweat. He tried to wipe his cheek on his shoulder, but his wet shirt just added more perspiration to the area. He glanced about the room again. His eyes stopped when he saw a piece of paper on the floor:

Hello, Michael.

Welcome to the land of consciousness. I hope you had a pleasant nap and an equally pleasant journey. Try to make yourself comfortable. Please do not try to escape. If by some miracle you were gone when I returned, I would hunt down your beautiful bride, fuck her, and then kill her.

Best wishes,
George

P.S. I have people downstairs, so don't try shouting out the window.

I'm having a nightmare, Michael said to himself. *That's what it is. A nightmare. Either that or I am losing my mind.*

He struggled and scraped his way toward the window. The chain just reached. He lifted his head, pushed his face under the shade with his nose and looked out. If he had been only confused before, he was completely lost now. There were tons of people on the streets. Neon lights splashed across the dark sky, "*LIVE* **Sex Shows!**" and "*LIVE* **Nudes!**" over and over again, as though some patrons would be confused and think that they performed sex shows with dead bodies. Dark, Asian men stood outside bars, opening the door every once in a while to reveal naked dancing girls on tables, hoping the view would entice customers into their establishment. A man stood in the middle of the street with three girls, each dressed in a red cape, blue boots, and yellow bodysuits with a giant *S* emblazoned upon the chest. The man kept yelling out, "Supergirl! Supergirl! Spend an evening with Supergirl! She fly you to the moon and back!"

Michael spotted a young Asian boy approaching an American couple in their sixties who looked liked they belonged on a farm in the Midwest. "You want go to sex show?" he asked in broken English, handing the couple a card. "Lookie at all these positions." He began to point to different parts of the card. "Woman on top. Two women with one man. Doggie. You name it. Lookie, big breasts. Use banana too. You like. Anything you want. Come with me. Live show."

Mr. and Mrs. Old MacDonald studied the card as if it were the fine print of a real estate contract, nodded eagerly, and then followed the Asian boy.

The street was packed, waves of people heading in both directions. There were other neon signs too. Some in English, some written in characters Michael did not understand. They were not, he knew, Chinese or Japanese. Not Hebrew or Arabic either. No cars were on the road, but he could hear them close by. On his right, he saw tables set up with watches, shirts, pants, sweaters, cassettes, everything. "Three dollars for LaCoste shirt," one vendor cried. Another shouted, "One dollar for favorite cassette. Six for five dollars. All favorites of you. George Michael. U2. Barbra Streisand. You name, we have."

What is this place?

The door behind him opened. "Well, well, we're awake."

Michael slid back to the floor. The man in the doorway was large and stocky. He appeared to be very muscular, though not as disproportionate as most weight lifters. His hair was slicked back like Pat Riley's, the former Lakers coach, and his suit looked like something off the cover of *GQ.*

"Welcome, Michael," the man began. "My name is George. Did you read my note?"

Michael nodded.

"It was for your own good," George continued. "Escape would be very dangerous. You see, I have already killed a lot of people. Killing your wife would just be one more."

Michael struggled, but the chains held him in place.

"Now, just relax a second, Michael." George knew a lot about the art of intimidation. Threatening a man's wife was one of his favorite tactics. It was connected to the whole possession thing, he guessed, and nothing demoralized a man more than the thought that his wife was balling another guy—by force or otherwise.

George grabbed the chair from the corner, sat down, and leaned toward his captive. "You look confused, Michael, so let me explain to you what's going on." His voice was relaxed, casual. A casual voice, George knew, was often more unnerving than the loudest of screams.

"We are in Bangkok. That's right, we are in the Far East, just you and me, pal. In fact, this building is on Patpong Street, the red-light district. Twelve-year-old whores suck off guys in this very room all the time, Michael, isn't that sick? Twelve years old and already they're hustling. A real shame."

George shook his head solemnly. "I tell you, the world is falling apart before our very eyes and nobody cares. Fact is, we're standing over a topless bar right now— bottomless too if you pay the right price."

George laughed maniacally at his joke. Michael stared back in horror.

"Don't get so upset, Mike. Can I call you Mike? Good. Maybe later we'll have time to see the sights. The Reclining Buddha is a must-see in my opinion. Same with the Grand Palace. Maybe we'll even take a little boat trip through the floating market. Would you like that?"

Michael just continued to stare.

"But first, let's talk business. If you do what I say, no one will be hurt and you will be free very soon. We might even have some fun. If, however, you do not cooperate, my reaction will be swift and painful." George smiled again. "Let me give you an example."

Without warning, George's hand shot out. It moved so fast it was barely a blur. His knuckles landed on Michael's nose. Michael heard a crunching, squelching noise and he knew that his nose had been broken. Blood trickled out of his nostrils.

"You see what I'm saying?"

The pain engulfed Michael's entire face. Since his

mouth was still covered with the tape, he had no choice but to breathe through his broken nose. *What do you want?* Michael tried to scream, but the tape muffled his voice.

"Now let me tell you something else," George continued. "I have things to do, so I can't sit here and watch you all day. Besides, it's too hot in here. Bangkok is always so humid, Michael, but you get used to it after a day or two. The thing is, my employer told me to make you as comfortable as possible. So I would like to loosen some of those chains and take the tape off your mouth. But I need your promise you won't try anything. Do you promise, Mike?"

Michael nodded.

"Good. If you leave this room or do something cute, my men will spot you, and Sara will suffer. I am good at making people suffer. And Sara is such a delicate little flower, Michael. You wouldn't want me to attach electric cables to her clit, would you? Juice her up good and then let my boys take turns with her?"

Michael quickly shook his head.

"I'm also pretty handy with explosives. If the police did by some miracle find you and decide to try a rescue"—he paused, smiled, and nodded toward the sticks of dynamite by the door—"ka-boom! Michael all gone. Blood, limbs, screams—very messy stuff. Follow me?"

Another nod.

"I'm going to take the tape off your mouth now. If you scream, I'll break your jaw. No one will pay attention anyway. People are always screaming on this street." George reached out and ripped off the tape.

Michael caught his breath. With some effort he worked his vocal cords. "What do you want?"

"Don't worry about it."

"I'll pay you anything you want."

"Forget it, Michael."

Michael managed to sit upright. "Can you take off the handcuffs?" he asked. "They're killing my shoulders."

"Sure, but the ankle chain stays on." George used a small key to unlock the handcuffs. They opened with a click. "Better?"

Michael nodded. He rubbed his wrists, eyeing George in the process. His head still swam; his vision still blurred. George sat no more than a yard away.

Now or never, Mikey boy.

Later, Michael would claim that pure fear clouded his brain and distorted his rational thinking. It was the only explanation for what he did next.

With something approaching horror, Michael realized that his fingers were forming a fist. His eyes watched helplessly while he cocked the fist and launched it toward George's face.

The punch moved at a pitifully slow pace. The drugs George had pumped into Michael's body continued to extract a heavy toll on his physical prowess. George's right forearm knocked the blow to the side with a casual wave.

"You are a brave man, Michael Silverman," George said. "You are also very foolish."

George's hand reached out and took hold of Michael's broken nose between his thumb and index finger. Michael screamed.

Then George twisted.

Tiny fragmented bones began to grate against one another, making a horrid grinding noise like someone was tap-dancing on a thousand beetles. George increased the pressure. Tendons and tissue ripped. Blood sprayed in different directions. Michael's eyes widened and then closed, his body falling slack.

"Try something like that again," George said, "and it will be Sara who pays the price. Understand?"

Michael could barely nod before he passed out.

CASSANDRA looked at her sister. Sara's bright green eyes seemed to have sunk deeper into her skull. Dark circles surrounded them. The beaming look of life had been replaced by a bleak look of incomprehension and shock. Three days had passed since she had been knocked unconscious in Michael's room—three days of depression, sadness, fear, and confusion. But now it was as though those emotions had hardened into something more concrete. During the last three days Sara's hurt had transformed itself into something more powerful, something more . . . useful.

Anger. No, rage.

"Hiya, baby sis."

Cassandra's smile was broad, too broad. It looked fake and Sara knew it.

"What's wrong?"

"Wrong?"

"Just come out and say it."

The smile fled Cassandra's face, leaving behind no

traces it had ever been there. Her expression was hard, serious. She sat down on the bed next to Sara and took her hand.

Sara looked down at their hands and then up into her sister's eyes. "What is it?" she asked gently.

"I know I haven't been the best sister in the world," Cassandra said.

"Neither have I."

"But I love you."

Sara tightened her grip on Cassandra's cold hand. "I love you too," she said.

Tears began to slide down Cassandra's cheek. "I think Dad is mixed up in this whole Gay Slasher thing."

Sara felt her body stiffen. "What?"

Cassandra nodded. "I think he's involved in some kind of plot to destroy the clinic."

"What are you talking about?"

"I overheard him arguing with Reverend Sanders in his study the morning after the charity ball."

"But Dad said he didn't know him."

"I know. Harvey told me that. So I became suspicious. I went through his desk when he wasn't around. There were letters saying that the funds Dad wanted for the new wing at the Cancer Center were going to Sidney Pavilion instead. One was from a guy named Markey—"

"Dr. Raymond Markey?"

"That's him. Assistant Secretary of something."

"Health and Human Services."

"Right."

Sara tried to swallow, but her mouth had suddenly

dried up. "But that doesn't mean he's involved with Sanders."

"That's what I thought . . . until the morning Michael was kidnapped. When Dad kept trying to make sure I would be out of the house that morning, I became suspicious. So I hid in his closet. Reverend Sanders came by again."

Sara sat up and stared directly into her sister's eyes. "Tell me everything they said, Cassandra. Everything."

BANGKOK at night.

The Thai locals approached every white-faced person who walked down Patpong, whispering promises of sexual fulfillment that would have made a porn star blush. But no one approached George. One or two of the Thais knew him personally; some had met him on occasion; many knew his name; all feared going anywhere near him.

Despite the enormous crush of people, the locals parted when George walked by, letting him pass, fighting to get out of his way. It was past midnight already, but Patpong was just beginning to stretch out its arms and prepare for the evening that lay ahead. George brushed past a group of Japanese businessmen who were negotiating rates and terms with a local pimp as if they were sitting in a Tokyo conference room.

When George reached Rama IV Road, he hailed a *tuk-tuk*, the native taxi of Thailand. A cross between a car and a scooter, the *tuk-tuk* had its good points—it was small, quick, used up next to no fuel, and was open-air. It also got crushed in an accident, had no headroom, and was open-air.

The driver gave George the customary Thai greeting. He clasped his hands in a praying position, bent his head forward until his nose touched his fingertips, and said, *"Sawasdee, kap."*

George returned the greeting, though not bending nearly as far as the driver. *"Sawasdee."*

"Where to?"

"Wats," George barked.

The driver smiled and nodded. George climbed into the bright blue *tuk-tuk*. The driver continued to smile. Typical Thai, George mused. Thailand, Land of Smiles. Everybody smiling. They might be griping, whoring, thieving, murdering, but they always smiled. George liked that.

They stopped at a traffic light on Silom Road. A voice shouted, "Hey, mate!"

George glanced to his right.

"Yeah, that's right, mate," a red-faced, inebriated Australian shouted, pointing at George, "I'm talking to you." The Aussie looked to be about fifty years old. There were six prostitutes jammed into a taxi with him—young Thai girls no more than thirteen, fourteen tops, giggling and rubbing the man with fast, vigorous hands.

George's face registered disgust. "What do you want?"

"Well, mate, it's like this, right. Seems I bit off a bit more than I can chew here, you see. Wanted to know if you wanted to go halfsies."

"Halfsies?"

"You take three and I'll take three—unless we want to

do an eight-person thing. Kind of a lick-'em and luv-'em orgy. Might be up for that."

"Degenerate," George spat.

"Hey, that's not a nice thing to say," the Aussie slurred. "'Specially as I don't know what it means."

The man laughed hysterically at this. The young women (kids really) joined him. The Aussie laughed harder, spurred on by the realization that the girls found him so amusing. The girls, George knew, did not understand a word of English, with the exception of some sexual terminology.

"Go to hell," George called back.

The light turned green and the *tuk-tuk* moved onto Charoen Road. It noisily began its journey along the Chao Phraya River. In Thai, *wat* meant temple or monastery, and Bangkok had more than four hundred temples of breathtaking beauty. Color was the key word in Thai architecture. Red, yellow, green, blue, and most especially gold—all reflecting the bright sun in an amazing kaleidoscope of nature and man.

There was Wat Po, which housed the Reclining Buddha—a statue so immense it stretched across an area larger than half a football field. Another enormous Buddha image, cast in well over five tons of solid gold, sat upon the altar of Wat Traimit, and Wat Arum, the Temple of Dawn, appeared to be suspended above the Chao Phraya River as though held there by the gods, its towering spires reaching up and scratching the very heavens with pointy claws.

But Bangkok's most spectacular temple was known to the Thai people simply as Wats, though it was far more than just a temple. Tourists knew it as the Grand Palace, though it was far more than that too. The Grand Royal Complex might be a better name. Everything King Rama I, ruler of the Chakri Dynasty, could have wanted was housed within the walls that enclosed his palace, including one of the most sacred images in all of Buddhism— the Emerald Buddha. In this bastion of awe-inspiring color and beauty, the Emerald Buddha stood out only for its rather startling unimpressiveness. The statue was only a few feet high, was made of jade, and showed no real signs of unusually brilliant handwork. You could buy an exact reproduction for a few baht in any Thai trinket store.

"We're here, boss."

"Swing around to the other side."

"Okay, boss."

At night, spotlights illuminated the many spires and pagodas of the Grand Palace, creating an impression both bright and haunting. In a word: mysterious. Like the most seductive woman, Bangkok hinted at unparalleled delights while always keeping part of itself covered, hidden from view, a secret.

"Stop here."

"Yes, boss."

The *tuk-tuk* chugged to a halt. George paid the driver and crossed over toward the Chao Phraya River. He walked along the river's edge, watching the wooden rice barges drift lazily by as though they had no particular destination in mind, the drivers still wearing their enormous straw hats though the blazing sun had settled in the west hours ago. The Chao Phraya was more than

a river to Bangkok. It was her lifeblood. The waterway
was used for transportation, for floating food markets,
for bathing. Families had lived for centuries in huts that
were more in the river than on it.

Through the darkness a long, narrow sampan glided
silently to the shore. The boat—closer to a canoe really—
was being steered from the back by a skinny boy. An el-
derly man with only one arm and a wisp of a mustache
sat in the front.

"George?" the man whispered.

Right on time as always. George climbed aboard the
sampan, sat and clasped his hands together. He bowed
respectfully. *"Sawasdee, kap."*

"Sawasdee, kap."

"How is business, Surakarn?"

"Brisk," the old man said. "But, alas, we have had
to close down our profitable Malaysian operation. Too
much heat from the state police. They are not, I'm afraid,
as receptive to gifts as they used to be."

"So I've heard." George looked at Surakarn's weather-
beaten face, his skin brittle like dry brown leaves. The former Thai boxing champion must be nearing seventy now,
George thought, and worth countless millions of dollars.
Yet Surakarn did not slow down, nor, it seemed, did he
do anything with his vast wealth. He still lived in a modest hut along the Chao Phraya, though he had long ago
allowed creature comforts to enter his dwelling. From the
outside, the hut looked like something from a Vietnam
War documentary; inside were two big-screen televisions,
VCRs, a GE refrigerator, a dishwasher, a washer and
dryer, a microwave, central air-conditioning, the works.

Surakarn smiled. "You've been away for a long time, old friend."

"Too long," George replied.

Surakarn waved his one arm toward the boy, and the sampan began its slow journey down the Chao Phraya. Surakarn's other arm had been sliced off in Chiang Rai almost twenty-five years before by a fellow competitor in the smuggling industry named Rangood. Rangood, however, had made the mistake of allowing Surakarn to live. After he captured his nemesis, Surakarn tortured him mercilessly in ways that were beyond imagination. Rangood begged Surakarn to kill him, but Surakarn would listen only to his shouts of agony, not his words. By the time Rangood's heart gave out several weeks later, his mind had long since snapped.

Surakarn was as trustworthy as they came, but George did not tell even him about Silverman's kidnapping. This was too big, too risky, to trust anyone. George had decided not to solicit the help of the usual local cutthroats he worked with, despite what he had written in the note to Michael. He had even gone so far as to put a mask on Michael's face when he sneaked him into the Eager Beaver.

The Chao Phraya area was quiet this evening. The gentle splashing sounds from an occasional boat enhanced the feeling of calm, of solitude. There was no mist in the air, only the stifling humidity, and yet there always seemed to be a fog rolling across the city, as though mist and fog could be detected by some sense other than sight and smell.

"Nothing changes here," George said.

Surakarn nodded. "Bangkok is a constant."

"I need to use the safe phone."

"Of course." Surakarn pointed to a radio with a microphone. "The radio leads to a cellular phone aboard one of my vessels near Hong Kong."

"I see."

"You asked to make a call that could not be traced. This is it." Surakarn moved toward the far end of the boat. "You need not fear. I will not listen."

George checked his watch. He called in the number to the captain of the drug boat in Hong Kong, who proceeded to hook him up with the United States. No matter what Surakarn claimed, the call was still, after all, traceable. The authorities could, in theory at least, figure out the call was made from a cellular phone (no doubt a stolen one) in Hong Kong. But to find out who made the call and then to find out that there was a radio hookup to Bangkok, well, that would be nearly impossible. Worst-case scenario: it would take weeks.

A few moments later George heard the voice. "Hello."

"Perfect," George said. "You're right on time."

"I can barely hear you," the voice said.

"Don't worry about it. We won't be on long."

"Is he all right?"

"Fine. We're having a ball together. Did you transfer the money?"

"Yes."

"All of it."

"Every last penny," the voice replied.

"How did you get it?"

"That's not your concern."

"I'll check my account tomorrow morning just to be sure. If it is not all there, my houseguest will be missing a few fingers by tomorrow afternoon."

"It's all there." The voice faltered for a moment and then said, "Why did you have to kill the nurse?"

"Excuse me?"

"The nurse. Why did you have to kill her?"

"She saw me."

"But you're supposed to be an expert. How could you let that happen?"

The words stung because George knew that they were true. He had miscalculated. That was rare. And very bothersome. "It was just a freak thing."

"Listen to me closely: I don't want any 'freak thing' to happen to Michael Silver—"

"Don't use names, imbecile! Someone could be listening."

"What—oh, sorry."

The voice was extra-taut tonight, George thought, like somebody wound so tightly he would either snap or stretch into something unrecognizable. George had not liked it when the voice was nervous. Now he feared that his employer was beginning to lose control completely.

That was not good. It was, in fact, very bad.

"I guess I should be thankful," the voice continued. "At least you didn't kill Sa—uh, his wife."

"I was able to sneak up behind her," George replied evenly. "She never got the chance to see me."

"Otherwise?"

"Otherwise she would be lying on a cold slab too."

"No one else is to be hurt without my say-so. Absolutely no one. Just keep a hold of you-know-who. Make sure you treat him well."

"I'll do what I have to do."

"No. You listen to—"

"Good-bye," George said.

"Wait. How can I reach you?"

"You can't." George had trusted his employer too much already but no more. It was time to take control. "Just follow our plan." He snapped off the radio. "Surakarn?"

"Yes?"

He tried to smile, but he was still distracted. "I feel good. Let's take a little ride."

"Where to?"

"I just came into a lot of money."

"Congratulations."

"Tell me, Surakarn, can a man still buy anything in Bangkok?"

Surakarn smiled toothlessly. "Do you still like them older?"

He nodded. "She has to be at least twenty."

JENNIFER Riker's whole body shook. Over the past three days she had read the press reports, seen the news of Michael's kidnapping on the television, witnessed the outrage of a country. But Jennifer felt more than outrage.

She felt fear.

Susan was going to be home in another two days, but Jennifer now knew that she could no longer wait until then. She had been wrestling with her decision for three days now and had come to the decision that the stakes were too high for her to hold back. Michael's life might depend upon her actions.

But when she reached over and picked up the packet, her mind started to vacillate again. No evidence, after all, linked this mailing with the Gay Slasher or the kidnapping. No evidence at all. These were just standard medical files and lab samples. Period. That was it.

Then why had Bruce mailed them the day he committed suicide? And why had three of the patients listed in the files—Trian, Whitherson, and Martino—been murdered? Coincidence?

She thought not.

She'd wavered long enough. The note written to Susan, well, that was Susan's and there was no way Jennifer was going to open it. But the other contents in the packet were not personal. The files were not, she knew, for everyone's eyes, but there was one person who might make sense of it, one person who might be able to piece together why Bruce felt the need to mail it to a seldom-used address on the day he died.

Jennifer picked up the phone and dialed Harvey's private extension.

ENOUGH lying around.

Sara threw the blankets off her body, stood, and took hold of her cane. The inactivity, the babying, the looks of pity were all behind her now. She had to stop crying. She had to get up and act. She had to find out what was happening and who was behind all of this.

She had to save her husband.

"Where are you going?" Cassandra asked.

"To speak with Max and Harvey. They're at the clinic."

"Wait a second," Cassandra said. "You can't tell anyone about this yet—not even Max and Harvey. This is still Dad we're talking about."

Sara nodded. "I know. I won't say a word about him until we speak to him tonight. I'll meet you at the house at eight o'clock."

The sisters embraced. Then Sara left for the clinic. She arrived at the door of the third-floor lab a half hour later.

"I want to know everything," she said.

Max and Harvey turned toward the lab door.

"Sara," Harvey began, "what are you doing here? You should be—"

"I should be right here," she interrupted.

"Max and I are doing all we can," Harvey continued in a calm voice. "Why don't you go back home and rest? We'll let you know if anything changes."

"Don't patronize me, Harvey."

"I'm not patronizing. I'm trying to do what's best for your health."

She continued to stare at them, her eyes both wide and defiant. "I'm fine. I want to know what you've learned."

Harvey's next protest was cut off by Max. "Then come over and sit down," Max said. "We don't have time to argue."

Sara limped over to the table and pulled out a chair. "Okay, what have you got?"

"A few things," Max said. "First, we've been going over the files of the murdered patients."

"Learn anything?"

"Maybe," Max said, his leg shaking up and down. "Maybe not. They were killed in almost the same order they got here. Trian and Whitherson were both original patients at the clinic and Martino came in a couple of months later. The other three cured patients—Krutzer, Leander, and Singer—all came in about a year later."

"What's that mean?"

Max hesitated, his fingers entwined in his own hair. "I don't know," he said. "It might mean nothing, but something about it bothers me."

"How does Bradley fit in?" she asked. "Or . . . or Michael?"

"They don't, really. They have no similarity to the other three victims or for that matter to the three who are still alive. In fact, the only similarity I can see is that both Bradley and Michael were VIP patients."

Harvey snapped his fingers. "But maybe that's it. Maybe the killer is after the important patients, not merely the cured patients."

"Could be." Max shrugged. "But that raises the larger question—why kill four patients, one nurse, and presumably one doctor and not kill Michael?"

Harvey looked at Sara hesitantly. "Excuse me for suggesting this," he began carefully, "but we really don't know if Michael is alive, do we? The killer may have just moved his body."

"It wouldn't make sense," Max replied. "Kill him at the clinic and then move him out? Very risky."

Harvey was about to point out that Bradley Jenkins

had met a similar fate but chose not to push it in front of Sara. "Okay, let's move on."

The intercom on the table buzzed. A woman's voice said, "Dr. Riker?"

Harvey lifted the receiver. "Yes?"

"Mrs. Riker is on line six," the receptionist said.

"Take a message."

"She said it's urgent."

"Sure. Her alimony payment is probably a week late. Tell her I'll call her back." Harvey replaced the receiver in its cradle. "Nothing important. Go on."

Sara nodded, struggling in her ongoing battle against coming apart. "How do you think the kidnapper got in and out of the clinic?"

"We think he used a secret entrance," Max replied. "There is a small tunnel in the basement that leads to an apartment building two doors down. Somehow, he found out about it."

"How?"

"I don't know," Max said.

"Then someone has to be giving out information on this place," Sara said. "And what about the timing, Max? Markey decides to use Michael as a guinea pig and the next thing you know he vanishes. It has to be related."

Max quickened his pace, his teeth working on a stubborn hangnail. "Agreed."

"Hold on a second," Harvey interrupted. "This makes no sense. No one has access to that kind of information, except . . ." He stopped.

Max stopped. "Except whom?" he prodded.

Harvey shook his head. "No one."

As if on cue, Winston O'Connor came around the doorway. "Hey, gang," he drawled. "What's going on?"

"Where the hell have you been?" Harvey almost shouted.

Winston looked confused. "No reason to bite my head off, Harv. Hell, I went fishing. Stayed in the family summer cabin on the lake. Caught the hugest humdinger of a fish—"

"Don't you get a newspaper?"

"Shit, no. We don't even have a phone out there." He stopped, looked around. "Now, what in the hell is going on around here?"

Max walked toward the chief lab technician. "Will you excuse us a moment?" he said to Harvey and Sara. "I'd like to speak with Winston alone."

18

IN Bethesda, Maryland, four powerful men sat in a plush office in a picturesque baronial structure on the campus of the National Institutes of Health. One was powerful in the religious world; one in the political realm; two in the medical community.

It was a beautiful day. The sky was dark blue and clear. The well-manicured grounds outside were alive with green. The whole area resembled the most exclusive of country clubs.

But the four men were oblivious to their resortlike surroundings.

Arguments raged. Accusations were hurled. Fingers were pointed. And in the end nothing was resolved. Through it all, one man had not raised his voice. One man had not engaged in the bitter debate. One man—a normally very verbose man—had not said a word.

But the man had listened. And the man had made a decision.

As the meeting broke up, the man pulled Dr. John Lowell to the side and said five words: "We have to talk alone."

To which Dr. Lowell nodded and replied, "Let's get back to New York first."

M A X closed the lab door. "So how were the fish biting?"

"Pretty good," Winston drawled. "I caught one of the biggest bass ya ever did see. She must have weighed a good—"

"Great. Congratulations. Now, why don't we stop playing games?"

"Playing games? I don't getcha, Lieutenant."

Max renewed his pacing with surprising vigor. "Would you mind telling me why you were in Washington three days ago?"

"How do you know—"

"Don't worry about how. Just tell me why."

Winston's expression remained cool, his tone impatient. "While I don't reckon it's any of your goddamn business, I stopped in Washington to visit some friends on my way home. Happy?"

"Your home in Alabama?"

"That's right."

"The cabin by the lake and all that."

"Yep."

"Tell me something else, Winston—what parts of Washington did you visit?"

"I don't see why that's important."

"It's not really. I just want to know why you went to the National Institutes of Health."

Winston tried to glare at his interrogator, but Max had his back turned. "You had me followed?"

"Yes."

"Well, I hate to disappoint you, Lieutenant, but there is nothing very sinister in that. I was visiting a couple of former coworkers. I used to work there."

"Interesting," Max replied. "Then how come there is no mention of it in your résumé?" Max reached into his coat pocket, withdrew his hand, reached into his front pants pocket, withdrew again. "Damn, I had it here someplace."

"Lieutenant . . ."

"Here it is." Max took out the crumbled piece of paper and unfolded it with quick fingers. "Now, this résumé covers your work history from your undergraduate studies to the present day. When exactly did you work for the NIH?"

Again the silence. Then: "I have a friend who works for the NIH, okay? Is that such a crime? I didn't want to say anything because I knew he would jump—"

"Now, there are two ways we can play it," Max said, ignoring Winston's shifting explanations. "One, you can tell me what I want to know. Two, you can continue your little charade and I can arrest you."

"On what charge?"

"Murder in the first degree. Breaking and entering. Assault."

"You're out of your cotton-pickin' mind. Who am I supposed to have murdered?"

"Riccardo Martino."

"Who?"

Max smiled. "The patient who was murdered in the clinic."

"I don't know the name of any patients. Harv must have told you that."

"Riccardo Martino was mentioned in the story on *NewsFlash* a few nights back."

"I don't recall the name," Winston said with a dismissing wave of his hand. "And anyway, you got nothing on me."

Max leaned forward. O'Connor's expression was relaxed, but Max had seen the familiar scared shadow cross his face briefly. "Sure about that, Winston?"

"Whadda ya mean?"

"We have a witness who will swear under oath you were in the hospital at the time of Martino's death, even though you claimed to be home."

"Get lost."

"The same witness saw you hit Dr. Riker over the head. We also know you were in the lab breaking into Dr. Riker's files."

"You're bluffing," he said.

True, Max thought, but now he noticed that O'Connor's voice was not as confident as it had been. Max decided to give him another little push.

"And one other thing." Max turned his head so that his back was to Winston. "Drop the Southern drawl. It's insulting."

"What the hell are you talking about?"

Max turned around, his eyes toward the floor, pencil

between his teeth. Something close to a smile passed his lips. "No one who has lived in New York for the past twenty years has a Southern accent that thick. You sound like somebody on *Hee-Haw*."

Again, silence.

"We know you work for the NIH," Max continued. "We assume you're CIA-trained. And we know what you've been up to."

"You don't know shit." The Southern accent was weaker now, less pronounced. Winston's Adam's apple bopped up and down continuously as he swallowed.

Max took the pencil out of his mouth and examined it. "I know I have the authority to drag your ass down to headquarters, book you for murder, and seal you in a cage. If you think your CIA or your NIH buddies are going to rescue you, you are very much mistaken. This case is too hot. They'll let you rot before admitting you're one of them."

"I don't know what you're talking about," Winston said, but there was now a clear waver in his voice.

"Then just humor me by listening to your other option," Max continued. "You might find it interesting."

"I told you I don't know—"

"Option two: you can tell me what you know," Max interrupted. "In return, I will promise to keep our conversation confidential—it'll just be between you and me. Washington will never know anything about it. Think about it. The choice is yours."

There was a stony silence that Max interrupted by taking out his handcuffs and a plastic card from which he read: "You have the right to remain silent. Anything you—"

"Hold on a minute."

Max looked up from his card. "Something you wanted to say?"

Winston rubbed his face. "How do I know I can trust you?"

"You don't. But if you don't cooperate, I'll pin Martino's murder on you. That's a promise."

For a brief moment Max and Winston locked eyes. It was Winston who looked away. "What do you want to know?"

"Who are you working for?"

"All confidential, right?"

"Right. Who are you working for?"

Winston took a deep breath and released it. "I don't know. I'm a CIA operative, but I report to the Department of Health and Human Services."

"To whom?"

Winston shook his head. "No names."

"Raymond Markey?"

"I said no names."

"What is your function?"

"Gathering information on the clinic."

"What kind of information?"

"Any and all."

"And how do you go about it?"

"What do you mean?"

"How do you gather your information?"

Winston shrugged. "Simple. I snoop around. I break into the confidential files. Whatever it takes."

"Is that what you were doing the night Harvey stumbled across you?"

Winston paused. He took a cigarette out of his pocket and put it in his mouth. "You gotta light?"

Max shook his head. "I don't smoke. It's bad for you."

"Yeah, sure, and chewing pencils is healthy, right?"

"Were you in the clinic the night Martino was killed?"

"I'd rather not answer that."

"Then I'll take that as a yes."

Winston O'Connor found a set of matches near a Bunsen burner. He lit the cigarette and inhaled deeply, as though the cigarette were an oxygen mask and he were caught in a fire. "Take it any way you want, Lieutenant. But I did not kill anyone."

"Why did the NIH want all of this information?"

"I don't like to theorize, Lieutenant."

"Try."

Another deep puff. "I assumed that the NIH wanted to check up on the clinic's progress independently. They got a big investment here, and Harv and Bruce can be pretty damn secretive."

Max thought for a moment. "Okay, tell me this: why did you report to Washington in person three days ago?"

"My contact was worried."

"About what?"

"He didn't like the positive media reports about the clinic."

"Why not?"

Winston shrugged. "He wanted to know what Harvey was up to—what he was going to do next."

"What did you tell him?"

"The truth. I can break into files and I can snoop

around, but I cannot read another man's mind. I told them I had no idea."

"What has the NIH said to you about Michael Silverman's kidnapping?"

"Not a thing. I haven't spoken to them since the day I flew into Washington."

"Has your contact ever mentioned the Gay Slasher?"

"Never."

"Do you think your employers are behind it?"

Winston smiled, the cigarette dangling from his lip. "How fuckin' crazy do you think I am, Lieutenant?"

Shrug. "How often did you break into the clinic's confidential files?"

"About once a week, I guess."

"During the daytime or the night?"

"Night usually. When I thought no one would be around."

Max nodded, pacing. "Except you didn't know Michael was on the third floor, did you, Winston?"

"Huh?"

Max walked toward him. "A few hours before Martino was murdered, a new patient had been secretly whisked into the room down the hall—Michael Silverman. Naturally, you wanted to find out who he was. So you broke into Harvey's private files that night."

"Now, hold on a minute."

"But you screwed up," Max continued. "Dr. Riker was on the floor at the time. He heard you in the lab. So you knocked Harvey out."

"Slow down a second."

"Then you went downstairs, killed Martino—"

"I didn't kill anybody!" he interrupted. "Okay, I admit it. I was in the lab that night. I broke into the file cabinet and saw Silverman's name. I knew the NIH boys would be interested in him, so I tried to find out more. That's when Harv interrupted me. I guess I panicked a little. My instructions were not to get caught under any circumstances. So when Harv came in the lab, I hit him in the back of the neck. But I didn't kill Martino—I swear it."

"You're a martial arts expert." It was more of a statement than a question.

"Yeah, so?"

"And the blow to Sara's neck was delivered by a martial arts expert."

"Whoa, back up a second, Lieutenant. I didn't touch Sara Lowell. For that matter, I never touched her husband or Janice or that Martino guy. Christ, I felt awful when I heard about Janice. She was a fine woman." Winston lowered his head into his hands. "I never hurt anybody, I swear. I was just trying to gather information for a branch of the government that has every right to know what was going on in here. There is nothing illegal in that."

"What else do you know?"

"Nothing. I swear."

Max stopped his pacing and restarted his nodding. "You better not be holding out on me. Or else."

He had tried to sound tough, but it came out too whiny. Damn.

*   *   *

"FUCK me, big stallion. Oh yeah, that's it. Yes. Ohhhh, ohhhh, I'm cominnngggg!"

Michael tried to ignore the continuous cries of the prostitute in the next room and consider his options.

One, he could try to break the chain manacled to his ankle. The problem lay in the fact that the steel was rather secure; more to the point, it would not budge.

Two, he could yell out the window for help. But suppose George or his accomplices heard him?

Three . . .

There was no three. He stood and tested how far the chain would allow him to roam. He could get close to the window but not to the door. George probably did that on purpose. The door was a scrawny-looking thing with rotted wood and a lock that a strong gust of wind could break in two.

He sat back down, his nose throbbing painfully. Downstairs, the topless bar was in full swing now. The music was considerably louder than earlier, the vibrations from the deep bass potent enough to reach inside Michael's chest. Prostitutes and their clients walked about freely in the hallway. Michael heard doors shut on both sides of his room. Then a woman yelling:

"Fuck me, big stallion. Oh yeah, that's it. Yes. Ohhhh, ohhhh, I'm cominnngggg!"

The woman screamed into her fake orgasm. The man grunted into his real one.

The sessions never lasted more than a couple of minutes. Then it would all start again. The prostitute would come upstairs with a new john. There would be the same giggling. The same fake orgasm. The same

"Fuck me" words shouted at the same rehearsed pitch. Over and over. Performance after performance. The woman's high-pitched squeals of delight were incessant, monotonous, passionless, as though Michael were listening to a robot or an actress who had learned her lines too well.

Okay, let's think this through. Harvey tells me Raymond Markey wants to use me as the clinic's guinea pig. Next thing I know, I'm in the Orient with a psychopath. So what can we conclude from all this? Just one thing: I have to get the hell out of here.

Cramps ripped through his stomach. The cause, he knew, could be his hepatitis or withdrawal from the addictive SR1 or . . . or something new.

Something AIDS-related.

"Fuck me, big stallion. Oh yeah, that's it . . ."

The very air had mingled with the sleazy surroundings, giving everything around him a dense and seedy feel. Breathing nauseated him. The women's cries were maddening in their repetition, hour after hour, endless. He put his hands to his ears and tried to block them out, but the sounds were right outside his door:

"Come on, Frankie," a whore purred with a thick Asian accent.

"Right behind you, sweetheart. Damn, I spilled my drink."

"This way, Frankie. Tawnee going to show you good time, you see."

"Might just be the other way around, honey," the man, an American, slurred. He was clearly inebriated.

"I take care of your big cock. You see."

"Bet your ass you will." The man stumbled, bumping into walls like a pinball.

"You like that, Frankie?"

"Yeah, that's wonderful."

"You want to go in room now, Frankie?"

"Sure thing, sweetheart."

"Okay, but money before is for boss man. You give Tawnee big tip, yes?"

"Let's talk about it in the room."

Michael froze. He saw the doorknob turn.

"No, Frankie, this way," the whore said.

The door shook. "Damn door is stuck."

"Over here, Frankie. That sign say no enter."

"Fuck the sign, sweetheart. I'll get us in. You just keep rubbing my balls."

"No, Frankie, wrong room." Her warnings were more urgent now, but Frankie did not pay heed. "That's boss man's room, Frankie. He get mad. Come over here. Frankie!"

Frankie threw his shoulder against the wood. The lock grudgingly gave way. Michael's eyes widened as the door began to swing open.

"No, Frankie, wrong room." The whore quickly reached through the portal. She maneuvered Frankie out of the way, fixed the lock, took hold of the door, and began to swing it closed. For the briefest of moments she looked at Michael, her eyes stained with fear and sympathy. Then she turned away. Michael's heart sank as the door closed.

"Come on, Frankie," the whore tried to enthuse. "We go have fun. You like too much."

"I hope so, sweetheart. Let's party!"

Then Michael heard another door open and close.

FRANKIE'S penis remained flaccid.

"What's the matter, Frankie?" Tawnee asked. "You no like me?"

Frankie looked down. The whore was licking his balls—and doing a yeoman's job of it too. Still, no hard-on. Super-strange. Frankie's sexual dysfunctions usually came from the flip side of a softy: premature eruption of ol' Mount Vesuvius. Not being able to achieve a serviceable, gargantuan erection was something new to him.

Super-strange.

It wasn't the alcohol either, though he had drunk enough to knock out a battalion. Shit, Frankie had been blitzed plenty of times. Plenty. But his "Throbbing War-head" had never had any trouble engaging in the past. The Big Fella was usually swollen to the size of a Louisville Slugger by now, splitting the little lady in two nice, even pieces. And it wasn't the chick's fault either. She was a pro in every way, her tongue licking gently at him like a kitten near a saucer of milk. A beautiful thing really. Screw the cream-colored ponies and crisp apple strudel—getting sucked off by a working pro was one of his favorite things.

But suddenly the dog had bitten, the bee had stung, he was feeling sad. Check that. He was feeling unhorny. And why?

Because he was a basketball fan.

"Lie down, Frankie. Relax."

He obeyed, but his mind was elsewhere. He had read in the *International Herald Tribune* a couple of days ago about the kidnapping of Michael Silverman. Super-strange stuff. It had happened in some AIDS clinic on the East Coast of the USA.

So then why the hell was Silverman chained to the floor of a Thai whorehouse?

Simple, Frankie. You're drunk. Check that: you're shit-faced, you thick-dicked macho hunk. You imagined the whole thing. How long was the door open, Super Stud, two seconds? You barely saw the guy.

Good point, except for one thing. Frankie never hallucinated. Drinking loosened him up. Drinking made him feel good. Drinking made him pass out and pee in his pants. Drinking did not, however, cause him to imagine kidnap victims chained to a floor. He had to tell the police, and he had to tell them right away. Could be a reward in it for him.

"Whoa, honey, slow down a second," he said.

The whore lifted her head. "Something to please you, Frankie?"

He stood and grabbed his pants. He zipped slowly, making sure he kept his Trouser Snake from running wild and getting caught in the metal teeth. "Don't take it personal, sweetheart, but I gotta go. Maybe next time."

"But, Frankie—"

"Here's fifty bucks. I'll tell boss man you were great. Don't worry."

He winked and then headed out the door.

Tawnee shrugged and picked up the fifty-dollar bill.

Poor man, she thought. It was sort of sad. She had seen more than her share of penises in her day, but the thing in that guy's pants looked like a baby's pinkie.

So sad.

SARA arrived at the family estate a few minutes before eight. Cassandra met her at the front door.

"Hi," Sara said.

"Hi."

That was the extent of their conversation.

They sat on either side of the den and waited in silence. Their eyes never met. They seemed to be avoiding each other, like teenagers left alone on a first date, but above all they looked weary. The clock on the mantelpiece ticked away, the only noise in the still surroundings. Sara began to tap her leg and sing an old classic from Thin Lizzy, but the words died away quickly.

"Sara?"

"Yes."

"I hope Michael is okay."

Sara nodded, a thin smile on her lips. "He is."

They heard the familiar sound of the Mercedes diesel engine. Their father was home. With great effort Sara made her way to her feet. Cassandra did likewise. As they headed down the corridor, past portraits of ancestors and the fine wooden paneling, John Lowell entered.

John saw his two daughters immediately and stopped. He did not call out to them or try to back away. He just stood there for a moment, staring, a defeated look on his face.

Cassandra stepped forward. "I told Sara. I'm sorry—"

John interrupted his daughter with a raised hand. "You did the right thing," he said.

"What's going on, Dad?" Sara asked.

"Perhaps we can explain."

"We?" Cassandra repeated.

John lowered his head and stepped aside. From behind him Senator Stephen Jenkins entered the room. His appearance had changed radically since the Cancer Center gala nearly two weeks ago. Bradley's father looked drawn. His eyes were unfocused and bewildered.

The senator tried to smile. "Hello, ladies."

The sisters shared a confused glance. "Dad," Sara began, "I don't understand what's going on."

"I know you don't, honey," John said gently. "Maybe we can explain it to you in the study."

HARVEY'S eyes were red. He had not been home in five days, and he had not seen Cassandra since their brief tryst in his office the day Michael had been kidnapped. His sleep came in infrequent periods of semiconsciousness at his desk, more like airplane dozing than genuine REM sleep. For several minutes at a time he had managed to push Michael from his mind and focus on work. But the minutes never lasted very long before his attention reverted back to Michael. Still, he felt keyed up by new developments. The changes in the SR1 formula— enhancements, really—were going to achieve the desired effect; he was sure of it. He just had to buckle down a little more, push himself a little more.

As anyone who knew or worked with him could attest, motivation had never been a problem for Harvey. More than anyone, he understood the ramifications of his work. That knowledge spurred him on when others—almost all others—would quit.

The intercom buzzed. "Dr. Riker?"

"Yes?"

"Mrs. Riker called again. She wanted me to remind you to call her as soon as possible. She said it was urgent."

Harvey sighed. Urgent. Yeah, right. To be fair, Jennifer probably wanted to know how Sara was doing and if they had learned anything new about Michael. He really didn't have the time to go into all that with her. Besides, thinking about her still distracted him, and the last thing he needed was a distraction. "Okay, thanks. I'll get back to her."

"Would you like me to place the call for you?"

Harvey thought for a moment and decided he might as well get it over with before Jen became hostile. "That would be fine, thanks."

"I'll connect you."

A few moments later Harvey heard the phone ringing.

19

LIEUTENANT Max Bernstein sat at his desk and pondered the latest developments in the Gay Slasher case. Of course, Max never actually sat. He stood, paced, squatted, juggled day-old doughnuts (he was trying to master four at the same time), and drove those around him nuts.

He kept replaying his conversation with Winston O'Connor, the first big break in days. Clearly the National Institutes of Health had a strong interest in Sidney Pavilion. The question was why. O'Connor's explanation that the NIH wanted to keep an eye on its interests rang hollow. Why single out the Sidney Pavilion? There had to be a reason.

But what?

Okay, forget that for a moment. Move on to the murder of Riccardo Martino. Winston O'Connor claimed that he had nothing to do with Martino's death, and Max believed him. In an odd way it solved something that had puzzled Max from the moment they found Martino's body.

The timing.

Okay, let's reconstruct. Harvey Riker had seen Riccardo Martino alive a few minutes before Winston O'Connor knocked him unconscious. Ergo, Martino was murdered after Riker was attacked. In order for that to be the case, the killer had to surprise Harvey, go downstairs, kill Martino, and then make his escape—all of which seemed very unlikely. No matter how cool a customer the Gay Slasher was, chances were he would have taken off as soon as Harvey stumbled onto the scene, saving Martino for another day.

So what was the explanation?

Simple. The person who killed Martino was not the same person who attacked Dr. Riker.

Well, if Winston O'Connor did not kill Martino, who did?

The Gay Slasher.

Then why didn't the Slasher stab him like the others?

Hmmm. Good question.

Like that one, Max? I got a million more for you. Is the person who hired the Gay Slasher targeting the cured patients like Trian, Whitherson, and Martino? Or is he (or she—let's not be sexist) after the secret patients like Jenkins and Michael? Or both? And what about the order of the deaths of the cured patients—the three early patients dead, the three later patients alive? Is there any significance in that or is it just a faulty wire in the brain that keeps bringing you back to that seemingly irrelevant point?

And the bigger question, which Max doodled on the top of his desk repeatedly:

Who benefits from the murders?

Good question. Crucial.

The phone on his desk rang. Max dropped the doughnuts onto the floor. He reached for the receiver without bothering to pick them up.

"Bernstein here."

"Good," Sergeant Willie Monticelli said, "you're still there. You ain't gonna believe this."

The tone of Willie's voice told Max that this was no routine call. "Where are you?"

"Downstairs. I got a police station in Bangkok on the phone. A guy named Colonel something. I can't pronounce it."

Bangkok! Max sat down. "What does he want?"

"I still have him on the line, Twitch. I want you to hear this for yourself."

"What is it?"

"I'd rather let him tell you himself."

"Patch him through."

"Just hold on. Damn, which button do I push?"

"The yellow one."

"Oh, right. Here goes."

Click. Static. Then: "Hello."

"Hello, Colonel," Max said, speaking slowly. "My name is Lieutenant Max Bernstein. I am with the New York Police Department. With whom am I speaking?"

"Colonel Thaakavechikan. Bangkok Special Forces."

"Colonel Thaka—"

"Colonel will suffice, Lieutenant. I went to school in California, so I know that Thai names are difficult for Americans."

"Thank you, Colonel. You have some information for us?"

"I believe so. I understand that you are in charge of the Gay Slasher homicides and the disappearance of Michael Silverman."

"Yes."

"Well, something has come to our attention which might be of interest to you. Have you ever heard of George Camron?"

"No."

"He is a professional hit man who lives in Bangkok, though he travels frequently. He is quite good and very deadly. We estimate that he has killed over two hundred people in the past decade."

"Jesus."

"When Camron is in Bangkok, he works out of a bar called the Eager Beaver on Patpong Street. He has been seen there quite frequently in recent days."

"Just recent days?"

"Yes. According to our sources, George Camron arrived in Bangkok within the week."

"Interesting," Max remarked.

"It gets more interesting, Lieutenant Bernstein."

"How so?"

"I have an American named Frank Reed sitting beside me. Mr. Reed is a patron of the Eager Beaver Bar."

"Oh?"

"Let me preface this by mentioning that Mr. Reed admits to being drunk at the time he was in the bar."

"Go on."

"It seems that Mr. Reed was engaging in sexual activities with a prostitute in the upstairs section of the Eager Beaver. He accidentally opened the wrong door and saw a man chained at the ankle."

"I see," Max said. His fingers plucked at his hair and mustache. "Isn't that fairly normal? Whips and chains at a whorehouse?"

"Oh, yes, quite normal," the colonel agreed. "Mr. Reed, however, swears that the man he saw was Michael Silverman."

The words slammed into Max's solar plexus. "What?"

"He claims Michael Silverman is being held captive at the Eager Beaver Bar."

"Have you checked out his story?"

"That might not be as easy as you might think," the colonel explained. "George Camron is more than a dangerous hit man, Lieutenant Bernstein—he is very clever and careful. If Michael Silverman is being held in the Eager Beaver—and it would not be the first time Camron has kept someone there—it will be nearly impossible to get him out. Camron probably has the place wired with explosives, and if he gets even slightly suspicious, he will blow the place up."

"Can't you take him out by surprise?"

"It is too risky, Lieutenant Bernstein. If we failed to kill Camron immediately or if he is working with an accomplice, I assure you that Mr. Silverman's life would be forfeited. Because Mr. Silverman is something of an international celebrity, our government would frown upon such actions. That is why I am calling you. I am not saying that the place is definitely wired. I am just giving you Camron's past history."

"I appreciate it. Willie, are you listening in?"

"Yeah, Twitch, I'm here."

"Get me booked on the next plane to Bangkok."

"Already did it. I have you booked on Japan Airlines flight 006, which leaves Kennedy in about two hours. You connect in Tokyo with JAL flight 491 that'll bring you into Bangkok in the evening. Problem is, I don't think the department will pay for it."

"I'll worry about that when I get back. Colonel, do you mind my coming over?"

"Not at all, Lieutenant, as long as you understand that we are in charge of the situation."

"Understood."

"Then we have no problem. In the meantime we will do our best to monitor the Eager Beaver as inconspicuously as possible."

Max rifled through his drawers until he found his passport underneath a jar of mayonnaise. He wiped it clean with an old napkin.

"Then I'm on my way."

THEY were all seated in the study.

John Lowell sat behind his large oak desk with Senator Jenkins on his right and a few feet behind him. Facing them on the other side of the desk were Sara and Cassandra. For a moment they all just studied one another. Then Sara broke the silence:

"Is Michael still alive?"

John glanced at the senator and then back toward his daughter. "We don't know, honey."

"But you know something about his kidnapping?"

"We *may* know something about it," Senator Jenkins corrected. "We can't say for sure."

Sara shook her head. "Dad, what's going on?"

"I'm not sure where to begin, actually." Dr. John Lowell rose and moved toward a bookshelf filled with large medical volumes. His eyes passed over the titles, but they read nothing. "You know how I feel about the Cancer Center, don't you?"

"Of course we do," Sara replied, "but what does that have to do with—"

"Everything, Sara," John said simply. He pulled out a book, glanced at the binding, and put it back on the shelf. "You see, focus can be a dangerous thing. Your view of the world narrows. You grow obsessed. Blinded. You see everything in terms of your obsession and nothing else. You cannot accept defeat. You cannot understand why everyone else does not share your passion. Don't get me wrong. Concentration and focus are good and necessary. But when they slide unchecked, they can distort your perspective. In the ultimate pursuit of knowledge, you can easily become ignorant."

Sara and Cassandra shared a confused glance. "I still don't understand."

John smiled sadly. "You will. This is not easy for me

to say, so just give me a little time. I'll get to the heart of the matter eventually."

The sisters nodded.

"I wanted that new wing at the Cancer Center so badly I ached physically," he continued. "It could help so many people—people suffering the worst medical curse known to mankind. Diseases and plagues come and go, but cancer is a constant. I thought the new wing and the additional finances would be a gigantic step toward unlocking the secrets of cancer and, ultimately, to curing it. I would have done anything to get that new wing. Anything."

He paused here, letting his meaning sink into the still surroundings. "When the additional finances for the new wing were rejected, it was like a spear through my heart. Those damn fools, I raged. How could they be so stupid? I tried to save the idea. I threw all the money I could into it, and tried to raise more privately. But it was not enough. We had needed the grant, and now that was gone. The new wing was dead. And why? Where had the money gone? To AIDS. To Harvey and Bruce's clinic. To a gay disease. To a drug addict's disease. To a disease I still believe will never run rampant in the normal heterosexual community."

Sara opened her mouth, but John stopped her by raising his hand. "I don't want to argue with you, Sara. I know you feel differently. Suffice to say that this is how I see it. Yes, some non-intravenous-drug-abusing heterosexuals have come down with AIDS, but the number is small, especially relative to the number of people who die from cancer. This is how I see it—right or wrong, it doesn't matter anymore."

He caught Sara's eyes then. A small smile appeared on his face. "You remember when we watched *Damn Yankees* on the video? Remember how the guy sells his soul to the devil in order to get what he wants? That's what I did. I didn't realize it at the time—or maybe I did but I didn't care. Who knows anymore? I only know that I signed on with the devil and there was no looking back."

"What did you do?" Sara asked, her tone distant.

"My rage consumed me. I started to look for any way, legal or not, to get the money away from the clinic and into the Cancer Center. Raymond Markey—he's the Assistant Secretary—"

"I know who he is," Sara interrupted. Her voice was cold. "Go on."

John cleared his throat. "Anyway, Dr. Markey contacted me. He said that there were other people who felt the way I did, people who felt too much emphasis was being placed on AIDS, people who wanted to bring down the Sidney Pavilion."

"What other people?"

John took a deep breath. "Reverend Sanders, to name one."

Sara glared at her father. "You signed on with that con man?"

"Listen to me, Sara. We both knew that we did not share the same ideology—just the same enemy. Sanders had his reasons for wanting to destroy the clinic, and I had mine. His reasons did not matter to me. The only important thing was getting the money for the new wing—even if that meant working with Sanders."

"And who else joined you?"

"Me," Senator Jenkins replied from behind John. "I was the fourth member of the conspiracy."

She turned her glare toward his. "And what was your reason, Senator?"

"A strange one," he replied in an oddly calm voice. "Love."

"What?"

"Let me explain," Senator Jenkins began, his voice hollow as though he were speaking through a long tube. "I was readily accepted by Sanders because of my right-wing affiliations, but politics had nothing to do with why I joined."

"Then why?"

"Sara, you've covered political campaigns before, am I correct?"

"So?"

"So I don't have to tell you that politics is a strange game. The strangest. Like it or not, a candidate must compromise to win elections. I am the leading senator in the Republican Party. I agree with most of the party's platforms, but let's say, for example, that I came out against the death penalty. Do you know what would happen?"

Sara folded her arms across her chest. "Why don't you tell me?"

"I'd be finished. Wiped out. All my years of service would go right down the drain. I wouldn't get elected dogcatcher. Let me give you a better example: our current president's position on abortion. He used to be pro-choice. Now he has magically shifted to pro-life. Do you honestly believe he had a change of heart? Of course not. He just accepted reality. He knew that if he ran as a pro-choice candidate, he would have never won the Republican nomination. And it's not just Republicans. The Democrats do it too. Do you really believe that every liberal senator is for abortion or against tax cuts? Of course not. They are just trying to get elected. Like I said before, you have to compromise. You have to compromise your very values and beliefs. It is not necessarily the politician's fault. It's just the system. Play the game or don't get elected."

"I don't see the point in any of this," Sara said.

"I am just saying that a man cannot be so neatly labeled as right or left wing. At times we are all hypocrites. At times we all do things that others would consider sinful." He glanced at Cassandra quickly and then continued. "What I am trying to say is this: despite popular belief, I do not agree with a good many of Reverend Sanders' views."

"Then why did you join him?"

"For my son," he replied.

"You joined up with Sanders for Bradley?"

The senator nodded. His eyes were moist, but his voice did not waver. "I was just trying to save my boy. When I found out that Sanders wanted to destroy an AIDS clinic, I figured that it must be making strides in discovering a cure. So I contacted Sanders and told him I was interested in enlisting in his 'Holy Crusade' against the unnamed clinic. Sanders welcomed me aboard. Truth was, I just wanted to find out more about it so I could enroll Bradley there."

"Which you did."

"Yes. Dr. Riker and Dr. Grey promised to keep it a secret."

"So," Sara said, "you joined this crazy conspiracy to help your son, my father wanted to help the Cancer Center, and Reverend Sanders so he wouldn't have to explain a cure for 'God's Plague' to his parishioners. Does that cover it, gentlemen?"

Both men nodded.

"So where does Assistant Secretary Markey fit into all of this?"

"I can't say for sure," John began. "Markey has known Harvey for a long time. He claims he doesn't trust him. He says Harvey cuts too many corners, but I think there's more to it than that. I think Sanders is blackmailing him with something."

"And on top of that," Jenkins added, "Sanders' influence got Markey his job with the government and his office on the NIH campus. It's nice and quiet there. Markey likes it."

"A political payback?"

Her father cleared his throat. "I guess you could say that, yes."

Sara felt her head spinning. She focused on the faces in front of her. Her father and Senator Jenkins looked a mix of embarrassment, fear, and anxiety, like children waiting outside a principal's office. Cassandra remained silent, her eyes watching her sister with uncommon concern.

"Do you know what is so odd about all this?" John asked, his voice near a plea. "I think Harvey Riker and Bruce Grey would understand what I did."

Sara continued to glare. "I doubt it."

"No, Sara, I think you're missing my point. Harvey and Bruce felt the same way about their clinic as I feel about the Cancer Center. But I let it get out of hand. I let it consume me. And I was lied to. Sanders and Markey tricked me. They led me to believe that Riker and Grey were not even close to finding a cure."

Sara's voice was unforgiving. "I think we've wasted enough time listening to your self-justification, Father. Just tell us what you did."

Again John looked over to Stephen Jenkins before speaking. Then he said, "Very little."

"Very little?" Sara shouted. "You call the murder—"

"We never killed anyone," John interrupted. "At least, we never sanctioned any deaths."

Sara looked at him in disbelief. "Am I hearing you right? You never 'sanctioned' any deaths? What the hell are you talking about? Patients were murdered. The senator's own son was murdered. Are you trying to tell me that your little conspiracy had nothing to do with any of that?"

"No," John said, "we are trying to tell you that we didn't know anything about it. We learned about the murders for the first time on *NewsFlash* the other day."

"And you never knew about them beforehand?"

"That's right."

Sara shook her head. "Then tell me, Senator, what did you make of Bradley's murder?"

"The same as everyone else," Jenkins said slowly. "I thought Bradley was the random victim of some homophobic psychopath. I had no idea that his murder was connected to the Sidney Pavilion until the newscast."

John nodded his agreement. "All we did was try to pressure the people in Washington to take back the grant. We went so far as to falsify reports to make it look like the Sidney Pavilion was illegally usurping funds."

Sara almost smiled. "So while Raymond Markey accused Harvey of falsifying reports, you four were the ones who were really tampering with the evidence."

"Yes," her father said. "In many ways the *NewsFlash* report almost buried the clinic. By revealing that Bradley was a patient at the clinic, you left Harvey wide-open to charges of purposely misrepresenting the facts. Theoretically, Markey could have taken away the clinic's grant."

"So why didn't he?"

"Because we live in the real world, not a theoretical one. Can you imagine the outcry if Markey had tried to close the clinic after the show? The media would have had him for lunch. A full investigation would have ensued, and none of us wanted that—"

"So," Sara interrupted, "all of you decided to stall the clinic for a couple of years by using Michael as a guinea pig."

"It was Sanders' plan," John corrected, "and frankly speaking, it was a damn good one. Michael would be able to receive treatment, and the cure would be delayed until Sanders could think of another way of destroying them."

"Then what went wrong?" Sara asked. "Since Sanders got his way, why did he have Michael kidnapped?"

"That's just it, honey. We don't know. Markey and

Sanders both swear they have nothing to do with the Gay Slasher or Michael's kidnapping. Sanders says he's as unhappy with the development as we are."

"And you believe him?"

"I don't know what to believe. I was just in Washington, screaming at him like crazy. He continues to swear he had nothing to do with it. In fact he says that the Gay Slasher and all the publicity has actually strengthened the clinic, not hurt it."

Sara shook her head. "But don't you see? Without the cured patients, there is no proof that SR1 works. By killing the cured patients, the Gay Slasher is doing your work for you."

Neither man responded.

"Are you going to expose the conspiracy?" Sara asked.

"If only it were that simple," John replied.

"It is that simple," Sara said coldly. "All you have to do is stop worrying about yourselves."

"Sara," John continued, "I know you are angry with me. I know that a part of you even hates me right now. I would feel the same way if the situation was reversed. Believe me, I have learned my lesson. I don't care anymore about my personal reputation—you have to believe that. But if I go out now and tell the world what I have done, it could destroy the Cancer Center. Charities cannot survive scandals nowadays—you know that. You did a story on that house for teenage runaways—a fine institution destroyed by one man's indiscretions. I'm sorry, Sara. I cannot risk the Cancer Center. It's too important."

Sara just stared. "Then you are not going to do anything, are you, Father?"

"I didn't say that."

"You didn't have to." Sara grabbed her cane and stood. The silent Cassandra stood with her. "I'm going to do whatever it takes to find the truth behind this whole mess. And I don't give a shit if I have to drag down my own father, half of Washington, and the damn Cancer Center to do it."

She stormed out of the room.

JENNIFER picked up the phone on the third ring. "Hello?"

"Hello, Jen."

She recognized Harvey's voice instantly. "Hello, Harvey. How are you?"

"Been better."

"I can imagine. How is Sara holding up?"

"As well as can be expected, I guess."

"Give her my love, will you?"

"Sure. How is everything out in Los Angeles?"

"Good."

"You're doing okay?" he asked.

"Yes."

Pause.

Harvey cleared his throat. "Listen, Jen, I hate to rush you off the line—"

"I have a package from Bruce," she interrupted.

"What?"

"On the day he died," she continued slowly, "Bruce sent himself a package to his post office box at the main branch of Los Angeles' post office."

"Did you open it?"

"Yes. There were medical files in it."

"How many?"

"Six."

"Do you have them right there?"

"Yes."

"Can you read me the names?"

She picked up the files. "Krutzer, Leander, Martino, Singer, Trian, and Whitherson."

Another pause. Then a whisper: "Jesus."

"Harvey, are you all right?"

"I'm fine," he said, but his voice still sounded dazed. "Was there anything else in the package?"

"Blood samples. Two vials for each patient, labeled A and B."

Harvey thought for a moment. "Listen to me very carefully, Jen, okay? I need you to send me the entire package here by overnight mail."

"Does this have something to do with Michael's kidnapping?"

"I can't say for sure until I see the entire package. Jen, you have to send me that package right away, okay?"

"It's after six. The post office is closed."

Harvey looked at the clock, realized the hour, and cursed himself out loud.

"I tried to reach you earlier," Jennifer added.

"I know. It's my fault."

"I can send it to you special delivery first thing tomorrow morning."

"Thanks, Jen."

"Will you let me know what happens?"

"Sure." He paused. "I hope you're happy, Jen. I still care about you, you know."

"I care about you too."

Jennifer hung up the phone, afraid of what more might be said. Then she picked up the white envelope marked "Susan" and stared at it for a very long time.

20

SARA'S mind churned in confusion and anger as her fingers dialed the Eighty-third Street Precinct.

"Police department."

"Lieutenant Max Bernstein, please?"

"Yeah, hold on a sec."

Her father. Stephen Jenkins. Raymond Markey. And Ernest Sanders. An unholy alliance who had done . . .

. . . what exactly?

She could not say for sure. And what should she do now? How should she follow it up? She was not sure. She knew that she needed to do something, anything, before she lost her mind completely. Max would know. He would have a good idea what their next step should be.

Sara had considered confronting Sanders and Markey head-on, but in the end she had decided against it. If the sons of bitches had denied any wrongdoing to their own coconspirators, they were certainly not going to tell her anything new—more likely, she would either warn them of impending danger or, worse, scare them into doing something catastrophic.

The sergeant manning the desk came back on the line. "Sorry, lady," he said. "Lieutenant Bernstein is not around."

"Can you page him for me?" Sara asked. "It's important."

"No can do. He is on official police business and cannot be reached."

Cannot be reached? "Do you know where he is?"

"Can't say, ma'am. I'm not at liberty to discuss his whereabouts."

"But I need to reach him."

"That's just not possible right now. If you would like to leave a message, I am sure Lieutenant Bernstein will be calling in."

Sara scratched her head. Where could Max be that he could not be paged on his beeper? "Please ask him to call Sara Lowell immediately. Tell him it's important. If I am not at home, he can reach me at the clinic."

"At the clinic. Okay, Ms. Lowell, will do."

"Thank you." She replaced the receiver and considered her next move.

NARITA Airport.

Max gladly disembarked the Japan Airlines' Boeing 747-300 that had carried him nonstop from New York to Tokyo for the past fourteen hours, checked the departure screens, discovered that his connecting flight was leaving from a nearby gate, and walked toward it. To be fair, the flight had been comfortable; in fact, the on-board service had been second to none. It was just that being trapped in any metallic tube 30,000 feet above the earth for four-teen hours had a way of wearing on a person—even if they did show two movies and serve three meals.

As Max walked through the terminal, he glanced out the floor-to-ceiling windows and saw a dozen or so JAL Boeing 747-300s lined up by their respective gates. Each plane had a boarding tunnel running from airport to air-craft like some gigantic umbilical cord that would have to be cut before the plane could be set free.

Max was not as tired as most of his fellow passengers. Though his mind had whirled with thoughts of how to free Michael, he had managed to sleep a good six hours. He checked his watch and realized that he still had about an hour before his connecting flight took off for Bang-kok, the exotic capital of Thailand. Just as well. He had some important things to do in the meantime.

He followed the yellow sign that read "Overseas Tele-phone," conversed with the operator for a moment, then went into a small booth and lifted the receiver. Within seconds the call was connected. One ring later the phone was picked up.

"Hello?"

Sara's voice came in a nervous half shout. It was late in New York, almost two in the morning, but Sara Lowell sounded very much awake. That did not surprise him. He debated what he was going to say and decided to be as vague as humanly possible.

"Sara?"

"Max? Where the hell are you? I've been trying to reach you all day."

"I'm sorry. I've been indisposed."

"Where are you?"

"In Tokyo."

"What?"

"Well, technically speaking, I'm not in Tokyo. I'm at Narita Airport. That's about an hour and a half from downtown Tokyo—"

"I don't need a geography lesson," she interrupted. "What are you doing in Tokyo?"

Max began to wrap the phone cord around his arm. "I'm on my way to Bangkok."

A small pause. "Why?"

"Something has come up."

"Involving Michael?"

Vague, Max. Don't want to get her hopes up. "Maybe. Look, I don't know what it means. I'm just tracking down a lead."

"What kind of lead?"

"Stop playing reporter. I don't have the time. I'll call you if anything happens."

"How long will you be gone?"

A good question. "I hope to be coming home right away. Anything new?"

"A lot."

"I'm listening."

Sara recounted her conversation with her father and Senator Jenkins. Max listened in silence. He wrapped the telephone cord around his mouth now and gnawed.

Tasted rubbery. The Japanese woman in the next booth frowned at him. Max smiled apologetically and let the wire fall loose.

When Sara finished, Max told her about his conversation with Winston O'Connor.

"Now we know how they were getting all that inside information," Sara said.

"I guess so," he said. "But there is still a lot that doesn't make sense."

"Like what?"

"Like why would Sanders do it? What does Sanders gain from the murders?"

"He wipes out the evidence," Sara replied. "No cured patients, no cure."

Max shook his head. "There have to be easier ways than going through all this Gay Slasher stuff. Like your father says, the press from the Gay Slasher has strengthened the clinic. More donations, more media support— even Markey couldn't close them down anymore."

"So what do you make of it?" she asked.

He thought. He thought about the murder victims. He thought about the AIDS clinic. He thought about the Washington conspiracy and Winston O'Connor's connection to it. He thought about the Gay Slasher. He thought about George Camron holding Michael in some whorehouse. "I don't know," he said, "but I better go now. I'll call you if anything comes up."

He replaced the receiver before Sara could protest, walked into the airport pharmacy, and purchased a can of shaving cream and a disposable razor. He headed into the bathroom and wet his face. Ten minutes later his mustache was gone.

BANGKOK'S Don Muang Airport.

As Max headed down the steps and into the Thai night, the humidity hit him first—sticky, like small droplets of syrup hanging in the air. It was late now, almost eleven p.m., and Max felt revved up. He wanted to act fast.

The plane from Tokyo to Bangkok had been a carbon copy of the one he had taken from New York to Tokyo. Same size, same seating configuration, same interior design, same distortion over the loudspeaker so that he could not tell when the captain was speaking Japanese and when he was speaking English. He had been a bit surprised to see how few passengers were seated in economy class. In fact, he had counted the seats: 100 in economy class, 128 in business class, 32 in first class. The first-class area was incredible. The spacious recliners reminded Max of his father's favorite TV chair in the family den, complete with leg rests. Dom Pérignon and beluga caviar were being served. Each passenger wore a Japanese happi coat. Very nice. Of course, when you are paying approximately $5,000 for a round-trip flight from New York to Bangkok you'd better be getting very nice.

Max was traveling economy class, which cost nearly $1,500, a sum total greater than Max's entire financial portfolio. Since there had been no time to appropriate the funds from the police department, Max had gone to Lenny.

Lenny made pretty good money—very good, in fact. He was, after all, one of New York's top criminal lawyers. Ironic really. Max's mother had always wanted him to become a handsome lawyer; instead, he was living with one.

Not exactly what his mom had had in mind.

Though seated in the back of the plane, Max had wandered around during the billion hours he was in the air. He always got a kick out of the curtains pulled between the classes, turning an airplane into a microcosm of modern society. *I paid less than you, ergo I am pond scum, not fit to look at you or breathe your air.* And just for laughs, try to use the bathroom in the first-class section when you are traveling economy class. The stewardesses attack like Muslim extremists. The reading lights were another problem. How come they were never aimed right? The beam was always too far to the left or to the right or too far in front of you or too far back so that it worked like a spotlight aimed at the top of your head. And who invented that medieval torture device known as the movie headset? They felt like someone was jamming pointed ice tongs through your eardrums.

Once inside the terminal Max spotted a sign with his name on it. He approached the man holding it. The man was tall for an Asian, over six feet, and very thin. He stood perfectly still, only his eyes moving, as if he wanted to conserve his strength.

"Colonel?"

"Yes."

"I'm Max Bernstein."

The Thai colonel looked at him. "You are a police lieutenant?"

Max nodded.

"Pardon my surprise, but I was expecting someone older."

Max started to pull at his mustache. He stopped when he realized that he had shaved it off. "That's why I normally have a mustache. Makes me look older."

"Pardon me?"

"Never mind. Where can we talk?"

"Come. I have a car waiting outside."

"Where is Frank Reed?"

"Mr. Reed is waiting for us in the car. We can talk on the ride."

The colonel led the way, walking effortlessly and without any wasted motion. He opened the car door and they both got in the backseat. Like the police vehicles in New York, the air-conditioning was not working. Max wasted no time. "You're Frank Reed?"

"Yep." The man stuck out his hand. "Call me Frankie."

Max shook the hand as briefly as possible and continued. "Mr. Reed, I need you to give me an exact layout of the area where Michael Silverman is being held."

"Nothing to it. You really a New York cop?"

"Yes."

"You look like a school kid."

"I joined the force when I was four. Tell me about the upstairs area."

"Well, Silverman is being kept on the second floor," Frankie began. "There must be about a dozen rooms up there. Looks like a sleazy motel or something. He was in a room in the left-hand corner at the end of the hall. There was a 'Do Not Enter' sign on the door. I couldn't believe my fuckin' eyes. I opened the door and wham! There he was. Super-strange, you know? I saw Silverman play at the Garden last year against the Bulls. Fantastic—"

"Can you draw it for me?"

"A 'Do Not Enter' sign? Sure thing."

"No, a map of the floor."

"Oh, yeah, sure."

"And you said he was chained to the floor?"

"Looked that way," he replied. "I only got a brief look—"

"Lieutenant," Colonel Thaakavechikan interrupted, "do you have something in mind?"

Max nodded, his fingers twisting braids in his hair. "George Camron is familiar with most of your good people, correct?"

"Yes."

"I don't think he is familiar with me. Just in case, I shaved off my mustache on the plane."

"I see."

"I want to go in myself."

"When?"

"As soon as Camron leaves the bar. Michael is very ill. We have to get him out right away."

The colonel nodded. "Tell me what you have in mind."

DR. Eric Blake checked his appearance in the mirror. As always, everything was in place. When people were asked to describe him, they rarely used terms like *handsome* or *ugly* or even *nondescript*. They usually said *neat*.

Tidy. Immaculate. Every hair in place, shoelaces tied, every button buttoned. Eric's shirttail never hung out, his socks always matched, his face was always clean-shaven. Even now Eric looked cool, unemotional, detached. But inside, under the fastidious grooming—well, that was another matter.

His head ached horribly. The pressure mounted until he was sure something was going to burst through his forehead. Suddenly, everything was falling apart and Eric was not sure what to do.

Do whatever is necessary . . .

He walked purposefully toward the lab room. Harvey, he knew, was downstairs, injecting Kiel Davis with SR1. Then Harv had rounds. He would not be on the third floor for some time now.

It was safe.

Eric crossed the room and unlocked his private file. Once again he slipped open the bottom drawer and withdrew the blood samples. He carefully lifted them free and placed them on the table. Then he examined them.

Nothing yet.

He sighed. Well, that was to be expected. The results would not be in for a little while yet. Thinking he could see something now had been little more than wishful thinking on his part. He would just have to be patient.

With not-so-steady hands, Eric returned the samples to the drawer, locked it, and went back to work.

MAX and Colonel T (as he liked to be called) sat in a taxi on Rama IV Road not too far from Patpong. Through the static of the car radio, a voice blurted out something unintelligible to Max. Colonel T picked up the receiver and blurted back something equally unintelligible.

"Camron has left the bar," the colonel explained. "He hired one of our *tuk-tuk*s."

"*Tuk-tuk*s?"

"Think of it as a taxi."

Max nodded. "Then I guess it's showtime."

"I will set up *tuk-tuk*s wherever he is dropped off. We will try to stall him if he returns before you have a chance to free Mr. Silverman, but there is no guarantee."

"I understand."

"You will signal us if the room has an explosive device?"

"I'll raise and lower the shade," Max said. "If I give you the signal, don't try to stop him. He might blow the place sky-high."

The colonel nodded. "And you have the layout memorized?"

"Yes."

"Then good luck."

"Thanks." Knots began to form in Max's stomach. "One last question."

"Yes?"

"How do I go about hiring a prostitute?"

The colonel smiled. "Sit at the bar and hold up a ten-dollar bill, Lieutenant. The rest will take care of itself."

SARA woke up late. For a brief moment she blindly reached out for Michael and clawed at the pillow before she remembered that he would not be there. Then she withdrew her hand and began to get ready to visit Harvey.

An hour later she knocked lightly on the door to Harvey's office and peeked in. "Can I come in?"

He looked up from his desk. He smiled at her in a tired way and took off his reading glasses. "Of course."

"I don't want to interrupt."

"No," he said, "you're not interrupting. I need a break anyway."

"When was the last time you got some sleep?" she asked.

"Oh, let's see. What year is it?"

"You look awful."

He nodded, still smiling. "I've seen you look better too."

She limped toward the wooden chair in front of his desk and sat down. Her eyes were immediately drawn to the poster of Michael that Harvey had plastered on the wall behind him. Seeing his image soaring to the basket was oddly comforting. She adjusted her spectacles and stared for a few more moments, watching him glide in midair, seeing the mask of concentration that covered his face. Then she said, "I have something to tell you. Something involving my father and Reverend Sanders."

He leaned back in his chair. "Oh?"

"You are not going to like it."

"When something involves your father and Sanders, I rarely do. What is it, Sara?"

She told him everything. Harvey's mouth remained still while she spoke but his body language was another matter. It altered completely. His fists slowly closed and then tightened to the point where the knuckles turned white. His face grew scarlet, his features twisting in smoldering anger.

"Sons of bitches!" Harvey shouted at long last. "Those ignorant, bigoted bastards!"

Sara said nothing.

Harvey stood up, his rage mounting with each passing second. "How could I have been so stupid? I knew it and I didn't do a goddamn thing. Of course Markey was working for them, the callous son of a bitch." He shook his head. "Sanders and Jenkins, I expected it from—but your father, Sara—he calls himself a man of medicine. A healer. Yet he joined forces with them. What kind of man is he?"

Her voice was soft. "I don't know."

"They're going to pay. The world is going to know what they did." His shoulders slumped, and the tired aura surrounded him again. "It's a constant battle, Sara. It never ends. Bigots, homophobes, naive people. AIDS has so many strikes against it, I sometimes wonder if we will ever be able to rid the world of it."

He moved back to his chair and sat down heavily. He spun the chair one hundred eighty degrees and stared at the photograph of his brother. "Do you remember when the AIDS scare first began?" he asked.

"Yes."

"There was talk of locking the carriers in concentration camps, remember? There was even talk of quarantining all known homosexuals. Nazi tactics, Sara. That's what it started with. You don't hear much talk about that now, but in a way the threat to gays is greater now than ever."

"What makes you say that?"

"Guys like Jerry Falwell and Ernest Sanders have become more subtle now. They have the same bigoted aim, but they take a different approach. And it works. People fall for it. We are bombarded by arguments that say AIDS will never become an epidemic in the heterosexual community. Respected doctors like your father say it every day. But the larger question is not the severity with which AIDS will strike the heterosexual community, but why we feel it is necessary to argue the point so vehemently."

"I don't understand."

Harvey's voice was both passionate and pained. "Okay, let's assume for a moment it is true. It's not. But for the sake of argument, let's assume your father is right and that AIDS will be a true epidemic only amongst homosexuals and intravenous drug abusers. So what? If your father and his cohorts are not being discriminatory, as they claim, why should it matter what segment of the population is being killed by the virus? If we found out that AIDS was only killing little girls between the ages of five and twelve, would someone dare come out and say, 'Don't worry. It won't affect you'? Of course not. Homophobia fuels these people, Sara. It's a battle we constantly wage. The tune has changed but the song is still the same."

"So what do we do?"

"We scrape and claw and battle back. We do everything we can to fight them. We go to the media and destroy them."

"But it might make them panic. If they are holding Michael . . ."

He nodded, stepped back. "I see what you are saying. Have you told Lieutenant Bernstein?"

"Yes."

"What did he say?"

"Not to do anything until he gets back."

"Where is he?"

"In Bangkok."

"What is he doing there?"

"He said he might have a lead on something."

"Christ, I hope so. We could use a break." Harvey leaned forward. "So what are we supposed to do in the meantime? Sit around and let the murderers stay free?"

"Max isn't so sure that Sanders is behind the murders or the kidnapping."

"Then who?"

"He doesn't know. He just said he has his doubts."

"And what about you, Sara? Do you have your doubts?"

"I guess I do."

"Well, it makes sense to me," Harvey said. "Sanders kidnapped Michael to stall the clinic, plain and simple. Markey knew that I was the only person who had worked on Michael—"

"And Eric."

Confusion crossed Harvey's face for a brief moment. "No, Sara. I mean, as far as having physical contact with the patient. I gave Michael all his SR1 injections. I always drew his blood. I—"

"Eric took his blood too."

Harvey stopped. "When?"

"I don't know. A day or two before he was kidnapped."

"Are you sure?"

"Of course. I was right there. Is that a problem?"

He shook his head. "It's just weird," he said slowly. "I left strict instructions for no one to do any lab work or give any medication to Michael except me."

"Maybe he didn't see them," Sara said. "Or maybe he forgot."

"Maybe," Harvey agreed, but he did not sound convinced.

"Why don't you ask him?"

"I will," he said, "as soon as he gets back." Harvey looked up and tried to smile reassuringly. He failed. "Don't look at me like that, Sara. I'm sure it's nothing."

"HEY, Joe, you want live sex show? Pea shooting contest, huh? Sound good, Joe? Pea shooting contest?"

"Pea shooting contest?" Max repeated.

"Yeah, sure, Joe. You like pea shooting contest. She aim straw and bust balloon. Guess what she blows with. Huh, Joe?"

Max, no stranger to quirky sexual situations, was not sure he understood what the Thai teenager was talking about. He also wasn't sure he wanted to know. Years ago, before he had met Lenny, Max and a couple of friends spent a week in Amsterdam's red-light district. They had seen a show where a woman projected various objects across a room using a certain part of her anatomy. Admittedly, most people would consider Max's sexual orientation bizarre, but he failed to see the show's eroticism no matter which particular sexual persuasion you happened to follow. More like watching an amazing pet trick or a strange magic show.

"What you say, Joe? You want nice woman. Make your head spin all the way around."

An interesting image. "Which head?"

"Huh, Joe?"

"Never mind. No, thanks."

He forced his way through the clusters of sex merchants, keeping his eye on the pink neon sign that read "Eager Beaver." Two men stood at the door. The smaller man greeted Max with a wide smile and a firm handshake; the larger greeted him with a menacing glare. Mutt and Jeff.

"Welcome," the little one shouted above the loud disco music. "Please come in. You find everything you want here. No cover charge."

"Thanks."

Max ducked past the sumo-sized doorman and entered the Eager Beaver. The interior decorator must have worked on the original *Dating Game*. Very sixties. Very go-go-bar-like. *Mod Squad* decor. Psychedelic, multicolored lights.

The music was strictly *Saturday Night Fever*. The singer screamed about a burning, burning disco inferno. Despite the fast beat, the topless women (a string bikini bottom made them topless rather than fully naked) danced slowly on the bar, the same steps over and over again. Max stared at their faces, but none looked back. Each wore a bored expression—dead, unseeing eyes that lit up only when money was jammed into their crotches.

Michael is in here somewhere . . .

"Swing it, baby!" a man yelled.

The girl smiled and obliged. She got 100 Thai baht (four dollars) for her trouble. She lowered herself toward the man, enticing him to add to her booty, but he waved her off.

The crowd was a mix. Hard-core hard-ups. Curious tourists. Married couples. Thais, Japanese, Americans, Italians, Germans, Australians—a horny United Nations. In a corner, people cheered a sexual act that defied both belief and biological realities. Ripley's, Max thought. Or even Guinness. Two naked women were on their hands and knees, one Asian, one black. They were—Jesus, he couldn't believe it—shooting bananas across the room with their vaginas. Bananas, for chrissake. A man marked the spot where they landed, measuring the distance traveled like he was working the discus toss at the Olympics. Another man kept loading their vaginas with bananas, as though the two women were human grenade launchers. Banana after banana rocketed across the room to the roar of the crowd.

Max turned away.

Michael is close by . . .

He sat at the bar in a seat that spun all the way around. Max liked it and began to twirl himself like a kid at a diner. Nearly two seconds passed before a Thai girl approached him, dressed in Classical American Hooker Drag. Tank top with satin shorts that not only rode up the crotch but actually dug a deeper crevice. The whores varied in age, but this one looked like she had just gotten a hold of Mommy's makeup case.

"Hi," she said.

She was no more than fifteen and had smooth, beautiful skin. Her looks were startling fresh and engaging, in the baby-doll mode so many men found attractive.

"Hi."

Her smile was wide, bright, and somehow cunning. "You buy me drink?"

"Why not? What would you like?"

"What you having?"

"Vodka on the rocks."

"I have same, please."

Max signaled the bartender and gave him the order. The bill came to twelve dollars—five dollars for his drink, seven for the girl's. Before Max could protest, the bartender pointed to the sign. "Beer—$3 Liquor—$5 Hostess Drinks—$7."

Hostess?

"What your name?" she asked.

"Max."

"Nice name. You live in America, Max?"

He began to twist his hair around his finger. "Yes."

"Nice place, no?"

"I like it."

"How come you always moving, Max?"

"We call it fidgeting."

"How come you always fidgeting, Max?"

"Don't know."

"You in Bangkok on business or pleasure?"

Max tried to smile, tried to get into the role of adventurous womanizer. It wasn't him. "A little of both, if you get my meaning." He winked pitifully.

Jesus.

Her tiny hand found its way to his leg. "You like me, Max?" She licked the air as though it were an ice-cream cone and leaned forward. Her eyes burrowed into his until he had to turn away.

"Very much."

"How much pleasure you want, Max?"

"A hundred dollars' worth," he said, "to start."

She nodded. "What you like?"

Max cleared his throat. "The Kink Room."

She froze. "You been here before, Max?"

"No. A friend told me about it."

She nodded again, more professional now. "Kink Room expensive."

"I can pay."

Yet another nod. Her hand was about a millimeter away from his groin now. Her very long, red-painted fingernails skimmed the surface of his pants with a feathery stroke. Surprisingly, something close to arousal crept in. Her touch was soothing, relaxing. It felt frighteningly good—sort of strange for a man who usually got excited by male bodybuilders. Not that Max had never been with women. He had. He just preferred men, that's all.

She moved her hand away. "Pay man over there, Max, and then we go upstairs. We have much fun together. I tear you whole world apart."

He nodded, wondering if that was better than having his head spin all the way around. Tough choice.

He bit down on a little piece of skin hanging off his
fingertip and did as he was instructed. The young pimp
looked like a welterweight contender—small, muscular,
without an ounce of body fat.

"How kinky you want it?"

"Very."

"You sure you want Kink Room?" the pimp asked.
"Very expensive. Very dangerous."

"I'm sure. How much?"

"Two hundred dollars for entrance. But if you want to
use red wall, extra. Much extra. You let me know, okay?"

The red wall?

After a few moments of negotiating, they settled on a
price tag of $175.

Max paid the money. Immediately, the Thai girl appeared at his side and led him up the stairs, whispering
the usual whore expressions about what fun they were
going to have and what a hunk he was.

"What is your name?" he interrupted her.

"Bambi."

A traditional Thai name.

"How old are you?"

"Old enough."

"For what?"

Again, the ice-cream-cone lick. "To make you happy."

"Why do you do this, Bambi?"

"Do what?"

The oppressive heat was even worse here than downstairs. They were in the darkened hallway now, the
painting chipped, the lighting nearly nonexistent. Max
shuddered as they passed the door in the corner with a

"Do Not Enter" sign stapled to it. He managed not to hesitate. "Prostitute yourself."

She looked at him. "Why?"

"Just asking. You seem like an intelligent—"

For a brief moment the smile disappeared and he could see the naked hatred underneath it. "You going to take me away from all this, Max?" A touch of scorn had slipped into her voice. But then the moment was over. Like a candle that had flickered, the smile came back and seemed to brighten. "Come," she said. "I will be your fantasy. Then you go home happy, okay?"

She opened the door. The first thing that hit him was the odor. Some sort of cherry room freshener had been sprayed in heavy doses, trying to conceal the still unmistakably foul smell of . . . of sleaze. Sleaze permeated every part of the room, as if the very acts had nestled into the walls like thousands of tiny cockroaches, rotting the foundations. Max shivered.

Where did his unease come from? he wondered. He had been in bathhouses, even heavy-duty mass orgies, and yet something about this room intimidated him. There was just something so . . . so blatantly dehumanizing about it.

As far as the physical layout, well, suffice to say that room was aptly named the Kink Room. On one wall hung dildos, lots of them, of shapes and sizes that boggled the imagination. Some were barely phallic. Whips, chains, handcuffs, ropes, straitjackets, leather masks, bondage and submission devices of all sorts covered shelves on his left. And then straight ahead, on a red-colored wall . . . He walked over to get a closer look.

"Jesus."

The red wall.

He spun back toward Bambi, who was huddled in a corner now. The smile was still there, but her eyes had suddenly filled with pure terror. "Red wall extra, Max." Pause. "You want?"

He looked again, not believing what he was seeing. A stun gun. A goddamn police stun gun. Enough volts of electricity to make a body spasm like an epileptic's during a seizure. "People use this on you?" he asked.

She did not respond for a few seconds, only smiling. "Not on me. Other girls."

He put the stun gun back and picked up a . . . Jesus Christ . . . an electric cattle prod. Kinky was one thing, but this went beyond simple sadism. He had heard about such things, men who enjoyed zapping nipples or even a clitoris, but his mind had dismissed it as mind-boggling fiction.

"Sometimes," Bambi said, "they want me to use."

"Huh?"

"On them," she continued.

Max looked at the prod and tried to imagine it pressed against his balls and prick. His muscles stiffened and something flipped over in his stomach. He continued to look at the shelves in disbelief. Nipple clamps. Sharp, pointed studs. Torture devices that looked like something from the Middle Ages. Nausea swept over him.

The Kink Room? Chamber of Horrors is more like it.

"What you want, Max?"

"I want to tie you up."

"You going to use . . . the red wall?"

"No."

Her relief was palpable. She started to undress, but Max stopped her. "Don't strip."

"You don't want me naked?"

He shook his head. "Lie on the bed," he said, trying to make it sound like a lustful command.

The girl eyed him strangely but obeyed. Max knew plenty about knots and tying people up. He bound her arms and legs three different ways, making sure they were secure but not cutting into her flesh. There was no reason to hurt her.

"Open your mouth," he said.

The young prostitute did as he asked. She was surprised when he stuffed only a cloth into her mouth. He wrapped a rope around her mouth and the back of her head repeatedly, effectively gagging her.

"Can you breathe okay?" he asked.

She nodded.

He wanted to leave with some words of everlasting kindness and wisdom, but he knew it would sound hollow. Instead, he leaned forward and gently kissed her forehead.

"Good-bye."

He stepped back toward the door. Bambi's eyes followed him. He opened the door slightly and glimpsed through the crack. The corridor was empty. He slipped out and headed toward the room where Frank Reed said Michael was being held. When he reached Michael's door, he grabbed hold of the knob. He turned it and pushed hard.

The door gave way and Max entered.

*   *   *

GEORGE held the phone close to his ear. "Then I'm going to kill Michael Silverman right now," he said.

"Wait!" the voice cried. "I am paying you to destroy the Bangkok supply building and—"

"And I'll do that," George interrupted, "but first Silverman must die. He is a loose end now, and I cannot let him go. He knows too much."

"Now, just a second. I made it clear—"

George hung up the phone. The sampan coasted through the still waters of the Chao Phraya River, but George did not really feel its calming effects. For the first time since the Gay Slasher killings, George was seriously worried. His employer was unraveling and worse, holding out on him. To want him to close up shop all of a sudden, to destroy the clinic's storage house and to return Michael Silverman made no sense unless . . .

. . . unless something had gone wrong. Very wrong.

Had he, George Camron, made a mistake?

Impossible.

"Thank you, Surakarn. I appreciate your service."

"Not at all, old friend."

George rolled out of the boat and back to dry land. In front of him the silhouette of the Grand Palace sat in monumental silence. George moved toward the *tuk-tuk*s.

"Need ride, sir?" the bald driver asked him.

George strolled toward the driver and suddenly veered in the other direction. Better safe than sorry. He jogged a few long blocks, hailed a taxi on Lak Muang Street and climbed in the backseat.

"Patpong."

The taxi driver nodded and started off.

Back by the *tuk-tuk*s the bald driver picked up a radio. "Colonel?"

"Go ahead."

"George Camron bypassed us and took a taxi. He could be there in a matter of minutes."

The colonel put down the radio microphone and waited for Bernstein's signal.

MICHAEL looked up through bleary eyes. "Max?"

Max signaled Michael to keep quiet while his eyes traveled about the room, probing, searching.

"Did Camron mention anything about an explosive?" he asked.

Michael's voice was weak, barely audible. "Behind you. Ceiling."

Max turned, looked up, and saw the sticks of dynamite tied together. "Damn," he said out loud.

His hand opened and closed the window shade, signaling the colonel and his men to stay away. "We have to get you out of here."

Michael tried to focus on Max's face, but his eyes would not obey him. Sweat pasted his hair against his forehead. His lower lip quivered as though from a fever.

"It's okay, Michael. You're as good as home."

"Home."

Max stood on a chair and examined the explosives. Then he jumped off and knelt in front of Michael. From the inside of his boot Max pulled out a long-toothed hacksaw and began to work on the chain around Michael's ankle. The steel was thick and strong, making progress dangerously slow. The heat in the room was sweltering, like a sauna on overdrive. Max had trouble breathing.

"You been in here this whole time?"

Michael nodded.

Max continued to saw away. One floor below him George Camron entered the Eager Beaver.

COLONEL T saw two things at almost the exact same time. He saw Lieutenant Bernstein's signal telling him that there was indeed an explosive device in Michael Silverman's room, and he saw George pay the taxi driver.

"Shall we detain him, Colonel?"

"You saw the lieutenant's signal. It is too risky."

"Then what shall we do?"

"Do?" the colonel repeated.

"We are waiting for your orders."

But the colonel knew there was nothing he could do. If they tried to stop him, George Camron might blow up the building. Lieutenant Bernstein was on his own. All the colonel and his men could do was watch helplessly while George disappeared into the Eager Beaver.

MICHAEL had never known such complete exhaustion. It was as if some sci-fi villain had drained all his life energy, leaving behind nothing but an empty carcass. His limbs were like blocks of lead, impossible to move. The pain that had engulfed his nose was gone now, replaced by a tingling numbness that was equally uncomfortable. The swelling had clogged his nasal passages, each drawn breath like inhaling flames.

George had fed him only a chunk of bread once a day. He had given him a bit more water, enough to prevent complete dehydration. The ceiling seemed lower now, the walls closer together. Delirium had begun to settle in. Michael wanted very much to scream, to scream until everything snapped and he could scream no more.

And then Max opened the door.

At first Michael had been sure it was an hallucination. Even now the room's dreamlike quality remained fixed. Strange sounds seemed to come from inside Michael's head—Max's saw munching through the chain, the bomb going tick, tick, tick, though he knew that the ticking was only in his head. No timer on the bomb. Still, tick, tick, tick, tick . . .

Ka-boom.

"Max?"

"Almost got it, Michael. Hang in there."

"Sara."

"She's fine."

"Our child."

"Safe in the womb. You'll be with her soon."

Michael tried again to focus on Max's face. Skinny face. Long nose. Clean-shaven. "No mustache."

A tight smile from Max. "I shaved it. Almost there, Michael. Almost . . ."

"Almost," Michael repeated.

"Got it!" The chain fell apart. "Michael, can you walk?"

"Sure."

Michael made it to his knees before his head began to spin like a plane taking a nosedive.

"Lean on my shoulder," Max urged. "We have to hurry."

With a lot of help from Max, Michael managed to stand. His legs were wobbly, but he was able to take a step forward.

"That's it. You're as good as home."

Michael nodded.

Max moved another step. He stopped suddenly when he felt something cold touch his neck. He looked down.

A stiletto blade rested against his throat.

Before Max could react, a giant biceps wrapped itself around his forehead. The arm gripped his skull and pressed it against a chest as solid as asphalt. Max could not move. George adjusted the blade. The sharp point now touched down on the voice box, nearly piercing the skin.

"Hello, boys!" George said. "How's it going?"

21

DR. Eric Blake looked up at the clock.

It was time.

Something nestled in Eric's throat, but he managed to swallow it away. He straightened the papers on his desk, lined up the pencils neatly, and stood. He checked his appearance in the mirror, tightened the Windsor knot in his tie, and gently patted his hair with both hands. Then he studied his face for a long time. Something about it was different today. It was as if his thoughts had surfaced, altering his appearance.

Everything I have worked for, everything I wanted to achieve . . .

Could it all be gone?

He took out a neatly folded handkerchief, dabbed his forehead, and then headed for the lab.

"Good morning, Dr. Blake."

"Good morning."

Eric tried to remember the nurse's name but could not. He recalled that she was the youngest and least experienced member of the staff. Her access to patients was strictly limited to the most recent arrivals, and her chores were usually the most mundane. Only one nurse had had access to all the patients and all the floors.

Janice Matley.

As quickly as the name had formed in his mind, Eric pushed it away. No use thinking about that now. Dead was dead. No comeback. No reprieve.

Nothing.

Eric entered the elevator and pushed the button. His eyes swerved about, trying to find something that might distract him. He settled on the signature of the elevator inspector. He tried to make out the name but the penmanship was too sloppy—looked more like an EKG reading than an actual signature. The inspector, Eric decided, should have been a doctor.

A minute later he arrived at the lab door. Part of him wanted to stall now that the moment had arrived, but the rest of his body propelled him into the room and over toward his file cabinet. He took out his key, unlocked the drawers, opened one, and reached back. His hand gripped the item. He took a deep breath, pulled it out and looked.

Silence.

Eric's face registered no emotion. He returned the glass dish to the back of the drawer and carefully closed it. He locked the cabinet, picked up the telephone and dialed a number in Bethesda, Maryland. After three rings, the phone on the other end was picked up.

Eric cleared his throat. "Dr. Raymond Markey, please."

I fucked up. Me. George Camron . . .

He could not believe it and yet he was holding the evidence against his chest. They had found Silverman. Shit, they had found him. Not even George's employer knew where he had hidden Silverman.

George held the point of the blade in place. When the man swallowed, George felt the stiletto vibrate in his hand. His mind raced for answers, but none came to him. He had fucked up. Badly. But how? When?

Get control of yourself, George. Show you're still in control.

Listening to the voice in his head, George forced himself to smile. It gave the appearance, he was sure, of being in complete control.

"So, gentlemen," he began, both his grip and grin strong and steady, "how are we today? Lovely weather, don't you think?"

Max managed a shrug. "Tad warm for my taste, George."

The man knew his name!

"Sorry about that," George replied. He wrestled with his tone in order to keep out any hint of panic. A droplet of sweat trickled down his neck and into the collar of his shirt. "Mind identifying yourself before I slice your goddamn head off?"

"Lieutenant Max Bernstein. NYPD. You are under arrest for the—"

"Spare me, Lieutenant." A cop! He looked like some goddamn college kid. George could not believe it. They had sent a snot-nosed kid after George Camron. Incredible.

"I have to read you your rights," Max continued.

"Try to move, and you're dead." With the point of the blade still against Max's throat, George released his powerful grip and reached into his pocket. He took out something resembling a small television remote. He held it in front of Max's face.

"Do you know what this is?" George asked.

Max looked at the device. "Are we going to watch TV?"

"You're very funny, Lieutenant," George said, but he did not like Bernstein's attitude. Here he was, holding a knife against the kid's throat, and this asshole was making jokes.

He knows something, George. You missed something else . . .

"This button right here"—George placed his thumb on it for emphasis—"sets off that little explosive up there. Very noisy stuff, I'm afraid. Ka-boom."

That seemed to shake up the cop. He suddenly looked pale. "Explosive?"

George gestured with the remote. "Right up there, my friend."

Max's eyes followed the gesture. "Jesus."

George was feeling better now. *Not so confident now, are you, kid?* "Yes. Powerful stuff. Bits and pieces of us will end up in Singapore. If I see even a hint of trouble, it's ka-boom time."

Max's eyes darted in every direction as if searching for a quick exit. "Forget it, Camron," the young cop said, but his tone no longer held the same bluster as before. "It's over. The place is surrounded."

"Guess I have no choice," George said with fake regret. "Looks like I'll have to blow the place up."

"You'd kill yourself too."

"No big deal."

"Wait!" Max shouted. When he did, the point of the blade broke the skin. A small cut opened up. Blood began to trickle down Max's neck.

"What?" George asked.

Max closed his eyes. He did not like bloodletting, especially his own. "I have an idea," he said.

"Oh?"

"An exchange, actually."

"What kind of exchange?"

Max thought a moment. "Information for freedom. I'll have the charges dropped in exchange for your testimony against the guy who hired you."

Panic again seized George. He knew almost nothing about his employer—no name, no address, nothing. Damn it! He knew he should have investigated this new employer more thoroughly. Why had he failed to follow his standard background check? Stupid! And another goddamn mistake.

What the hell was wrong with him?

He could fake it, of course. Stall. Make up a name. Lie. But George was realistic. There was no way the

Thais were going to let him walk—not after an incident like this. The Thais were not like the Americans. They did not work that way.

"No dice," George answered slowly. Like a well-trained surgeon, George scraped at Max's wound with the point of the blade. More blood flowed. A plan—a brilliant, surefire plan—began to take shape in his mind. His smile returned, radiant. "But I have another idea," George ventured.

"Yes."

"I am going to walk out of here. In exchange, I guarantee that no one will get hurt."

Max shook his head. "The place is surrounded—"

"Don't worry about that," George interjected. "I have a way out. You are going to wait five minutes. If you leave this room before then, I'll detonate the bomb. After five minutes you are free to go."

"Max," Michael interrupted. It was the first time he had spoken since George had entered the room. "Don't listen to him. He's lying."

Max nodded, but he seemed unsure. "How can we trust you?"

"You have my word," George said.

"Max—"

"Then it's a deal," Max said, "under one condition."

"Max, listen to me. You can't—"

"You have a better idea, Michael? He's got a blade on my throat."

Michael just stared at him. "You can't trust him."

"What choice do we have? Huh?"

George liked what he was hearing. "We are wasting time. What is your condition?"

"You give us some information before you leave."

"No."

"Then no deal," Max said.

"I am the one holding the stiletto and the detonator—"

"No deal unless you talk. I just want information, George. I'm not interested in capturing you."

George considered his options. His employer had, after all, screwed things totally. George no longer owed him any loyalty. Why not talk? The cop would be less likely to try anything if he had information he thought was useful.

Besides, Lieutenant Max Bernstein was not going to live long. Neither was Michael Silverman.

"Ask your question."

"Who hired you?"

"I don't know. I got anonymous calls."

"What was the purpose of the murders?"

"Purpose?"

"Why did you target people at an AIDS clinic?"

"I don't know that either."

"Come on, George, you're going to have to do better than that."

"I kill for hire," George explained. "The less I know, the better."

"You must have heard something."

"Nothing."

"Then why did you make the murders look like the work of a serial killer?"

"Those were my instructions," George said. "I was told to slash them all up in an unmistakably similar fashion—make it as bloody as possible."

"Why did you dump Bradley Jenkins behind a gay bar?"

George shrugged. "I just did what I was told." As George spoke, his plan crystallized. As soon as he hit the street, he would set off the explosives, killing Silverman and the cop while providing him with the ideal diversion for his escape. "That's what I get paid for, Lieutenant—even if the payments did come a little late. I thought I was being stiffed until yesterday—"

"Did you kill Dr. Bruce Grey and make it look like a suicide?"

"Yes."

"Why?"

"Orders."

"Were all the other victims mutilated?" Max asked.

"Yes."

"Stabbed repeatedly?"

"Yes."

"None killed any other way?"

George sighed impatiently. "All were stabbed except Dr. Grey."

"And Riccardo Martino?"

"Never heard of him."

For the first time since the questioning began, Max paused. Then: "Why was Michael kidnapped?"

George rolled his eyes. "How the hell am I supposed to know? I got a call in the morning telling me to nab Michael Silverman before the day was over. That's what I did. I paid off a friend in customs, loaded him on a cargo jet, and we flew over here. I do not like to repeat myself, Lieutenant, so I will say this for the last time—I do not know, nor do I care, why my employer ordered any of these jobs."

"What were your last orders?"

"Blow up a building and let Michael go."

"What building?"

"A storage house."

It was Michael who spoke. "The clinic's storage house," he said. "All Harv's lab work would have been destroyed."

"I am leaving now," George said, "but before I do, let me remind you that I have my thumb resting on a detonator. If you try any heroics, I'll push the button. If you plan on having a sniper take me out, he better make sure I die instantly. Otherwise my thumb presses down. Do you understand?"

Max nodded.

"Good. I'm going to let you go now. Don't move for five minutes."

George shoved Max across the room. Max stumbled and fell. He turned around, still on his knees.

"One last question," Max said.

"No more questions, Lieutenant. Good-bye. And re-member"—he held up the detonator—"ka-boom."

"Just one more."

George stepped toward the door. "Good-bye."

Max reached into his boot and took out his gun. It was the first time he had ever done that in the line of duty and he was surprised at how smooth his movements had been. "Would you please put your hands up?"

George looked amused. "Are you joking, Lieutenant?"

"Put your hands above your head now."

George laughed. "Go ahead. Fire. I'll blow this whole fucking block to kingdom come."

"No, you won't."

"And why not?"

Max smiled. "Because you fucked up, George. Again."

George's smile disappeared. "What are you talking about?"

"I disconnected the explosives before you got here."

George's mouth dropped open.

"You do terribly crude work, George. No trip wire, no nothing. Any idiot could have disengaged it in two seconds. Very sloppy work."

George shook his head. "The Thais would have busted in if that were true."

"The Thais think the explosives are still intact," Max said. "I wanted them to."

"Why?"

"If they stormed us," Max continued, "somebody might have gotten killed. And you were the most likely candidate. I needed your information first."

"You're lying."

"Then go ahead. Push the button. As soon as you do I have my reason to waste you. Either way you are a dead man." Max steadied his aim. "So go ahead. You already told me everything you know. You're worthless to me now. Push the button."

It's over. I fucked up. I really fucked up . . .

George's mind flailed wildly, grasping for any rescue

float. "If I surrender," he began tentatively, "will I be extradited to the United States?"

"Yes."

Maybe I can still swing a deal. The Americans will want someone to testify against my employer. I still have valuable information. Wouldn't be the first time they let the hit man go to catch the big fish . . .

"Okay, then," George said, "here." He held out the detonator.

"That's worthless now, George. Take out your knife and put it on the ground. Then put your hands above your head."

Max opened the window shade. Within seconds the cops were in the room. They cuffed George and dragged him downstairs. Max immediately ran for the detonator. He picked it up gently as if it were made of expensive crystal.

"Max?" Michael called.

"Yeah."

"You don't know anything about explosives, do you?"

Max did not look up. "Not a damn thing."

22

HARVEY watched yet another sunrise from the window at the clinic. He had managed to catch a few hours of sleep on the couch last night and had woken up with a major Excedrin headache. Why, he could not say. Anxiety probably. Patience, a requirement in his field, had never been one of his virtues. And now the stakes had been raised astronomically. Something was going to happen today; he was sure of it. Something big.

Something in Bruce's package.

It would be only a matter of time before it arrived. He tried to temper his excitement and unease. The package, he continuously reminded himself, could be nothing important. Bruce might have mailed himself those files for a variety of reasons. For example, he might have wanted to . . .

Harvey thought hard, but nothing unimportant came to mind.

He massaged his temples and tried to relax, but something else kept nudging at him, something that could be even more critical than the package. He did not want to think about it, did not want even to consider the possibility. And yet the facts were clear. Eric Blake had taken a blood sample from Michael's arm when he had specifically been told to keep away. Why did he do it? Eric had always been big on protocol and following the rules. Why had he gone against their common practices to take Michael's blood?

Frightening questions. Might be even more frightening answers.

Harvey looked at his watch. Eric was supposed to arrive soon. He would confront him then.

The intercom sounded. "Package for you, Dr. Riker."

"Send it in."

A UPS driver entered the room. With a trembling hand Harvey signed for the package, locked the door behind the driver, and carried it to his desk. He could feel something flutter in his heart. His breath grew shallow.

Harvey opened the package and began to examine its contents.

"TIRED?" Max asked.

Michael looked up from his cot. Only a few hours ago he had been George Camron's prisoner. Now he, Max, and a Thai doctor shared the closed-off back section of a Thai Airways jet that was somewhere over the Pacific.

"More like anxious."

"Don't blame you." Max put the pencil in his mouth

and began to gnaw. "But in a way, it's better Sara wasn't home. This isn't the kind of thing you want to tell someone over a phone."

Michael managed to sit up. "That was a hell of a bluff you made back there."

"What choice did I have?" Max said. "If I let Camron go, he would have blown us up."

"I know, but still—"

"Besides, I didn't do that much. I just made the decision to live or die his own."

"What do you mean?"

"George never thought I'd risk pulling a gun on him," he explained. "He counted on that fact. Once I did, he had no choice. If he pushed the button, he was dead— either by the explosives or by my gun. George Camron did not want to die. It's as simple as that."

Michael nodded. "How's your neck feel?"

Max touched the bandage on his throat. "Just a flesh wound," he said. "Kinda gross, though."

"Can you fill me in on what's happened?" Michael asked.

"I can try."

"Why was I kidnapped?"

Max paced the tight aisle. He recounted all he knew about the Gay Slasher case. Michael's eyes never left him. His face registered no emotion, even when he heard about his father-in-law's involvement with the Washington conspiracy.

"So who do you think is behind all this?" Michael asked.

"I'm not sure."

"What about Sanders' group? They seem the most likely suspects."

Max tilted his head back and forth like a pendulum swing. "Yes and no," he said. "I don't think it's the conspiracy, per se, or Reverend Sanders. If Sanders was willing to commit murder to destroy the clinic, there would have been no reason for all this fancy footwork—just murder a few doctors or blow up the clinic."

"What do you mean 'conspiracy per se'?"

"Well, it could be one of them—Markey, Jenkins, your father-in-law—acting on his own."

"What motive would they have?"

"Don't know."

"You said something before about the order of the murders?"

Max nodded. "It probably means nothing, but I keep focusing on that point. There were six cured patients." He took out a piece of paper and began to scribble:

> Trian, S.
> Whitherson, W.
> Martino, R.
> Krutzer, T.
> Leander, P.
> Singer, A.

"What about Bradley Jenkins?" Michael asked.

"He was never cured, so let's leave him out of this for a second." Max pointed to the list of names. "This is the order in which they became patients. Trian, Whitherson, and Martino—the Gay Slasher's victims—all came in between a year and a year and a half before Krutzer, Leander, and Singer. Whitherson was actually the first patient admitted."

"Then the order is wrong," Michael said. "Trian was killed first."

"True," Max agreed, "but the real question is this— how come the three patients cured first were killed and not the last three?"

Michael thought for a moment. "Given enough time, they might have been," he said. "Maybe you put the last three in hiding before George had a chance to strike."

"Maybe. But George's boss must have seen that possibility. He told George to make the killings look like the work of a serial killer. He purposely made the killings so obvious that even a moron would know he was targeting the clinic's cured patients. Why? He had to know that we'd catch on eventually, that he'd never be able to kill all six with the Gay Slasher routine unless . . ."

"Unless he never intended to have George kill all six," Michael finished.

"Exactly."

"So what separates the first three cured patients from the last three?"

"Interesting question. Let's have a look-see."

For the next hour Max went through Harvey's files while Michael watched from his cot.

"Interesting," Max remarked after the hour had passed.

"What?"

"Trian, Whitherson, and Martino were all admitted by Bruce Grey."

"Is that significant?"

Max shrugged and turned a page. "Something else."

"What?"

"Your buddy Eric Blake joined the clinic after Trian, Whitherson, and Martino were admitted, but before Krutzer, Leander, and Singer had arrived on the scene."

"I don't see the point."

"Neither do I. Yet."

"Who admitted the other three—Krutzer, Leander, and Singer?"

Max checked the files. "Harvey."

"All three?"

"Yes."

"Didn't Eric admit anybody?"

"Never. He could only assist."

"Anything else?" Michael asked.

Max continued to glance through the files. "Let's see how the blood work went with them."

"Okay."

"Let's see . . . Trian's, Whitherson's, and Martino's original blood work was all done by Bruce. Theoretically, this should mean that Harvey did the later blood work to see if they had changed from HIV positive to HIV negative."

"Did he?"

Max thumbed through the pages for a few minutes. "Yep, it checks out. Harvey handled all the later HIV tests. Now let's see if Bruce did the HIV testing for the patients Harvey admitted." He continued to skim through the files. When he finished, he put them down.

"Well?"

Max turned toward him. "Bruce Grey performed the

tests, just as he should have. They even let Eric do a couple on Krutzer and Leander to make sure everything was aboveboard."

"So everything was on the up-and-up."

Max nodded. "Guess so." He picked up a chewed-up pencil and drew a quick chart:

Patient	Original Blood Work	Later Blood Work
Trian, S.	Grey	Riker
Whitherson, W.	Grey	Riker
Martino, R.	Grey	Riker
*Krutzer, T.	Riker	Grey
*Leander, P.	Riker	Grey
*Singer, A.	Riker	Grey

*Patients who were admitted after Eric Blake joined.

"So what's wrong?" Michael asked.

"Nothing. Let's move on."

Michael sat up. Dr. Sombat, the Thai doctor, watched him warily. "What about the motivation of Sanders' coconspirators?"

Still distracted by the blood-work rotation, Max wrote the names on another piece of paper:

Assistant Secretary of Health and Human Services
    Raymond Markey
Senator Stephen Jenkins
Dr. John Lowell

Dr. Sombat stood and walked toward them. "Excuse me," he said, "but Mr. Silverman must get some rest. This whole experience has weakened him considerably."

"I'm fine," Michael replied.

"No, he's right, Michael." Max smiled. "Get some rest. You look awful."

"I'm too wound up."

The Thai doctor produced a needle. "This will help. Please lie still."

As Michael dozed off, Max continued to stare at the three names on the sheet of paper in front of him.

Markey, Jenkins, and Lowell.

Sounded like a New York law firm.

SARA hobbled through the door, leaning heavily against her cane. She pressed the answering machine rewind button, listened to the scratching sound and then waited for the tape to begin. The first two messages were hang ups. The third was from Harvey.

"It's Harvey, Sara. Give me a call at the clinic when you have a chance. It's . . . it's rather important. Bye."

She was about to reach for the receiver when the phone rang.

"Hello?"

"Hello, Sara? It's Jennifer Riker."

"Hello, Jennifer. How are you?"

"Fine, thanks." Pause. "Sara, have you heard anything . . . ?"

"Nothing," she said quickly.

"I wish there was something I could do."

"He'll be fine."

"I hope the package I sent Harvey will help."

"What package?"

"Hasn't Harvey called you?"

"He left a message for me on my machine, but I haven't had a chance to call him back yet. What package, Jennifer?"

"Bruce mailed a package to his California P.O. box the same day he committed suicide. It probably means nothing—"

"What kind of package?"

"It had all kinds of medical files and blood samples in it. Anyway, Harvey should have received it today."

"Thanks for calling, Jennifer. I hate to rush you off the line . . ."

"Say no more. Good luck, Sara."

Sara hung up and quickly dialed the clinic. "Dr. Riker, please. This is Sara Lowell."

"He is on rounds, Ms. Lowell. Would you like me to page him?"

"Just tell him I'm on my way over there."

"Of course, Ms. Lowell. Good-bye, now."

Sara grabbed her cane and headed for the door.

JFK Airport, New York.

Sergeant Willie Monticelli showed his ID, boarded the plane, and headed for the closed-off section in the back.

"Hey, Twitch."

"Hi, Willie."

"Got the ambulance for Silverman," he said.

"The press know anything?" Max asked.

"Not yet. We can sneak him out on the tarmac. It's dark as hell out there. No one will see him."

"Have you located Sara yet?"

"She's at the clinic."

"Did you speak to her?"

Willie shook his head. "You said not to."

Max began pacing. "Okay, good. I'll go with Michael and the doctor."

"Wouldn't advise it, Twitch."

"Why not?"

"I got a call from the county coroner's office. Ralph Edmund said he had vital information you wanted on Riccardo Martino. He also said that you would *definitely* want to see it. He's waiting for you at the morgue."

Max felt the familiar excitement rush through him. If his suspicions were right about Martino's tests . . . "The doctor here can escort Michael to the hospital," Max said hurriedly. "Willie, drive like a maniac to the morgue."

Willie smiled. "I'm your man."

"HERE you go, lady."

"Thank you."

Susan Grey paid the driver. After a long (too long) hiatus, she and her son, Tommy, were finally home. Home. A city. Lots of people. Real life. Susan had missed them all, and that was why they were home two days early. Vegging out in the woods had been fun at first, beneficial even. But then it began to wear on them both. She and Tommy had reached the stage where they craved some good old-fashioned civilization. Yes, American civilization. Electricity. Hot water. Men without beards. Women who shaved their legs. A television set. An episode of *Wheel of Fortune*. A Michelob Light commercial. One damn issue of *Cosmopolitan*. A mall. A conversation that did not employ the word *granola*.

But the retreat had worked. With absolutely nothing else to do, she and Tommy had been forced to confront their problems, to discuss Bruce's suicide, to try to make sense of their lives. Things were not yet perfect, but at least they were on the path to normalcy. Tommy no longer blamed her for the death of his father, and that was a good thing.

Now if only I could stop blaming myself . . .

Tommy reached down and grabbed his mother's suitcase. "I got it, Mom," he said. His smile, so like his dead father's, tweaked her heart.

"Thanks, sweetheart."

Tommy carried the suitcase to the door and turned the knob.

Why, Bruce? You were hardly the suicide type. Why kill yourself? Why leave your son without a father?

Susan had already asked herself those questions a million times, and there had been no answer. She guessed that she would never know, that one day she would stop asking herself and move on with her life.

Why . . . ?

They entered the apartment.

"Jennifer?" Susan called out.

"Susan? Is that you?"

"We came home a little early," Susan called back.

"The woods were starting to get to us. Anything new in the civilized world?"

Jennifer did not answer. Instead, she came out of the kitchen and faced them both. Susan was taken aback by her sister's appearance. Jennifer's face was ashen, her eyes deep dark circles that looked as though they had not closed for weeks. Her body looked frail, her posture slumped.

In her left hand she held a white envelope.

"Jen . . . ?"

Jennifer handed Susan the envelope. "This," she began, "came for you."

Susan took the note from her sister. She had to scream when she recognized the handwriting.

23

I WILL kill both of them in the lab.

I wish there were another way. I am not a killer. I do not enjoy it. I loathe it. I fear it. And yet what choice do I have?

None.

My hands can't stop shaking. Everything has gone so awry. My plan should have been simple and precise. But I got fancy. I went overboard. Getting Michael involved was necessary, but I should have seen the possible problems. Now I have my back against the wall and there is only one thing I can do.

Kill again.

I feel nauseous, but I know what must be done. There is no turning back now. I have to go on. Two more lives—the lives of a doctor and a beautiful woman—must be sacrificed too. Then everything will settle down. Everything will fall back into place.

*I must remain focused. I must remember why I am do-
ing this. I must rid myself of sentimentality. It is hard, but
I will have to perform these deeds myself. There is no George
Camron to do the work for me this time. On my own hands
will be the blood of the innocent man, the innocent woman,
and the child within her womb.*

Stop it!

*I must think of the positive, of my goal, of my dream.
And for Sara Lowell it may be for the best. Once Sara Lowell is dead, she will know no more pain. I can take some
solace in that. Sara Lowell is strong and has overcome ob-
stacles before. But she has never faced an agony like the one
that awaits her.*

*You see, I never wanted to kill any innocent people. But
look at the list of names:*

Bruce Grey . . .

Janice Matley . . .

Michael Silverman . . .

And now I have to add two more names.

When they get to the lab.

SARA knocked.

"Come in," Harvey called out.

Sara opened the door and stepped into the office.
Again, she was greeted with Harvey's tired smile. "Hi,
Sara. Hear anything from Lieutenant Bernstein?"

"Not yet. I got your message on my machine."

"Good."

"I guess you were calling about Bruce's package."

He nodded. "Jen told you about it?"

"I spoke to her an hour ago," she replied. "Did you get it yet?"

"It came in this morning."

"And?"

Harvey took a deep breath. "I don't know yet, Sara. I've been going through the files for hours now and I still don't know what to think."

"Can I take a look?"

"Be my guest." He handed her a stack of files from the top of his desk. "These are all the files from Bruce's package. Six of them."

"The six cured patients?"

He nodded. "There were also six containers, each containing two vials of a patient's blood. One vial was labeled A, the other B."

Her eyes scanned Trian's file and then Whitherson's. "What's this last entry mean?"

"You mean that 'DNA. A versus B'? I found that puzzling too."

She flipped to the back of all six files. "It's the last entry in all six files."

"I know. I am not sure of the significance. It is all very strange. I assume the A and B stand for the blood vials. But I can't imagine what DNA has to do with them."

Sara sat back and closed her eyes. DNA. A memory came to her like a deep, hard punch. She sprang forward suddenly, nearly shouting. "Do you remember the Betsy Jackson murder case a couple of years ago?"

"The one where the husband murdered his wife with the butcher knife?"

She nodded. "The case drew nationwide attention

because of its use of DNA testing. B negative blood was found at the scene—the same blood type as Betsy Jackson's husband, Kevin. But Kevin Jackson's attorneys claimed that many people had B negative blood and thus the evidence meant nothing."

"I remember it now," Harvey said. "Didn't the DNA test prove that the blood found at the scene was a perfect match with Kevin Jackson's?"

"Yes. When Jackson's attorney tried to question the validity of the test, the prosecution came back with evidence that proved DNA testing was 99.7 percent accurate."

"So what does this have to do with Bruce Grey?"

"Suppose," she continued, "that Bruce wanted to compare the two blood samples from the same patient and see if they matched."

"Why?"

"I don't know," she said. "Maybe he had some reason to believe that the blood in the vials labeled A would not match the blood in the vials labeled B. Maybe he thought that someone had tampered—"

"Whoa, slow down a minute, Sara. I explained to you and Lieutenant Bernstein that there were always two of us handling the blood. It would be impossible to tamper with the blood samples."

"But there is something else to consider," Sara said. "Eric took blood from Michael without your knowledge."

"So?"

"So he could have done it other times. Bruce could have done it too."

"To what end?"

"I'm not sure, but there has to be a connection here

somehow. First, Bruce sends himself blood samples with instructions about DNA testing. Then Eric takes a blood sample from Michael in direct defiance of your rules."

"So? You're not suggesting that Eric is somehow involved in all of this, are you?"

"I am not suggesting anything," Sara said. "The only way to know for sure is to run a DNA test on the blood samples. Where are they now?"

"The blood specimens? They're in the lab."

"Doesn't Eric have a key to the lab?"

"Of course."

Sara felt something cold prick at the base of her neck. Her voice sounded distant, hollow. "Is Eric at the clinic right now?

"Yes."

"You saw him?"

"A little while ago. Why?"

She swallowed. "Did you ask him why he took Michael's blood without your authority?"

"He said he needed it for treatment verification, that's all."

"And you believed him?"

Harvey looked at her. "Why shouldn't I?"

"Has Eric ever done anything like this before?"

Pause. "No," Harvey said slowly. "Never."

She stood. "We have to get to the lab."

"Why?"

"Eric could be in there destroying the evidence."

"Evidence? Sara, what are you talking about?"

"The blood samples," she urged. "Why would Bruce have mailed them out hours before he was killed unless they were important? Harvey, listen to me: somebody murdered Bruce to get that package."

Harvey opened his mouth to speak, but then closed it.

"Damn!" He stood and ran toward the door.

"What is it?" she asked.

Harvey stopped, turned, and told her the awful truth. "Eric is in the lab right now."

RALPH Edmund was standing over a corpse, biting down on a souvlaki, when Max stumbled into the morgue.

"Willie said you wanted to speak with me?"

Ralph looked up. The juices from the souvlaki spilled out of the pita bread, down his gloved hands and onto his arms.

"Hand me a napkin, will ya, Twitch?"

"Where are they?"

He signaled with his elbow, trying to hold back the gushing souvlaki. "Over there. Bottom drawer. Hurry—before this shit falls into this guy's intestines."

Max fetched the napkins and brought them to Ralph, his eyes averted from the still form on the table. Max was not good with corpses, and down here a casual glance was always an unpleasant surprise. An accident victim with no face. A homeless man found gnawed on by rats. An infant who had fallen from a fourth-floor window.

"Here, hold this."

Ralph Edmund handed the souvlaki to Max and took hold of the napkins.

"Look, Ralph—"

"Hold up a sec." Ralph wiped his hands and forearms,

changed gloves, and took back the souvlaki. "There, thanks."

Still fighting off the desire to look down at the corpse, Max said, "Willie told me you had the test results for Riccardo Martino?"

Ralph took another bite and nodded. "When you first asked me to run the tests, I didn't understand the relevance. It was clear that Martino did not die of something AIDS-related."

"I know."

"I mean, AIDS had absolutely nothing to do with the cause of death. But then I saw that report on TV the other night—the one that said Martino and a couple of other guys with AIDS had become HIV negative—and I got to thinking: Twitch is up to something."

"Ralph, I don't have the time. Was Martino HIV negative, yes or no?"

Ralph smiled. "No."

"Are you sure?"

"As positive as Martino's HIV test. I ran two Western blots and two ELISAs just to be certain. If Martino had been cured of AIDS, his tests had a funny way of showing it. I also ran a test on his T cells and the count was dangerously low."

"Then you're saying—"

"Riccardo Martino had AIDS."

Max felt his legs go weak.

"Where's the phone?"

"Over there."

Max sprinted, picked up the receiver, dialed the safe house, and waited for Dr. Zry to answer.

Zry answered. "Hello?"

"You get those HIV test results on Krutzer, Leander, and Singer yet?" Max asked.

"Yeah, they check out."

"All three of the patients are cured."

"Yep. HIV negative."

"You sure?"

"Of course, I'm sure. Krutzer, Leander, and Singer have all been cured of AIDS. It's a miracle, Twitch."

"How do they look to you?"

"Healthy as can be. Just a few side effects from the SR1."

Max hung up, his mind spinning. Fragments flew about his head, but for the first time Max was able to reach out, grab them, sift through them, and piece the important ones together. The first three cured patients. The blood work. Grey's patients. Riker's patients. Eric. Sanders. Sara's father. The senator. Markey. The blood work, the damn blood work. Martino HIV positive. Krutzer, Leander, Singer HIV negative.

The blood work.

Max reviewed the medical histories. Then he took out the chart he had made on board the plane:

Patient	Original Blood Work	Later Blood Work
Trian, S.	Grey	Riker
Whitherson, W.	Grey	Riker
Martino, R.	Grey	Riker
*Krutzer, T.	Riker	Grey
*Leander, P.	Riker	Grey
*Singer, A.	Riker	Grey

*Patients who were admitted after Eric Blake joined.

Max put down the chart. He felt like he was trying to read a record while it spun on a turntable—Michael as Markey's guinea pig. The night Michael was kidnapped. Sara seeing Eric Blake. Sara going upstairs. Taking something for Eric. Almost ruining everything for George and his employer. And George Camron said his payments came late, that he had finally been paid within the past few days . . .

"Oh no."

Cold, dark fear rushed over him in high, crashing waves.

Ralph took another bite. "This Gay Slasher thing keeps getting crazier and crazier, huh, Twitch?"

Max shook his head slowly. "No, Ralph," he began. "For the first time, things are beginning to make sense."

Ralph stuffed the rest of the souvlaki in his mouth and licked his fingertips. "Do you know who killed these guys, Twitch?"

Max nodded and ran for the door. "I do now."

SARA'S leg throbbed as she tried to hobble quickly after Harvey. Her heart fluttered wildly, as if a bird were trapped in her chest, but the fluttering was more from fear than exertion. She glanced sideways at Harvey. His face was set, his eyes straight and unwavering, his lips thin, his fists and jaw clenched.

"Did you tell Eric about the package?" she asked.

Harvey hesitated, then nodded. "He's supposed to be setting up some tests right now."

With his words they both increased their speed. Sara struggled to keep up with him, changing her steady limp into an awkward sort of one-step hop.

Harvey stopped in front of the lab door. "Are you okay?" he asked.

"Fine."

He nodded and reached for the knob. He tried to turn it. "Locked," he said.

"Is that normal?"

"Not if Eric is in the lab, it's not."

Harvey reached for his key, found it, and placed it in the lock. A moment later the door swung open with an unhappy creak.

"Eric?" Harvey called out.

No answer. The shades were pulled down, and the lights were out. The lab was blanketed in darkness.

Harvey flipped the light switch. The room was immediately illuminated with bright fluorescent lights. He stepped toward a table in the corner. "Damn!"

"What is it?"

"The blood samples are gone. I left them right on the table." He checked under the counter and in the nearby vicinity. Nothing. "Check the refrigeration room in the corner," he said. "I'm going to look in Eric's private file cabinet."

"I thought the private files were locked."

"They are. I'm going to bust the damn thing open."

Sara hobbled past several lab tables, past Bunsen burners, past test tubes, past the large periodic chart on the wall, past tables and adjustable stools, past countless charts and scraps of paper. The lab looked more like an eighth-grade science classroom than an ultramodern research center. Still, it had the feel of professionalism. Everything was spotlessly clean. The microscopes and other assorted gadgets looked high-tech and expensive.

When she reached the door to the refrigeration room, she turned around for a brief moment. Harvey had found a metal ruler and was working on the top drawer of Eric's file cabinet. She could hear him grunting from the effort. She turned back toward the door. She hoped the blood samples were in the refrigeration room. She hoped that her suspicions about Eric were wrong, that he had not done anything wrong, that he was still their friend . . .

The door handle was cold. She gripped it with her fingers and pulled back. The suction gave way and Sara was immediately greeted with a frosty breeze. Little pricks of terror began to rise on the base of her spine. She pulled the door all the way back, stepped into the doorway, and peered inside.

Sara inhaled sharply but could not move.

A scream built inside her throat, but only a strange, unrecognizable sound—a grunt of some kind—managed to push its way through her lips. She stared forward, her eyes wide and fixed.

Eric Blake's bloody corpse lay twisted on the floor in front of her.

Almost a full minute passed before she turned away from the dead body and looked toward Harvey. He looked back, pointing a gun at her. There was no surprise or panic in his face, just a look of exhaustion, aggravation, defeat—the look of a man whose car had just blown a tire on his way to work. Harvey sighed heavily, closed the lab door behind him, and tried to smile.

"I haven't had a chance to move him," he said by way of explanation.

24

SUSAN Grey's knees felt wobbly. She continued to stare at her name written in Bruce's familiar scrawl.

"Look at the other side," Jennifer said in a hollow voice.

Susan turned the envelope over:

TO BE OPENED UPON MY DEATH

She fell heavily onto the couch, her eyes still glued on the envelope. "Another suicide note?"

"I don't know."

"Mommy . . ."

"Come with me, Tommy," Jennifer said, steering the child away. "Let's go into the kitchen."

Left alone, Susan flipped the envelope back over.

SUSAN

Her name was written by her dead husband in large block letters. The familiar penmanship raked across her heart. She could look at pictures of Bruce, listen to him talk on a cassette, even watch him on a videotape. But there was something so personal about handwriting, something so individual, so eerie, that she had to look away for a moment.

She pushed back her long brown hair and fumbled open the envelope. Several pages of plain white paper slipped out and fell to the floor. She reached down, picked them up, and unfolded them. As her eyes traveled down the lines of written text, they widened:

Dear Susan,

If you are reading this letter, it means that my suspicions were correct. For much of the past two weeks I was hoping that I was merely paranoid or even a full-fledged nutcase. I wanted to be everything but right. I even hesitate in sending you this letter because like it or not, I have put you in danger. Someone will kill to get their hands on this package. Someone has already killed twice (and now that I am dead, three times) because of what has been occurring in the clinic.

I wish I could give you some sound advice about what to do with the contents of this letter, but I can't. I probably should have gone to the NIH or to the media and showed them what I had, but I was afraid of the results. I thought I could handle it on my own. Evidently, I was wrong. But if I had gone to the media and exposed the truth, I would have played into the hands of our enemies, the bigots who want to take away all AIDS financing. Now, it is your choice to make.

Where did it suddenly go wrong? I don't know. When did I first become suspicious? That too is a tough question to answer. I think it was after the first murder, the murder of Scott Trian, but more likely, it was after Bill Whitherson was killed in a similar fashion. The timing of the murders seemed such a strange coincidence to me. Harvey and Eric did not see it that way. They feared that someone was targeting our cured patients. But I saw something else unusual—the recent deterioration of both Trian and Whitherson. We had all assumed that they were suffering from SR1 side effects, but what if that wasn't so? Whatever was wrong with Scott and Bill had still been in its infancy, but what if it was somehow AIDS-related?

Now that they were both dead and buried, there was no way to check. I asked Harvey about the possibility, but he just shrugged it off, which was not like him. I tried to press the issue, but the more I did, the more hostile Harvey became. "Whose side are you on anyway?" he would ask. "If you think the cure isn't working, go retest Krutzer, Leander, and Singer."

I did. I was relieved to see that they were all still HIV negative. But then again, they had not been treated as long as Trian or Whitherson. That bothered me. I was going to confront Harvey again but decided against it. He was all worked up over the latest round of proposed budget cuts. The members of the medical budget committee were preparing to pounce upon us like so many vultures on a wounded animal. The competition for funds is incredible. We spend more time agonizing over budget cuts than on curing patients—a shame but that is reality.

I decided to sneak behind Harvey's back and draw blood from Riccardo Martino (you will find his chart enclosed in the packet). Then I had his blood tested. When the results of his Western blot and ELISA came back, I wanted to scream. Martino was HIV positive. He had AIDS. I panicked and ran toward Harvey's office to tell him the awful news. But something made me stop. Harvey's blind dedication has always intimidated me, but for the first time I was actually afraid of him. Our funding was about to be cut off, and I knew Harvey would do anything to keep us operating. But how far had he gone?

I walked into his office calmly and asked him when he planned on testing Martino again. He informed me that a result should be ready tomorrrow. I, of course, did not sleep that night. When I awoke in the morning, I sprinted into the lab, checked Martino's code number, and looked at the blood sample for myself. Imagine my surprise to find both the Western blot and ELISA test showed that Martino was HIV negative, not positive.

How could it be? Had one of the tests been wrong? Did SR1 work? Was it a permanent cure or merely a temporary one? And how did the murders of Scott Trian and Bill Whitherson fit in? Were the murders a plot to destroy the clinic? A terrible coincidence? Or was there something else going on?

On the other hand, I had tested Krutzer, Leander, and Singer myself, and they were all cured. There was no question about it. So what exactly was I afraid Harvey had done? Tampered with some patients and not others? That would make no sense. Besides, Winston O'Connor ran most of the tests. Sometimes Eric. Very rarely did Harvey do any lab work.

It took me a while, Susan, but eventually I figured out what he was up to. The proof of Harvey's crimes is in this packet.

My plane is landing, so I will have to wrap this up now. At the risk of sounding melodramatic, I do not know what will happen once I land. For that reason I will save the long explanations and give you some specific instructions. Enclosed are my private journals on each patient. I picked up the blood samples from our storage house in Bangkok. As per the clinic's rules, all tested specimens were packaged after each test by either Eric Blake or Winston O'Connor. You will notice that there are two blood samples for each patient, labeled A and B. Sample A was taken from the patient when he was admitted (hence HIV positive). Sample B was taken when he was cured (hence HIV negative). Have someone you can trust run DNA tests on the two blood samples. When they don't match, it will become clear what has been done.

The plane is on the ground now. I do not know if Harvey is acting alone or with some help. I cannot imagine he slaughtered Trian and Whitherson on his own, so I assume he has accomplices. I am sure that he is on to me. So tonight I will hide someplace. Tomorrow morning I will confront him in the clinic, where I know there will be a lot of witnesses and I will be safe. Since you are reading this letter, I guess I screwed up someplace. Know that I love you, Susan, and I am sorry for all the pain I caused. Please let Tommy know that his father will always love him and somehow I will always be with him.

Good-bye, Susan,
Bruce

She did not move. She just sat for a very long time. There was no need to reread the note.

"Susan?"

She turned toward her sister. "Bruce mentioned a package."

"I mailed it to Harvey yesterday. He thought it might be important."

Susan sat up. "Does anyone else know about this?"

"Just Sara. She's with Harvey now."

"I'M really sorry, Sara," Harvey said, moving the gun from his left hand to his right. "I never wanted to hurt you."

Sara stared at him with a mixture of disbelief and horror. "You?"

"Yes."

"You murdered your own patients?"

"Not murdered," he corrected. "Sacrificed. I'm not a monster, Sara."

She glanced at the still body behind her. "Tell that to Eric."

He smiled his weary smile. "You don't understand."

She said nothing.

"It was an impossible struggle from the beginning," he continued. "Powerful people tried to squash us. You can't imagine what we went through to get the initial funding for this place."

Her voice, when it finally came, sounded hollow. "You killed your own patients?"

"They were already dying."

"From what?"

"AIDS."

Pause. "I thought they were cured."

"No." He smiled sadly. "Please, Sara, you have known

me for a long time. I am not an evil man. I want you to understand before . . ."

"Before what?"

"I'm sorry. I wish there was another way, but there isn't. As soon as Jennifer told you about the package, the decision was out of my hands. I'll have no problem convincing her that Bruce's package had nothing to do with the Gay Slasher. But you would have insisted on the DNA tests."

"You're going to kill me." It was not a question.

"You will have to be sacrificed, yes."

"And you're going to kill our baby."

He winced. "I wish I didn't have to. You see, Sara, AIDS is a disease unlike any other. One minute the world is focused on it. The next, no one cares. I needed a way to maintain focus."

"SR1 doesn't work, does it? It never did. It was all a lie."

"It worked perfectly in the animal tests," he said. "Even the FDA agreed with that. The problem is we have not been able to get it to work on humans. But it's just a matter of time until—"

"Then Michael is doomed."

He shook his head. "I'm so close, Sara, so damn close. All I needed was a little more time to perfect the formula. But our grant was not going to be extended. Sanders and his fellow conspirators would have seen to that. Our funds were about to be cut off. I needed something, Sara. Some way of keeping the funds."

"So you faked a cure?"

"It was easy, really," he said. "I was the one who drew the blood from Trian, Whitherson, and Martino. All I had to do was switch test tubes—replace their blood specimens with someone's who was HIV negative. It went perfectly."

"Then why did you murder them?"

"Because they were dying," he said. "SR1 had managed to put the HIV into a sort of remission for a while, but eventually the treatment accelerated their deterioration. I could only dismiss their worsening condition as a drug side effect for so long. I had to get rid of the evidence. The AIDS virus would have killed them anyway in another month or two."

"So you had them murdered."

He shook his head. "I didn't have George 'murder' anybody. I had him speed up the inevitable."

"I can't believe this."

"I did it for them, Sara, not for me."

"For them?" she repeated incredulously. "You took away their last precious months of life for them?"

"I did not want them to die in vain. I wanted their deaths to mean something, to benefit the AIDS movement."

"What the hell are you talking about?"

His eyes gleamed now. "The publicity, Sara. The media doesn't focus very long on medical developments, but throw in a Gay Slasher and whammo, you have nationwide press. Look at the *NewsFlash* report. Parker spent more time on the serial killings than on the AIDS cure. The murders stirred up the masses in a way even Sanders would have been proud of. Record-setting donations have been flooding in since the show aired, not just because we are on the verge of finding a cure, but because people are outraged by the slashings."

Sara gripped her cane tightly. "You crazy bastard."

"No, Sara, I am rational. I am looking at it on a cost-benefit basis. Trian, Whitherson, and Martino were going to die awful, painful deaths from AIDS. Instead, they were killed mercifully while helping the development of a cure."

"You call mutilation and torture merciful?"

His smile evaporated. "That was never supposed to happen," he said quickly. "That was George's doing. As soon as I found out about it, I put a stop to it. It was a mistake."

"And what about Bruce and Janice? More 'mistakes'?"

"I never wanted to hurt them. Bruce stumbled onto the truth. He had to be silenced. And George killed Janice when she spotted him near Michael's room. They were both accidents. I mourn for them more than anyone. I can't sleep at night because of what happened to them. But I have to shut my eyes to my pain. When I think of the goal, Sara, when I think of the possibility of curing AIDS, I realize how insignificant a few lives are. I'm not talking about saving hundreds of lives here. I'm talking about saving thousands, perhaps millions, of people."

Her harsh glare did not waver. "So they were expendable?"

"I know it sounds cruel, but it's true."

"The end justifies the means?"

"When the end is something as important as an AIDS

vaccine, of course the end justifies the means. Wouldn't you sacrifice one person to save a thousand? If you could go back in time, wouldn't you murder Hitler rather than let him kill six million Jews?"

"Don't compare innocent victims with Hitler."

"That's not the point and you know it. I am talking about life-and-death realities here. Sometimes the innocent must suffer. It's a fact of life. But if we can stamp out AIDS, isn't it a small price to pay? Wouldn't any good person be willing to sacrifice his life to save thousands of others?"

"Why did you kill Bradley Jenkins? He wasn't one of your cured patients."

"But he was dying, and frankly speaking I was terrified of how his father would react if he died while under my treatment. It could have been disastrous for the clinic."

"And that's why you 'sacrificed' him?"

"Not just that." Harvey paused and took a deep breath. He tried to renew his smile, but it never reached his eyes. "Bradley was the third gay man murdered by the Gay Slasher, remember? The first two, Scott Trian and Bill Whitherson, were ignored by the media for the most part. Why? Because no one cared. Trian and Whitherson were nothing but a couple of unknown faggots. Ten Trians and Whithersons would have to die before the media really paid attention. But once the Gay Slasher killed the son of a United States senator, once Bradley's bloody body had been found behind a gay bar, then the media became outraged. You're a reporter, Sara. Think about it. When did the media become interested in the case? Not until Bradley was murdered. Then the sympathy began to build. All I had to do was let the world know about the connection to the clinic."

"That's where I came into the picture."

"Yes."

"And I fell for your bullshit hook, line, and sinker."

"You helped me finance the clinic."

"So why did you kill Eric?"

"Eric too became suspicious. Worse, he got proof from the blood sample he took from Michael. I tried to reason with him. I tried to explain why we had to do all this. But Eric wouldn't listen. He had already put a call in to Markey and was going to tell him everything. I had to stop him before Markey called him back."

Sara shook her head in confusion. "What does Michael's blood have to do with any of this?"

Harvey moved toward Sara. He grabbed a stool, sat down heavily, and turned toward her. "It's simple," he said. "Michael does not have AIDS."

Her heart constricted in her chest. She could barely breathe. "What?"

"Role reversal, Sara. Think about it a second. In order to make it look like Trian, Whitherson, and Martino were cured, I switched their HIV-positive blood with healthy blood. In Michael's case I did the opposite—I exchanged his healthy, HIV-negative blood with someone's who was HIV positive. He was diagnosed with AIDS, but he never had it."

"But what about his symptoms? What about the stomach pain and the jaundice?"

"Oh, Michael does have hepatitis," he said. "Do you know how easy it is to give someone hepatitis? All you do is jab him with a contaminated needle. Remember when he came to see me when he had the flu a few months back? The flu shot I gave him came from a contaminated needle . . ."

"You sick son of a bitch . . ."

"Then all I had to do was wait for the symptoms to crop up. If they didn't—that happens sometimes—I would have found some other way to make him think he was sick with something that could be AIDS. And even though Michael was neither gay nor a drug user, his blood transfusion in the Bahamas gave me the excuse to test him without raising too many eyebrows."

His words bombarded her from every direction, but there was no way to fend off the blows. "How could you?" she screamed. "What was the point. Why—"

"—did I pretend Michael has AIDS?" he finished for her. "Isn't it obvious?"

Her vocal cords would not work. She could only shake her head.

"Do you remember when we first diagnosed Michael as being HIV positive?" he asked. "I told Michael that he had a responsibility to go public. I told him that he could make the disease real to the millions of people who ignored the threat because they saw AIDS as just a gay disease. A healthy, handsome, popular basketball star like Michael could bring it out in the open, focus the world's attention on this tragedy like no one before him. To the world he is a fairy-tale prince. To me, he was Rock Hudson and Ryan White rolled into one. He could educate the world. His name alone could finance my research for years."

She gripped the cane ever tighter, her rage mounting. "He is your friend."

"But don't you see? I was right, Sara. Michael accomplished all of that and more. The fact that he was straight and married to the beautiful and famous Sara Lowell made it all the better—even though Sanders tried to take some shine off the apple by dragging out Michael's stepdad."

"You callous bastard," she shouted. "Then what? Were you going to 'cure' him and make yourself a goddamn hero?"

"Not me," he said. "Never me. It was all for the clinic. It was all in pursuit of finding an AIDS cure."

"How could you?" she hissed. "Michael loves you."

Harvey looked at her strangely. "And I love him. I would rather have torn off my own limbs than hurt Michael—you know that. But what good would it have done? I needed someone like Michael. And think about it, Sara: what was the big sacrifice? He never had AIDS. Hepatitis caught early is not very dangerous. His life was never in any real danger. Yes, he would have been out of basketball for a while, but so what? He was on his last legs anyway. And even if he wasn't, it was such a small price to pay for so much good."

"You're insane."

"You're not listening to me."

"I don't want to listen to you. I want to rip your eyes out of your head. I want to crush your skull with my cane."

He raised the gun. "Sara . . ."

"My father was right about you."

"Huh?"

"You are just like him—only worse. Blinded by your passion. I don't want to hear any more about how you murdered people and turned lives upside down. I want to know where my husband is."

His face clouded over. "I never planned on having George kidnap Michael. I thought I could keep him as a patient at the clinic for a month or two and then make him an outpatient so that he would lead a fairly normal life. In a year or so, when the AIDS vaccine became a reality, I would take an HIV test and declare him cured. But someone got in the way."

"Who?"

"Sanders and his coconspirators."

"What do they have to do with Michael?"

"After the *NewsFlash* broadcast, Markey visited me in the clinic, remember? The government wanted proof that SR1 worked. So they came up with the idea of making Michael a test case and monitoring his progress from the very beginning. Remember how upset I was? I screamed about how the government was trying to stall my progress. But in truth—"

"You were afraid they would learn you were a fraud."

He nodded. "All they had to do was run one HIV test on Michael and all my work would have collapsed around my head. And worse, Markey was sending in his men the next day. What choice did I have? I had to get rid of Michael. So I had George kidnap him."

"Where is he now?"

He did not answer the question. Instead, he stared down at his gun. "I have to kill you, Sara. I'm sorry."

"What is your plan this time, Harvey? How are you going to explain away my death? Or Eric's?"

"It won't be very difficult. Eric killed you because you discovered the truth about him. Then he ran away. Disappeared."

"What truth?"

"That Eric was the man behind the Gay Slasher plot. First, I'll blow the lid off Sanders' conspiracy. Cassandra will be so outraged by your murder that I am sure she will cooperate. From there it won't be any problem to convince the media that Eric worked for the conspiracy. The media will eat it up, make it sound like the Goliath right-wing government was picking on the little David clinic. The money will come pouring in."

Harvey cocked the gun's hammer. "The police will search for Eric. They may even find him wherever I dump him. I don't know. If they do, everyone will figure his coconspirators murdered him to keep him quiet. The media loves that kind of stuff."

Sara stared at him with a look that was nearly palpable. "You'll never be able to tie the conspirators to the murders."

"I don't have to. The speculation will be enough."

"Max will figure you out."

"You give him too much credit, Sara. All the evidence is gone. I killed Martino with the cyanide injection. The blood samples in Bruce's package have been destroyed. There's nothing left to tie me to the murders . . . except you."

A million questions ran through her mind, but the same one kept surfacing. "Where is Michael?"

Harvey stepped toward her. "When I found out that Lieutenant Bernstein knew about George, I realized that it was just a matter of time before he got caught. I had to cut my losses. So I told George to burn down the storage house in Bangkok—something else I could blame on the right-wing conspiracy."

His smile was back, his eyes bright and maniacal. "Don't you see the irony, Sara? Everyone thinks that the patients were murdered by fascists who wanted to stop me from proving there was an AIDS cure. But actually, it was the opposite—the murders made it impossible to prove that there was *no* cure."

Sara's eyes bored into his. "What happened to Michael?"

Once again the smile left his face. He lowered his gaze. "He's dead, Sara. George killed him. I begged him not to, but he hung up on—"

There was a sudden knock on the lab door. "Dr. Riker?"

A nurse.

Harvey turned to Sara, his face suddenly panicked. "If you call out, I will kill her too."

The nurse knocked again. "Dr. Riker?"

"I'm in the middle of an experiment," he said, his voice cracking. "Is it important?"

"Yes, Doctor."

"Hold on a minute."

He turned back to Sara. Her big green eyes were tear-filled now. There was no longer confusion or horror in them—just devastation and pure hatred.

"Get in the refrigeration room," he whispered.

"You killed Michael."

He glanced at the gun and then back at Sara. "Don't make me kill the nurse too."

She knew it was no idle threat.

"Drop the cane on the floor and move back. Now."

With her eyes still on him, she dropped the cane and slowly backed up into the refrigeration room. Her foot bumped into something and she realized with revulsion that it was Eric Blake's body.

"The room is soundproof so I wouldn't try screaming," he said. "Please don't bring any more innocent people into this. Enough have died."

The cold closed in around Sara as Harvey shut the refrigerator door and locked it with a padlock. Then he moved across the room, unlocked the lab door, and stepped into the hallway, closing the door behind him.

"What is it?" he asked the nurse.

"It's Michael Silverman," the nurse said excitedly. "He's here."

"What?"

"He just arrived from Bangkok."

THE sirens blasted.

"Drive faster, Willie."

"Jesus, Twitch, I can't drive through cars."

"Then drive on the sidewalk."

"Here." Willie handed him a pencil.

"What?"

"Suck on your pacifier and tell me what's going on."

"I was an idiot—that's what's going on." Max tossed

the pencil on the car floor. "I spent so much time trying to figure out who wanted to destroy the clinic that I
couldn't see what was so obvious."

"What?"

"The murders were helping the clinic, not hurting it."

"What the hell are you talking about?" Willie asked.

"I just got the test results. Riccardo Martino was HIV
positive. Krutzer, Leander, and Singer are HIV negative."

"Speak English."

"Martino had AIDS. The other three don't."

"I thought Martino was cured by this miracle drug."

"SR1 is not a miracle drug. It doesn't work. Harvey
Riker faked the whole thing."

"The head of the clinic?"

Max nodded. "At first I thought it might be his assistant, Eric Blake."

"So what changed your mind?"

"Something that happened the night Michael was kidnapped. Sara was about to go home for the night when
she bumped into Eric Blake. He was heading upstairs to
run an errand. Sara volunteered to do it for him, and he
let her."

"So?"

"If Eric Blake was behind the kidnapping, he would
have never let Sara go back upstairs. He would have insisted on running the errand himself."

"Let me get this straight—this Riker guy faked like he
had a cure?"

"Right."

"But he didn't run all the tests. I thought you said the
other docs ran blood tests too."

"They did. But look at the rotation. Our three murder victims were Trian, Whitherson, and Martino. All three were admitted by Bruce Grey. That meant that Bruce Grey took a blood test, concluded that they had the AIDS virus, and admitted them. Then Riker took over. He was the one who drew the blood that was used to determine if they were cured. He must have sent the lab someone else's blood—*someone who never even had AIDS*. Naturally, when the lab tested this blood, it came back negative. Ergo, they were 'cured.' A 'miracle.'"

"But I still don't get it, Twitch. Didn't Bruce Grey do the later tests with some of the patients? And didn't you just say the three guys Dr. Zry tested were all cured?"

Max smiled. "Krutzer, Leander, and Singer weren't cured," he said, "because they never had AIDS in the first place."

"Huh?"

"All three were admitted by Harvey Riker. So what did he do? He switched the blood samples right in the beginning—except this time he switched their HIV-negative blood for the blood of someone who had AIDS."

"Motherfucker," Willie exclaimed. "So it looked like they had AIDS when they never did?"

"Right. Then Harvey probably infected them with a few mild flu viruses to make it look like they were really sick. When the time came, Bruce Grey performed the blood tests. Since they never had AIDS in the first place, their tests came back negative. Ergo, they were 'cured.'"

"Un-fuckin'-believable. When did you start putting it together?"

"When George Camron was raving about being paid late. I didn't pay much attention at the time, but then I got to thinking—why was he paid all of a sudden? How did his boss get his hands on money so fast? Then I remembered my original question—who benefits? Who got the good press? Who put pressure on his foes to keep financing them?"

"The clinic."

Max nodded. "And all the donations solicited from *NewsFlash* went directly to the clinic."

"Riker used the money to pay off Camron?"

"Some of it. Camron also said he never killed Martino. So I got to thinking—who had the best opportunity to kill Riccardo Martino? Riker claimed to be the last guy who saw him alive. He probably injected him with cyanide a few minutes before O'Connor knocked him over the head."

"You got a motive for all of this?"

Max thought for a minute. "It's an unselfish, albeit warped, one—Riker thought he could cure AIDS. He tried desperately to keep his clinic financed, but after their first year he must have realized that he needed something big or their grant would get cut off. That's when he decided to fake the cure. But he also knew that Trian, Whitherson, and Martino would never stand up to close scrutiny and eventually they would die. So he had to find other patients who could stand up to any test. He had to find patients who would be legitimately HIV negative when tested by the government. That's when he brought in Krutzer, Leander, and Singer."

Willie swerved around a van. "It's a nice little theory, Twitch. Have any evidence?"

"I will. Riker's one problem was the storage house in Bangkok. All lab material was immediately packaged by either Eric Blake or Winston O'Connor and sent to Bangkok for safekeeping. If Riker had tried to divert it, it would have looked suspicious. But Riker really wasn't worried about it anyway. He figured he could always have the storage house destroyed if anybody got too close to the truth."

"Which is what he tried to do, except you nailed Camron first."

Max nodded. "Colonel T's men are guarding the building twenty-four hours a day. When we test the stored blood specimens, it will prove that the blood taken upon admittance could not possibly belong to the same person as the blood taken when they were supposed to be cured. That's one reason Riker wanted the safe house in Bangkok. It was far away and yet it was George Camron's hometown. Markey and the government would have a lot of trouble finding it. If they really tried, Riker could always have George destroy it."

"Case solved."

"I hope."

"Do you think Riker knows you're on to him?"

"I doubt it."

"So calm down. We're almost there."

"You don't understand."

"What?"

Max leaned down and picked up the pencil. "Sara is alone with him."

* * *

I T was so cold.

Sara wrapped her arms around herself but it did no good. The frigid air cut through her skin to the bone. She looked down, coughing. Eric's body was in a twisted fetal position. His eyes were closed, a bullet wound in his throat. She wondered how Michael had died. Had he been tortured or had it been quick and painless? She fought back tears and tried to think clearly. For the sake of their unborn child, she had to find a way out of this.

She tried the door, but it would not budge. Her cough had become relentless, racking her body with powerful jerks. She could feel the cold settle into the bottom of her lungs. She wondered if it was an infection. Her lips trembled. She felt weak, drained. She hunched her body into a small ball, her eyes darting about the small room. There were shelves filled with various codes. One test tube said 87m332. Another read 98k003. The beakers were labeled $NaOH$, SO_2, H_2SO_4, H_3PO_4, HCl and $CHCl_3$.

Michael. Her poor, beautiful Michael. Dead. How? Why?

The room was tiny. The walls and ceiling seemed to be closing in around her. Sara curled herself into a tighter ball, lowered her head, and sobbed gently. She had never known such loneliness, such despair. The cold grew unbearable. Her fingers became numb. She felt herself grow weaker and weaker. She tried to concentrate on a Blue Oyster Cult song in a bizarre attempt to keep herself awake.

But she felt herself slipping away.

Hold on, Sara. Hold on.

But it was no good. Harvey was coming back soon and then it would be over. Her Michael was dead. He had joined the Reaper, and in the end, so would she.

Her eyes began to close.

25

MICHAEL was still unconscious when they wheeled him into his room on the third floor. Dr. Sombat patiently filled Harvey in on everything that had happened.

"Your Lieutenant Bernstein is a brave man," the Thai doctor said. "He saved Mr. Silverman's life."

"Did they capture the man who kidnapped Michael?" Harvey asked.

"Yes. He is in custody."

"Has . . . has he said anything yet? Anything that might help solve this case?"

"I apologize, Dr. Riker, but I am not privy to that information."

Harvey nodded. "Where is Lieutenant Bernstein now?"

"He had an emergency," Dr. Sombat replied. "He drove off with Sergeant Monticelli. If there is nothing else, I have to get back to the airport."

"No, nothing else. Thank you for all your help."

"You are welcome. How can I get back to Kennedy Airport?"

"Ask the receptionist downstairs to call a taxi. Thanks again."

They shook hands and Dr. Sombat departed, leaving Harvey alone with Michael in the quiet, dark room.

"Michael?"

No response. Harvey could see that Michael's nose was broken. He had lost a considerable amount of weight.

"I'm sorry, Michael."

Harvey stared down at his young friend lying help- lessly in the bed. A tear ran down his cheek. He bent over and gently kissed Michael's forehead. Then he turned to leave.

"Harv?"

He turned around. Michael looked up through the darkness with groggy eyes.

"I'm right here, Michael. You're back now."

His voice was barely a whisper. "Sara?"

"She left a few minutes before you got here," he re- plied. "I left a message on the answering machine for her to call me."

"Feel . . . feel weak."

"I know. Try to get some rest. I'll wake you when Sara gets here."

Michael tried to nod. "Max got the Slasher."

"I know," Harvey replied, walking back toward the bed. He hugged his friend. "Go to sleep now, Michael. Everything is going to be okay. You want me to give you something?"

Michael shook his head and closed his eyes. Harvey quietly crept out of the room. Then he headed down the hallway, unlocked the door, and entered the laboratory.

"I'm sorry, Michael," he said out loud. But there was no one to hear his words.

He took the gun out of his pocket and wrapped a towel around the barrel, using it as a makeshift silencer. No matter, really. The refrigeration room was sound-proof once the door was closed. He had shot Eric in there and no one had heard a sound.

He crossed the lab. How was he going to get the bodies out? Harvey knew from firsthand experience how heavy deadweight could be. He would have to place the corpses in a plastic bag. Then he would instruct the nurses that he would take care of Michael for this evening on his own and that no one was to enter the third floor under any condition. That would give him the opportunity to drag the bodies to the elevator, head down to the basement, get them out through the tunnel George had used, and put them in the trunk of his car.

Then what?

He was not sure. Tie weights to their legs and dump them in the river. Wasn't that what they always did in the movies? He would have to be careful. Wear gloves. Clean the lab from top to bottom. *Wouldn't want the police to find a few strands of long blond hair in the refrigeration room, now, would we?*

He reached the door of the refrigeration room and leaned his ear against it. Cold. Well, what did he expect? And why did he put his ear against the door in the first place? What had he expected to hear through the thick door?

Idiot.

Stop putting it off, Harv. Stop stalling. Sara has to die. She'll never keep silent. Think of all the young men dying every day. Think of the thousands, maybe millions, you can save from an awful death. Look toward your goal.

A world with no AIDS.

Harvey nodded to himself. He reached down and unlocked the padlock. Then he opened the door and pointed the gun at Sara.

TWO floors below, Cassandra smiled at the security guard as she headed into the clinic. She tried to put a little bounce in her steps, tried to make her smile bigger, but it would not hold. In her right hand, she had a bag of Chinese takeout. Spare ribs, moo shu pork, General Tso's chicken (Chinese generals cook?), and beef with broccoli, all packaged in those little white boxes Chinese restaurants use. The bottom of the bag no doubt had about 850 packets of duck sauce, soy sauce, and that mustard hot enough to remove paint. Then there were the usual fortune cookies and, for some reason that always escaped her, they always gave you an orange for dessert.

Cassandra strolled down the hall toward Harvey's office. She had not seen him very much in the past few days and missed him terribly. Probably he had not been sleeping or eating properly. Between Michael's mysterious kidnapping, the Gay Slasher, and now her father's

Washington conspiracy—it was enough to make any man begin to unravel.

So Cassandra had decided another little surprise was in order. At the end of the hallway, she knocked on Harvey's door. "Hello?"

No response.

"Harv?"

Still no response.

She peeked in the doorway and saw that the room was empty. Maybe the receptionist would know where he went. She went back down the hall to the receptionist's desk. Cassandra smiled, and the receptionist smiled back, putting up one finger to signal her to wait.

"I'm sorry," the receptionist said into the phone, "but I can't locate Sara Lowell. She may have already left. Yes, Mrs. Riker, I know you said it's an emergency, but . . . Yes, I understand the importance. Would you like me to page Dr. Riker? No? Okay, okay, I won't. Calm down."

Cassandra leaned over. "A call for Sara?"

The receptionist put her hand over the mouthpiece. "It's Jennifer Riker, Dr. Riker's ex. She keeps ranting about an emergency."

"I'll talk to her."

Cassandra took the phone. "Hello?"

Jennifer's voice came fast. "Who is this?"

"Cassandra Lowell, Jennifer. I'm Sara's sister. We met a few years back at a party—"

"I remember," Jennifer interrupted. "Where's Sara?"

"I don't know. I just got here myself."

"Find her, Cassandra. She's in grave danger."

Cassandra held the phone close to her ear. "What are you talking about?"

"I'm talking about the letter," Jennifer explained.

"What letter?"

"The letter Bruce wrote."

SERGEANT Willie Monticelli veered right and exited off the Henry Hudson Parkway at One Hundred Seventy-eighth Street. He sped down Fort Washington Avenue, passed Hood Park, and turned left at One Hundred Sixty-seventh Street. He made a hard right on Broadway, accelerated past the main hospital building and Babies Hospital, and took a sharp left.

Ten seconds later the squad car arrived at the Sidney Pavilion entrance. Willie pulled the car up on the sidewalk, braking with a horrid screech, inches before hitting the cement stairs at the entrance. Max was out of the car before it came to a complete stop, Willie not far behind. The two sprinted up the stairs, badges out. The security guards, spotting the police IDs, stepped back to avoid being the victims of a two-man stampede.

"Any other police arrive yet?" Max asked without breaking stride.

"None," the guard yelled back.

Max continued to run, busting through doors like an Old West gunslinger in a saloon. He reached the reception desk.

"Where's Sara Lowell?" he asked.

The receptionist looked up quizzically. "And who might you be?"

Max tossed his badge on her desk. "Lieutenant Bernstein, NYPD. Where is Sara Lowell?"

"She is a very popular young lady today."

"What does that mean?"

"It means, Lieutenant, that you are not the first person in a rush to speak to her."

"Who else?"

"Jennifer Riker just called looking for Ms. Lowell. She said it was very urgent."

"Dr. Riker's wife?"

"Ex-wife," the receptionist corrected. "Anyhow, I couldn't find Ms. Lowell anywhere, so Mrs. Riker spoke to her sister instead."

"Cassandra? Where is she?"

The receptionist shrugged. "I couldn't tell you for sure. She spoke to Mrs. Riker, turned all white and funny, and then ran off without a word. Didn't even have the courtesy to hang up the phone."

"Where did she go?"

"She got in the elevator and went up. It stopped at the third floor."

Max turned toward the elevator. "Willie?"

The sergeant stood at the elevator, holding the door open. "One step ahead of you, Twitch."

"Then let's move."

HARVEY cradled the gun close to him as he swung open the door slowly.

He had considered the possibility that Sara Lowell might launch some sort of futile attack when he first opened the door. But when he looked in the cold room, he knew that he had worried needlessly.

Sara was slumped in the corner. Her eyes were closed, her head tilted back at a strange angle. Her normally pale complexion was frighteningly white, colorless. Her trembling lips were thin and blue. She looked so pitifully small and helpless, huddled in the corner like a wounded animal trapped in a cage.

"Sara?"

No response. Her breathing was labored and uneven. Her shoulder drooped into her chest; her arms hung limply at her sides.

"Sara?"

Still nothing. Her eyes remained closed. A choking noise, like something was stuck in her air passage, came from her throat. Part of him wanted Sara to stay unconscious, but most of him wanted her to be awake. He wanted her to be conscious when he killed her, to have the right to stare at him with accusing, hateful eyes as he pulled the trigger. The haunting image would never leave him, he knew. It would be his own way of serving penance.

He kept his distance on the off chance that she would regain consciousness and try to surprise him. From where he stood near the doorway, he would have plenty of time to raise his gun and fire should she try to cross the room. Not even someone with Michael's quickness would be able to cross a room that fast.

For a moment he considered using the knife in his pocket on her. It would, no doubt, be quieter. But no, he would stick to the gun. The gun was more impersonal.

It could kill from a distance. Stabbing someone, slicing their throat from ear to ear or jutting the long blade into the heart . . . only a certain sort of man could do such a thing.

Harvey found it too painful to stare at Sara's pathetic form crouched in the corner. He swerved his eyes toward the neat row of test tubes on the top shelf. He read the labels. So close was he to his project that he had each patient's code and every chemical in this room memorized.

87m332 was Ezra Platt. 98k003 was Kiel Davis. The next one should be, yes it was, 39kl0, Kevin Fraine . . .

"Sara?"

Still nothing. Her troubled breathing had deteriorated into struggled gasps and arduous intakes. Harvey felt tears push into his eyes, but as he had done when he ordered Bruce's death, he forced them back down. His eyes moved down the row of beakers.

$NaOH$, SO_2, H_2SO_4, next should be H_3PO_4, and then . . .

. . . where was the HCl . . . ?

Sara's slumped arm moved like it had been spring-released. The arm shot toward him as he raised his gun. In her hand Sara held a large glass beaker filled with HCl. Harvey's eyes widened.

HCl. Hydrochloric acid.

There was no time to react. The liquid flew across the room and splashed onto Harvey's face.

He screamed.

The acid ripped at him. It burrowed into his face, eating away at his flesh, shredding his corneas and pupils, tearing apart the milky whites of his eyes. Pain engulfed him, but the pain in his skin was nothing compared to what was happening in his eyes. Thousands of sharp flaming darts punctured the soft gel of his eyeballs.

His hands flew to his face; his fingers pulled at his eyes in a futile attempt to lessen the pain. He could hear his skin and eyes sizzle, smell the burning flesh on his own face.

As Sara struggled to her feet, she saw the gun fall from his hand and bounce underneath a shelf. She thought groggily of trying to get it but decided against it. It would probably take too long and give Harvey the time he needed to recuperate. Better to make a run for it.

Before she took a step, Sara heard Harvey manage his first words since the acid had landed on his face. They started low, almost inaudible, but they grew louder with each syllable. He repeated the same words over and over as though they were some sort of ritual chant:

"You must die, Sara. You must."

THE elevator moved so damn slowly. After thirty seconds of pushing the close-door button, the door grudgingly obeyed by sliding shut. With a grunt it began to ascend.

"You check the second floor," Max said to Willie. "I'll go up to the third. Yell if you see anything."

"Right."

The elevator stopped on the second floor. The door had not yet opened when Max and Willie heard what sounded like a long, primal scream.

"Third floor," Max shouted.

Willie repeatedly pressed the third-floor button, but the elevator's course had already been set and it was not about to be rushed by a human scream. The door opened slowly on the second floor and then paused.

Impatience overcame Max. He sprinted across the portal. "I'll take the stairway. Meet me up there."

Willie withdrew his revolver from its holster. "Got ya."

"Y O U must die, Sara . . ."

Sara wasted little time. Summoning up strength she did not have, she maneuvered past Eric's body, shoved Harvey aside, and hobbled toward the door. Even with the adrenaline flow, her movements were slow. The cold had stiffened her limbs and constricted her lungs. She had spent so much energy on the quick swing of her arm and pushing Harvey that she feared she might not be able to make it.

Have to. The baby . . .

A few minutes earlier Sara had been ready to give up. Trapped in the cold room, no way of escape, no hope of a last minute rescue . . . no Michael—in truth, she had almost welcomed defeat. There was nothing left. Her spirit had been crushed. Michael dead. What difference could survival make when there was no Michael?

She had begun to drift away. Delirium took control, and it too was welcome. Anything was better than reality. She would just drift and drift, not think about Michael, just drift, look around, let her mind replay "(Don't Fear) the Reaper." She could almost hear Buck Dharma singing about the Grim Reaper's visit . . . *"It was clear she couldn't go on, / Then the door was opened and the wind appeared, / The candles blew and then disappeared . . ."*

She was looking around, looking at all the test tubes and fancy equipment on the shelves, looking until too exhausted to look anymore, eyes beginning to close . . .

. . . *"the curtains flew and then He appeared . . ."*

. . . yes, there were all the various test tubes and glass dishes and beakers . . .

. . . *"saying 'Don't be afraid, come on, baby' . . ."*

. . . lots of beakers, so many sizes with all the fancy codes labeled on the front.

. . . *"and she had no fear . . ."*

. . . Sara had not held a beaker or test tube since tenth-grade chemistry. God, she hated that class. Seemed like all they did was the damn periodic table. She remembered very little of it now, like the Spanish she took for four years and never used again. A few words she remembered. *Hola* was hello . . .

. . . *"as she ran to him . . ."*

. . . *adios* was good-bye. *Buenos días* was good morning. The same with chemistry. H_2O was water. CO_2 was carbon dioxide and HCl . . .

. . . *"and they started to fly . . ."*

. . . HCl was hydrochloric acid.

Acid.

Harvey's tortured voice pursued her. "You have to die, Sara. You have to . . ."

Sara glanced behind her. Harvey had scrambled to his feet. He pried his hands off his face and took a knife from his pocket. His face was red and blotchy.

Sara turned back around and moved forward. Behind her Harvey began to lunge toward the lab door. He moved like a maniac—without reason, without concern for what might be in his way. And like a maniac, he moved fast.

"You have to die. You have to . . ."

She tried to hobble faster. Her eyes fixed on the doorknob. Just a few more seconds, just a few more steps, almost there, almost . . .

She reached out. Her hand touched the doorknob and then closed around it. Harvey was right behind her now, just a few yards back. He stumbled and dove forward, landing inches away from her. Sara turned the knob.

The door was locked.

Her heart sank. Her fingers quickly moved to the dead bolt . . .

"You have to die, Sara . . ."

. . . and twisted it clockwise. She heard the bolt slide back. Her hand moved back to the knob again.

That was when she felt cold fingers wrap around her ankle.

From the floor below her. "You have to die, Sara. You have to."

She screamed, trying to pull her bad foot free, but he held on. He suddenly tugged hard and Sara toppled to the floor beside him. Pain rushed up her leg. She kicked at him, but the blows did not seem to bother him. He was beyond pain now, beyond any form of rationality. He was like some robot set on destroy and nothing she could do would deprogram him. He had to silence her. He had to save his clinic. There was nothing else.

He pulled her ankle and her body slid toward him.

Her fingers reached out, trying to grasp anything that might slow him down, but there was nothing but the slick tile.

". . . have to die . . ."

He grabbed her hair and tugged harshly. Holding her in place, Harvey raised himself up. He lifted the knife above his head. Sara made a fist and swung. It landed in Harvey's groin. He made an oofing noise and fell off her.

Sara scrambled to her feet. She twisted the knob. The door opened. She heard Harvey scream.

"NO!"

She fell out into the hallway as Harvey stumbled to his feet after her.

Then Sara heard somebody say, "It's over, Harv. Drop it."

They both froze.

The voice, Sara thought . . . *but it can't be.*

Her line of vision traveled past Harvey. It traveled down the corridor until it reached the spot where the voice had come from.

"Michael!"

STILL holding the knife, Harvey spun toward the voice. The acid had rendered his right eye useless, but his left could still make out shapes. A man was standing about ten feet away from him. It was Michael. And the figure behind him . . . He squinted, trying to make out the face. . . .

His tormented voice said her name. "Cassandra."

With tears running down her face, Cassandra turned away.

"Let go of the knife," Michael said. "It's over."

Lieutenant Bernstein came flying around the corner. Sergeant Monticelli followed with his gun drawn. He aimed at Harvey's head.

But Harvey had already dropped the knife. There was no point in continuing. Killing Sara would no longer benefit AIDS because Michael knew the truth. So did Cassandra and Lieutenant Bernstein and that other police officer. He could not kill them all. He could not hide the truth any longer.

So what should he do now?

His whole body went limp. The officer with the gun tackled him and flipped him roughly onto his stomach. There was no need. Harvey offered no resistance. Through his one good eye, he saw Michael pick up Sara. They embraced for a very long time.

He was cuffed and dragged to his feet. Cassandra still could not face him. A pity. He had really cared for her. He might even have loved her. But how could he make her understand that his happiness was irrelevant? How could he make her understand that he had become merely a shell, a tool, a valuable asset in the war against AIDS? His personal life was immaterial. It was Harvey the doctor and researcher that mattered; Harvey the man had always been superfluous.

His eyes still burned from the acid, but he was not thinking about that anymore. He was mulling over his options. He would get a lawyer, a lawyer who could stall for as long as possible. Just a few months of freedom was all it would take to perfect SR1 . . .

"You have the right to remain silent," the police officer was saying. "Anything you say . . ."

. . . and even if he had to spend time in jail, so what? He might be able to work on the formula in prison and correspond with researchers in the outside world. He had read about a doctor doing that somewhere. He could still make a contribution, still give the world his expertise.

But first, he would call a lawyer. A good, smart lawyer.

Yeah, that was it. That was what he'd do. That was exactly what he would do.

EPILOGUE

THURSDAY, APRIL 9

LENNY walked into the Eighty-seventh Street Precinct. He strode past the usual ugly glares and catcalls with a smile.

When he arrived at his destination, Lenny said, "Take that pencil out of your mouth."

Lieutenant Max Bernstein looked up. "Hi, Len."

"Ready to go visit Sara and Sam?"

"Let me just finish this up."

"What is it?"

"Paperwork. That's all I do now."

"Hang in there," Lenny said. "Someone has to blaze the trail."

Max began to fiddle with his new mustache. "I never thought of myself as much of a trailblazer."

"Sometimes greatness is thrust upon you."

"No one talks to me anymore," Max said. "All I get is shit detail."

"Being a leader is a lonely business."

"It's not funny, Len."

"Do you wish you never said anything?"

Max remembered the news conference seven months ago. Newspaper and television reporters from all over the globe were there to cover the capture of the Gay Slasher and the revelation that SR1 was a hoax. On that day Max had not planned on saying anything except the usual "this was a team effort" bullshit. His mouth, however, had other ideas.

A reporter had asked, "How does it feel to be a hero, Lieutenant?"

"I'm just glad the case is over."

"Do you realize that you're an idol? Parents consider you a role model for their children."

"I doubt that."

"Don't be so modest, Lieutenant. Do you think this case is an example of how far the gay community will go to deceive the American public?"

"I don't understand your question."

"Do you think this was a plot by a subversive gay group to get more money for AIDS?"

"There is no doubt that Dr. Riker acted on his own," Max said. And then he added, "Furthermore, since I am your hero of the week, I will tell you that it just so happens that I myself am . . ."

. . . and that was when he spilled it.

"Well?" Lenny said. "Are you sorry about coming out of the closet?"

Max shrugged. "I don't know."

"You've done a lot of good."

"My career is in the toilet."

Lenny smiled. "You take the good with the bad. Give it time."

"Have any other comforting clichés?"

"No. Just remember that legally the police department can't do a damn thing to you."

"Except assign me shit detail. I should have gotten a shot at that Masquerade Killer, but they put someone else on it. I only get the minor fag cases because, as the captain puts it, that's my 'field of expertise.'"

"He's a homophobic Neanderthal," Lenny said. "Want to go into his office and make out in front of him?"

Max chuckled. "I think not."

"Don't worry. They'll start accepting you soon. Trust me. Progress comes slowly."

Max took the pencil out of his mouth. "Doubt it."

"Hey, Twitch."

Max spun toward Willie Monticelli. He had not seen the sergeant since the day he had made himself a national gay celebrity seven months ago.

"Hi, Willie. Long time, no see."

Willie hesitated. "Who's this? Your boyfriend or something?"

"Lenny, this is Sergeant Willie Monticelli. Willie, this is Lenny Werner."

"I've heard a lot about you, Sergeant."

Snickers from nearby cops.

"What sort of things?" Willie asked suspiciously.

"That you are a good cop," Lenny replied.

Willie shrugged. "I do my job."

"What can I do for you, Willie?" Max asked.

A voice from the corner: "Careful how you answer that, Willie. Might get more than you bargain for."

"Shut the hell up, Owens," Willie shouted back.

Max's fingers plucked nervously at his shirt. "What's up?"

"Got me," Willie replied. "I was assigned to assist you on this Masquerade Killer. Seems the mayor was not happy about the results Owens and his buddies were getting. Wants to offer us a chance at it."

"You're kidding."

"Look, Twitch, let me put it on the line." Willie hitched up his pants by the belt. "I'm no fag lover, I gotta be honest. But I've seen a lot of cops in my day. Some are straight, some like to do it with whores in the basement, and yeah, some are fairies. So you like fondling balls instead of tits—as long as they ain't mine, I don't give a shit. I just want to solve the case, ya know?"

Lenny smiled at Max. "You see? Progress already."

"MAIL call."

The prison guard tossed the envelope threw the bars. "There you go, Dr. Loony Tunes. A letter for you."

Harvey scrambled for the envelope. His heart lifted when he saw the return address was from Washington. His hand quickly tore the seal.

Dear Dr. Riker,

Our staff at the National Institutes of Health has examined the files and evidence that you sent me. While we appreciate hearing from anyone who might expedite our search for an AIDS vaccine, we must confess that we no longer consider you a reputable scientist.

Moreover, I must take exception to the absurd and unsubstantiated accusations you level in your confidential letter to me. I categorically deny any and all such claims of a "conspiracy," but it seems to me that the government and AIDS movement would be best served by discouraging you from making false charges. For this reason, I believe we can reach an arrangement that we will both find satisfactory.

For my part I will be delighted to update you on the NIH's progress and pass on your suggestions to the board. I will do all I can to see that you are given information on the progress of AIDS research during your incarceration.

For your part you will never again make mention of your absurd and unsubstantiated accusations. The men you mentioned in your letter and I no longer converse. We no longer work together toward the common goal you described as "vile," and what they might do separately is of no concern to me. I have paid my debt to the man you call "pious scum" and hence will no longer be communicating with him.

Thank you for your time. It is encouraging to see that some prisoners wish to make productive use of their time while paying their debt to society.

With best wishes, I remain
Sincerely,
Raymond Markey, M.D.
Assistant Secretary of Health and Human Services

Harvey put down the letter, tucked it away neatly, and sat back.

That was when he spotted the back page of yesterday's *New York Herald* lying on the cell floor.

He had been so caught up yesterday in working out new calculations that he had not even glanced at the paper. Now he saw the gigantic back page headline.

DOUBLE VICTORY FOR SILVERMAN
Triumphs in Comeback Performance and Becomes a Dad in One Night!

Harvey read down the page.

(New York)—For the first time all season, the sound of classical music could be heard in the New York Knicks' locker room. It was a sweet sound for all.

"Did you see what he did out there?" close friend and teammate Reece Porter exclaimed after the game. "Mike is most definitely back!"

After a lengthy illness, Michael Silverman, the New York Knicks' veteran cocaptain, made a triumphant return last night in front of a Madison Square Garden capacity crowd, leading the Knicks to a 123–107 trouncing of the Chicago Bulls.

"Now that we're heading into the play-offs, we really need him," said Coach Richie Crenshaw. "He gives our team that extra lift."

"No one believed he'd make it back," added Jerome Holloway, the odds-on favorite to win this year's Rookie of the Year honors. "But he showed them tonight."

Basketball was only part of the story for Michael Silverman last night. Right after the game, Silverman got word that his wife, popular *News-Flash* cohost Sara Lowell, had gone into labor. The entire Knicks team followed Silverman to the hospital.

"We all paced around the waiting room like a group of nervous, expectant fathers," Porter later joked.

At 11:08 p.m., the suspense was over. A teary Michael Silverman came out to announce that Sara had given birth to their first child, a healthy baby boy named Sam—7 pounds, 6 ounces.

Harvey put down the paper and smiled.

It was wonderful news.

Then he went back to figuring out why the T cell receptor was not reacting the way he had predicted.

Perhaps if he changed the compound . . .

#1 *New York Times* bestselling author
Harlan Coben
is back with another thriller.
Read on for a preview of

LIVE WIRE

THE ugliest truth, a friend once told Myron, is still better than the prettiest of lies.

Myron thought about that now as he looked down at his father in the hospital bed. He flashed back sixteen years, to the last time he had lied to his father—the lie that caused so much heartbreak and devastation, a lie that started a tragic ripple that, finally, disastrously, would end here.

His father's eyes remained closed, his breathing raspy and uneven. Tubes seemed to snake out from everywhere. Myron stared down at his father's forearm. He remembered as a child visiting his dad in that Newark warehouse, the way his father sat at his oversize desk, his sleeves rolled up. The forearm had been powerful enough back then to strain the fabric, making the cuff work tourniquet-like against the muscle. Now the muscle looked spongy, de-

flated by age. The barrel chest that had made Myron feel
so safe was still there, but it had grown brittle, as though
a hand pressing down could snap the rib cage like dried
twigs. His father's unshaven face had gray splotches instead of his customary five o'clock shadow, the skin around
his chin loose, sagging down like a cloak one size too big.

Myron's mother—Al Bolitar's wife for the past forty-
three years—sat next to the bed. Her hand, shaking with
Parkinson's, held his. She too looked shockingly frail. In
her youth, his mother had been an early feminist, burning her bra with Gloria Steinem, wearing T-shirts that
read stuff like "A Woman's Place Is in the House . . . and
Senate." Now here they both were, Ellen and Al Bolitar
("We're El-Al," Mom always joked, "like the Israeli airline"), ravaged by age, hanging on, luckier by far than
the vast majority of aging lovers—and yet this was what
luck looked like in the end.

God has some sense of humor.

"So," Mom said to Myron in a low voice, "we agree?"

Myron did not reply. The prettiest of lies versus the
ugliest truth. Myron should have learned his lesson back
then, sixteen years ago, with that last lie to this great man
he loved like no other. But, no, it wasn't so simple. The
ugliest truth could be devastating. It could rock a world.

Or even kill.

So as his father's eyes fluttered open, as this man Myron treasured like no other looked up at his oldest son
with pleading, almost childlike confusion, Myron looked
at his mother and slowly nodded. Then he bit back the
tears and prepared to tell his father one final lie.

*   *   *

SIX DAYS EARLIER

"Please, Myron, I need your help."

This was, for Myron, a bit of a fantasy: a shapely, gorgeous damsel in distress sauntering into his office like something out of an old Bogey film—except, well, the saunter was more of a waddle and the shapeliness was coming from the fact that the gorgeous damsel was eight months pregnant and really—sorry—that kind of killed the whole fantasy effect.

Her name was Suzze T, short for Trevantino, a retired tennis star. She had been the sexy bad girl of the tour, better known for her provocative outfits, piercings, and tattoos than for her actual game. Still, Suzze had won a major and made a ton in endorsements, most notably as the spokeswoman (Myron loved that euphemism) for La-La-Latte, a chain of topless coffee bars, where college boys loved to snicker for "extra milk." Good times.

Myron spread his arms. "I'm here for you, Suzze, twenty-four/seven—you know that."

They were in his Park Avenue office, home of MB Reps, the M standing for Myron, the B for Bolitar and the Reps because they represented athletes, actors, and writers. Literal-Moniker-R-Us.

"Just tell me what I can do."

Suzze began to pace. "I'm not sure where to begin." Myron was about to speak when she held up her hand. "And if you dare say, 'Start at the beginning,' I will rip off one of your testicles."

"Just one?"

"You're engaged now. I'm thinking of your poor fiancée."

The pace turned more into a stomp, picking up speed and intensity so that a small part of Myron feared that she might go into labor right here in his recently refurbished office.

"Uh, the carpet," Myron said. "It's new."

She frowned, paced some more, started biting her exuberantly polished fingernails.

"Suzze?"

She stopped. Their eyes met.

"Tell me," he said.

"You remember when we first met?"

Myron nodded. He had been just a few months out of law school and starting up his fledgling firm. Back then, at the inception, MB Reps had been known as MB SportsReps. That was because initially Myron represented only athletes. When he started representing actors and writers and others in the field of the arts and celebrity, he dropped the Sports from the name, ergo, MB Reps.

Again with the literal.

"Of course," he said.

"I was a mess, wasn't I?"

"You were a great tennis talent."

"And a mess. Don't sugarcoat it."

Myron put his palms toward the ceiling. "You were eighteen."

"Seventeen."

"Seventeen, whatever." Quick memory flash of Suzze in the sun: blond hair in a ponytail, a wicked grin on her face, her forehand whipping the ball as though it had offended her. "You'd just turned pro. Adolescent boys hung your poster in their bedrooms. You were supposed to beat legends right away. Your parents redefined pushy. It's a miracle you stayed upright."

"Good point."

"So what's wrong?"

Suzze glanced down at her belly as though it had just appeared. "I'm pregnant."

"Uh, yeah, I can see that."

"Life is good, you know?" Her voice was soft now, wistful. "After all the years when I was a mess . . . I found Lex. His music has never been better. The tennis academy is doing great. And, well, it's just all so good now."

Myron waited. Her eyes stayed on her belly, cradling it as though it were its contents, which, Myron surmised, it kind of was. To keep the conversation going, Myron asked, "Do you like being pregnant?"

"The actual physical act of carrying a child?"

"Yes."

She shrugged. "It's not like I'm glowing or any of that. I mean, I'm so ready to deliver. It's interesting though. Some women love being pregnant."

"And you don't?"

"It feels like someone parked a bulldozer on my bladder. I think the reason women like being pregnant is because it makes them feel special. Like they're minor celebrities. Most women go through life without the attention, but when they're pregnant, people make a fuss. This may sound uncharitable, but pregnant women like the applause. Do you know what I mean?"

"I think so."

"I've already had my share of applause, I guess." She moved toward the window and looked out for a moment. Then she turned back toward him. "By the way, did you notice how huge my boobs are?"

Myron said, "Um," and decided to say no more.

"Come to think of it, I wonder whether you should contact La-La-Latte for a new photo shoot."

"Strategically angled shots?"

"Exactly. Might be a great new campaign in these puppies." She cupped them in case Myron wasn't sure what puppies she was referencing. "What do you think?"

"I think," Myron said, "that you're stalling."

Her eyes were wet now. "I'm so damned happy."

"Yeah, well, I can see where that would be a problem."

She smiled at that. "I put the demons to rest. I've even reconciled with my mother. Lex and I couldn't be more ready to have the baby. I want those demons to stay away."

Myron sat up. "You're not using again?"

"God, no. Not that kind of demon. Lex and I are done with that."

Lex Ryder, Suzze's husband, was one half of the legendary band/duo known as HorsePower—the much lesser half, to be frank, to the supernaturally charismatic front man, Gabriel Wire. Lex was a fine if troubled musician, but he would always be John Oates to Gabriel's Daryl Hall, Andrew Ridgeley to Gabriel's George Michael, the rest of the Pussycat Dolls next to Nicole Scherz-i-something.

"What kind of demons then?"

Suzze reached into her purse. She plucked out something that from across the desk looked as though it might be a photograph. She stared at it for a moment and then passed it to Myron. He took a quick glance and again tried to wait her out.

Finally, just to say something, he went with the obvious: "This is your baby's sonogram."

"Yep. Twenty-eight weeks old."

More silence. Again Myron broke it. "Is there something wrong with the baby?"

"Nothing. He's perfect."

"He?"

Suzze T smiled now. "Going to have my own little man."

"That's pretty cool."

"Yeah. Oh, one of the reasons I'm here: Lex and I have been talking about it. We both want you to be the godfather."

"Me?"

"Yep."

Myron said nothing.

"Well?"

Now it was Myron who had wet eyes. "I'd be honored."

"Are you crying?"

Myron said nothing.

"You're such a girl," she said.

"What's wrong, Suzze?"

"Maybe nothing." Then: "I think someone is out to destroy me."

Myron kept his eyes on the sonogram. "How?"

And then she showed him. She showed him two words that would echo dully in his heart for a very long time.

AN hour later, Windsor Horne Lockwood III—known to those who feared him (and that was pretty much everyone) as Win—swaggered into Myron's office. Win had a great swagger, like he should be wearing a black top hat and tails and twirling a walking stick. Instead he sported a pink-and-green Lilly Pulitzer tie, a blue blazer with some kind of crest on it, and khakis with a crease sharp enough to draw blood. He had loafers, no socks, and basically looked as though he'd just gone yachting on the SS *Old Money.*

"Suzze T just stopped by," Myron said.

Win nodded, jaw jutted. "I saw her on the way out."

"Did she look upset?"

"Didn't notice," Win said, taking a seat. Then: "Her breasts were engorged."

Win.

"She has a problem," Myron said.

Win leaned back, crossed his legs with his customary coiled ease. "Explain."

Myron spun his computer monitor so Win could see. An hour ago, Suzze T had done something similar. He thought about those two small words. Harmless enough on their own, but life is about context. And in this context, those two words still chilled the room.

Win squinted at the screen and reached into his inside breast pocket. He plucked out a pair of reading glasses. He'd gotten them about a month ago, and though Myron would have said it was impossible, they made Win look even more haughty and stuck-up. They also depressed the hell out of him. Win and he weren't old—not by a long shot—but to use Win's golf analogy when he had first unveiled the glasses: "We are officially on the back nine of life."

"Is this a Facebook page?" Win asked.

"Yes. Suzze said she uses it to promote her tennis academy."

Win leaned a little closer. "Is that her sonogram?"

"Yes."

"And how does a sonogram promote her tennis academy?"

"That's what I asked. She said you need the personal touch. People don't just want to read self-promotion."

Win frowned. "So she posts a sonogram of a fetus?" He glanced up. "Does that make sense to you?"

In truth, it did not. And once again—with Win wearing reading glasses and the two of them whining about the new world of social networks—Myron felt old.

"Check out the picture comments," Myron said.

Win gave him the flat eyes. "People comment on a sonogram?"

"Just read them."

Win did. Myron waited. He had pretty much memorized the page. There were, he knew, twenty-six comments in all, mostly various good wishes. Suzze's mother, the aging poster child for Evil Stage (Tennis) Mom, for example, had written: "I'm going to be a grandma, everyone! Yay!" Someone named Amy said, "Aww cute!!!" A jocular "Takes after his old man! ;)" came from a session drummer who used to work with HorsePower. A guy named Kelvin wrote, "Congrats!!" Tami asked, "When's the baby due, sweetie?"

Win stopped three from the bottom. "Funny guy."

"Which one?"

"Some turdlike humanoid named Erik typed"—Win cleared his throat, leaned closer to the screen—"'Your baby looks like a sea horse!'" and then Erik the Riot put the letters 'LOL.'"

"He's not her problem."

Win was not placated. "Old Erik still might be worth a visit."

"Just keep going."

"Fine." Win's facial expressions rarely changed. He had trained himself in both business and combat to show nothing. But a few seconds later, Myron saw something darken in his old friend's eyes. Win looked up. Myron nodded. Because now Myron knew that Win had found the two words.

They were there, at the bottom of the page. The two words were in a comment made by "Abeona F," a name that meant nothing to him. The profile picture was some sort of symbol, maybe Chinese lettering. And there, all in caps, no punctuation, were the two simple yet wrenching words: "NOT HIS."

Silence.

Then Win said, "Yowza."

"Indeed."

Win took off his glasses. "Need I ask the obvious question?"

"That being?"

"Is it true?"

"Suzze swears that it's Lex's."

"Do we believe her?"

"We do," Myron said. "Does it matter?"

"Not on a moral basis, no. My theory? This is the work of some neutered crank."

Myron nodded. "The great thing about the Internet: It gives everyone a voice. The bad thing about the Internet: It gives everyone a voice."

"The great bastion for the cowardly and anonymous," Win agreed. "Suzze should probably delete it before Lex sees it."

"Too late. That's part of the problem. Lex has sort of run off."

"I see," Win said. "So she wants us to find him?"

"And bring him home, yes."

"Shouldn't be too difficult to find a famous rock star," Win said. "And the other part of the problem?"

"She wants to know who wrote this."

"The true identity of Mr. Neutered Crank?"

"Suzze thinks it's something bigger. That someone is truly out to get her."

Win shook his head. "It's a neutered crank."

"Come on. Typing, 'Not his'? That's pretty sick."

"A *sick* neutered crank. Do you ever read the nonsense on this Internet? Go to any news story anywhere and look at the racist, homophobic, paranoid 'comments.'" He made quote marks with his fingers. "It will make you howl at the moon."

"I know, but I promised I'd look into it."

Win sighed, put the glasses back on, leaned toward

the screen. "The person who posted it is one Abeona F. Is it safe to assume that's a pseudonym?"

"Yep. Abeona is the name of a Roman Goddess. No idea what the F stands for."

"And what about the profile photograph? What's this symbol?"

"I don't know."

"You asked Suzze?"

"Yep. She said she had no idea. It looks almost like Chinese lettering."

"Perhaps we can find someone to translate it." Win sat back and resteepled the fingers. "Did you notice the time the comment was posted?"

Myron nodded. "Three seventeen a.m."

"Awfully late."

"That's what I was thinking," Myron said. "This could just be the social-networking equivalent of drunk texting."

"An ex with issues," Win said.

"Is there any other kind?"

"And if I recall Suzze's rambunctious youth, there could be—conservatively speaking—several candidates."

"But none that she imagines doing something like this."

Win continued to stare at the screen. "So what's our first step?"

"Really?"

"Pardon?"

Myron moved around his renovated office. Gone were the posters of Broadway plays and Batman memorabilia. They'd been taken down during the paint job, and Myron wasn't really sure if he wanted to put them back up. Gone too were all his old trophies and awards from his playing days—his NCAA championship rings, his *Parade* All-American certificates, his College Player of the Year Award—with one exception. Right before his first professional game as a Boston Celtic, as his dream was finally coming true, Myron had seriously injured his knee. *Sports Illustrated* had put him on the cover with the tagline IS HE DONE? and while they did't answer the question, it ended up being a big fat YUP! Why he kept the framed cover up, he wasn't quite sure. If asked, he said that it was a warning to any "superstar" entering his office how quickly it can all go away, but Myron somehow suspected it went deeper than that.

"That's not your usual modus operandi," Myron said.

"Oh, do tell."

"This is usually the part where you tell me that I'm an agent, not a private eye, and that you don't see any purpose in doing this because there is no financial benefit to the firm."

Win said nothing.

"Then you usually complain that I have a hero complex and always need to rescue someone in order to feel complete. And last—or I should say, most recently—you tell me how my interfering has actually done more harm than good, that I've ended up hurting and even killing maybe more than I've saved."

Win yawned. "Is there a point?"

"I thought it was pretty obvious but here it is: Why suddenly are you willing—enthusiastic even—about taking on this particular rescue mission when in the past—"

"In the past," Win interrupted, "I always helped out, didn't I?"

"For the most part, yes."

Win looked up, tapped his chin with his index finger. "How to explain this?" He stopped, thought, nodded. "We have a tendency to believe good things will last forever. It is in our nature. The Beatles, for example. Oh, they'll be around forever. *The Sopranos*—that show will always be on the air. Philip Roth's Zuckerman series. Springsteen concerts. Good things are rare. They are to be cherished because they always leave us too soon."

Win rose, started for the door. Before he left the room, he looked back. "Doing this stuff with you," Win said, "is one of those good things."